Praise for ...son Packard

"*Love in the Afternoon* is enjoyable, interesting and charming.... Highly readable and enjoyable."
—*Romance Around the Corner*

"I think that this may be my favorite debut novel of 2012! Anyone who likes Jill Shalvis, Carly Phillips, Susan Mallery or Victoria Dahl will probably fall in love with this book as much as I did."
—*The Book Pushers* on *Love in the Afternoon*

"A fun, sweet easy read.... I really enjoyed myself while reading this one."
—*FictionVixen.com* on *Love in the Afternoon*

"I liked everything about this book.... I hope readers pick this up. I think they'll be thrilled with the adult romance. It's one of my favorite books of the year."
—*Dear Author* on *The Winning Season*, recommended read

"I pretty much liked everything about Matt and Kelly's story.... This romance really worked for me and I will definitely be recommending."
—*FictionVixen.com* on *The Winning Season*

"I absolutely adored this book, it was so fun and sexy and everything I love about romance."
—*The Book Pushers* on *The Winning Season*

Also available from Alison Packard and Carina Press

The Winning Season
A Christmas for Carrie

And stay tuned for a new Alison Packard novel coming in 2014!

Love in the Afternoon

ALISON PACKARD

ISBN-13: 978-0-373-00227-6

LOVE IN THE AFTERNOON

This edition published by arrangement with Harlequin Books S.A.

www.CarinaPress.com

Printed in U.S.A.

Dear Reader,

My debut novel, *Love in the Afternoon,* revolves around the fictional soap opera *A New Dawn.* Soap operas have been around for decades, and although the number of daytime dramas on network television has declined, soap operas still have millions of die-hard fans who have a deep emotional investment in the characters they love, and love to hate.

Although soap operas have gotten a bad rap over the years for their over-the-top story lines, their one constant has always been romance. That's why we who love the genre will never give up on our shows. We'll keep tuning in to see our favorite characters travel that exhilarating—and oftentimes rocky—road to true love.

Speaking of true love, when the characters Sean Barrett and Kayla Maxwell play on *A New Dawn* are suddenly paired with each other, it doesn't take long for sparks to fly between them in real life. And soon, Sean and Kayla are living their own soap opera, complete with a jealous coworker, a controlling father and a mysterious stalker who just might want Kayla dead.

I hope you enjoy *Love in the Afternoon.*

Happy reading!

Alison Packard

Acknowledgments

This book would not have been possible without the support, encouragement and suggestions I received from Chrissie Humphrey, Jennifer Vincent and Christie Auschwitz. Thank you, ladies, for believing I could do this.

Hugs and thanks to everyone at *Trusted Hearts,* where it all began.

I can't leave out the following individuals: Elizabeth "Bess" Shelton, Laura Kelly, Jodi Henley and Keena Tomko. They all had a hand in this book, and I appreciate their help and guidance more than I can say.

And last, but not least, a big thank-you to Angela James, editorial director at Carina Press, who uttered the words every author longs to hear: "We'd like to publish this."

Love in the Afternoon

One

Shay: You can tell me anything, Stefan.
Stefan: I'm sorry, Shay. But I'm going back to my wife.

"YOU SLUT!"

Since Kayla Maxwell was the only other person in the produce section, there was no doubt the scathing insult was meant for her. Or to be more precise, her alter ego Shay McKade.

Turning from the refrigerated vegetable display, she pasted on a fake smile and found herself looking into the eyes of one very pissed off woman who, sadly, was dressed in a garish hot pink jogging outfit that looked like someone had attacked it repeatedly with a Bedazzler gun.

"Excuse me?" She tossed a bag of baby carrots into her cart. "Did you just call me a—"

"How could you?" the woman interrupted, her close-set eyes blazing with contempt. "You...you tramp."

"Actually, I'm not *really* a tramp. I just play one on TV." She flashed another smile. Maybe a little actress humor would appease the woman. This wasn't the first time she'd been accosted by an overzealous soap opera fan that had it in for her character.

"You slept with a married man." Her face mottled with anger, the woman pointed at her with a pudgy finger. "I've waited years for Stefan and Cassie to get together and then, when they finally do, you slither into town and lure him into your bed."

"Slither?"

The woman's beady eyes narrowed. "Like the snake you are."

"Snake?" Kayla's voice rose. "Now, wait just a minute—"

"No! You wait." The woman moved closer. Kayla could smell the cloying scent of old lady perfume. It permeated the air, just like the woman's outrage. "Stay away from him, or else."

"Or else what?"

"Or you'll be sorry." The woman's nostrils flared before she gave Kayla a final glare and then turned and pushed her cart toward the deli counter.

"Believe me," she muttered at the woman's retreating back. "I'd love to stay away from him."

Kayla's cell phone rang as she pushed her cart toward the tomato display. Pulling it from her purse, she saw her publicist's name on the caller ID.

"Hi, Lisa. What's up?" Lisa had not only been her publicist for the past seven years, but was also a good friend.

"Great news. You're going to be on the cover of *Soap Opera Journal* in three weeks. I just got a call about the photo shoot."

"The cover? Is something going on I don't know about?"

"You tell me."

"There's nothing to tell." Kayla stopped her cart in front of the vine-ripened tomatoes. "But I have a few scripts at home I haven't read yet. Maybe something big is going to happen between Shay and Stefan." She paused. "Oh, hell no. You're going to ruin this by telling me I have to do the shoot with Marcus, aren't you?"

"Unfortunately, yes." Lisa's voice was sympathetic. "Although I'm not sure there's a lens wide enough to capture both him *and* his over-inflated ego."

"Tell me about it. Oh, and get this, we had a love scene last week. It was all I could do to get through it without puking."

"Did he try to shove his tongue down your throat again?"

"He did. But I took care of it," Kayla said with a grin. "Thanks for the tip."

"Anytime. By the way, Sean will be there too."

Kayla's jaw dropped. "Sean Barrett?"

"Yep. Maybe his character is going to be involved in the story with Stefan and Shay. Look, I've got to go. I need to call Sean and give him the news. I'll call you later with more info. And let's try to meet for lunch this week."

"I'm off on Thursday," Kayla said. "We can meet at…" She stopped. Lisa had hung up. She smiled at the phone. "And…I guess we'll talk later." Shoving her phone back into her purse, she tore off a plastic bag from the roll next to the tomatoes.

The cover of *Soap Opera Journal.* How cool was that? Pretty freaking cool except for the part about Marcus. But Sean would be there too. *Why?* She picked up a tomato and tested its firmness with her fingers.

Sean and his character, Jared Madison, were even more popular than Stefan Cabot, although Marcus would never admit it. Jared was a detective and a recent widower—soon he would need a love interest. It couldn't be Shay though. *Could it?* They'd never even been onscreen together, except for the time the big tornado hit town, and, of course, the funeral for Jared's wife.

The crackle of the intercom jolted her from her thoughts as the store clerk announced the daily special. She picked a few more tomatoes, and after putting the bag into her cart, she turned to find a smiling teenage girl standing next to her.

"Excuse me?" the girl said with a high squeaky tone of excitement. "You play Shay McKade on *A New Dawn*, don't you?" The girl's smile widened, revealing braces.

Kayla nodded. "Yes," she said, relieved the girl was friendlier than the crazy woman who'd just confronted her.

"I told my mom it was you but she didn't believe me." She giggled. "Can I have your autograph?" The teenager held out a scrap of paper and a pen.

"You sure can." Kayla smiled, and while signing her name answered a few questions the teen had about the show, and about acting in general. Now these were the kind of fans she liked. The ones who could separate her from the character she played on television.

Kayla knew Shay wasn't going to be a permanent fixture in Stefan's life. Stefan and his estranged wife Cassie were way too popular to be apart for long. Perhaps the writers were gearing up for a storyline between Shay and Jared. If that was the case then she would be working with the most talented actor on the show. Her stomach churned at the thought. She'd come to terms with being a second tier character on *A New Dawn*. Being paired with Sean Barrett would change all that. Could she hold her own with him? Or would she prove herself to be a rank amateur? A few years ago, she wouldn't have doubted her acting abilities, but she'd been in Hollywood for seven years now, and other than a couple of horror movies, she didn't have much to show for it.

After she'd finished her shopping and stood waiting in the checkout line, she noticed the latest issue of *Soap Opera Journal* on the rack. On the cover was a picture of Sean and Nikki Andrews, the actress who had played his wife, Rebecca. The banner above their picture said it all:

A New Dawn actress axed! What's next for Jared as he mourns his soul mate?

SEAN BARRETT KNEW he should be memorizing his lines for the next day's taping, but the lure of his favorite team playing their arch rivals was far more interesting than whatever Jared Madison, his character on *A New Dawn,* would be saying and doing. The script would have to wait. The Dodgers on his big screen and an ice cold beer in his hand were taking precedence over work. Just as it should be on a Sunday afternoon.

"Come on, Scanlon," Sean muttered as Matt Scanlon, his best friend, strode from the on-deck circle to the batter's box. "You're due," he said as if Matt could hear him. Lifting the icy bottle to his lips, Sean watched as Matt gave the pitcher his patented stink eye and then stepped up to the plate. "Don't swing at the first pitch," he said, lowering his beer and then groaning when Matt did just that. "That's why you're leading the league in strike outs." Sean shook his head in disgust.

Just as Matt hit a foul ball into the stands at Dodger

Stadium, Sean's cell phone rang. Leaning forward, he picked it up from the coffee table, checked the screen and saw it was his new publicist, Lisa Harrison.

"I've got good news," she said, not bothering with the customary pleasantries after he'd greeted her. "You're going to be on the cover of *Soap Opera Journal*."

"You call that good news?"

"It's publicity, Sean," she said with a hint of testiness. "And in your profession getting a cover is a good thing."

"If you say so." He watched Matt hit a ground ball straight to the shortstop who fielded it easily. "Damn it to hell."

"Excuse me?" Sean could almost see Lisa's arched brow and steely blue eyes.

"Sorry. The Dodgers are losing." Sean set his half empty bottle on the table and hit the mute button on the remote. "Look, I've been on the show for almost ten years. My face has been on the cover of *Soap Opera Journal* so many times I've lost count. It's not that big of a deal to me."

At Lisa's heavy sigh, Sean realized she was only doing her job. A job she got paid very well to do, and one she took seriously, which was why he'd hired her to replace the asshole who'd planted false stories about him in the media.

"When's the photo shoot?" he asked. Why would he be on the cover now? His last storyline arc had just wrapped up, and since the producers had fired Nikki Andrews, his onscreen wife, he expected his character to be on the back burner for a while mourning her untimely death from a tragic car accident.

"Are you available Thursday? I just talked to Kayla and she's got the day off."

"Kayla Maxwell?" Sean asked with surprise. "But her character's banging Stefan right now."

After a slight pause Lisa said dryly, "Well, that's one way to put it. In any event, all three of you are going to be on the cover."

"That's weird. Kayla and I haven't had any major scenes together since she joined the show."

"Maybe the executive producer has plans for the two of you. I got the call from the network's publicity department. They know I represent both you and Kayla. And from what I understand Marcus is available any day this week."

Sean almost snorted. "I'm sure he is. The guy never met a camera he didn't like."

"True, that," Lisa said with amusement. "So, are you available on Thursday? I'd really like to get this squared away tonight."

"Yeah. I'm available." Sean stared at the television and bit back another curse when the catcher for San Francisco hit a ball deep into left field. The Dodgers' left fielder sprinted, but before he could get to the warning track, the ball went over the wall. Sean watched as the young catcher pumped his fist in the air and loped around the bases. After passing Matt at home plate, he raised his arm and pointed to the sky as if thanking God for his fortuitous swing of the bat.

"Great. I'll get back to you tomorrow with the time and location of the shoot," Lisa said. "And don't be late."

"I'm never late," he said before he realized Lisa had hung up. Annoyed, he tossed the phone on the sofa and grabbed the scripts from the coffee table.

Lisa's comment got him thinking about his upcoming scenes. He'd been in the business long enough to know that if he and an actress on the show started doing photo shoots together the producer and head writer were contemplating pairing them up. The scenes could be a chemistry test after which the producer's staff would monitor the show's comment line to see what the fan reaction was.

Soap fans were nothing if not vocal. And while the show's producers didn't always listen to what the fans wanted, they knew the main draw of soaps was romance. Now that his character was a widower, it seemed like they were barely letting the guy mourn before having him embark on a new relationship.

Flipping through his script for the next day's taping, he didn't see any scenes between Jared and Shay. The same for Wednesday. He was off on Thursday, so the third script was for Friday. He turned the pages and read that he had two scenes with Kayla. So it was true. He was going to be stuck with a damn newbie. And one who more than likely had been hired because of her looks rather than her talent. At least Nikki could act. As for Kayla Maxwell, he'd been in a couple of scenes with her and since their characters didn't have any interaction, he couldn't remember anything particularly outstanding about her performance.

"This is bullshit," he said after reading the lines. He tossed the scripts on the table. Although he didn't have storyline approval in his contract, he was damn well going to make sure Jared Madison didn't do anything out of character. It was time for a little chat with the head writer.

Sitting at the table in her cozy yellow and white kitchen, Kayla ate the last bite of her chicken enchilada and watched the local news.

Eying the scripts on the end of the table, she pushed her plate aside and grabbed them and her yellow highlighter. She flipped open the top page, pulled the cap off the highlighter, and began marking the sections of dialogue she needed to memorize for tomorrow's taping.

She'd just finished marking the last page when her cell phone's musical ringtone blared. Picking it up, Kayla smiled when she saw the familiar number. "Hi, Mom," she said, replacing the cap on the highlighter.

"Hi, honey," Patricia Maxwell replied warmly. "How was your week?"

Kayla rose from her chair and moved into the living room. "It was good," she said, sinking onto the plump cushions of her overstuffed chair. "Busy." She curled her legs to the side and got comfortable. "How was yours?"

"Hectic." Patricia sighed. "I think it's time to retire."

"Mom, you'd go crazy if you were home all day. I think you should stick to the plan and retire when Dad does."

"Speaking of your dad, he wants to know how the car is."

"The car?" she asked with mock indignation. "What about me?" Kayla laughed and then continued, "Tell him the Mustang is fine. I took her in for an oil change last week. They checked everything, including the air pressure in the tires."

"He'll be happy to hear that. You know your father and cars."

"Is Dad home?" Kayla asked.

"No. He went to look at a '69 Corvette he's got his eye on. Another restoration." Patricia switched gears, moving on to her favorite subject. "I read the spoilers for next week and it sounds like Shay is starting to see that Stefan isn't over Cassie."

Looping a lock of hair over her ear, Kayla couldn't help but smile. Her mom was a huge fan of the show and, every day, drove home from the doctor's office where she worked to watch it while she ate her lunch.

"Are you still going on those online message boards?"

"Oh no. I stay away from those. Some of those people are vicious. I can understand them not liking your character, but to blame you personally for what the writers write is just plain ridiculous. They're crazy."

"You don't know the half of it," Kayla muttered.

"What really bothers me is when they criticize your acting ability. You're a wonderful actress."

"You have to say that. You're my mom."

"I'm saying it because it's true." There was a long silence before her mom continued, "You never used to doubt yourself, Kayla.

Tears pricked Kayla's eyes. That was true. There was a time when she'd believed in herself and her talent. "It's a tough business, Mom. It can wear you down."

"I know what wore you down and it wasn't Hollywood."

"Let's not talk about Greg," Kayla said, hearing the hostility in her mom's voice. "I'm done with him. I haven't seen him in months. He's out of my life."

"Praise the Lord for that," Patricia said vehemently. "That man was never good enough for you. And I want you to remember this—you have more talent in your little finger than he has in his whole body."

"Thanks, Mom."

"Don't mention it. That's what moms are for."

"I have some good news," Kayla said, putting her ex out of her mind. "I'm going to be on the cover of *Soap Opera Journal.*"

"What?" Patricia exclaimed so loudly that Kayla winced and had to pull the phone from her ear for a second. "Oh my God, honey. That's wonderful."

"The photo shoot is on Thursday."

"Is it you and Marcus Bertrand?"

"Yes. And Sean Barrett," Kayla said. That, she knew, would send her mother into a tizzy.

"Sean Barrett." Patricia sighed dreamily. "Is he as good looking in person as he is on television?"

Kayla imagined Sean's sandy blond hair and muscular body and felt a fluttering in her stomach. "Yes." Sean Barrett was hotter than hell. Television didn't do him justice.

"Does this mean you're going to be working with him on the show?"

"I'm not sure, Mom."

"Jared just lost his wife," Patricia mused. "Maybe Shay is going to be his next love interest."

"I doubt it." Kayla frowned. She didn't want to tell her mom what she'd read in Friday's script. She had a couple of scenes with Sean, but after reading the dialogue it was obvious she wasn't going to be his love interest. In fact, if the writers were going where she thought they were, she wouldn't be *anyone's* love interest for a good long while.

Two

Jared: It can't be that bad.
Shay: Yes, it can. I'm pregnant.

ON THURSDAY MORNING, Kayla sat in the make-up chair while Sandy, one of *A New Dawn's* make-up artists, applied mauve eye shadow with easy strokes. Sparing a quick glance across the hall to the photography studio, she tried to squelch the butterflies fluttering wildly in her stomach but wasn't having much luck. She'd woken up uncharacteristically nervous, and even her daily run hadn't put her back on an even keel.

"I know I say this all the time, but you have the most amazing eyes," Sandy said as she stepped back and admired her handiwork. "I hope the camera picks up the gold flecks." Sandy tilted Kayla's head and surveyed her with a critical eye. "Sometimes brown eyes can look flat in still photos, but Leo knows a few tricks to make them pop without making you look like an alien."

Kayla smiled. "That's good. I'm sure my mom is going to give copies of the magazine to all of our family and friends so I'd rather not look like something from outer space."

Sandy laughed, returning the eye shadow case to her make-up kit. "You're going to look gorgeous. With those eyes and that bone structure I'm surprised you're not a model."

"I'm not tall enough. *And* there's a little too much junk in the trunk. If you know what I mean," Kayla said with a grin. "Besides, it sounds as boring as hell."

"It can be tedious, but I love transforming the models. When I was a little girl I used to beg my mom to let me put make-up on her. I guess I knew what I wanted to be at a young age." She smiled. "Okay, we're done. I'll go get Lance so he can finish your hair."

After Sandy left the room, Kayla could still feel the butterflies knocking around inside of her stomach. It'd been a long time since she'd felt this edgy. In fact, the last time she was this nervous was when she'd first come to Los Angeles and auditioned for a part in a Steven Spielberg movie. She'd been pretty green back then and to this day she was still mortified at how she couldn't stop her body from trembling as she auditioned in front of the great director. The man was one of her film idols and she'd totally embarrassed herself by giving the worst audition of her career. He'd been very kind but, of course, she didn't get the part. She didn't blame him one bit. Her reading had been atrocious.

And now here she was feeling just as nervous over a stupid photo shoot. Something she'd done countless times without a second thought.

It was because of Sean Barrett. Kayla didn't even bother to deny it. The man was an amazing specimen of masculine good looks. His blond hair, brilliant green eyes and killer smile embodied the California surfer look. Kayla could easily picture him on a surfboard, or on the beach surrounded by bikini-clad groupies who would do anything he asked just to be near him. What normal woman wouldn't be nervous?

"Hello again, my darling." Lance, a stylist who

owned a salon in West Hollywood, and her friend for ages, breezed into the room. He stood behind her chair and rested his hands on her shoulders. "Shall we take those curlers out and get you all dolled up?" He leaned down and lowered his voice. "Trust me. You're going to want to look your best when you see the gorgeous hunk I just saw in the lobby." Lance lifted a hand and fanned himself. "Good Golly, Miss Molly, I almost fainted dead on the spot."

Kayla smiled at his theatrics. "Every time I see you, you're swooning over some man."

Lance began to pull the curlers from her hair and dropped them on a tray by the chair. His fingers stilled on a curler as he met her gaze in the mirror. "Darling, swooning over a man is one of life's most enjoyable pastimes. You should try it."

Kayla rolled her eyes. "Oh, I've swooned, Lance. And trust me, it wasn't worth it."

"One bad apple doesn't spoil the whole bunch. Or is it bushel?" Lance asked with a tilt of his head. He removed the last curler and then picked up a brush. Frowning, he shook his head. "Never mind. Look, sweetie, I know dickhead—"

"His name isn't dickhead," Kayla interrupted, although why she bothered was beyond her. Greg Alamo, her former boyfriend, didn't deserve any kindness from her and was the reason she'd sworn off dating actors for good. And the last thing she needed was another man who was jealous and controlling. She'd had more than enough of that with Greg. It was nice not worry about everything she said or did. Even the most casual glance at another man would have Greg accusing her of cheating on him. But it was okay for *him* to leer at other women to his heart's content. What a hypocrite.

"He's always been dickhead to me," Lance shot back with a smirk. "As I was saying before I was…*ahem*…interrupted. Just because dickhead cheated on you doesn't mean you should give up on love—or sex." Holding the brush above her head, he smiled wickedly. "When was the last time you got laid?"

"Now there's a question you don't hear every day."

Startled by the deep male voice, Kayla almost jumped out of her chair and Lance let out a girlish squeal as Sean Barrett sauntered into the room with his hands thrust into the pockets of his faded jeans. The collar of his white cotton shirt was open at the neck and his sleeves were rolled up to the elbows revealing his tanned forearms. The man oozed raw sexuality almost effortlessly. She tried not to stare but, *damn*, he was hot.

"Goodness gracious, clutch the pearls," Lance whispered in awe, holding the hairbrush to his lean chest as he stared at Sean, mouth agape.

With the grace of an athlete, Sean moved to the chair beside Kayla and lowered his muscular frame onto it. "Don't stop on my account," he said, meeting her stunned gaze in the mirror. He settled back in the chair. "I believe you were just asked a question."

Kayla felt her face warming. Swallowing hard, she couldn't seem to speak.

"If you have to think about it I guess it's been awhile," Sean drawled and then flashed a wicked grin.

"Well, for me, it was Friday night," Lance said, gathering his composure more quickly than Kayla was able to. "Turn your head, doll face." He put his hand on her head to direct her attention back to the mirror. "*And*

Saturday night," he added with sly grin. "Let's just say it was an excellent weekend."

"And they say actors have all the fun," Sean replied with a smile, looking at Lance. "I've seen Kayla at the studio, but I don't think we've met before. I'm Sean Barrett."

"Lance Del Rey. It's a pleasure to meet you," Lance gushed, and somehow managed to infuse the word "pleasure" with extra meaning.

Kayla rolled her eyes. "Please tell me you didn't change your last name again?"

Lance swung his gaze to her and nodded. "Girlfriend, St. James was way too pretentious."

"And Del Rey's not?"

Lance shrugged and started brushing out her hair. "Hey, if you were born with the last name Funkhauser you'd have a last name complex too."

Kayla looked at Sean and smiled. "I guess he's got a point." As Sean flashed a grin, she directed her attention back to Lance. "So, is Lance really your first name?" Lance averted his gaze and stared at a smudge on the mirror. "Oh, my God." Kayla giggled. "It's not, is it?" She glanced over at Sean who regarded them with amusement. He appeared relaxed and comfortable, his forearms resting on the arms of the chair. Kayla could see a fine coating of blond hair on his tanned skin and had to tamp down the sudden urge to reach over and touch him. "Spill it, Lance," she ordered. But Lance continued to avoid her gaze. His brush strokes turned rough indicating she'd struck a nerve. "That bad, huh?"

"No comment," Lance said, and then pressed his lips together in grim line. "Suffice it to say that some of us weren't given names like Kayla or Sean." He gathered her hair in his hands. "Do you want it up or down?"

"Down," Sean said before Kayla could respond. Both she and Lance turned to look at him. "I've been doing this a while. You'll look better on the cover if your hair is down." His gaze locked with hers and a gush of feminine awareness flooded her body. She'd never met anyone with emerald green eyes before. Up close they were amazing—hypnotizing even.

"I saw you in the grocery store," Kayla began, not able to tear her eyes from his. Sean's brows lifted. "On the cover of the current issue of *Soap Opera Journal,*" she clarified. "So I guess you know what you're talking about." Forcing her gaze back to the mirror, she looked up at Lance. "I'll wear it down."

Sandy rushed into the room, "Sorry, Sean. Marcus is here and he's been talking my ear off."

"Better you than me," Sean said dryly.

Sandy dropped her make-up kit on the counter and rummaged around in it before pulling out a bottle of foundation.

"Sandy, is that your Mustang in the parking lot?" Sean asked. "I've seen it over at the studio a few times."

"No," Sandy said as she abandoned the foundation for a jar of loose powder from her kit.

"If you're talking about the red Mustang, it's mine," Kayla said.

"'67, right?"

"'66." She tried to turn her head to look at him but felt Lance's fingers press into her scalp.

"Don't move," Lance warned. "I'm creating magic here."

"Yes, sir," Kayla said, amused. She watched as he

arranged her hair so it curled around her shoulders in soft waves.

"V-6?" Sean asked.

"V-8 with a 225 horsepower engine and a four-barrel carburetor. And the grille is the original free-floating pony emblem surrounded by horizontal grille bars." Glancing sideways at him in the mirror she could see the surprise on his face and smiled sheepishly. "My dad is into classic cars. He restored the Mustang and gave it to me for graduation. I think I know just about everything there is to know about '66 Mustangs."

Was she babbling? Of course she was. Being so close to him unnerved her.

"Automatic or stick?"

"Stick, of course."

"I *do* like a vertical stick," Lance chimed in. His eyes gleamed with mischief.

Sandy turned and glared at him. "Lance, please. Not before lunch." Shaking her head, she brushed some loose powder on Sean's face. "I'll just use a bit of mineral make up. With your skin tone you don't need much else."

Kayla watched Sean covertly in the mirror. Even though they'd been on the set together a couple of times she'd never been this close to him. Now he was three feet away and she couldn't seem to control her reaction to him. Yes, it had been awhile since she'd been with a man. But that was no excuse for the sexual energy humming through her body. Digging her fingers into the arms of her chair, she reminded herself she was a professional, and no matter how sexy Sean Barrett was, she would remain that way. Besides, he was an actor and there was no way in hell she was going down that road again.

Sean smiled at something Sandy said and the sheer wattage of it sent a jolt of electricity straight to Kayla's core. Okay, that was definitely *not* professional.

STANDING SEVERAL FEET away from the brightly lit backdrop, Sean couldn't take his eyes off Kayla Maxwell. She was posing with Marcus Bertrand while Leo, the photographer, gave them instructions.

"Marcus, loosen your arms. You're crushing the poor girl. Kayla, turn your head to the right just a smidge."

"Sorry, Leo," Marcus said and relaxed the death grip he had on Kayla. Sean was sure no one else noticed the flicker of relief in Kayla's eyes, but he caught it immediately. Marcus, as usual, was oblivious. "Is that better?"

"Much," Leo intoned. He leaned forward and put his eye to the camera sitting atop a tripod in front of him.

"There isn't a shadow on my cheek from my nose is there?" Marcus asked. "Maybe we should change positions. This really isn't my good side."

Behind him, Sandy and Lance tried unsuccessfully to stifle their giggles. Kayla must have heard them as well. Her lips twitched a bit as if she wanted to laugh with them, but she didn't. She remained professional, keeping a neutral expression on her face.

And what a face it was.

Living in Los Angeles, Sean had seen more than his fair share of beautiful women, but Kayla Maxwell was one of those rare women who was beautiful without even having to try.

Her hair flowed silkily around her shoulders and, like her eyes, was the color of rich dark chocolate. Her nose was small and fit her heart-shaped face perfectly. But it was her mouth that had caught his attention. Full and sensuous, it was a mouth that begged to be kissed. A mouth made for sin.

That mouth, and her womanly body, pushed his buttons in all the right ways. Unlike the majority of actresses in Hollywood, Kayla wasn't stick thin. She showcased that curvy body in a pair of black jeans that clung to her hips and thighs, and hugged her firm round ass to perfection. Her clingy turquoise top, while not low cut, couldn't disguise her full and lush breasts.

Sean watched with amazement as Marcus inched his hand up Kayla's midriff toward her breasts. He was close to copping a feel when Kayla, without even a flicker of change in her expression, reached up and pushed his hand back down.

Sean wasn't surprised by the asshole's actions. Marcus's character was one of the most popular on the show and he was pretty much allowed to get away with murder. Evidently popularity beat out talent. Why else would they allow a mediocre actor and womanizer like him to stay on the show?

"Great. I got some good shots," Leo said and turned. "Sean. I'd like to get some shots of you and Kayla and then we'll finish up with all three of you." Leo looked past him. "Sandy, Kayla's a little shiny."

"I'm on it, Leo."

Marcus let go of Kayla and moved toward Sean.

"Sean," he offered with a nod as Sandy headed for Kayla with a jar of powder and a brush in her hand. Kayla smiled at Sandy. He'd noticed Kayla smiled a lot. It seemed genuine, but he'd been fooled before and didn't plan on making that mistake again.

"I read that your father is getting rave reviews for his role in King Lear," Marcus said, drawing Sean's attention away from Kayla.

"Has he?" Sean asked, not trying to conceal his annoyance. The only reason Bertrand talked to him at all was because of his burning desire to meet James Barrett. Sean had already worked on *A New Dawn* for three years when Marcus joined the show. On his first day he'd marched right up to Sean and declared that James Barrett was the reason he'd become an actor. And then he'd gone on to say that James Barrett was the greatest actor of his generation.

Although Marcus was right, Sean recognized bullshit when he heard it and shut him down immediately. He never talked about his father with anyone and wasn't going to start with Marcus. But Marcus, being the self-absorbed idiot that he was, didn't seem to get the hint, and always managed to drop James Barrett's name whenever he could.

"There's talk of another Tony award." Marcus flashed his famous dimples.

"We're ready, Sean," Leo said, moving to his place behind the camera.

Marcus grinned while leering at Kayla. "Enjoy. She's the hottest piece of ass we've had on the show in years. Damn, I'd like to tap that."

Sean clenched his fist and resisted the urge to punch Marcus's smug face. "How's your wife?" he asked instead.

"Fine," Marcus said stiffly, his face suffusing with color. "In fact, I should call her. Excuse me." After pulling his phone from the pocket of his khaki pants,

Marcus moved toward a row of chairs at the back of the studio.

Sean turned and strode toward Kayla. Sandy brushed passed him and gave him a sunny smile. He nodded and then halted next to Kayla. She was taller than he'd realized. He'd worked with Nikki for a long time and whenever they did photo shoots together she had to stand on a box next to him so he wouldn't have to stoop. That wouldn't be the case with his new co-star. If Kayla possessed at least half of Nikki's talent maybe it wouldn't be so bad working with her.

"Okay, let's start with a standard pose," Leo said. "Kayla, step into Sean's embrace. Sean, I want you to loop your arms around her waist. Kayla, put your right hand on Sean's arm."

It was indeed a standard pose, and both he and Kayla moved to do it automatically, but the moment Sean put his arms around her he caught a whiff of the soft fragrance she wore. It was subtle but intoxicating—vanilla with a hint of spice. A spike of heat caught him low in his gut, catching him off guard.

"Good. Very good," Leo said. "You two look great together."

Sean had done hundreds of photo shoots during his tenure on the soap. Over the past ten years his character had had several different love interests, but he sure as hell couldn't remember being this physically affected by any of them. The pose was chaste yet he was intensely aware of her.

Leo lifted his head from the camera. "Kayla, I want you to turn with your back to Sean. Sean, you know the drill."

Kayla glanced up at him and he realized he still

had his arms around her. “Sorry,” he muttered, letting her go. She turned around and stepped back. His arms snaked around her, and the moment her soft curves pressed against him, his body reacted. Heat curled inside him, threatening his control.

Again, he inhaled her alluring scent and his body tightened anew with sexual awareness. Her breasts curved out just above his clasped hands. Right there, waiting for him to…

Baseball.

Think about baseball, not breasts. Let’s see, as of today the Dodgers were in first place. The season was young but anything could happen by the time October rolled around.

“Sean. Loosen up.” Leo’s voice penetrated his consciousness and Sean realized he’d tensed. Expelling a breath, he tried to relax.

In his arms, Kayla seemed totally unruffled. He was the one affected by their close proximity, not her. As she had been with Marcus, she was totally professional. Just as Nikki had always been. The only difference was, in the three years he’d worked with Nikki he hadn’t once lusted after her.

He thought about the relationship he’d ended last year. It had been with an actress, and after discovering she was just one more woman who had wanted to use him to further her own career, he’d vowed never to date another woman in his profession again—no matter how attracted to her he was. And there was no doubt he was attracted to Kayla Maxwell. No doubt at all.

KAYLA PULLED HER Mustang into a coveted parking spot across from Cheech’s Pizza and turned off the ignition. Glancing at her watch, she saw she was ten minutes early for her lunch date with Lisa. Just as she was about to open the door her cell phone rang. Digging into the side pocket of her purse she pulled it out and saw Lisa's name on the screen.

"I'm on Hillhurst," Lisa said before Kayla could speak. "Are you there yet?"

"I just got here."

"I'll be there in five minutes. Order my usual." Kayla waited for Lisa to continue but all she heard was silence. Unable to suppress a grin, Kayla shoved her phone back into her purse and opened the door. She climbed out of her car and waited for the traffic to pass before crossing the street.

Cheech's was in the central Los Angeles neighborhood known as Los Feliz. Lantern Studios, where *A New Dawn* was taped, was in the same part of town but Kayla had discovered the place long before she'd landed her role on the soap. She lived nearby in Atwood Village and had been coming to Cheech's for years. The prices were affordable and the food delicious, the perfect combination for a struggling actress. But even after she started working steadily and was making more money she still preferred Cheech's to some of the more trendy pizzerias, the kind of places where people went to be seen. Definitely not her style.

Once she'd placed her and Lisa's orders, she brought their drinks outside and snagged the last unoccupied table. She hung her purse over the back of the chair, sat down and sipped her soda. It was a gorgeous spring day—sunny and warm, the kind of day that drew so many people to California with the promise of year round sunshine.

Her thoughts drifted to the photo shoot. And to Sean Barrett. Even now, she could feel his strong arms around her and, just like in the studio, her body tingled with awareness. His clean male scent had made her almost lightheaded. She couldn't remember ever being so drawn to a man before. It had taken everything inside her to remain professional and to not let on just how affected she was by his hard body touching hers.

Lisa's silver BMW roadster zipped by. Craning her neck, Kayla watched Lisa expertly maneuver into a small open spot across the street. When Lisa opened the door and stepped out Kayla saw the two men at the table next to her turn and stare—something that happened quite often.

"I'm famished," Lisa said when she reached the table. She sat down in the chair opposite Kayla and took off her oversized black sunglasses. She hooked them over the edge of her tote and then stowed it beside her. "How did the photo shoot go?" After brushing back her long white-blonde hair, she reached for the soda Kayla had bought for her. "Did Marcus touch the girls again?" Lisa asked, lowering her gaze briefly to Kayla's breasts.

"No. Thank God." Kayla shuddered, remembering the photo shoot she'd done with him just after she'd joined the show. To this day he maintained that touching her breasts had been *accidental*. Just like his tongue had *accidentally* slipped into her mouth during their first kissing scene.

"He's a pig." Lisa took a sip of her soda just as the owner of Cheech's brought out their order. "I've been dying for one of these for days. They make the best vegetarian meatball sub in L.A. Just one slice?" she asked, eying Kayla's plate with puzzlement.

Thinking of the lines she had to memorize tonight, Kayla shrugged. "I guess I can afford to eat two. I won't be wearing leather bustiers and halter tops on the show much longer. Shay's pregnant."

Lisa looked up at her. "What?"

Kayla picked up her pizza. "It's in tomorrow's script. Jared comes across Shay in a park near the cemetery. She's very upset and he tries to help her. She blurts out that she's pregnant with Stefan's baby."

"So that's why they wanted shots of you, Marcus and Sean. Now it makes sense." She paused, tried to suppress a grin and failed. "How do you feel about working with Sean?"

Kayla met Lisa's shrewd gaze. "He's the best actor on the show," she said, hoping she didn't sound as apprehensive as she felt. Not only was Sean the best actor on the show but he was the son of Hollywood royalty. It was intimidating, and what was even more unsettling was that during the photo shoot he'd awakened something that had been dormant inside her since she'd broken up with Greg.

Her sexuality.

"You didn't answer my question."

Kayla shrugged, not wanting to acknowledge just how much Sean had affected her. "I think I'll prefer him to Marcus."

Lisa snorted. "Working with a trained monkey is preferable to working with Marcus. Not to mention Sean is very easy on the eyes."

"Is that why you took him on as a client?"

"You know I never mix business with pleasure. I

took him on because, like you said, he's the best actor on the show. He's going to be around a long time. And I think he has the potential to transition out of soaps and into film work. If he wants to."

"I wonder why he's never been nominated for an Emmy."

"From what I've heard he never submits his name."

"That's unusual."

Tilting her head, Lisa met her gaze. "I've only worked with him for a short time. He's nothing like I expected."

"What do you mean?"

"He couldn't care less about fame or publicity. He doesn't want to do fan events at all, and getting him to a red carpet event is like pulling teeth."

"That must make your job difficult."

Lisa grinned. "That's why I get paid the big bucks. I finally convinced him to go to *A New Dawn's* fan club luncheon next month."

"I'm really looking forward to that."

"I think you'll be pleasantly surprised at the reaction you'll get. I've been doing a little surfing on the internet. You've got a fan base out there. It's small but growing."

"I've been afraid to go online. My mom, bless her heart, got into it with some fans on a message board. Evidently, they were saying some really nasty stuff about Shay and about me as well." Kayla smiled. "Mom tore them a new one and got banned from the website."

"That sounds like Patricia. She's very protective of you and Kelly."

Lisa's mention of her sister reminded Kayla she needed to call Kelly. Her sister was almost three years older, a publicist like Lisa, and worked in the media relations department of the San Francisco Blaze Major League Baseball organization.

"So, back to Sean…" Lisa was saying.

"Right. Tomorrow will be the first day we actually share a scene with dialogue."

"You up for it?"

Kayla hoped her primal reaction this morning was just a fluke. If not, working so closely with him was going to prove just how good an actress she was.

Or, more to the point, *wasn't.*

"I'll have to be."

Three

Jared: I want to help you. If you'll let me.
Shay: You don't even know me. And besides, I'm in love with Stefan.

EARLY THE NEXT morning, Kayla made her way down the brightly lit hallway at Lantern Studios holding a much-needed cup of coffee. As she passed framed head shots of past and present cast members from the show, she noticed her picture was now among them—coincidentally—right next to Sean's.

When she reached the last office at the end of the hallway, she paused at the doorway. "Hi," she said to the show's stage manager, Amanda Todd. "Are you ready for the weekend?"

Amanda looked up from her desk and smiled. "I'm always ready. Jim and I are taking a break from the kids and driving up to Santa Barbara."

"That sounds fun." Kayla leaned against the doorframe. "Do you have scripts for me?"

"Not yet. I should get them before taping is finished. I'll drop them by your dressing room or you can stop by before you leave today." Amanda leaned back in her chair. "I looked over today's script. It looks like you might be working with Sean for a while." She paused. "And I hear Rachel isn't too happy about it."

"Why would she care?"

"She's been lobbying to be Sean's next love interest." Amanda picked up a stack of envelopes on her desk held together tightly with a rubber band. "These are for you." Kayla stepped forward and took them. "Fan mail," Amanda continued. "I saw them in the production office."

"Wow. There's a lot this week." Kayla looked up from the letters. "Wait. Did you say love interest? It's just a couple of scenes. I don't think I'm Sean's—I mean *Jared's*—new love interest."

Amanda's brows furrowed. "I thought you said you watched soaps."

"I did. I watched *A New Dawn* when I was in high school. But not since I moved to L.A."

"Okay, I'll give you a pass then." With a good-humored grin, Amanda folded her arms on her desk. "There aren't any random scenes, Kayla. They're chem testing you and Sean. If they like what they see then you can bet your ass Jared and Shay will be hooking up."

"But…but Shay's pregnant."

Amanda shrugged. "Doesn't matter. Besides, she's not even past her first trimester. Anything could happen to that baby. It's a soap. Outrageous stuff happens all the time."

"That's true," Kayla said. "I mean how many people do *you* know who've come back from the dead?"

"Or had a baby they forgot they gave birth to," Amanda deadpanned.

Kayla laughed and then noticed the clock on the wall. "I'd better go. Rehearsal is in five minutes."

Since she was running behind schedule, instead of relaxing in her dressing room like she usually did, Kayla rushed to put away her purse and fan mail. With her cup of coffee and script in hand, she left the dressing room and headed for the set. She'd never been late and didn't want to start now and risk angering the show's director. So rather than stopping to chat with the crew she just gave them a friendly wave and stepped onto the set.

"Good morning, Kayla," Bill Caruso said as she came around the gazebo that made up part of the park set where she and Sean would be doing their scenes.

"Hi, Bill," she said and then glimpsed Sean on the other side of the gazebo. He was on his cell phone, so engrossed in his conversation he hadn't seen her come on set.

Kayla let her gaze roam over him and, *damn it*, he still looked as hot as he did yesterday at the photo shoot. Last night she'd tried to convince herself she'd only imagined his blond good looks. But she hadn't. Wearing jeans and a blue chambray shirt, Sean looked so gorgeous her heart started racing.

Swallowing, she tore her gaze from his muscular frame. She tried to steady her erratic heartbeat but couldn't. And that worried her. Because if Amanda was right, and Jared and Shay were going to hook up, then she and Sean would be spending a lot of time together on the set. And not only that—there would probably be love scenes. It nerved her up just thinking about it.

She had worked for seven years in Hollywood and kissed more actors than she could count. Not one of them had ever made her skin tingle and her stomach flutter when she looked at them.

Only Sean Barrett had ever elicited that reaction.

SEAN GRIPPED HIS phone tightly and wished he hadn't answered the damn thing to begin with. Talking to his father was never his idea of a good time, but he'd been avoiding his father for quite some time and felt obliged to take the call.

"The play is going well," James Barrett said.

"I hear you're getting rave reviews," Sean said, remembering Marcus's attempt to suck up to him yesterday.

"You've read them?" His father sounded surprised.

"No. One of my co-workers mentioned it."

After an uncomfortable silence, James continued, "I'll be here in New York until the end of the summer. If you don't mind, I'd like you to go out to the house occasionally. The housekeeper will be there once a week but it would put my mind at ease if you kept an eye on the place."

"I can do that," Sean replied, running a hand through his hair. Out of the corner of his eye he noticed Kayla had arrived on the set and immediately his pulse spiked.

"I assume you still have your key."

"Somewhere," Sean said absently, watching Kayla talk to their director, Bill. Her hair was pulled up into a loose ponytail and she wore a pair of sweats and a T-shirt that couldn't disguise her curvy body. His gaze rested on her full breasts and he felt a pull in his groin.

"You sound distracted."

"I'm at work." He could hear the annoyance in his father's tone and didn't care. Sean braced himself for what was coming next. It was always the same.

"You've wasted ten years of your life on that dreadful show. Don't you think it's time you start taking your career seriously and admit that you're staying there just to spite me?"

"I do take my career seriously." Sean felt his temper

rise but worked to keep it in check. "And I'm not on this show to spite you. Quit trying to control my life *and* my career."

"I just think you can do better, Sean," James said after several tense seconds.

Sean let out an exasperated sigh. "I'm tired of having this same conversation over and over. I'm not leaving the show. So get the hell over it." He hung up, shoved the phone into the pocket of his jeans then let out a controlled breath before crossing the set. Forcing his father from his mind, he met Kayla's dark eyes. She smiled at him as he halted next to Bill.

"Good morning," she said cheerfully.

"Morning." Sean nodded, letting his gaze roam over her face. She wasn't wearing a drop of make-up, yet she looked even more beautiful than she had at the photo shoot.

"Okay, guys," Bill said, looking from Sean to Kayla. "The blocking for your scenes today is pretty simple. Kayla, you'll be sitting on the bench. For the first part of the scene we'll be replaying Shay's break-up with Stefan. Later today, I'm going to have you do a short scene showing Shay taking a home pregnancy test. It will read positive. There won't be any dialogue, just a reaction shot. It'll run after we replay the break-up scene. Sean, Jared will come from around the gazebo. I want you to stop in front of it when you see her. Jared doesn't know her. He's seen her with Stefan but they've never spoken. But he's concerned because she's visibly upset. You'll pause for several seconds and then go over to her. After your first two lines of dialogue I want you to sit next to her. We'll do the rest of the scenes with the two of you sitting on the bench. Right now I don't have any script changes." Bill looked down at his clipboard. "Let's do a run through before you go to hair and make-up."

Sean pulled his script from the back pocket of his jeans. He'd memorized his lines and didn't think he'd need it, but just in case he always kept it handy during the run through.

As Kayla moved to the bench Sean walked to a spot just beyond the gazebo. He watched as she sat down and set her coffee and her script next to her.

"Let's do it," Bill said, backing away from Kayla. "Sean, I'll motion when I want you to enter the scene. Kayla, when we're taping, the camera will be on you. Shay is upset. She's just lost the man she loves and is pregnant with his baby. She has no one to turn to and nowhere to go. I want that pain and desperation evident on your face."

Kayla grinned. "Not asking for much, are you?"

Bill laughed. "Just the moon and the stars, darlin'."

Sean looked at Bill with astonishment. He didn't remember Bill ever being so jovial before. What was up with that?

"Remember there'll be clips playing for the viewers to see, but we're going to edit you in. You'll need to sustain what Shay's feeling for about two minutes. On three, Kayla," Bill said and then counted down.

The moment just before Bill counted to one the expression on Kayla's face changed dramatically. Sean had never seen anything like it. One second she was smiling at Bill and the next her face was a mask of misery. Tears welled in her eyes and her body trembled. He watched—transfixed—as she became Shay and without a saying a single word was able to make him believe her heart was breaking.

After a minute or so had passed, Bill pointed at him. Sean moved forward slowly and then paused at his mark. Jared had just come from the cemetery visiting his wife's grave. He was in pain. The moment Kayla noticed him she wiped her eyes and turned away quickly. She looked so distraught that Sean couldn't help but do exactly what Jared was about to do. Try to help her.

"Are you okay?" he asked, moving toward the bench. "Is there anything I can do?"

"I'm fine."

"Most people don't cry when they're fine." He paused. "May I sit down?" She nodded and then looked away as if she were embarrassed to be caught crying. "I've seen you with Stefan Cabot. And you were at my wife's funeral. Did you know her?"

She turned to him, her eyes still glistening with tears. "I met her at the hospital. I needed someone to talk to and she…she listened." She wiped her cheeks. "I saw her a few times. The last time…" Her voice broke and a beat later she continued, "The last time she gave me some really good advice."

"Rebecca was good at that."

"I wish I'd taken that advice," Kayla said. "You loved her a lot, didn't you?"

"Yes. I did." He turned away from her sympathetic eyes, feeling Jared's pain.

"What you said…at her funeral." She put her hand on his arm, her fingers warm and soft. An electric charge shot through his body. He swung his gaze back to hers as she said, "Your eulogy was so beautiful…so loving."

"That was Rebecca. Beautiful and loving," he said,

blinking back the sudden moisture in his own eyes. “And that’s how I want her to be remembered.”

“She told me about you.” She gave him a tremulous smile.

“What did she say?”

“That you were the best man she’d ever known.” Kayla squeezed his arm. “Oh. And that she was the luckiest woman in the world.”

“I was the lucky one,” Sean whispered, so in the moment that his eyes were indeed welling up.

“There aren’t any words to make what you’re going through any easier, but I’m so very sorry for your loss.”

“Thank you,” he said, and reached up to wipe his eyes. He was tearing up in rehearsal. When was the last time that happened? “You were upset. Why?”

“It doesn’t matter.” She shook her head, sadness etched on her face.

“Maybe I can help.”

She withdrew her hand from his arm. “I don’t think so.”

“Try me. Whatever it is, it can’t be that bad.”

“Yes, it can.” Her lower lip trembled. She bit it as fresh tears filled her eyes and spilled down her cheeks. “I’m pregnant.”

“And cut.” Bill’s voice broke the silence. “Excellent work, you two.”

Still staring into Kayla’s eyes, Sean barely heard Bill’s words.

Son of a bitch.

She was good.

STILL REELING FROM the emotional scenes she and Sean had just finished taping, Kayla stepped into her dressing room and closed the door behind her. She collapsed onto the cushions of the small sofa near the door and, leaning her head back, she closed her eyes and tried to shake off Shay McKade.

Until recently, she'd been able to completely lose herself in whatever character she was playing. But somewhere during her two year relationship with Greg, she had lost that ability as well as great deal of confidence. Landing the role of Shay had given her hope that she wasn't as untalented Greg believed she was.

Today with Sean she'd felt a connection. There was no denying it. The difference between Sean and Marcus Bertrand was astounding. Marcus was a lazy actor. He had a hard time remembering his lines and always seemed mentally absent from their scenes. The phrase "phoning it in" definitely applied to Marcus. The only time he was invested in their characters' interaction was when they had a love scene.

Her eyes flew open when a light knock at her door startled her. "Kayla, it's Sean. Can I talk to you for a minute?"

Kayla bolted upright, her heart pounding. "Come in," she called out, brushing her hair away from her face. Sean opened the door and stepped inside. The room was small and his virile presence seemed to overwhelm it. He'd changed out of his character's clothing into his own and had washed the stage make-up off his face. He closed the door behind him.

"Would you like to sit down?" she asked, then realized that would be a mistake.

The sofa was actually more of a love seat, and if he sat next to her he would practically be on top of her. Considering the effect his green eyes were having on her right now, being that close to him might cause her to do something extremely foolish.

"No. Thanks. I'm good." Sean rested against the door and shoved his hands into the pockets of his jeans. Kayla couldn't help but notice how the faded blue denim accentuated his muscular thighs. Idly, she wondered if he was a boxers or briefs kind of man. Probably briefs. In fact, she could almost picture his Calvins or BVD's lovingly cupping his…

"Kayla." The sound of her name cut through her wayward thoughts. She lifted her gaze to his and hoped he couldn't read her mind.

"Sorry, I zoned out for a sec." Her face was hot.

Good Lord, what the hell is going on? She was acting like she'd been without a man for years.

The corner of his mouth quirked in a half smile; Kayla could see why millions of women all over the country had voted him the sexiest male soap star in *People* magazine. That smile, along with his stunning eyes, would tempt any woman to drop her panties.

"I wanted to talk to you about Jared and Shay," Sean said, seemingly unaware of the affect he was having on her.

"Jared and Shay? What about them?"

"The scenes we taped today make it pretty obvious that Ken has decided to put them together."

"You think so?"

"Don't you?"

Kayla leaned back against the sofa. "Truthfully, I thought my days on the show were numbered. But this morning Amanda told me she's pretty sure I'm your new love interest." Pausing at the flicker of amusement in his eyes, she corrected herself. "I mean *Shay* is

Jared's new love interest. Amanda mentioned something about a chem test."

"It was," Sean said, "and when I first read the scenes I wasn't happy about it."

That bothered her. "May I ask why?" Was there another actress on the show he'd rather work with? Did Sean, like Greg, think she was a mediocre actress?

"Because Jared has just lost the love of his life," Sean said. "I've been playing this guy for almost ten years. I know him. He wouldn't bury his wife and then hook up with another woman so quickly."

"It would also anger the fans who watched Jared and Rebecca fall in love."

"Exactly. But the fans wouldn't have any trouble believing that Jared would help Shay. That's the kind of character he is." Sean paused. His gaze shifted above her head, to where she'd hung a portrait of her family taken during the Christmas holidays. "So the other day I talked to Ken," he said, looking back at her.

"You did?" Kayla asked, amazed at his boldness. "I'm afraid to talk to him. I hear he gets really ticked off if the actors try to talk to him about their storylines."

Sean gave her a lazy smile and shrugged. "He does. He definitely didn't appreciate me putting in my two cents, but I think I got my point across."

Kayla tilted her head, curious. "And that was?"

"I've noticed in the last year or so that the writers have gotten into the habit of rushing things."

"I know what you mean. Shay wasn't even in town a week before she and Stefan were hitting the sheets." She hadn't been happy about it, but she was new to the show and thrilled to get the part, so she'd kept her thoughts to herself.

"When I read the scenes, I had a pretty good idea where the writers were going. And when I talked to Ken he pretty much confirmed it."

"Okay, I'm curious," Kayla said, leaning forward. "Where *are* the writers going with Jared and Shay?"

"Jared and Shay are strangers. They're both dealing with the loss of the people they love. Jared is grieving for Rebecca, and Shay has been dumped by Stefan only to find out she's pregnant with his baby. Jared believes he'll never fall in love again so he offers to help Shay. He takes her in and tells her he's willing to be a father to her child."

Kayla frowned. "Is that really believable?"

Sean let out a short laugh. "Kayla, it's a soap."

"Right." Kayla chuckled. "I forgot for a minute. Okay, so even though Shay moves in with Jared she's still in love with Stefan. But then Jared and Shay start to have feelings for each other, right?"

"Now you're catching on," Sean said with a grin. "What I told Ken was that it shouldn't happen overnight."

"I agree," Kayla said. Sean's eyes lowered briefly to her chest and suddenly she remembered she was still wearing her character's wardrobe. Reaching up, she tugged at the neckline with her fingers so it wasn't so revealing. "My mom is always complaining about how fast the characters hop into bed these days. She says the best part is watching a couple fall in love." Kayla's pulse sped up as Sean lifted his gaze to hers. "She loves soaps," she added to fill the lengthy silence that fell between them.

"Your mom is right," Sean said as he moved to the sofa. He sat down next to her, his knee brushing hers.

The contact was casual but it caused goosebumps to rise on her skin.

Just as she'd thought, the sofa was far too small. He seemed to realize it too and shifted his body away from hers as he continued. "Not only have Jared and Shay been through a lot, but it would insult the audience's intelligence if they fell madly in love in just a month or two. Plus, Shay is still a new character. The audience needs to connect with her. To get to know her as a character in her own right, and not just as the woman who had an affair with Stefan."

Kayla was impressed with Sean's ability to see the big picture. She certainly hadn't seen it. But then Sean had been on the show for ten years. If anyone would know the intricacies of the storylines, he would.

"Kayla, I think this could be a story the audience could really buy into—" he paused "—if it's not rushed. And after today I have no doubt Ken will go ahead with it."

"What do you mean, after today?"

Sean's genial expression turned serious. "I'm going to be honest with you. Before you were cast on the show, I'd never heard of you. And since you've been here, we've only been in a couple of ensemble scenes together. I had no idea if you could act or if you were hired because of your looks."

"So what's the verdict?" Kayla asked. "Can I act, or am I just a bimbo who got hired because I look good in lingerie?"

"Is that a trick question?" Sean grinned. "Because I'm pretty sure you look good in lingerie."

"Just answer the question," she said, almost afraid to hear his answer.

Sean's grin faded. "Are you telling me you didn't feel it?"

"Feel what?"

"They don't call it a chemistry test for nothing. Not all actors have it. But we do. You heard Bill. He couldn't stop raving about our scenes today."

Kayla was speechless. And surprised. Until now she didn't have a clue if Sean had felt the same connection she'd felt between them. Obviously, he did.

"Kayla, I've been doing this a long time. Ken's going to look at those scenes and see the same thing Bill saw."

Kayla swallowed the sudden lump that seemed to be lodged in her throat. "What did he see?"

"What all of America will see when those scenes air in a few weeks," Sean said with a confident grin. "Magic."

Four

Jared: I've been giving the situation a lot of thought. I think we should get married.
Shay: Are you delusional?

SITTING ON HIS surfboard in the chilly water off of Huntington Beach, Sean watched his best friend paddle toward him. Lying flat on his board, Matt used his powerful arms to cleave into the gray water of the Pacific Ocean. After he'd glided past Sean and maneuvered around to face the shore, Matt pushed himself up and straddled his board.

"The waves are pretty mild today," Matt commented. Sean stared at the beach front stores just across the Pacific Coast Highway. Huntington Beach, as always, bustled with people. Although the sun would be setting soon, the mid spring day had been warm. The ocean—not so much. "There's not a lot of daylight left. I wish I'd been able to get here earlier," Matt added when Sean didn't reply.

"I'm surprised you're here at all." Sean looked at his friend. "I thought you weren't supposed to participate in any dangerous sports during the season."

"Surfing isn't dangerous," Matt grumbled. "Shit, we've been riding waves since we were kids. And besides, what the suits don't know won't hurt them."

"I listened to the game on the way over this morning," Sean said, not sure if he should bring up the free-for-all Matt had started by going after the Padres' star pitcher after being hit by a wild pitch.

"So I guess you know I got tossed." Matt grinned as if being ejected from the game was a good thing. Two years ago Matt wouldn't have batted an eye over a getting hit by a pitch. He'd take his base and hope that the pitcher's mistake would result in the Dodgers scoring a run. But now he seemed almost proud of his bad boy reputation. Sean was worried that his friend's behavior was going to cost him his career.

"I heard." Sean adjusted the zipper of his wetsuit. In the distance he saw several seagulls fly toward the shore and heard their faint cawing. "Why'd you go after him?" he asked, shifting his gaze back to Matt.

"He fucking hit me. With his fast ball," Matt snapped, his dark eyes flashing with anger.

"You've been hit dozens of times and never charged the mound. Did something else happen?"

"No," Matt said with a terse edge in his voice. "Nothing else happened."

"If you want to talk about it..."

"I don't."

Sean knew Matt well enough not to press him. His friend had gone through a hell Sean wouldn't wish on his worst enemy. Matt kept insisting he was fine but his actions told a different story. Unlike Matt, Sean listened to sports radio. The latest buzz was that Matt's behavior on and off the field might end with him being traded. Sean hoped that wouldn't happen.

"I caught your show the other day." Matt rested his hands on his thighs. "Some of the guys watch it in the clubhouse," he added. "Is Kayla Maxwell as hot in person as she in on television and in the movies?"

Hotter, Sean thought. Just the other day wardrobe had her dressed in a skimpy black halter dress that sent his temperature through the roof. Her character, Shay, was pregnant but not showing yet and Jared had followed her to a party to try to convince her to marry him.

"Movies? What movies?" he asked, forcing thoughts of Kayla's hot body from his mind.

Matt grinned. "Not porn, if that's what you're thinking. She was in a couple of slasher flicks."

"Which ones?"

"*Trick or Treat,*" Matt replied. "And the sequel, *Halloween Hell*. They're both classics."

"Never saw them," he said, although he vaguely remembered the titles.

"You should. Trust me. She wasn't naked but there are a couple of scenes where she might as well have been."

For some reason the lascivious look on Matt's face irritated Sean. "I've been working with her for the past few weeks. She's a good actress," Sean said, and then almost lost his balance in the choppy water. He put his hands on his board to steady himself and stay upright.

"Of course she is." Matt rolled his eyes "That's why all the guys in the clubhouse watch the show. For her *acting*." Matt laughed, annoying Sean even more. "Think you'll have any love scenes with her?"

"Probably."

Until Matt brought up Kayla's name Sean had been doing a pretty decent job of not thinking about her. They'd been working together at least three or four days a week for the past three weeks, and the more he worked with her the more he appreciated her talent. For the first time in several years he felt challenged by his acting partner. Watching her transform completely into the character of Shay showed a dedication to her craft he admired. What surprised him the most though, was the fact that she didn't seem to grasp just how good she was. Most actresses were drama queens or had egos the size of the Goodyear Blimp. So far, Kayla hadn't exhibited either trait. But if experience had taught him anything, she would; it was just a matter of time.

"Man, I envy you sometimes." Matt grinned. "How many guys get to kiss women as a part of their job?"

"There's like a million people standing around."

"Did you ever get a boner when you were kissing one of your co-stars?"

"When I was nineteen," Sean said. Glancing behind him, he noticed the bank of gray-tinged clouds that—as they did every day—would roll in to shore after sunset. "It was embarrassing."

"But you're able to control yourself now, right?"

Sean nodded and then grinned at his friend. "But Kayla *is* smokin' hot."

"Do you still have those two rules you told me about?" Balancing himself on his board, Matt squinted at him. "No tongue...and what was the other one?"

"No groping."

"So you've never slipped one of your co-stars the tongue?"

"Actually, I did. And she was *not* amused." He paused. "Why do you think I came up with the rules?"

Matt threw back his head and laughed. For a moment Sean was reminded of the scraggly dark-haired kid he'd met in first grade, the friend who had helped Sean through the toughest time in his life. The death of the mother he adored.

"I think I'll try to catch a few waves before sundown." Matt eased himself down on his board. "I'll see you on the beach," he said as he paddled away.

Looking up at the sky, Sean figured he had about an hour of daylight left. He hadn't been surfing in a while but today he'd decided to brave the cold waters of the Pacific. The ocean never failed to relax him. Today however, he found it hard to relax and keep his mind off work. Or more specifically, off Kayla Maxwell.

SITTING IN HER kitchen, Kayla half listened to the six o'clock news while she opened her fan mail. Just as she sliced open an envelope with her letter opener, her cell phone played "Who Can It Be Now," startling her. Setting the opener and the envelope down, she reached for her phone and saw her sister's name on the caller ID.

Kelly's naturally husky voice greeted her. "How's my favorite sister?"

"Your only sister," she said with a wry smile. "I'm fine. How about you?"

Kelly let out a long sigh. "Stressed. One of the players got pulled over by the highway patrol last night. Drunk driving. There was a little too much celebrating after the team's win yesterday. We've been doing damage control all day."

"And here I thought you just sat around all day surrounded by hunky baseball players." Glancing at the television, she saw the sports segment was on and the station was running a clip of the Dodgers game. Kayla watched the batter get hit by a pitch. He threw his bat to the ground and sprinted toward the pitcher. When he reached him, he punched him square in the face. In seconds, both dugouts had cleared and punches were being thrown left and right. "Holy cow," she said, unable to look away. "I'm watching the news and they're showing a hell of a brawl between the Dodgers and the Padres."

"I saw that," Kelly said. "I'm glad Matt Scanlon isn't with the Blaze. I'd never get a day off. The rumor is that the Dodgers are going to cut him loose. Oh, by the way, I'll be in L.A. in early July when the Blaze play the Dodgers. It's a four-game series so we'll get to spend some time together."

"Do you want to stay with me? I finally fixed up my guest room."

"Sure," Kelly said. "I'll rent a car so you don't have to drive me around. And if you want to come to one of the games I'm sure I can arrange it."

"I'd love to." Kayla glanced down at her fan mail and saw an envelope addressed to her character rather than to her.

"By the way, I saw Greg on one of those Hollywood gossip shows." Kelly's voice hardened. "I really hate that asshole."

"You never did like him, did you?" Kayla asked as she studied the precise block lettering on the envelope.

"No. The first time I met him I knew what a controlling bastard he was."

"You didn't tell me."

"I tried, but you had stars in your eyes." Kelly sighed. "I knew you'd figure it out eventually. You're a smart cookie."

"Not smart enough. I spent nearly two years with him."

"He didn't break you, Kayla," Kelly said after a lengthy silence.

Kayla's eyes grew moist. "He almost did. I was ready to leave Hollywood and my career behind because of him."

"But you didn't," Kelly reminded her. "And you showed him. You're on the number one daytime show in the country. And what's he doing?" Kelly's snort was derisive. "Voiceovers."

"You can make good money doing voiceovers," Kayla pointed out.

"But Greg wants to be a movie star. He's got the ego of Tom Cruise but only a fraction of the talent." Kelly's laugh was devilish. "I would love to run into him and give him a piece of my mind. I know exactly what I'd say to him."

"I'm sure it involves a lot of cussing."

"You know me too well," Kelly said dryly.

After promising to talk on the weekend, she and Kelly said their goodbyes. Kayla put her phone aside and looked down at the small white envelope she still held in her hand. It wasn't unheard of for her to get fan mail addressed to her character. Just like the woman in the grocery store a few weeks ago, there were people out there that confused her with Shay McKade.

Slipping the piece of paper from the envelope, Kayla opened it and sucked in a shocked breath as she read the bold block print written in blood red ink.

WHORE! LEAVE TOWN OR YOU'LL BE SORRY!

Quickly, her shock turned to puzzlement. It wasn't like she hadn't received letters similar to this one before. After all, her character wasn't exactly Snow White. But really? Did this so-called fan think a letter like this would accomplish anything? All it did was prove that some people took their soap operas way too seriously. Folding the letter, she tossed it and the envelope on the table and reached for another one. She opened it quickly and started reading.

"Why, thank you…" she glanced down at the signature "…Janice, my number one fan in Ocala, Florida. I think Shay is too good for Stefan too." She put the letter on the stack with the ones she would send a personal reply to and grabbed the next one. The cute little pink envelope was adorned festively with hand-drawn smiley faces. It had to be a nice one, right?

Wrong.

"Holy crap," she muttered after reading it. "For the last time, people, Nikki wasn't fired because of me. I liked Nikki." Kayla threw the letter down, done for the evening. She rose from the table, picked up the small stack of nasty letters and moved into the kitchen, where she tossed them into the trash and didn't give them a second thought.

Five

Shay: I can't marry you. I don't love you, and you don't love me.
Jared: I know. It's perfect.

THE SECOND KAYLA walked into the make-up room after Monday morning's rehearsal she wished she hadn't. Sitting in one of the four chairs was Rachel Hixson, and Kayla had no desire whatsoever to engage in polite chit-chat with her. Sandy, who was applying foundation to Rachel's pale cheeks, shot her a quick smile as Kayla sat in the chair farthest from Rachel.

"Hi, Kayla," Sandy said cheerfully. She smoothed the make-up sponge over Rachel's jawline. "Did you have a nice weekend?"

Settling back in the cushioned chair, Kayla noticed the sidelong glance Rachel gave her. "Yes. How was yours?"

"Busy," Sandy said. "I did make-up for a runway show on Saturday night."

"I went to the premiere of the new Ben Affleck movie," Rachel said, inserting herself into the conversation. "Ben and I are friends, you know," she added with a smile more practiced than genuine. "There were paparazzi absolutely everywhere. We couldn't get away from them."

Kayla noticed Sandy trying to hold back a smile.

"They usually do come out in droves for those red carpet events," Kayla said, refusing to take the bait regarding the famous actor. Rachel claimed to be friends with a lot of movie stars but Kayla highly doubted it. Rachel also claimed to be a natural blonde and everyone knew *that* wasn't true either.

Sandy put the make-up sponge on a small towel and picked up one of her many blush compacts. "So, Kayla, I'm hearing good things about the scenes you and Sean have been taping." She opened the compact and then grabbed a brush.

"Really?" Kayla was surprised. She glanced at Rachel and saw her fake smile had disappeared.

"I saw Bill and Ken in the break room on Friday. Bill was telling Ken that you and Sean have been kicking ass."

Kayla's jaw dropped. "He actually said that?"

Sandy shrugged. "More or less. I could be paraphrasing."

"You must be," Rachel said. "We all know Sean is an excellent actor but…" Rachel's eyes met Kayla's "…you've only been on the show a short time. You still have a lot to learn about acting." Kayla bristled but decided to keep her mouth shut. Rachel's words were nearly identical to the ones Greg had told her countless times. A part of her knew that Rachel was a spiteful person, but still, another part of her wondered—was Rachel right?

"Sean's an excellent actor," Kayla said, keeping her voice neutral. There was no way she was going to let Rachel know she'd struck a nerve. "I'm very fortunate to be working with him."

"It won't last," Rachel said. "The fans won't accept

Shay with Jared any more than they accepted her with Stefan." Rachel's mouth twisted in a smirk. "The letter writing campaign they organized forced the writers to bring Cassie and Stefan back together."

Kayla pushed her insecurities away and met Rachel's gaze, her smile just as fake as Rachel's had been. Two could play this game, after all. "I'm sure you're thrilled to be working with Marcus again. After all, when it comes to talent, you're evenly matched."

Rachel's eyes narrowed and Sandy made a noise that sounded like a giggle but quickly covered it with a cough. "You're done, Rachel." Sandy's choice of words seemed to have a double meaning, but her expression was benign as she stepped back and spun Rachel around in the chair. "Off to hair you go." Sandy pulled the black cape from around Rachel's neck.

Rachel rose from the chair and admired her reflection in the mirror for several seconds before turning to meet Kayla's eyes. "I saw in tomorrow's script that we have a scene together," she said, gazing down at her with a look of superiority Kayla knew all too well.

"It appears so." She'd read the script last night and wasn't looking forward to it.

"Maybe you can pick up a few pointers," Rachel said, then breezed out of the room.

Kayla met Sandy's stunned gaze before they burst out laughing. "Oh, my God." Sandy shook her head. "Could she be any more full of herself?"

"Sadly, I think she could."

"She's just jealous." Sandy patted the now empty chair. "Can you sit here? I don't want to move my stuff."

"Sure." Kayla moved to the other chair. "Why would she be jealous of me?"

"*Hello?* Look in the mirror." Sandy put the make-up cape around her and fastened it behind her neck. "Rumor has it she got Nikki fired because she was jealous of her. She hated the fact that the fans loved Nikki's character more than hers. And I'm sure she thought something was going on between Nikki and Sean even though Nikki's married and totally crazy about her husband."

Kayla frowned. "But Rachel's gorgeous. And she has a huge fan base."

"She's threatened by other women. Especially beautiful and talented women. So, my friend, be warned."

"How could Rachel get Nikki fired?" Kayla didn't think any one person could have that much power on the show. "Everyone loved her."

"Which is why it's so odd she got canned." Sandy moved to the side and picked up a bottle of foundation. "Like I said, it's just a rumor. But as with most rumors, there's probably a grain of truth to it."

"What rumor?" A masculine voice asked.

Kayla, along with Sandy, turned to see Sean lounging against the doorframe. A slow grin spread over his handsome face. "Sorry, I couldn't help but hear what you were saying." He moved into the room and settled in the chair next to hers. "Please don't tell me someone else is getting the axe."

"Not that I've heard," Sandy said, reaching for a clean make-up sponge. "We were just talking about Nikki."

"Oh, yeah…*that* rumor."

"I've got to be the only person who didn't hear it." Kayla glanced at Sean. He was dressed in jeans and a

Dodgers T-shirt that displayed the powerful outline of his chest to perfection.

"Do you think it's true?" Sandy asked.

Sean shrugged. "Anything's possible. Do you really think Rachel has that much power?"

"I don't know. But I hope not."

"Me too," Kayla chimed in with a grin. "Because if she does, I'm next."

"I guess Marcus is safe then." Sean folded his arms across his chest. The move caused the hem of his T-shirt to rise up just a tad to reveal a sliver of his taut stomach. Suddenly it felt very warm in the make-up room and Kayla had to force herself to look away. "I think Rachel is the only person at the studio who can stand the guy."

"They both joined the show around the same time," Sandy said as she dabbed some foundation on Kayla's face, then used the sponge to blend it on her skin. "Maybe that's it. Hey, did you see the fight yesterday at Dodger stadium?"

"I heard about it, but I didn't see it until I got back from Huntington and watched it on the news," Sean said, crossing his leg over his knee. Kayla noticed he was wearing sneakers without socks and somehow it seemed to fit him. "It was one of the worst brawls I've seen in years."

"What's up with Scanlon?" Sandy asked as she worked on Kayla's forehead.

"I wish I knew." Sean's voice sounded sad. "All I know is if he keeps it up, the Dodgers will trade his ass to San Francisco, or some equally pathetic team."

"Hey!" Kayla exclaimed, jerking her head toward

him. "The Blaze aren't pathetic. They made the play-offs last season."

"By the skin of their teeth. They were lucky to get the National League wild card spot. And then they were swept in the divisional series."

"And where were the Dodgers during the play-offs?" Kayla cocked her head and met his gaze. "At home eating pizza and drinking beer, that's where."

"Uh-oh." Sandy sighed. "I forgot you were a San Francisco fan."

Sean stared at her as if she'd grown two heads. "You can't seriously be a Blaze fan? This is L.A."

"I grew up in the Bay Area."

Sean shook his head in disgust. "I don't think I can work with you anymore," he continued, his expression solemn. "Maybe I should talk to Rachel about getting you fired."

Kayla stared at him speechlessly and then noticed the corners of his mouth twitch. "Very funny," Kayla said as Sean burst out laughing. "You should do comedy."

"Comedy is hard. I'm not sure I'm that talented." Sean rose from the chair. "Off to wardrobe. I'll be back in a few minutes for make-up," he said and then turned and left the room.

"If I wasn't engaged to the most wonderful man in the world, I'd be all over him," Sandy said as she opened up an eye shadow compact.

"I'm done with actors."

"Not all actors are jerks, you know. I snagged a good one." Sandy began to apply the shadow to her eyelids. "Speaking of which, have you seen Greg lately?"

"Not since I came to my senses and broke up with

him. He goes to one of the stylists at Lance's salon but we've never run into each other."

"I'm surprised Lance hasn't barred him from the place."

"He wanted to. But I told him it would only cause more trouble." Kayla suppressed a shiver, thinking of the night in Malibu when she'd ended their relationship. The malevolence in Greg's eyes had scared her and for weeks afterward she'd been on pins and needles worrying he would try to badger her into getting back together. "The last thing I want is for Greg to start bad mouthing Lance's salon, or Lance. You know how gossip travels in this town. It doesn't take much for someone's reputation to get trashed."

"MARRY YOU?" KAYLA's dark eyes were filled with surprise. "I can't marry you. I don't love you, and you don't love me."

"I know," Sean, as Jared, said. "It's perfect."

He turned as Kayla moved past him to her mark. As usual, the wardrobe department had her in one of Shay's trademark low-cut clingy tops. It was a testament to her skill that she had engaged him so completely in the scene that the only thing he was focusing on was trying to convince Shay to marry Jared.

"Why is that perfect?" she asked. "Marriage is based on love. You should know that better than anyone." She paused for three beats per the script and then continued. "It's what you had with Rebecca."

"You're right. I love Rebecca," he said in a low voice. "I always will."

"And I love Stefan."

"Rebecca's gone. Stefan went back to Cassie." Sean moved toward her. "And you're pregnant."

"You don't need to remind me of that." She placed her hand on her abdomen. Anguish filled her eyes. "God, I never planned for this to happen."

"But it did."

"I'm grateful you've given me a place to stay but, Jared, you don't have to marry me." Kayla gazed up at him, only it wasn't Kayla. It was Shay. As usual, she'd become her character. "In fact, the more I think about this…about your offer to help me, the more I think it's a really bad idea."

"Why?"

"What if we get married and then you fall in love with someone else? You won't be free to be with her. You'll be tied to me and a baby that isn't yours."

"I'm not going to fall in love again." He turned from her and moved to the table behind the sofa to look at a framed photo of him as Jared, and Nikki as Rebecca. He picked it up, stared at it for a few seconds and then put it back on the table.

"How do you know that?"

"I just do." He tore his gaze from the photo and returned to his mark in front of her. "Your baby needs both of us." He put his hand on her shoulder; she trembled slightly.

She stared at him for several seconds. Had she forgotten her line? It didn't happen often, and never once while they were actually taping.

"I need to think about it," she finally said. "Can you give me some time?"

"Of course." He squeezed her shoulder. "Take all the

time you need. Just know that I want to do this, Shay. I don't have any doubts and I won't have any regrets."

"You say that now." Kayla's voice was sad. "But sooner or later, we all have regrets."

It was the end of the scene, but he held her gaze for the required time so that the tape could be edited with a long fade out.

"Cut," Bill said. "And that's a wrap. Thanks, everyone. See you tomorrow."

Still staring into Kayla's eyes, Sean realized his hand was still on her shoulder. Reluctantly, he lowered it, but couldn't seem to move. He still felt the connection they had as Jared and Shay. He was close enough to smell the faint spicy vanilla scent of her perfume. It made him want to bury his face into her neck and drink it in.

Then Kayla blinked and, just like that, Shay was gone. "Nice touch, picking up the picture. You didn't do that in rehearsal."

Behind them the guys on the camera crew were talking and laughing as they rolled the cameras from the set. Kayla gave them a wave and then turned back to him.

"So I guess a wedding is in our future," she said and then quickly amended her words, "I mean in Jared and Shay's future."

"I told you so," he said and she laughed as they walked off the set. They parted ways at her dressing room and as Sean walked to his, he felt almost guilty that he enjoyed working with Kayla much more than he had with Nikki. Nikki was sweet, and a competent actress. But she wasn't in Kayla's league. Hell, he wasn't even sure *he* was in Kayla's league.

After changing out of his character's wardrobe and

washing the stage make-up off his face, Sean picked up his scripts for the rest of the week from Amanda, and left the studio. Walking across the parking lot, he noticed Kayla's Mustang parked next to his Jeep. The trunk was open and she was bent over it, peering inside.

Unable to resist, Sean let his gaze roam over her body. Her luscious curves, which were fit snugly into a pair of shorts, gave him an excellent view of her perfect ass and shapely legs. Just looking at her lit a powder keg in his gut. It was accompanied by a tug of arousal in his groin.

"Damn it." He heard her mutter.

"Something wrong?" he asked, halting just behind her. She jerked her head up and smacked it on the lid of her trunk.

"Owww." Her hand flew up to the back of her head. Turning, she pinned him with accusing eyes. "You scared me."

"Are you okay?"

"I'll be fine," she said with a grimace, rubbing her head. "My tire, on the other hand, is flatter than a pancake."

Because he'd been checking out Kayla's delectable body Sean had failed to notice that her car was leaning slightly to the left. He walked around her and saw that the front left tire was completely flat. "You probably have a nail in it," he said, looking back at her. "I can change it for you."

"I can't ask you to do that. Besides, my dad made sure both Kelly and I learned how to change a tire."

"You didn't ask, and I'm sure if your dad was here he'd change it for you. Just let me put my scripts in the Jeep," he said and unlocked his passenger side door.

It didn't take him long to change the tire, but rather than a nail, it almost looked like someone had stuck a knife in it. There was a ragged gash near the tread. Luckily, the spare appeared to be brand new. He put the jack and lug wrench back in the trunk along with the flat tire.

"Thanks," Kayla said after she'd closed the trunk. "Was it a nail?"

"You may have run over a large piece of metal," Sean said, looking at his hands, grimy from the tires.

"I've got some wipes in my purse." She turned and leaned over the door—treating him to yet another view of her firm backside—and grabbed her purse. She rummaged through it and pulled out a pack of hand wipes. "This should help."

"Thanks." He took the packet from her outstretched hand. Tearing the packet open, he pulled out the moist cloth and wiped his hands.

She opened the car door and tossed her purse inside and then shot him a grateful smile. "Thanks again for coming to my rescue."

"Hey, how about..." he began and thought about inviting her to grab a pizza with him at Cheech's, one of his favorite places. He squelched the thought immediately even though it felt as natural as breathing. He'd given too many people the benefit of the doubt only to be proved wrong when it was revealed their motives weren't quite so pure. He was the son of one of the most revered actors in Hollywood, and there were women, and men, who weren't above trying to get close to him to get to his father. He couldn't take the chance of getting involved with another person who was only trying to use him.

"Sean?" Kayla's voice startled Sean from his reverie. He met her quizzical gaze, grateful he'd come to his senses before making another mistake. While Kayla appeared to be normal and down to earth, Sean knew all too well that many people weren't what they appeared to be. There would be no more users in his life. "What were you saying?"

"Nothing," he said quickly. "Have a good night." He turned and rounded the back of his Jeep.

Before he could change his mind, Sean climbed inside, started the ignition and then backed out of his space. He drove away but couldn't help but look in the rear view mirror and watch Kayla get into her car. Turning the corner, he headed for the security gate and tried to put Kayla Maxwell out of his mind.

TWENTY MINUTES LATER, Sean was sitting at an outdoor table at Cheech's waiting for his pizza when he saw Kayla maneuvering her Mustang into an open spot just down the street.

His first thought was that she'd followed him. It wouldn't be the first time that had happened. He picked up his soda and watched her get out of her car, wait for traffic to clear, and then cross the street. She made her way toward Cheech's, smiling cheerfully at an elderly man walking his dog. After she'd passed him, the old guy turned around and eyed her appreciatively, proving that, despite his age, he wasn't too old to ogle a beautiful woman.

The second Kayla spotted him, her steps faltered and her eyes widened in surprise. If she'd followed him, she was doing a good job of acting like it was a coincidence. “Long time, no see,” she mused, stopping beside his table near the door “How do you know Cheech’s?”

“I live near here.” He set his cup on the table.

“So do I,” she said, adjusting the strap of her purse over her shoulder.

“Really? Where?”

“Atwater Village,” she said, brushing her hair back over her shoulder. “I come here all the time.”

He’d never seen her. And he definitely would have remembered if he had.

“I’m here at least once a week.” She shifted as she shoved her keys into her purse. “I love their pizza and since I don’t have anything in the house right now, I thought I’d grab a couple of slices to take home.”

“Why don’t you join me?” he asked before he could stop himself. What the hell was he doing? Had he learned nothing at all from trusting the wrong people?

Kayla’s dark eyes held his for several seconds before she nodded. “Okay. I’ll just go inside and place my order. Be right back.”

After she disappeared into the restaurant, Sean leaned back in his chair and contemplated his actions. It was dangerous—given his stance on dating actresses—to invite her to sit with him. But one impromptu dinner at Cheech’s didn’t mean anything, did it? He was curious about her, that’s all. He’d worked with her almost every day of the week for the past three weeks yet barely knew anything about her. Was it a crime to satisfy his curiosity?

SITTING AT A table outside Cheech’s across from Sean, Kayla wished she’d taken a little more time with her appearance before she’d left the studio. Thinking she was going home after a quick stop for pizza, all she'd bothered to do was wash off her stage make-up and change into a pair of shorts, a simple cotton top and flip-flops. Not exactly what she'd wear on a date. Not that this was a date. If she'd met another one of her co-stars here they'd probably end up sharing a table just like she was doing with Sean. Unless it was Marcus or Rachel. In that case she'd grab her pizza and run. Literally.

"You said you grew up in the Bay Area. Where exactly?" Sean asked.

"A small town in the East Bay. About 30 miles or so from Oakland."

"And you're a Blaze fan rather than an Oakland A's fan? Explain that."

Kayla smiled. "My dad grew up in the city and lived there until he went to college." She paused. "That's what we call San Francisco. The city. No one in the Bay Area calls it Frisco. It's usually how you can tell if someone isn't from Northern California."

Sean raised his hand, a sheepish expression on his face. "Guilty."

Kayla laughed. "My dad's a sports nut. He loves the Blaze and the Forty-Niners." She reached for her soda, feeling more at ease. "He passed his love of sports on to me and my sister, Kelly. She works for the Blaze. She's in their public relations department."

"Your dad must be excited about that." Sean brushed a lock of hair from his forehead, drawing attention to his hand, long-fingered and strong. Her response reminded her of how she had almost flubbed her line when he'd touched her during taping and how it had taken several seconds for her to regroup.

"Oh, he is." Kayla nodded. "Kelly was able to get a discount on season tickets. Dad took full advantage of that."

"I'll try not to hold it against you that you're a Blaze fan." Sean's eyes held a mischievous sparkle.

"And I'll try not to hold it again *you* that you're a Dodgers fan."

"Do you get a lot of people asking to buy your Mustang?"

Kayla put her cup down. "I can't tell you the number of times I've come out to my car when I've been running errands and found a note on the windshield from someone offering to buy it." She paused to smile. "The first time it happened I thought I got a parking ticket."

Sean grinned, his eyes crinkling at the corners. "I've had that happen once or twice with the Jeep."

"A parking ticket or an offer to buy it?"

Sean's grin widened. "Both."

She glanced at his Jeep. It was rugged and outdoorsy. Just like he was. "That's a 1970 Wagoneer, right?"

Sean lifted his brows "'69. I'm impressed. Not a lot of people would know that."

"Again, my dad's influence," Kayla admitted. "I used to spend hours with him in the garage when he was restoring cars. And I have a good memory."

"You *do* have a good memory. I've noticed you barely have to look at your script in rehearsal." He leaned forward, his expression curious. "How do you do that?"

She shrugged. "I have a photographic memory. I can read the script once or twice and remember everything I've read."

A jovial waiter came out with Sean's pizza and her

two slices. He set them on the table along with a pile of extra napkins. She was about to pick up a slice when she heard the familiar strains of her cell phone. Sean met her gaze and smiled. "Your purse is singing."

Kayla laughed. "That's my family ring tone. My sister downloaded it for all of us at Christmas," she said, reaching back for her purse. "Let me just check to make sure there isn't some sort of emergency." She pulled her phone out and glanced at the caller ID before answering it. "Hi, Mom."

"Hi, honey," Patricia replied warmly, "I just wanted to call and tell you I saw your scenes today. You and Sean Barrett have some major chemistry. More than you ever had with Marcus Bertrand." Patricia paused. "I called *A New Dawn's* comment line after the show. I wanted them to know that I liked what I saw today and I want more of it."

Kayla let out a short laugh. "But you're my mother."

"That doesn't matter. I want a couple I can root for. I think Jared and Shay have the makings of a supercouple."

"Supercouple?" Kayla echoed as Sean's eyes met hers. "Mom, don't get carried away."

"Did I ever once refer to Shay and Stefan as a supercouple?"

"No."

"Then give me a little credit, please," Patricia said dryly. "Kayla, I've seen you do some excellent work. But today in the park scenes, I was crying right along with you. And when you see Sean Barrett, tell him he was just as good. I'll bet even those Shay haters out there were shedding a few tears."

"I'm with Sean right now. I'll tell him you liked the scenes."

"You're with Sean Barrett?" Patricia exclaimed shrilly. Kayla pulled the phone away from her ear. "Are you still at the studio?"

"No. We're having pizza at Cheech's and speaking of which, I should go. You're the one who's always telling me it's rude to talk on a cell phone when you're at dinner."

"Are his eyes as green as they are in HDTV?" Patricia asked in a dreamy voice.

"Yes, Mom. I'll call you on Sunday, okay? My pizza's getting cold."

"Bye, honey. I love you."

"I love you too," she said and then shoved her phone back into her purse. "Sorry," she said as she reached for a slice. "My mom saw our first scenes. They aired today."

"Amanda told me the comment line got quite a number of positive calls," Sean replied as he sprinkled parmesan cheese on his pizza.

"My mom was one of those calls. She thought you were great by the way," Kayla said with a grin.

"I'm sure she thought you were great too. Because you were." He paused, holding her gaze. The intensity in his eyes caused her stomach to flutter. She wasn't used to the praise. All she'd heard for the past year and a half was how her line readings were forced, her timing sucked and her facial expressions were exaggerated.

Sean picked up his pizza. "Did your mom start watching the show when you were cast?"

"Oh no," Kayla said. "She's been watching the show ever since I was a kid. She's thrilled I'm on it."

"It sounds like your family is really close," Sean said before taking a bite of his pizza. "That must be nice."

"It's wonderful," she said but didn't elaborate after seeing the smile fade from his face.

"Are you going to the fan club luncheon?" Sean asked after they finished their first slices of pizza. The haunted look in his eyes was gone.

She nodded. "Lisa told me she talked you into it."

"She twisted my arm. I really hate those kinds of events. I just want to act. I don't care about publicity and all that hoopla."

"Yet you cared enough about the fans to talk to Ken about our storyline," Kayla noted. "If you don't care, why bother?"

Sean regarded her thoughtfully. "Talented and astute. I think I have to be careful around you, Kayla Maxwell."

She smiled. "Trust me, when the fans see you, they're going to go nuts."

"That's what I'm afraid of." Amusement gleamed in his eyes. "Luckily, you'll be there. You can fend them off for me."

Kayla burst out laughing. "They'll mow me down to get to you."

"Then maybe we should sit together. We can keep each other safe."

"Deal," she said. After taking a sip of her soda, she set it down and reached for another slice of pizza. As she took a bite, she wondered just who in the hell was going to keep her safe from Sean Barrett.

AN HOUR LATER, Kayla was stopped at a red light on Los Feliz and Hillhurst. The radio was tuned to her favorite '80s station and she was humming along with a Duran Duran classic while replaying the dinner with Sean in her mind.

If anyone had told her way back when she was a teenager hooked on *A New Dawn* that one day she'd be working with Sean Barrett she would have laughed in their face and called them crazy. Now here she was, not only working with him, but she'd just shared pizza with him. It was as if all of her schoolgirl fantasies were coming true. Talk about surreal.

Glancing up at the rearview mirror, she noticed a black Mercedes convertible behind her. A flicker of apprehension coursed through her. Greg had a car exactly like that—or at least he had when they'd been dating. Her gaze went straight to the driver. It was a man wearing mirrored sunglasses. He was staring straight ahead but it was hard to make out his features. Logic told her it couldn't be Greg. As far as she knew, he was still living in Malibu. Plus, he hated this part of L.A. He'd told her more than once that she should leave Atwater Village, or "the ghetto," as he'd sneeringly called it.

The driver inched the Mercedes closer even though the light hadn't changed. Kayla gripped her steering wheel, unable to tear her gaze from his mirrored sunglasses. Just when she thought he might hit the Mustang, the light changed and the car in front of her moved forward. Letting out a sigh of relief, she eased off the clutch, hit the gas and then turned right on Los Feliz. The Mercedes continued straight ahead on Hillhurst, leaving Kayla to feel more than a bit silly for imagining Greg Alamo was following her.

Six

Shay: Give me one good reason why I should marry you.
Jared: Because I can help you give your baby a good life.

SITTING AT AN umbrella-covered table next to Lisa's swimming pool, Kayla pulled a stack of fan mail from her tote bag and dropped it on the table. She watched Lisa do her laps in the crystal clear water and admired her devotion to the sport. Lisa swam seven days a week come rain or shine.

She picked up the top envelope and her letter opener, opened the envelope, and pulled out the sheet of paper inside. Reading it, she smiled at the fan's thoughtful comments. More and more, the fans were warming to Shay. There were still a few negative letters, but the good were definitely outweighing the bad.

Kayla looked up to see Lisa climbing out of the pool. Water ran down her slender body and her feet left wet footprints on the concrete as she moved toward the table. Grabbing a colorful towel from the back of one of the chairs, Lisa wiped her face with it, then draped the towel over her chair and sat down.

"When are you going to get someone to help you with your fan mail?"

"Soon." Kayla set the letter aside. "I've decided to

check out that fan service you recommended a while ago."

"I know it's hard for you to let it go, but you're spending all your free time answering your mail."

"I've come to that realization myself." Kayla picked up another letter and opened it. "I'd still like to answer a few but I can't do them all."

Lisa reached for the small white envelope on top of the stack and slid her finger underneath the flap to open it. "Are you hungry? I made a vegetarian taco salad for lunch."

"Does that mean it has tofu in it?" Lisa didn't answer. "What is it?" Kayla asked when she noticed Lisa's brows drawn together in a scowl.

"Check this out." Lisa held out the note she'd been reading.

Kayla took the note, saw the blood red ink and felt a sickening wave of apprehension course through her body. *Not another one.*

SLUT! I TOLD YOU TO LEAVE TOWN. DO AS I SAY OR YOU'LL BE SORRY.

"You don't look surprised." Lisa studied her with shrewd eyes.

"I'm not."

"How many of these have you gotten?"

"This is the third one. The first one was right before the photo shoot and then I got another one last week. I threw them both away."

Lisa's expression was troubled. "Don't throw them away."

"I got some hate mail when Shay had the affair with Stefan. I tossed all of it."

"Hate mail because of a storyline and threats like this one are two different things. In the future, you should keep a file of anything that's in any way threatening."

Kayla tried to ignore the frisson of fear. However, with the arrival of this third letter, it was a little more difficult to do. "If I worried about every letter like that I'd be afraid to leave the house."

Lisa held her gaze. "I think you should consider moving."

"Move?" Kayla exclaimed, shaking her head. "No way. I love Atwater Village. Besides, I have an alarm system."

"An alarm won't stop someone who really wants to get in," Lisa argued.

"I'm not moving. I refuse to let a few letters force me from my home."

Lisa leaned back. "Will you at least upgrade your alarm system?"

"Yes. I'll call the alarm company and ask them to send someone out to evaluate the system." She paused. "I know it's not what you want, but I don't want to live in some sterile gated community behind ten foot walls."

"Fame has its price, Kayla." Lisa held up the envelope. "And whether you like it or not, you're becoming more famous. You're in people's living rooms at least four days a week. More people will see you on *A New Dawn* than ever saw you in those slasher flicks, or the Lifetime movies you did."

"I just want to act."

"Now you sound like Sean."

"What's wrong with that?" Kayla countered.

"Nothing. But you can do it and still be safe." Lisa snatched the note from her fingers. "Have you forgotten what happened to Josie?"

"No," Kayla said. Josie had been Lisa's first client, and just as she was starting to make a name for herself in Hollywood, she'd been brutally murdered.

Lisa's expression was sober. "Josie didn't take her ex-husband's threats seriously."

"I don't have an ex-husband, and I haven't seen Greg in over six months." She paused as she remembered the black Mercedes. But that couldn't have been Greg, could it? No. He wouldn't be caught dead in Los Feliz, or Atwater Village. "He was pissed when I dumped him but I haven't heard a peep out of him since that night."

"It doesn't have to be someone you know. Does the name Rebecca Schaeffer mean anything to you?" Lisa asked as she stuffed the offensive note back into the envelope.

"Everyone in Hollywood knows what happened to that poor girl," Kayla said, thinking of the young actress. "She was murdered by a psychotic fan."

Psychotic fan.

She stared at Lisa, finally comprehending why her friend was so worried. "He came right up to her door," she whispered as it sunk in that she'd been far too blasé about the letters, Lisa's mention of both Josie and Rebecca Schaeffer were blatant reminders that she needed to take them seriously. If she didn't, she could end up dead. "And it wouldn't be that hard for someone to find out where I live."

"That's what I've been trying to say. You're an easy target, Kayla."

"I get it." Kayla's stomach churned. "I just didn't want to believe it could be that serious."

"It may not be, but it's better to be safe than sorry," Lisa replied gently. "Will you call the alarm company tomorrow?"

"First thing in the morning," Kayla promised. "What are you going to do with the letter?"

"Keep it. And if you get any more I want to see them." Lisa paused. "I mean it, Kayla," she added in a firm, no nonsense voice. Lisa glanced at the envelope. "The postmark is Los Angeles." She looked up. "That means whoever is sending you this garbage lives in the area. I'm going to check in with you tomorrow to make sure you've called your alarm company."

Kayla managed a weak smile. "You sound like my mom."

"I'm your best friend. Your mom is counting on me to look out for you, and that's exactly what I intend to do."

"Thanks for slapping some sense into me," Kayla said. "But can we change the subject? This whole thing is creeping me out."

"It should. But as long as you're taking action we don't have to dwell on it." Lisa's grim expression relaxed. "How about that taco salad? I'm starved."

"You didn't tell me if it has tofu in it." Kayla wrinkled her nose.

"Yes, it has tofu in it." Lisa slipped her feet down from the chair and stood up. "Will you at least try it?"

"Okay. Do you need any help?"

"Nope. Just relax. I'll be right back."

After Lisa disappeared into the house, Kayla let her gaze rest on the envelope containing the threatening note and couldn't squelch the uneasiness that swept over her. She hoped it was nothing more than a ticked off fan playing a malicious prank. And while that was disturbing in and of itself, it was infinitely better than the alternative.

THE TACO SALAD was actually pretty good. Kayla settled back in her chair with a happy sigh and met Lisa's sly smile.

"So what's up with you and Sean? I saw your scenes this past week. The chemistry between you two is off the charts. And I happen to know that the issue of *Soap Opera Journal* with you and Sean on it has been their biggest seller so far this year."

"That's because my mom bought about a hundred copies." Kayla laughed. "And she's matting and framing the cover so I can hang it my hallway."

Lisa chuckled and adjusted the strap of her swimsuit. "I'll bet Marcus had an absolute hissy fit when he saw that the picture of you and Sean dominated the cover, and his picture was a mere thumbnail." Her lips twitched in amusement. "God, I would have loved to have seen his face."

Kayla let out a soft chuckle. "You're so bad."

"Okay, spill it. How do like working with Sean?" Lisa lifted her feet to the chair and looped her arm around her bent knees.

"I'm learning a lot from him." Kayla hesitated, not quite sure how to explain it. With each scene she shared with Sean she found her confidence in her acting abilities returning.

"I see a connection between you and Sean that I never saw in your scenes with Marcus." Lisa pushed a strand of damp hair behind her ear. "Those two scenes when Jared finds Shay in the park were pretty emotional."

"It *was* intense." Not that she would admit to Lisa that a lot of the intensity was due to her attraction to her co-star.

"I think you should prepare yourself, Kayla. Shay and Jared are going to be the hottest couple on daytime," Lisa said. "The network called on Friday to let me know that both you and Sean are invited to attend Fab Fan Weekend in July."

Taken aback, Kayla couldn't speak. Fab Fan Weekend was the nickname for an annual event called the Fabulous Soap Fan Extravaganza. It was held in a different venue every year. Last year it had been held in Orlando, Florida, and this year it was in Savannah, Georgia. Only the network's most elite and popular soap stars were invited to attend. And they wanted her?

"But I've only been on the show about six months."

"That's irrelevant. The network brass knows a good thing when they see it. I spoke with Amanda the other day. It turns out that Shay and Jared have struck a chord with a lot of viewers."

Kayla was flummoxed. "But only a handful of scenes have aired."

"The fans see the same chemistry I do. You and I both know some of the most popular couples on daytime were never meant to be together. But the actors just had that special something. I think a good barometer of Jared and Shay's popularity will be at the fan club luncheon next weekend."

"I had dinner the other night with Sean. He told me you twisted his arm into going."

"I told you that's why I earn the big bucks," Lisa said with a laugh and then her eyes widened. "Wait a minute. *Dinner?* You and Sean went on a date?"

"It wasn't a date. He helped me change a flat tire and then I ran into him at Cheech's. He invited me to sit with him."

"Sounds like a date to me." Lisa grinned.

"It was just pizza," Kayla clarified. "And it turns out he lives in Los Feliz."

"I know. When he hired me I dropped off some papers at his house."

"Why didn't you tell me in lived near me?"

Lisa's lips curved in a shrewd smile. "Why do you care where he lives?"

"I don't," she said, feeling her face growing warm. "What's his house like?"

"Spanish style. I think you'll like it."

"I doubt I'll ever see it."

Lisa grinned. "Wanna bet?"

SEAN STARED AT his big screen in disbelief as—once again—Matt got ejected from a game. The Dodgers were in Arizona taking on the Diamondbacks, and Matt had just made the mistake of shoving the home plate umpire. And in baseball, you never, *ever*, laid a hand on the umpire.

The D'Back's runner was out at home. The replay proved that, but the umpire didn't have the luxury of instant replay and, from his vantage point, had missed the tag Matt laid on the runner's ankle with his glove. It happened. Umpires were human and sometimes made the wrong call. Every baseball player—and fan—

knew it, yet Matt went ballistic the minute the ump had flashed the safe sign.

After finishing his beer, Sean picked up the remote and turned off the television. He hated watching his friend self-destruct, but there wasn't much he could do about it. Maybe a fine by the league would get Matt's attention. Something had to and soon, or the Dodgers would make good on those trade rumors. Sean would hate to see that happen.

Just as he got up to take his empty bottle to the kitchen, his cell phone rang. He fished it out of the pocket of his jeans and saw Lisa's name on the caller ID.

"I have good news," she said before he could speak.

Shit. He hoped it wasn't another fan event, or photo shoot. "I'm afraid to ask," he said, entering the kitchen.

"You've been invited to Fab Fan Weekend."

"Thanks, but no thanks." He set the bottle on the counter near the sink and then turned to lean against it. Seeing one of the houseplants in the garden window was limp, he made a mental note to water it.

"Sean, why did you bother hiring me?" Lisa's tone was cool. "This is an important event. You need to go."

"I hired you to handle my publicity, not to accept every damn event I get invited to." He ran a hand through his hair and wished he hadn't answered the phone.

"I haven't accepted it. That's not my call. I'm letting you know about it." Lisa paused. "And I'm advising you to accept the invitation."

"I'm going to the fan club luncheon next weekend." Sean tried to keep the irritation out of his voice, but wasn't succeeding. "Isn't that enough?"

"Fab Fan Weekend is important to the show, Sean. The network honchos want you and Kayla there."

"Kayla?"

"Yes. She's also been invited, and unlike you, she's honored to be included."

"She's going?"

"Yes."

"Where is it?"

"Savannah." Lisa paused. "In Georgia."

Sean rolled his eyes. "I wasn't raised by wolves, Lisa. I know where Savannah is."

Lisa let out an amused snort and then continued, "I watched your scenes with Kayla this week. Both of you were amazing. The show is getting a lot of positive feedback."

"Yeah, I heard."

"The event isn't until July, and the network is picking up the tab."

"Money isn't the issue."

"Look, by July the fans will be clamoring to see you and Kayla. In fact, I'll bet that at the fan club luncheon next weekend both you and Kayla will be surprised at the number of fans Jared and Shay already have."

"Our scenes just started airing. Don't you think you're getting ahead of yourself?"

"No, I don't," Lisa said. "Seventy-five percent of my clients are soap actors. And I've been doing this for seven years. Soap opera fans are the most vocal, *and* the most loyal, in the business. And when they fall in love with a couple, they can get pretty zealous."

"That's true," Sean said, thinking of how the fans had fallen in love with Jared and Rebecca three years ago.

"I shouldn't play this card, but I will," Lisa said. "Kayla could use your support. If the fans feel in any way that you don't support your character's involvement with hers they won't accept her. She hasn't been on the show as long as Nikki was. And even that didn't save Nikki."

Lisa had a point. Nikki Andrews was beloved by everyone, and yet she, and her character, was given the boot without a second thought. Kayla had only been on the show six months. If this storyline didn't pan out, she could be axed just as Nikki was. And for reasons he didn't care to examine right now, Sean wasn't going to let that happen.

"I'll go."

"Excellent," Lisa said. "I'll call you when I firm everything up."

Sean heard a decisive click and then silence. "And you have a nice evening too," he said and grinned. Lisa was an odd duck, there was no doubt about that. But she was good at her job, and he supposed he should take her advice a little more seriously and not be so contentious with her. After all, she was only doing what he paid her to do.

Slipping his phone back into his pocket, he watered his plant and then slid onto a stool at the edge of the island where he had his laptop set up. After powering it on, he navigated to the search engine and typed in Kayla's name. When the search results came up on the screen, he selected her Wikipedia page and, although he felt a bit voyeuristic, he began to read.

Some of it he already knew, like where she was from and that she'd been in two classic horror films. What he didn't know was that her birthday was on Christmas Day, she was twenty-seven, and her first role was seven years ago in a Lifetime movie. She'd done several of them apparently, and over the years had done quite a number of guest shots on several different television shows. He scrolled down trying to find what he was most interested in. Was she dating anyone?

During their dinner, he'd noticed a number of men checking her out. Even without make-up and dressed simply, she was beautiful. She had to have guys lined up to date her, but even though they spent a lot of time together on the set she'd never talked about any guy except Lance. At Cheech's she'd only mentioned her father, that was it.

He found a small blurb about a two-year relationship she'd had with a fellow actor—Greg Alamo. He clicked on the link and up popped a picture of Kayla standing next to the guy. The name didn't sound familiar and Sean had never seen him before. But that wasn't unusual, L.A. was filled with actors. There was no way to know or have seen them all.

Greg Alamo wasn't much taller than Kayla and had dark brown hair and eyes. His smarmy face was smiling into the camera and his arm was around Kayla, holding her possessively. Kayla was smiling, too, but the smile didn't seem to reach her eyes. Sean went back to the original text and read that they'd dated for two years and had broken up seven months ago. He shut down the website satisfied. At least as far as the internet world knew, she wasn't dating anyone right now.

Sliding off the stool, he grabbed his script for tomorrow's show and headed for the back yard. He sat at the table on the patio and opened the script. Instead of reading it, though, he thought about Kayla.

He enjoyed her company. A lot. There was a genuineness about her he found very appealing. Obviously, she was close to her family. The love she felt for them was evident whenever she talked about them. He envied her that.

Not long ago, he'd made a conscious decision to never get involved with another actress and now, here he was, letting Kayla invade his thoughts on a daily basis. He was trying to fight his attraction to her, but it was getting harder every day. There was something about her he was drawn to. Every time he looked into her eyes he found himself thinking less about the reasons why he should keep his distance and more about how he looked forward to coming to work every day just so he could see her.

More than anything, he wanted to believe Kayla wasn't like the other leeches who had tried to attach themselves to him. Was it fair to her to assume she was? No, it wasn't. But he'd been burned badly in the past. There was no way he would risk going down that path again. Ever.

Seven

Shay: Fine. I'll marry you. But I don't want a church wedding.
Jared: Why?
Shay: Because church weddings are for people in love and that's not us.

TWO HOURS BEFORE *A New Dawn's* fan club luncheon was scheduled to begin, Kayla greeted the receptionist in Lance's West Hollywood salon and headed to the back of the salon where Lance was texting on his cell phone.

"Hello, darling," Lance gushed as she approached. He set his phone on the gleaming black counter of his station and then gave her a hug, in addition to kissing both of her cheeks. He pulled back and gave her the once over. "Girl, you look hot." He put his hands on his hips. "But in a tasteful, not slutty way," he added with a grin.

Kayla smiled. "Thanks. I think," she said, looking down at the simple black sheath dress and red heels she'd chosen for the luncheon.

"Love the pop of color," he said. "Do you think they make those shoes in my size?"

Kayla burst out laughing. "I doubt it. You have huge feet."

"That's not all that's huge." Lance raised his brows and treated her to a wolfish grin.

"Stop." Still laughing, Kayla put up her hand. "Too much information."

Lance shrugged. "Hey, if you've got it, flaunt it." He paused, studying her hair. "So, what did you have in mind?"

"I was thinking one of your chic ponytails," she said, looking past him and into the mirror. "I don't like my hair down with this dress."

"I agree. It hides those sexy shoulders of yours. I think a ponytail is a fabulous idea. Not a severe one though. I'd like to keep it casual, but with a touch of elegance."

"Work your magic."

"Have a seat, doll." Lance turned the chair in front of the station around so she could sit down. "How's that gorgeous hunk of man doing?" Lance asked as he spun her around.

Kayla didn't have to ask who he was referring to. "Sean's fine."

"Oh sweetie, he *is* fine." Lance waved his hand in front of his face. "Is there any chance he's batting for my team?"

Meeting his hopeful eyes in the mirror, she shook her head. "I'm pretty sure he's straight. The gossip at the studio is that Rachel Hixson is after him."

Lance let out a loud snort. "That bag of bones?"

"Lance." She tried to suppress her chuckle. "That's not very nice."

"I'm just saying." Lance shrugged. "I saw her on *Access Hollywood* last week. She could eat a sandwich." He paused as he gathered her hair in his hands. "Or two."

"The camera adds ten pounds," Kayla said, although why she was defending Rachel was beyond her.

"Then she must be absolutely skeletal." Lance let go of her hair and reached for a brush. "Uh-oh." His face blanched. "Incoming."

"What are you...?" she began and then her heart dropped to her stomach when she saw Greg Alamo's reflection in the mirror. She twisted in her chair to look up at him. The scent of his expensive cologne surrounded her, filling her with memories that were far from pleasant. He was dressed to impress, as usual. His black jeans were new and obviously designer. The same with his crisp pale blue button down shirt. There was no way in hell Greg would be caught wearing faded Levi's or a T-shirt, especially if he believed the paparazzi might be nearby.

"Kayla," Greg said in his smooth-as-silk voice that was in great demand for voiceover work. "It's good to see you." The words sounded sincere, but his dark eyes were cold. Her skin prickled and she fought to keep a neutral expression on her face. He gave Lance a cursory glance and a nod but, as usual, didn't address him. "I heard you landed a soap gig." His tone was derisive. He'd told her repeatedly during their relationship that only actors of the lowest caliber worked on soap operas. No doubt he was thinking she was exactly where she belonged.

"You heard right," Kayla said, and while courtesy dictated she ask about him, she didn't. She didn't care about him or what he was doing and she wasn't about to pretend she did.

"I'm up for a role on a new show called *Vampire Nation*," he said as if she'd asked. No surprise there. *His* career had always been his favorite subject. "The audition went great."

"That's nice," she said, casting him a smile just as fake as his spray tan. Clearly he was expecting more enthusiasm. His mouth flattened into a hard line.

"Are you seeing anyone?"

"That's really none of your business." She felt Lance's protective hand on her shoulder and was reassured by his presence.

Greg's eyes narrowed as he stared down at her, but then, like a chameleon, his hard expression changed and he flashed one of his charming smiles. "You're right. It's not." He checked the expensive watch on his wrist. "I've got an appointment." He paused and met her gaze. "It was nice seeing you, Kayla."

Before she could reply, he turned and headed for the exit. Kayla expelled a deep breath and relaxed the rigid control she'd had on her posture. "That was awkward," she said looking up at Lance.

"Tell me about it," Lance said, gazing at Greg's retreating back. "I wonder why he was here. I always check the books when I know you're coming in so you don't have to run into him."

"Maybe he came in to buy some products," Kayla said. "He's fussy about his hair."

"Maybe." Lance echoed, and then looked at her with a wily grin on his face. "So back to the hunk. I checked out your soap. And if I do say so myself, you're rockin' it, girlfriend."

"Thanks."

He ran the brush through her hair. "You and the hunk have some major chemistry."

"His name is Sean." Although Kayla had to admit, he *was* a hunk.

"You say potatoes, I say po-tah-toes." Lance smirked. "Do you think you might ditch that stupid moratorium you have on dating actors and go for it?"

"We did have pizza one night after work."

Lance's hand stilled. "You went on a date?" His eyes lit up. "Did he kiss you?"

"It wasn't that kind of date. He helped me change a flat tire on the Mustang and then we ran into each other at Cheech's. He invited me to sit with him."

Shaking his head, Lance sighed. "You *really* don't know men, do you?"

Kayla frowned. "What does that mean?"

"It means, if he wasn't interested he wouldn't have asked you to join him."

"I think he was just being polite," Kayla protested, even though a part of her found Lance's observation just the tiniest bit thrilling. Just because she'd sworn off actors didn't mean she'd checked her ego at the door.

"Polite, my ass," Lance said with a grin. "I might be gayer than a fruit cocktail, but I'm still a man. Mark my words, the hunk is interested. I'd bet my best pair of leather chaps on it."

"You have more than one pair?" Kayla asked, trying to block out the mental image of Lance wearing leather chaps.

Lance shrugged. "Doesn't everyone?"

OUTSIDE THE HILTON Hotel in Universal City, Sean sat in his Jeep and listened to the Dodgers game on the radio. The score was tied four all in the third inning. Today's game was Matt's first day back after serving a three-day suspension for pushing the umpire in last weekend's game against Arizona. So far Matt was on his best behavior, and had even scored a run. Maybe the suspension and the fine had knocked some sense into him. Sean hoped so.

While he'd been listening to the Dodgers game, he'd seen Marcus and Rachel arrive together. He'd also been scanning the parking lot for Kayla's Mustang, but so far, there was no sign of her.

At the end of the inning, Sean turned off the radio and pulled the keys from the ignition. Grabbing his sport coat, he climbed out of the Jeep and locked it. As he was crossing the parking lot, he saw Kayla's red Mustang turn down the aisle and then zip into a parking spot nearer to the hotel.

Stepping up his pace, he made it to her car just as she was locking the door. Looking at her, Sean felt a hammer blow to his chest. She looked absolutely stunning. Her long silken hair was pulled back in a ponytail, revealing her smooth shoulders and graceful neck. Her short black dress fit like a glove, emphasizing her luscious body. Her legs were bare, sleek and lightly tanned, and on her feet were a pair of red high heels that could only be described as sexy as hell.

Trying to ignore the thick beat of awareness in his blood, Sean cleared his throat. "Hey," he said. Startled, she turned toward him, a sudden luminous smile lighting her face. His pulse kicked as their eyes met. "You look great."

"Thank you," she said, opening her small black purse and dropping her keys inside. "So do you," she said, moving toward him. "I think I've only seen you in jeans. You clean up nice."

He pulled on his sport coat. “Thanks. At least I don’t have to wear a tux.”

“What is it with men and tuxes?” She slipped the slim strap of the purse over her shoulder as they began walking toward the hotel. “You guys hate them but you look so good in them.”

“They’re like straightjackets,” Sean said with a grimace. Kayla just laughed and shook her head.

As they approached the entrance, Sean noticed two women near the double glass doors watching him and Kayla. By the rapt looks on their faces, he assumed they were fans. His assumption proved to be correct when they clutched each other’s hands and squealed in delight.

“I told you he’d come,” the taller of the two, a blonde, said.

“Oh, my God. I can’t believe this,” the brunette said in a loud voice. “May we have your autograph?” she asked, gazing at him with adoration.

He slowed his pace and glanced at Kayla. She smiled and nodded. “Go ahead. I’ll wait.”

He moved toward the women. The tall one held out an autograph book. “We were hoping you’d come this year,” she said, handing him a pen. “We love the show.”

“And you’re our favorite character,” the brunette said and looked past him. “Do you think Kayla would sign an autograph for us too?”

“I’m sure she’d be happy to,” Sean said, and turned to look at Kayla standing by the door. “Kayla,” he called to her. “Could you come over?” He turned back to the women and signed his name in the autograph book.

“Hi, Kayla,” the shorter brunette said when Kayla

joined them. "Would you mind signing an autograph for us?"

"Not at all." Kayla's tone was friendly. "Are you going to the luncheon?"

"No. We couldn't afford the tickets."

"Oh, I'm sorry to hear that," Kayla said as the brunette handed her an autograph book and a pen. "What's your name?"

"Donna."

Kayla signed the book. Sean noticed she personalized it with a message and then signed her name. She glanced at him. "Trade you." She smiled and handed him Donna's book. He gave her the other woman's book. "What's your name?" she asked the blonde.

"Stephanie."

Sean signed Donna's book while Kayla signed Stephanie's. "There you go." Kayla handed Stephanie the book. "How much were the tickets?"

"Seventy-five dollars," Donna answered. "We've been to every luncheon for the past six years but both of us were laid off three months ago."

"Things are kind of tight money wise." Stephanie stuck her book back in her purse. Her expression brightened. "But we got to see you guys *and* get your autographs."

Donna nodded. "You really made our day," she said as Sean gave her back her book. "Thank you *so* much."

Sean met Kayla's eyes. "We should go inside."

Kayla nodded and then looked at Donna and Stephanie. "Did you get Marcus Bertrand's autograph?"

Donna's smile faded. "No. He didn't notice us."

More like ignored them, Sean thought. Marcus only paid attention to his fans when it suited him. And since he'd arrived with Rachel, who thought anyone who wasn't in the business was beneath her, he was sure Marcus deliberately avoided the two fans like the plague.

"If you don't mind waiting a few minutes, I'll have him come out and sign your books."

Sean admired Kayla's gracious offer, but he was pretty sure Marcus would refuse to do it.

"We don't mind at all," Stephanie said, gazing at Kayla with wide eyes.

Kayla touched his arm. "Let's go. I want to find Marcus before the luncheon starts. Don't leave," she called back to the two women as they moved toward the double doors.

"How the hell are you going to get Marcus to sign their books?" Sean asked her as they crossed the crowded lobby.

Kayla shot him a glance and smiled. "Don't worry. I have a plan."

Sean grinned. "Isn't that what Lucy always said to Ethel?" he said as they followed a sign that read: A New Dawn Cast Members Enter Here.

"Just trust me," Kayla said with a laugh. They entered the room and she said, "I'll be right back." Sean watched her walk away, enjoying the sway of her full hips, and the stride of her sexy legs.

"Sean?" He recognized the incredulous feminine voice and turned to fine Rachel staring at him in disbelief. "What are *you* doing here?"

"The same thing you are," he said, "attending the luncheon."

"But you never come to these boring affairs," Rachel said, disdain evident in her expression.

He shrugged. "There's a first time for everything."

Rachel smile was brittle. She'd always been slender, but in the last year she'd dropped at least ten pounds. She was painfully thin and looked like she might break if someone hugged her. He hoped she would eat the lunch they were serving today. She obviously needed it.

"How are you?" she asked. "We haven't talked in a while."

"I'm good." He looked past her and saw Marcus talking on his cell phone, but didn't see Kayla.

Where the hell had she gone to?

"So I'm sure you heard the rumors that I'm the one who got Nikki fired."

That got his attention. He swung his gaze back to hers. "Are you?"

Rachel's eyes narrowed. "Do you think I have that much power?"

"I don't know. Do you?"

"If I did I wouldn't tell you." Rachel shot back with a toss of her head. "I'm sure you can't be pleased to be paired with Kayla Maxwell."

"Why would you think that?"

"Because she's as phony as a three dollar bill." Rachel's tone was cold, just like her eyes. "She's not as sweet as she pretends to be. It's all an act."

Any other time Sean would tell her where to stick it. Rachel had just reminded him why he gave her a wide berth at the studio. She'd also reminded him that he didn't know Kayla all that well. Was she a phony as Rachel claimed? It wasn't like he hadn't been duped before.

Across the room, he spied Chris Winters, the actor who played his friend on the show. "Excuse me. I need to talk to Chris." Without waiting for her reply, Sean brushed past her and headed for Chris. He surveyed the room but still didn't see Kayla. Marcus hadn't left, so either Kayla's plan had backfired or something else was going on. And he was damn curious as to what it was.

Fifteen minutes later, just as the emcee of the day's event was getting ready to introduce the cast members, Kayla joined him at the double doors that led into the main ballroom.

"Where have you been?" he asked, keeping his voice low.

Kayla's dark eyes met his. "Taking care of business."

"Did you get Marcus to sign their autograph books?"

"No." Her smile was luminous. "Better than that."

He stared at her but she didn't elaborate.

"Sean, you're up." Chris came up behind him. "Will you guys save me a seat at your table?" Chris asked. "I don't want to get stuck at Marcus's table again."

"Of course we will," Kayla said.

Chris let out a sigh of relief. "Thanks. I owe you."

Sean watched as Kayla peeked inside the ballroom. "This is so fun." Her face was lit with excitement. "He's introducing you," she said. "Get ready, Sean."

"Get ready for what?" he asked and then heard the emcee start the introduction.

"You'll see," she said and then put her hand on his back. She gave him a push just as his name was announced.

The second he stepped into the room, the fans erupted with applause and whistles. The continuous flashes from the cameras almost blinded him as he made his way from the back of the room toward the front where round tables covered in white linen tablecloths were reserved for the cast members. Amazed, he saw that the fans were out of their chairs, clapping and yelling.

For him.

Astounded by the crowd's reception, he shook several outstretched hands and then found himself at the front of the room. He turned to his left to go to the table he'd been told to sit at and was surprised to see Donna and Stephanie there, clapping and cheering with the rest of the crowd. Not sure what the protocol was, he turned and gave a wave to the crowd and then moved next to Donna and sat down when everyone else did.

"Thank you." Donna put her hand on his arm as the crowd quieted.

"For what?"

Had the two fans crashed the luncheon?

"For getting us in." Stephanie craned her neck to look at him. "It was you, wasn't it?"

He shook his head. "No. It wasn't me."

"But..." Stephanie's mouth gaped.

Donna looked from Stephanie to him, her eyes wide. "It had to be Kayla."

At that moment, the emcee announced Kayla's name. Sean turned from Donna and Stephanie. The crowd didn't go as crazy for her as they had for him, but there were loud whistles and a good round of applause. As she glided gracefully toward him, waving to the crowd and shaking hands with several fans along the way, Sean's eardrum was pierced by the sound of a loud penetrating whistle. He turned to find Donna and Stephanie on their feet, clapping wildly, happiness etched on their faces.

Getting to his feet, Sean joined the applause and watched Kayla walk toward the front of the room. Her smile was radiant, her dark eyes bright and shining. When she reached the table she rounded it, and instead of sitting by him she walked toward Stephanie, who threw her arms around her. Kayla returned the Stephanie's bear hug and met his eyes. When she winked at him, Sean knew one thing for sure.

Kayla Maxwell was no phony.

Eight

Jared: As weddings go, that wasn't so bad.
Shay: Sorry about running out like that. Who knew morning sickness could last all day?
Jared: That's okay. At least you came back.

AFTER SHE'D FINISHED her lunch, Kayla thanked the waiter when he set a sinfully delicious French apple tart in front of her. It wasn't often she indulged in rich desserts but it wasn't because she didn't care for them. It was because what she'd told Lance earlier was true. The camera added at least ten pounds.

"If you don't want that I'll take it off your hands."

Kayla picked up her small fork and looked at Chris Winters, who sat to her left and was eying the tart like he hadn't just practically inhaled his own dessert. "Back off," she warned and then gave him a quick smile. "I love dessert. If you want another one, ask the waiter."

Chris regarded her with a look of surprise. "Wow. An actress who actually eats dessert. Color me shocked."

"I'll run it off tomorrow."

"Where do you run?" Sean asked. He was seated next to Stephanie's friend, Donna.

Meeting his gaze, her body tingled with awareness. In fact, it had been tingling ever since she'd found him standing by her car in the parking lot looking like he'd come straight from a GQ photo shoot. The man was seriously hot. And judging by the number of woman in the room who'd been staring at him, she wasn't the only one who thought so.

"On work days I run near my house and on my days off I usually go over to Griffith Park."

"Have you ever done any surfing?" Sean asked.

"No. My parents used to take my sister and me to Santa Cruz when we were kids. I could handle a boogie board pretty well, if I do say so myself."

"Lightweight," he said with a good-humored grin.

"Surfing is hard," Donna said, looking from Sean to Kayla. "My boyfriend loves it. He tried to get me to learn but I got knocked in the head with the board."

Stephanie picked up her glass. "And she hasn't been back to the beach since," she said, casting an amused glance toward Donna.

Donna nodded. "I told him he can have the surf. I'll stick to the turf."

Kayla laughed at the wry expression on Donna's round face and then took a bite of her tart. The two women appeared to be very close. Over lunch, Kayla had learned more about them. They met, and became friends, while working for the phone company. Stephanie was married to her high school sweetheart, and Donna had been with her boyfriend for several years. When the economy took a downturn, they'd both been laid off and were still trying to find jobs.

As Donna pointed to one of their cast members at another table and then whispered something to Stephanie, Sean sought Kayla's eyes. "Surfing isn't that hard," he said, pushing his plate to the side. "It just takes a little practice."

"Do you guys know what's going to happen between

Jared and Shay?" Stephanie asked. "Are they going to fall in love?"

"I bet they will," Donna said, picking up her water glass. "Once Shay realizes she isn't in love with Stefan."

"Why do you think they're going to fall in love?" Kayla asked.

"Because Jared's going to help Shay, and that means they'll start spending a lot of time together," Donna said. "If you've watched soaps at all you know what that means." Donna paused and met her gaze. "I have to be honest. When Shay first showed up I didn't like her."

Kayla didn't take offense. "You aren't the only one who felt that way."

"I don't now," Donna clarified. "Shay was duped by Stefan. He made her believe he cared about her when it was obvious he'd never gotten over Cassie."

"And Shay believed him," Stephanie added. "After all, he was legally separated from Cassie."

Kayla gave Sean a cursory glance. He was listening intently.

Donna grimaced. "You guys probably think we're nuts. Going on about your characters like they're real people."

"Oh, I don't think that at all," Kayla said. "My mom has watched the show for practically forever. Now that I'm on it she calls me all the time for spoilers. I used to watch the show when I was in high school so I know what it's like to get so involved with the characters."

"You watched it?" Donna's eyes lit up. "Did you have a favorite character?"

Kayla forced herself not to look at Sean. Talk about being put on the spot. She searched her mind for a character that was on back then but couldn't come up with one to save her life.

"There were a few I liked," she said, knowing it was a lame answer. But what could she say? That she had a huge crush on Sean? Or that she rewound his scenes over and over again just to watch him? *Hell no,* she wasn't going to admit that.

"Who's your favorite character?" Chris directed his question to both Donna and Stephanie. Kayla let out a breath of relief, glad the spotlight was off her. She shot a glance toward Sean. His eyes flickered with amusement, and she wondered if he somehow knew he was the sole reason she had watched the show. But how could he? It wasn't like he was a mind reader.

"Jared." Both Stephanie and Donna said at the same time and then looked at each other and laughed.

Donna sipped her water and then looked at Sean. "Do you like working with Kayla?"

Taken aback by the question, Kayla glanced at Sean and found his eyes on her. "Very much," he said, turning his attention back to Donna. "We're lucky to have an actress of her caliber on the show."

A hot blush crept over her face as Donna and Stephanie beamed at her. "Thank you," she said, her stomach fluttering. "I paid him to say that," she joked and then tore her gaze from his before she drowned in those dazzling eyes of his.

Donna and Stephanie laughed, but it was Stephanie who spoke. "Sean's right, *A New Dawn* is lucky to have you, Kayla…" she paused "…and I'm not just saying that because you somehow finagled a way to get us into the luncheon." The blonde's eyes were filled with sincerity. "Don't bother to deny it, Sean already fessed up that it wasn't him."

Kayla shrugged. "I just checked to see if they had a couple of extra spots open," she said, picking up her iced tea, "and as luck would have it, they did."

Stephanie opened her mouth to say something but then the emcee's voice boomed over the speakers announcing the Q&A portion of the event. Kayla sipped her tea, grateful for the interruption. Getting them into the event wasn't a big deal. She was lucky to be employed.

It was obvious Stephanie and Donna weren't looking for a handout. They were just two loyal fans who, for the first time in years, were going to miss the fan club luncheon due to a financial hardship not of their own making. But they weren't bitter about it. Instead, they'd waited outside the hotel in hopes of getting glimpse of their favorite soap stars. Anyone would have done the same thing she did.

As the emcee explained the Q&A segment, Kayla let her gaze wander over the packed ballroom. Everyone was laughing and smiling, enjoying the event. Everyone except Rachel and Marcus. They were sitting next to each other at a table just across the aisle. Marcus looked bored to tears, and Rachel had such a petulant look on her face that Kayla wondered why she had even bothered to attend the event. Rachel must have sensed someone watching her. She turned her head and their eyes met. Immediately, her mouth tightened and her eyes glittered with a sharpness that could cut glass.

Looking away, Kayla amended her earlier thought. *Anyone with a heart* would have done the same thing.

HOLDING THE AWARD he'd received for best actor, Sean walked beside Kayla, Donna and Stephanie as they crossed the Hilton's expansive lobby. The majority of his cast mates had left the hotel the moment the awards presentation was finished. Chris had hung out for a while, and then left, citing plans with his girlfriend. Chris's departure could have been Sean's cue to leave as well, but instead he'd stayed. And while he could say it was because he wanted to mingle with the fans, the bottom line was he stayed because of Kayla.

Although Donna and Stephanie sat between them at the table, Sean was aware of Kayla's alluring presence all afternoon. He couldn't seem to help but notice everything about her. From the soft sheen of her dark hair to the red polish she wore on her fingernails. She'd laughed often and with ease, and had engaged everyone at their table in conversation. Especially Donna and Stephanie. She treated them like friends, and he was pretty sure he heard Stephanie ask her if she could start a fan club for her.

As they reached the double glass doors, Sean quickened his pace to hold the door open for the women. Kayla caught his eye and smiled as she brushed past him and out into the late afternoon sunshine. He followed closely behind the three of them as they strolled to the parking lot. Letting his gaze roam over Kayla's hot body, he appreciated the way she moved—with fluid grace despite the four-inch heels she wore. Her ponytail swung back and forth, brushing her shoulders. He had a sudden urge to pull the band from her hair and run his fingers through it.

Feeling a tug in his groin, he jerked his gaze from her and forced himself to think about baseball.

Did the Dodgers win? Do I give a shit?

Right now, no. And that pretty much told him that Kayla Maxwell was affecting him much more than he cared to admit.

He stopped short as Stephanie halted and turned toward Kayla. “Our car is that way,” she said, pointing in the opposite end of the parking lot from where he and Kayla were parked. Stephanie smiled as she reached out and gave Kayla’s arm a brief squeeze. “Thank you again for getting us into the luncheon.”

“And for letting us sit with you,” Donna added. “We had a blast.”

Kayla smiled at them both. It was a genuine, not practiced like Rachel’s. “You’re welcome,” she said. “I had fun too.” She gave them each a quick hug, and then turned her attention to Stephanie. “Email me your ideas on the fan club. I’ll let you know what I think.”

“Come on, Steph,” Donna said and then turned to Sean. “Bye, Sean. It was great to meet you.”

“Same here,” he said and meant it. The women who had been just random fans to him earlier in the day had turned out to be two of the nicest people he’d ever met.

“Congrats on your award.” Stephanie grinned at him. “We voted for you.”

“I appreciate it,” he said, glancing at the clear Lucite award with his name engraved on it.

“See you,” Stephanie said before she and Donna headed in the opposite direction.

He stared after them a moment and then turned to find Kayla’s dark eyes on him. “What?” he asked not missing the gleam of amusement in them.

“Admit it,” she said with a wide smile. “You had fun today.”

He held up his award. “I got an award. What’s not to like?”

“Don’t worry. Your secret is safe with me. I won’t tell Lisa you enjoyed yourself,” she said as they began heading in the direction of their cars.

“Thanks. She might try to sign me up for more of these things.”

“Well, there *is* a fan event in a couple of weeks. Chris and I are going. You’re welcome to join us.”

“Fan event? Is it another luncheon?”

Kayla opened her purse and pulled out her keys. “No. From what Chris told me, it’s more of a meet and greet type of thing. He’s real big on events. Lisa’s his publicist too.”

“She must *love* him,” Sean said as they approached her Mustang.

“She does. She says he’s the perfect client.”

“Unlike me,” Sean said and then grimaced.

“Totally unlike you.” Kayla let out a soft laugh.

“Lisa’s…different…but I like her,” he said, and then put his hand on her arm. Her skin was as soft as silk and he found he wanted to find out if every inch of her was that soft. She turned and met his gaze, her eyes questioning. “What you did today was pretty amazing,” he said, still impressed with her selfless gesture.

Her cheeks turned a light shade of pink, making her even more beautiful. “It was nothing.”

“Yes, it was.” He squeezed her arm gently. “You paid for Donna and Stephanie to attend the luncheon, didn’t you?”

She bit her lower lip. “Yes.”

“That was very generous of you.”

“Let’s consider it my good deed for the year.”

"Was it another to be the last cast member to stay and talk to the fans?"

She gave him a sly smile. "But I wasn't the last cast member to stay. You stayed too."

He opened his mouth but then quickly snapped it shut. She had him there. But he'd only stayed because of her, not because he wanted to talk to the fans. And while his motive to stay hadn't been altruistic, he was glad he did. He normally steered clear of events like the luncheon. Not because he didn't care about the fans, but because he couldn't fathom why they would want to talk to him. He was just an actor doing his job. Nothing more, nothing less. But today he found talking to them very rewarding. And that was something he hadn't expected.

Just like Kayla Maxwell.

"You're not at all like I thought you'd be," he said, noticing the gold flecks in her dark eyes. Their eyes met and the air around them suddenly turned electric.

"What did you think I'd be like?" she asked, her voice low, husky and sexy as hell.

"Like most of the actresses in this town." He paused. "But you're not."

She laughed. "Why? Because I eat dessert?"

He couldn't help but laugh with her and then the intimate moment passed. "Among other things." Reluctantly, he let go of her arm. "You did a really nice thing today, Kayla."

"I'm just glad I could do something for them. I have a job. And they don't."

She swung around to unlock her door. Just like his Jeep, there was no automatic lock for the Mustang, she had to use the key. It was the only thing about owning an older model that was inconvenient, but Sean didn't mind. The Wagoneer was perfect for hauling his surfboards and other athletic equipment around. It also harkened back to a time when surfing was all the rage. It still was for a lot of people. Only Hollywood didn't make stupid movies about it anymore.

Kayla opened the car door and turned to meet his gaze. "Did you see all the dialogue we have on Monday?"

He nodded. "I haven't memorized any of it."

"Me either," she said, tossing her purse into the car. "Normally I'd start on it tonight but I have plans."

Plans? What kind of plans? Did she have a date?

Of course she does, you idiot. She was too damn beautiful to be sitting home alone on a Saturday night.

Sean had plans too. He was driving to Pacific Palisades to check on his father's house. His script was in the Jeep and he'd been planning on going over it while he was there. But now he had a better idea and plunged ahead. "Since we both won't be able to study our scripts tonight maybe it would help if we got together tomorrow and ran lines together."

Her eyes widened just a bit; he held his breath waiting for her answer.

"Where?" She rested her hand on the car door.

"How about my house? Around noon. I'll even provide lunch."

"That'll work."

After he'd gotten her cell phone number and entered it into his phone, Sean's gaze lingered on Kayla's bare legs as she slid into her car. He closed the door for her and stepped back as she fired up the Mustang. She gave him a wave, backed out of the parking space and drove toward the exit. As her Mustang disappeared from view, Sean didn't bother to deny his invitation didn't have a damn thing to do with work. Yes, there was a lot of dialogue in Monday's script, but it wasn't anything he couldn't handle. In fact, there'd been a number of days in the past ten years when he'd had that much dialogue and more.

The truth was everything about Kayla intrigued him. The more he got to know her, the more he wanted to know. At this moment he wasn't thinking of all the reasons why he shouldn't spend time with her. Instead, all he wanted to do was satisfy his burning curiosity about her. Tomorrow, after spending time with her, he might realize that all he was feeling was physical attraction. And that he could deal with in other ways.

But what if it was more than physical attraction?

Nine

Shay: It's our wedding night. What do we do now?
Jared: Let's go to bed.
Shay: What?
Jared: I didn't mean with each other. I haven't forgotten this is a marriage of convenience.

PICKING UP HER script from the kitchen table, Kayla shoved it into her purse. A quick glance at the digital clock on the microwave showed that, despite changing her clothes four times before finally deciding on what to wear, she wasn't running late.

On a normal Sunday she usually wore her favorite shorts, or a pair of comfy jeans along with a T-shirt and flip flops. But this wasn't a normal Sunday. In five minutes she would be on her way to Sean's house. And while she kept reminding herself it wasn't a big deal, the fluttering in her stomach told a different story.

The last thing she had expected yesterday was for Sean to ask her if she wanted to run lines with him. It wasn't an uncommon practice among actors. But she and Sean rarely had to do it because both of them were always prepared and ready to go by dry rehearsal. And while she could easily memorize her lines by tomorrow morning, she hadn't been able to resist accepting his offer.

The evening they had shared a pizza at Cheech's,

Sean had directed the conversation so expertly that she'd been the one answering all the questions. Most men—at least the ones she knew—were more than happy to talk about themselves. But not Sean.

Of course, his reluctance to talk about himself only intrigued her more. Today she was hoping to satisfy her curiosity.

As she searched in her purse for her sunglasses, her cell phone rang. Digging it out of the side pocket, she saw Lisa's name on the caller ID. Knowing her friend, she was probably checking in to see how the fan club luncheon went.

"Good morning," she said, pressing the speaker-phone button.

"How was the luncheon? Did Sean show up?"

"Yes," Kayla said as she rummaged in her purse and found her sunglasses.

"How was the turnout?"

"The ballroom was packed. The crowd went nuts when Sean was introduced. No one was expecting him be there."

"And how did the crowd respond to you?"

"I didn't get the thunderous applause that Sean got, but it was decent. I think Shay's starting to catch on."

"I told you so," Lisa said, her tone more than a bit satisfied. "I'm actually calling for another reason. I know you normally read your fan mail on the weekends. Have you received any more of those threatening letters?"

Glancing at the four stacks of fan mail on the other end of the table, Kayla said, "No. But I haven't gone through the stuff I picked up on Friday."

"And did the alarm company come out yet?"

Kayla had called them just as she promised Lisa she would, but she'd forgotten to call her to let her know. "No. They're sending their consultant out on Thursday. I don't have to be on set that day."

"I wish it was sooner," Lisa said. "Remember that cop I was seeing a few years ago?"

"Luke Slade?" Kayla said, surprised Lisa had brought him up. "Yes, I remember him." How could she not? A man that gorgeous would be hard to forget. But Lisa apparently had. This was the first time she'd mentioned him since their brief affair ended. "Are you seeing him again?"

"No." Lisa's tone was cool. "But if you get any more of those letters I'm going to contact him."

"Why him?" Kayla asked. "Does he even work in this part of L.A.?"

"I'm not sure where he's assigned now but despite how things ended with us, I trust him. He's a good cop."

Kayla glanced at the clock. "I promise I'll let you know if I get any more letters." Picking up the piece of paper she'd written Sean's address on when he'd called earlier, she slipped it into the pocket of her pants. "Sorry, but I've got to run. I have somewhere to be at noon," she said, deliberately not mentioning where she was going. Dealing with Lance and his assumptions about Sean was enough. She didn't need Lisa chiming in with her opinion as well.

"I'll be in touch," Lisa said and hung up.

Slipping her phone into her purse, Kayla crossed the kitchen to the living room. Before opening the front door, she checked her reflection in the mirror. The outfit she'd decided on was a pair of white capri pants and a yellow tank top. Of all the clothes she'd tried on this combination seemed to be the one that didn't scream she was trying too hard. After all, contrary to what Lance thought, it wasn't a date. Today was all about work.

Yeah right, who are you kidding?

"Shut up," she muttered, thoroughly annoyed with her subconscious.

Reaching for her keys in a shallow bowl on an antique table placed beneath the mirror, Kayla opened the door and tried not to think about Lance's theory that Sean was interested in her. She and Lance had gotten together last night to see a movie and he'd grilled her mercilessly about the fan club luncheon. Then, of course, she'd made the colossal mistake of telling him about Sean's invitation to run lines today. The triumphant look on his face made her want to deck him. She had no doubt he'd call her tonight looking for juicy details. For someone who supposedly had his own hot and heavy love life, Lance was way too interested in her non-existent one.

After using the keypad just above the light switch to activate the alarm, she left the house and locked the door behind her. Slipping her sunglasses on, she headed for her car, all the while telling herself it wasn't a date.

SEAN HAD JUST finished washing down the backyard patio when his cell phone vibrated in the pocket of his jeans. Dropping the spray nozzle on top of the hose he'd just wound into a circle next to the house, he fished for his phone and scowled when he saw his father's name on the small brightly lit screen. *Shit.* The last thing he needed was another lecture about his career choice, or another job offer from one of James Barrett's powerful

Hollywood friends. Okay, so maybe he'd gotten a little too comfortable on the soap, but he'd leave the show when he was damn well ready to, and certainly not at the prodding of his father. The old man was lucky Sean hadn't totally cut him off. Oh, he'd thought about it, but out of respect for his mother, who had loved James Barrett with everything in her, he couldn't quite cut the cord.

"Yeah," he answered the call as he surveyed the yard, pleased with his efforts.

"Did I call at a bad time?" James Barrett's tone was polite and distant. As usual.

"Sort of." He glanced at his watch. Kayla would be arriving in about fifteen minutes.

"I won't keep you long," his father said. "But I wanted to let you know that your agent will be getting a call from the casting director for Steven Spielberg's production company."

Sean's fingers tightened on the phone. "Why would Spielberg's casting director be calling my agent?"

"You probably know that Steven and Tom Hanks have collaborated on two mini-series on HBO. Steven was in New York and dropped by my dressing room after yesterday's matinee. He was quite excited about a new HBO project he and Tom have in the works."

Sean had met the director and the actor several times. They were friends of his father, and both lived in Pacific Palisades. Sean hadn't seen either of them in years. Not since he'd moved out of his father's house.

"Please don't tell me you asked him to put me in his production." Sean crossed the wet patio, and after wiping his feet on the mat by the door, entered the living room. "You know how I feel about using your name to get parts."

"It's just an audition, Sean," James said and sighed. "I don't see why you have such an issue about using my name to at least get you in the door. It doesn't guarantee anything. You still have to impress them with your talent."

Sean closed the screen door. "I'm happy where I am."

"You're working on a soap opera, for Christ's sake."

"I'm not having this conversation again," Sean said, running a frustrated hand through his hair.

"Are you saying you won't even consider it?" James asked. "Most actors would kill for a role in one of Steven's productions.

"I'm not most actors."

"Are you afraid, Sean?"

"Afraid?" he exclaimed. "Of what?"

"Of being compared to me."

He bristled. "This isn't about you. If I wanted to leave the soap, I would." Sean's jaw tensed. He hated that his father could make him so angry. "Why can't you get it through your head that I make my own decisions about my career? I don't need you running interference for me with Steven Spielberg, or anyone else for that matter."

"I just want to help you," James said, his voice low. "I'm your father, Sean."

"You haven't been a father to me since Mom died," Sean ground out. His heart pounded as all the memories of that day flooded him.

It had been a beautiful summer day, perfect for surfing. Back then surfing was all he wanted to do and he'd even imagined himself as the next Kelly Slater—the pro surfer he and Matt worshipped. He was so caught up in the sport that when his mom had asked him to do one simple thing, he'd blown her off and rushed out of the house without even giving her a kiss goodbye.

There was a tense silence and then his father spoke. "We shouldn't talk about this over the phone."

"I couldn't agree more. In fact, I don't think we need to talk about it at all. It doesn't change a damn thing."

"That's one thing we agree on. But this conversation is far from over. You and I are going to continue this when I get home from New York." Before Sean could reply, his father changed the subject. "Were you able to check the house?"

"I went out there yesterday afternoon." Sean moved to the kitchen. "Everything's fine. I have to go," he said brusquely. "I'm expecting someone in a few minutes."

"Very well. But I wish you'd reconsider Steven's project. It's a wonderful opportunity."

"Goodbye." Not waiting for a response, Sean ended the call. Setting the phone on the counter, he scrubbed a hand over his jaw.

Of all the memories he had of his mother, the one he couldn't forget was the one he wished he could go back and change. A do-over. He'd sell his soul for one. Only there was no such thing.

Glancing again at his watch, Sean forced the memory of that day and his father from his mind. Dwelling on the past didn't change that fact that if it wasn't for his selfish actions, his mother would still be alive.

That's what his father had told him, and in his heart, Sean knew it was the truth.

KAYLA PARKED HER Mustang in front of the Ambrose Avenue address Sean had given her. Like most homes in the Los Feliz area, the architecture was Spanish. For several moments, Kayla sat in the car and admired the house. It was a single story house with a terracotta tile roof, which contrasted nicely with the pale orange stucco. An arched portico, as well as arched windows, gave the home tremendous curb appeal. The front yard was nicely landscaped with two medium size palm trees on either side of two brick pedestals with what looked like old fashioned gas lamps on top of them.

After getting out of her car and locking it, she walked up the tiered brick walkway to the front door and pressed the doorbell. As she waited, she removed her sunglasses and slipped them into her purse.

When the door opened, Kayla met Sean's eyes and, in what was becoming a regular occurrence, the physical attraction she felt for him flooded her body. Tightening her grip on her purse, she tried to ignore the way her pulse was suddenly racing at a dizzying speed and returned his famous grin. The same grin that had every woman at the luncheon yesterday practically drooling. Her included.

"Hey." He held the door open so she could enter. He was wearing faded jeans and a white cotton shirt with the sleeves rolled up. His hair was tousled and sexy. She wondered what it would feel like to run her fingers through it.

"Hi," she said. Brushing past him, his clean male scent traveled along her nerve endings. "This is a beautiful room," she said as she stopped to take in the large living room. It really was lovely, with a gleaming hardwood floor and the muted yellow walls. A mocha colored leather sofa was placed across from a white brick fireplace, and mounted above the mantle was a large flat panel television.

"Thanks." Closing the door, he moved to stand next to her. Turning, she lifted her gaze to his. "I was thinking we could run lines in here, or out on the patio." He nodded toward the screen door that led to his backyard. "Whichever you prefer."

"It's a beautiful day," she said with a smile. "How about the patio?"

Trailing after him, she couldn't help but admire the snug fit of his jeans. He was powerfully built and moved with the grace of an athlete. She could almost picture him on his surfboard, mastering the waves with ease. Biting her lower lip, she tried not to imagine what else he could master with that body of his, and then almost plowed into him as he stopped by the screen door.

Lifting her hand, she braced it on his back to steady herself. "Sorry," she said. "I wasn't watching where I was going." Quickly, she withdrew her hand. But not before feeling the warmth of his skin through his shirt.

He opened the screen door and motioned with his hand for her precede him to the patio. "Do you want anything to drink?"

"Got any beer?" she asked.

"You bet. It's one of the four basic food groups, isn't it?"

She laughed and turned to look at him. "That and chocolate."

He lifted one brow and grinned. "I've got that too."

"I may never leave," she shot back. As their eyes locked, a moment of sizzling awareness sent her pulse into overdrive.

"I'll be right back," he said after several charged

seconds. He motioned to the table. "Make yourself at home."

After he disappeared into the house, she moved to the round wooden table with a colorful sun umbrella shading it. She set her purse down and checked out the yard. While it wasn't as large as Lisa's backyard, just beyond the patio was a swimming pool with an adjacent hot tub. On the other side of the pool, along the fence, were oleander bushes in colorful bloom. The tall and manicured shrubs gave the yard a sense of privacy from the neighbors.

"What do you think of the yard?" Sean asked. She turned to find him approaching her holding two beers and two frosty beer mugs.

"It's lovely," Kayla said, pulling out one of the chairs tucked against the table. "It must be nice to come home from the studio and be able to take a dip in the pool, or sit in the hot tub."

Sean opened one of the beers and poured it into a mug and then slid it toward her. "When I decided to move here from Santa Monica I told my Realtor I had to have a pool," he said then sat down across from her. "It's the only way I can stomach not living by the ocean."

"I've heard the traffic is really bad coming in from Santa Monica."

He opened his beer. "One accident and you might as well forget getting anywhere on time. After two years of dealing with it I decided to move closer to the studio."

"I lucked out," she said picking up her mug. "I fell in love with Atwater Village the moment I saw it. And it's not that far from the studio either."

"How long have you lived there?"

"About four years. I was able to buy my house after

I did a couple of horror movies." She leaned back and sipped her beer.

"That must have been an interesting experience,"

"Very." Kayla smiled. "I've never screamed so much in my life."

Sean laughed, his eyes crinkling at the corners. "Did your character die in some over the top gruesome way?"

"I survived the first movie. But I wasn't so lucky in the sequel. My head was hacked off with a meat cleaver." Sean's eyes widened and she couldn't help but smile at the look of disgust on his face. "Not a fan of slasher flicks, I take it?"

"When I was twelve." He shot back with a boyish grin. "My tastes have evolved since then. What's your favorite movie?"

Kayla set her mug down. "There are too many great movies out there to pick just one." She wrinkled her nose in distaste. "Speaking of which, the movie I saw last night was just awful. Lance and I walked out about half way through it. Even *he* couldn't take it."

"Lance?" He paused. "From the photo shoot?"

Kayla nodded. "He did my hair before the luncheon yesterday. We've been friends for years and have a standing date to catch a movie once a month."

"He's quite…colorful," Sean said with a smile.

Kayla let out a laugh. "That's putting it mildly." Glancing at the script sticking out of her purse, she was reminded of why she was there. "Did you look at your script at all?"

"I read through it this morning. I'll go get it. I left it in the house." He rose from his chair. "Be right back."

Kayla watched him walk to the house and then reached for her script. Opening it to the first page of dialogue she stared at the page blankly thinking that, although the nervous fluttering that had plagued her all morning was gone, in its place was something far more unsettling. The more time she spent with Sean the more she liked him. And the more her physical attraction to him grew. She had vowed never to get involved with an actor again and at the time she'd meant it. But that was before she'd met Sean, before she'd looked into those bottomless green eyes of his and felt things she'd hadn't felt in a good long while.

Unlike Lance, she didn't assume that Sean was interested in her romantically. But if he was, there was one thing she knew for sure. Resisting him would be futile.

IN HIS BEDROOM, Sean grabbed his script from the bedside table. From the window he was able to see Kayla studying her script. Until she'd mentioned it he'd totally spaced on why she was at his house. The moment he'd opened the front door and seen her standing there, the only thing he could think of was how damn beautiful she was. Well that, and how much he wanted to kiss her full, sensuous lips.

As much as he'd wanted to do a more thorough internet search on her, he'd resisted the urge. Gathering information on her that way bordered on stalking—at least in his mind—and then there was the fact that he didn't want to get to know her in such an impersonal manner. Most of the stuff on the internet was bogus anyway. He'd found that out the hard way when his former publicist, Jerry, planted false information about his personal life. To read that he was involved with a stripper had shocked the shit out of him. A lot of actors gravitated to strippers and porn stars but he wasn't one of them. And while Jerry had retracted the information, it was still out there for anyone to read. And to believe.

Sean knew that if it could happen to him, it could happen to Kayla. So he preferred to get his information the old fashioned way. By talking to her. And besides, spending time with her was a lot more enjoyable than reading about her on the internet.

Tearing his gaze from her, he left his room with only one thought on his mind. And it wasn't running lines.

Ten

Shay: Would you mind putting on a shirt?
Jared: I just got back from a run. I'm hot.
Shay: Yes. Yes, you are.
Jared: What did you say?
Shay: I said you must have run far.

KAYLA SET HER fork down, unable to contain her blissful sigh. "That was delicious."

Sean's amused gaze met hers. "There's more in the kitchen," he offered, and then lifted his mug to his lips.

"Oh no," she said putting a hand on her stomach, "I'm stuffed." She glanced at her empty plate, hardly able to believe she'd eaten two helpings. "Did you make the pasta salad yourself?"

He nodded. "After I moved out on my own there was no cook to prepare my meals for me so it was either fend for myself or starve."

"You had a cook?" she asked, and then remembered who his father was. Of course they had a cook and probably more staff as well. "My mom would have killed for a cook," she said with a smile. "And, trust me, there were a few meals when my dad probably would have shelled out the money for one if he could have afforded it."

Sean's eyes softened. "Sally was a nice lady and very

good at her job. My dad hired her after my mom died. I ate more meals with her than I did with my father."

"Was your father gone a lot?" Kayla asked, surprised he'd brought up his parents.

Sean nodded. "He was gone for long stretches at a time. Either working on a movie, or doing theater in New York."

"That must have been tough."

"I got used to it." Sean shrugged.

"Is it hard having such a famous father?" Kayla asked. She was treading on shaky ground. Sean was known for not discussing his father with anyone.

"I've never known anything different. I'm sure a lot of people would love being the kid of a famous actor, but it's not all it's cracked up to be." His tone was matter of fact, but her instincts told her his nonchalance was a front.

"What happened to your mom?"

He paused and for a moment she wondered if this time she'd overstepped. "She died when I was thirteen," he said quietly.

"What do you remember about her?"

"She had blonde hair. And green eyes like mine." His lips curved in a sad, almost vulnerable smile. "And she always smelled good. Like sugar cookies," he said with such a wistful expression on his face that it tugged at her heart. It made her want to wrap her arms around him and comfort him.

Kayla blinked several times as moisture filled her eyes. "You were so young," she said softly. "It seems so unfair."

Sean shifted his gaze from hers when a bird flitted

past them and landed on the patio. "You're very lucky to have both your parents."

"Death is difficult to deal with. It's the one thing that happens to all of us, and yet it's the hardest thing to talk about."

Turning to look at her, Sean held her gaze without replying. A crackle of something almost electric passed between them, but then it was gone, and she wondered if she'd imagined it. "I normally don't talk about my mother with anyone," he said, leaning back in his chair.

"Not even your father?"

Sean's mouth twisted into a grimace. "Especially not my father."

"May I ask why?"

"We don't get along." Sean's tone was terse. "Among other things, he's not happy with my career choice."

"He disapproves of you being an actor?"

"No, he's fine with that. He just doesn't like that I'm on a soap. He doesn't consider it legitimate acting."

"Are you serious?" she exclaimed. "It's hard work." Kayla reached for her script next to her plate and lifted it. "This is our dialogue for tomorrow. This is almost as much as I had in *Halloween Hell*." She grinned. "But to be fair, I probably would have had more if I hadn't been decapitated halfway through the movie." Dropping the script back to the table, Kayla shook her head. "I don't understand why people look down on daytime. There are so many talented actors on the soaps."

"You're proof of that," Sean said and the sudden intensity in his eyes seemed to suck the air out of her lungs.

"Thank you." Her face was burning under his scrutiny. "So are you."

He shrugged a shoulder. "I was getting lazy. It happens when you do one character for so long. I've had to step up my game since we've been working together."

Flustered, she picked up her beer and took a slow sip as she tried to control the erratic beating of her heart.

"Have you ever thought of leaving the show?" she asked, wishing she could press the cold mug to her face to cool her warm skin. She'd never reacted to any man the way she was to him. Her gaze rested on the tanned skin where his shirt was unbuttoned at the collar and she took another sip of the ice cold beer. Just moments ago she wanted to comfort him, now she wanted to press her lips to his neck and nibble her way up—or down. Either destination was fine with her.

Seemingly unaware of the effect he was having on her, he answered her question. "From time to time. My father is always badgering me to quit and do some…" he lifted his hands and mimicked quotes with his fingers "…real acting."

"It could be worse." She smiled. "You could be doing porn."

Sean's jaw dropped, and then he threw back his head and roared with laughter. It was contagious, and she couldn't help but laugh along with him.

"THANK GOD THIS last scene is short," Kayla said looking up from her script after they'd done a cold reading of the lines. "It's in Jared's living room." She looked up at him. "Can we go to yours and do a little blocking?"

Sean drained the last of his beer from his mug. "Sounds like a plan." They rose from their chairs and Sean let her precede him into the house. They'd been running lines for almost three hours. He was pretty sure they could have done it in less time but going over the lines and talking about Jared and Shay's motivation had lengthened the process. He didn't mind though, he'd enjoyed every minute of it.

Stopping behind the sofa, he watched her as she rounded it, enjoying the gentle sway of her hips. The snug white pants she wore showed off her remarkable curves. She came to a halt on the other side of the coffee table.

"I think Shay is starting to notice Jared in a different way." She looked down at her script. A thick swatch of her dark hair fell over her shoulder. She brushed it back and cast him an amused look. "The only reason they're having you take your shirt off in this scene is because America voted you the sexiest soap star in *People* magazine."

He shifted uncomfortably. "I think my former publicist rigged that poll."

"I doubt it." She tilted her head and studied him with her dark eyes. "I know for a fact that my mom and a few of my aunts voted for you. They think you're hot."

"Whoa." He put his hand up. "Too much information."

She laughed. "You can be a serious actor and a hunk, you know."

"You think I'm a hunk?" he asked and then couldn't help but smile when her cheeks turned a becoming shade of pink. Her tendency to blush was cute.

"Uh…well…" She looked down at her script. "That's what they called you in the magazine." She was flustered and it was damn appealing.

"Good save." He unfurled his script. "Okay, so Jared comes in from his run…"

"Without his shirt."

"Right." He cocked his head. "Do you need me to take off my shirt now? You know, just to make the run-through more realistic?"

Her eyes widened. "Uh..." She bit her lower lip. "No need. I can imagine you with it off."

"Really?" He grinned.

"I have an excellent imagination."

"What a coincidence." He held her gaze. "So do I."

She held up the script, her cheeks still stained with pink. "Let's take it from the top. You can come in from the kitchen."

He headed for the kitchen. Once he was out of her sight he couldn't resist the idea of messing with her. Putting the script on the counter, he quickly unbuttoned his shirt and pulled it off.

"I'll be on the sofa," she called out. "The scene starts with Shay reading a book."

He put his shirt on the counter on top of his script. He wouldn't need it, there wasn't much dialogue. "Let's do the scene all the way through. No breaks."

"Works for me," she replied as he moved toward the living room. "Are you ready?"

"As I'll ever be," he said, grinning to himself.

"Action," she said.

When he walked into the room she had her head down, looking at the script. "What are you reading?"

"A book about how the baby develops over the course of the pregnancy. It's really pretty amazing." She looked up, turned her head and except for the slightest widening of her eyes, she stayed in character. "Where have you been?"

"At the park." He saw her gaze lower to his chest

and then jerk back up. He wiped his brow. They would spray him with water before the scene so he would look sweaty. "How's the morning sickness?"

"Better." She got up from the sofa and moved toward him. "Now I'm just getting it in the morning instead of all day." She halted in front of him and again her eyes lowered to his chest. "Would you mind putting on a shirt?"

"I just got back from a run. I'm hot."

"Yes." Her voice was low. "Yes, you are." She lifted her gaze to his and they were filled with something that looked a lot like…arousal. She moved to go around him; he reached out and grabbed her arm. She stopped beside him. Her skin felt warm; the soft scent of her perfume surrounded him. His heart started to pound.

"What did you say?"

"I said you must have run far." According to the script, she was supposed to pull her arm from his grasp. But she didn't, instead she made an imperceptive shift toward him. Her eyes burned into his as they paused for the required beats and then she said in a husky voice, "I'll go make breakfast and you can go shower."

"You don't have to do that…" he paused "…you know, make me breakfast every day."

"I want to." There were no more lines, nothing left but for her to walk away from him and for him to stare after her. It was in the script, only she wasn't following it. Several charged seconds passed. In those seconds all Sean was aware of was the curve of her cheek and the voluptuousness of her lips. It filled him with heat and desire, and drove all reason from his mind. Lowering his head, he heard the hitch of her breath just before his mouth covered hers. After that, nothing else registered, except for the fact that Kayla's lips tasted just as sweet as he had imagined. And they were soft…so soft as they parted and she returned his kiss with an urgency that surprised him.

Their lips tangled until he felt her hand against his chest. With a low groan, he pulled back. Her eyelids fluttered open and when their eyes met he felt an involuntary tightening low in his gut.

"That wasn't in the script," Kayla said in a husky voice that didn't do a damn thing to stop the blood running hotly through his veins. Her dark eyes gleamed with sudden amusement. "You thought you could get me to break character by taking off your shirt, didn't you? I can't believe you did that."

Supremely aware of her fingers resting on his bare skin, Sean grinned. "And like the pro you are, you didn't miss a beat."

"It takes more than a naked chest to rattle me," she shot back. "Don't forget, I was able to do love scenes with Marcus and not puke."

"You should get a reward for that."

"I did," she said softly. "I get to work with you."

The admiration in her voice took him by surprise. Before he could speak, she stepped back forcing him to let go of her arm. "I should probably go." She looped a loose strand of hair behind her ear. "It's getting late."

"Right," he said, even though he wanted her to stay. And the funny thing about that was he couldn't remember the last time he wanted to spend more than an hour with any woman. "Let me get my shirt on and I'll walk you to your car."

After she'd gathered her things and he'd put his shirt on, they walked together toward her car. All he could think about the kiss. He didn't know what the hell was happening to him, but he did know he felt totally alive in her presence.

"This was a great idea," she said as they stopped at the curb next to her Mustang. Her gaze lifted to his. "I like what the writers are doing with Shay." She reached into her purse and pulled out her keys. "I think she's going to follow Jared when he goes on that stakeout."

"That's what it sounds like."

"I hope so." Kayla grinned. "She's been moping around for a while now. I'm glad she's getting some of her spunk back."

"Jared is going to regret ordering her to leave the police work to him," he said, letting his gaze wander over her beautiful face. Was she feeling the same thing he was? Should he mention the kiss? Maybe it had meant nothing to her. "He means well, but Jared doesn't know how women think."

"You're right," she said, her brows arched in amusement. "We don't like being told what to do." As she turned to unlock the passenger side door, her script slipped out of her hand and fell to the curb. Instinctively, they both bent to pick it up. Sean heard a sickening crack as their foreheads butted together. "Oww," Kayla cried out, recoiling quickly. As pain shot through his head, he reached for her, but wasn't quick enough. She fell to the ground and he heard another crack when the back of her head hit the concrete.

Eleven

Shay: I signed up for Lamaze classes.
Jared: Great. When do we start?
Shay: Not until...wait...you want be my coach?
Jared: Of course. We're in this together, Shay.

"KAYLA?" IGNORING THE throbbing in his head, Sean bent over her, concerned by the dazed look in her eyes. She blinked rapidly but didn't speak. "Kayla? Are you okay?"

"I feel like I ran into a brick wall…" she paused "…twice," she said, her voice shaky. "You have a hard head." She tried to smile, but then grimaced and sucked in a painful breath.

"I've been told that a few times in my life," he said, keeping his voice casual despite his worry. "Let's go back in the house. I think we could both use some ice." He reached for her hands and gently pulled her up.

"I can't." She shook her head and then squeezed her eyes shut as if she was in pain. "I have to answer my fan mail."

Fan mail? She read and answered her fan mail? Damn, the woman continued to surprise him.

"I don't think you should drive," he said when she opened her eyes.

"I'm fine," she insisted but her eyes were too unfocused for his liking. "The pain is going away."

Sean let go of Kayla's hands and bent down to pick up her script. "I'll drive you home," he said as he straightened.

"No." She shook her head and raised her hand to her temple. "I'm fine. Really," she said and then blinked several times.

Sean frowned. "Sorry, but I can't in good conscience let you drive. Atwater Village isn't that far from here. I'll drive you home and then tomorrow I'll pick you up and we can stop by my house either before work or after so you can pick up your car."

She opened her mouth to protest, but then rubbed her temple and nodded. "I can't take a chance with the Mustang. If I totaled it, Dad would kill me."

"I'm sure he'd be more concerned about you than the car."

"But the car's a close second." Her slender fingers moved to touch her forehead. "I hope I don't get a bruise."

"I've got an ice pack in the freezer. You can put it on your forehead. That should help with any swelling or bruising." He put his hand on her shoulder, trying to ignore the throbbing in his head. "Let's go back inside to get it," he said as they walked slowly back to the house.

TWENTY MINUTES LATER, Sean pulled the Jeep into the driveway next to Kayla's quaint white stucco bungalow. As with most homes in the area, the garage was detached. However, unlike his home, the access to the garage was at the front of the house via a brick pathway that led from the front porch to the driveway. That bothered him. From a security standpoint, a rear access garage was much safer.

"Stay put," he said after he'd turned off the engine. Kayla lowered the ice pack from her forehead as he climbed out and rounded the front of the Jeep to help her out. "How are you feeling?" he asked, taking her hand to assist her after he'd opened the door.

"Like I've been kicked in the head." When her feet touched the ground, she swayed unsteadily. He put his arm around her shoulders. "Thanks," she said leaning against him. "I'm dizzy."

"I wonder if you have a concussion." Sean closed the door and then led her around the Jeep and toward the tiled porch. "Maybe I should take you to the emergency room."

"No." Her quick response was vehement. "I hate hospitals. I just need some aspirin and a good night's sleep."

When they reached the porch, he held her elbow with a firm grasp as they climbed the steps to the arched front door. She'd given him her keys earlier and he pulled them from the pocket of his jeans. There were about six or seven keys on the ring. "Which key?"

"The silver one," she said. He unlocked the door and pushed it open. "Thank you for driving me home." She gazed up at him, and while her eyes weren't as unfocused as they'd been earlier, she looked a bit shell shocked. "I'm sorry to be so much trouble."

"You're not any trouble," he assured her. "Let's go inside. Your alarm is beeping." She nodded and turned to enter the house. After she haltingly pressed the numbers on her security keypad, Sean followed her inside. She took several steps into the living room and then stopped.

"I think I should sit down." Her voice was almost a

whisper. Sean closed the door and then helped her to a chair in the corner of the room. She sank down on the cushions and dropped her purse on the pale green area rug that covered the dark hardwood floor. She pressed the ice pack to her forehead and sighed. "I'll bet Sandy's going to have to use a lot of make-up on me tomorrow."

Moving to the chair, Sean hunkered down in front of her. "Let me see your head." He reached for the ice pack and took it from her grasp. "There's a knot forming." He looked at her forehead. There was a lump, but it wasn't as bad as it could be. The ice had helped. He reached around and gently touched the back of her head with his fingers. She winced. "I think I should call the advice nurse at the hospital," he said, noting the pallor of her skin.

"It's just a couple of bumps on the head."

"You could have a concussion," he said and rose to his feet. He turned, looking for the kitchen and saw that it was through the archway behind him. He held up the ice pack. "I need to put this in the freezer and get you more ice." Without waiting for her to reply he moved to the kitchen.

"I'll call, and if they tell me to bring you in, you're going," he said as he opened the freezer side of her stainless steel refrigerator and tossed the ice pack inside.

"Sean, you're fussing over nothing." She sighed. "Really. I'm fine."

"Sorry, sweetheart." He shot her a grin. "I'm not convinced. If the nurse says there's nothing to worry about then I'll leave, but until then, I'm staying."

"All right then." Kayla flopped back in the chair. "Make the call."

MUCH LATER, SITTING on Kayla's sofa watching *Sports Center*, Sean checked his watch. Four hours had passed since Kayla had gone to bed. The nurse he'd spoken to hadn't been unduly alarmed however she did suggest that Kayla be monitored overnight.

Rising from the sofa, he headed down the hallway past the guest room and into her bedroom. He flipped the light switch by the door and saw her curled up on her side facing him. She was covered with a sheet and light blanket and her hair had fallen like a smooth curtain around her face. Her shoulders were bare except for the thin straps of whatever she'd changed into earlier. Moving to the bed, he touched her arm.

"Kayla."

She didn't stir so he slid his hand up to her shoulder. Her skin felt like satin. "Kayla," he said again and this time shook her shoulder. "Wake up."

Her body jerked and, lifting her hand, she brushed her hair away from her face. "What the…?" she muttered and then frowned. "What are you doing here?" she asked in a sleepy voice.

"I'm supposed to wake you every four hours, remember?" He straightened. "What's your name?"

"You know my name," she said and then rolled to her back. Looking sexier than hell, she smiled up at him. "You're really tall. How tall *are* you?"

"Six-two," he replied. "You need to tell me your name. I'm supposed to ask you a few questions to make sure you're thinking clearly."

Her hair fanned out on the pillow; dark against the crisp white pillowcase. It looked soft, silky and very touchable.

"Kayla Anne Maxwell," she said and then sighed softly. "Satisfied?"

He would be if he could kiss her again.

He held up three fingers. "How many fingers am I holding up?"

"Two," she said and then let out a delighted giggle. "Ha! Gotcha. It's three."

Sean shook his head and chuckled. "Great. I've got a comedienne on my hands. When's your birthday?"

"December 25th." She gazed up at him. "Can I go back to sleep now? I'm tired."

"How's your head?"

"Better." Her eyes were more focused now. "What time is it?"

"A little after nine. I'll wake you up in another four hours."

"Can't wait." She rolled over and closed her eyes.

THE SOUND OF something truly annoying jolted Sean out of a deep sleep. He silenced the alarm on his watch and then pushed himself up and climbed out of the bed in Kayla's guest room. Yawning and rubbing the grit from his eyes, he made his way to her room and flipped on the light.

His pulse kicked the second he saw her. The sheet and blanket were bunched down by her ankles. The sleep shorts she was wearing hugged her rounded bottom and exposed her shapely legs. She was sprawled on her stomach, her head turned to the side away from him.

Tearing his gaze from her hot body, he leaned down and tapped her shoulder. "Kayla," he said and tapped again when she didn't move. "Wake up."

"Go away," she muttered. "Sleeping."

"Just answer a few questions and then you can go back to sleep."

Kayla groaned and lifting her head, twisted around to her side. She rubbed her eyes and squinted at him. "What now?" she asked but Sean didn't answer. His eyes were locked on the small portion of her nipple that was exposed just above the low neckline of her camisole. Temptation rocked through his veins; he had to force himself to look away.

"What's your name?"

"Kayla Anne Maxwell." She yawned and lifted her hand to cover her mouth. The movement covered her exposed nipple.

Thank God.

"Born on Christmas Day," she said before he could ask. She wrinkled her nose at him. "Anything else, Sherlock?"

"Funny." He put his hands on his hips. "Favorite baseball team?"

She laughed. It was low and throaty and made him wish he could join her in that bed of hers. "Not the Dodgers."

He shook his head and grinned. "How's your head doing?"

"It hurts," she grumbled. "Can I take more aspirin?"

"Enough hours have passed. Where's the bottle?"

"Bathroom." She pointed to the open doorway in the far corner of her room.

He rounded the bed and went into the bathroom. After grabbing the small bottle sitting on the counter, he returned to the bed and reached for the bottle of water on her nightstand. "Do you need me to help you sit up?" he asked.

"No…fine…can do myself." She pushed herself up and brushed her hair away from her face. "This really sucks," she said as he handed her the water. He pried the top off the bottle. She held out her hand to let him shake two tablets onto her palm. She downed them quickly with a long gulp of water.

"Thanks." She handed him the water and then collapsed back on the bed, her breasts moving freely underneath the fabric of her top. Swallowing hard, Sean put the water and the bottle of pain reliever on the nightstand. "Are you gonna wake me up again?" she whispered with her eyes closed.

He glanced at watch. "Probably one more time before morning."

"Crap."

"My sentiments exactly." He stifled a yawn. "I'll see you in four hours, sweetheart."

THE SHRILL BEEPING of her alarm clock startled Kayla from a fitful sleep. Forcing her eyes open, she reached across the bed and hit the snooze button to silence the annoying reminder that she had to get up and go for her daily run. Shoving the sheet and blanket aside, she pushed herself up on her elbow and stared at her running shoes sitting beside her armoire.

Who was she kidding?

There was no way she was running this morning. Not with the remnants of the worst headache she'd ever had still lingering in her head like a low lying fog. And certainly not after the worst night's sleep she'd ever had.

Seriously, how could anyone get any rest when someone was waking them up every four hours to check if they were still alive?

Sitting up, Kayla swung her legs over the side of the bed and gingerly got to her feet. Brushing her hair from her face, she padded to the bathroom and hit the light switch. Peering into the mirror above the sink, she let out a sigh of relief when she saw that the only ill effects from her head butt with Sean was a small lump on her forehead, and dark circles under her eyes from her sleepless night.

After using the bathroom, she went back to the bedroom and slipped on her robe. Since she wasn't going to run, she could at least make some coffee. She definitely needed it, and Sean probably would too.

On her way to the kitchen, she stuck her head in the guest room and saw him stretched out on the bed, dead to the world. He was still wearing his jeans and white shirt, but his feet were bare. He was on his back with one hand up near his head and the other resting on his stomach.

Venturing into the room, she pulled a crocheted afghan from the back of a chair in the corner. Moving to the bed, she covered him with it. He stirred and muttered something unintelligible but didn't awaken.

Staring down at him, she let her gaze roam over his face. He was just as gorgeous asleep as he was awake. His powerful body seemed to dwarf the double bed. Everything about him was compellingly masculine, yet in sleep he seemed almost vulnerable. It reminded her of the look in his eyes when he'd briefly talked about his mother.

Sean let out a light snore and shifted his head on the pillow. She couldn't help but notice the yellowish bruise on his forehead. Grimacing, Kayla remembered the white hot pain that had seemed to explode in her head, and was amazed she hadn't passed out. Sean had to have been in the same kind of pain, but he hadn't shown it. He'd calmly attended to her without giving a thought to himself.

Then he'd stayed all night, waking her up throughout the night to make sure she didn't have a concussion. Not many men would do that. But Sean did.

Unable to resist, Kayla lifted her hand, and with her fingers, lightly brushed his hair from his forehead. "Thank you," she whispered, longing to feel his lips on hers again.

Her schoolgirl crush now seemed so innocent and safe. When she was seventeen, he was someone she'd never dreamed she would meet. Her teenage fantasies were nothing more than him taking her to the senior prom, or escorting her to some big Hollywood premiere. But now, her fantasies were far from innocent, or tame. They had nothing to do with proms or premieres, and everything to do with hot, sweaty, knock-your-socks-off sex. That's how sex with Sean would be, she was sure of it. If that kiss they'd shared was a preview, the main attraction would be hotter than hell.

Her gaze wandered from his face to where his shirt was unbuttoned at his chest. Resisting the urge to touch his golden brown skin, she turned and left the room.

After putting the coffee on to brew, and taking a very hot and much needed shower, she dressed in a pair of khaki cargo pants and a white tank top. She slipped into a pair of sandals, pulled her hair into a ponytail and left her bedroom intent upon her first cup of coffee of the day.

Passing by the guest room she saw that it was empty and then heard the sound of the cupboard closing. Evidently, Sean had woken up while she was showering. When she walked into the kitchen, his back was to her and he was pouring himself some coffee.

"Good morning," she said cheerily.

"Morning," he said, turning around. "How are you feeling?" he asked as he held the cup out.

"Much better than yesterday." She moved toward him and took the cup from his outstretched hand. "Thanks," she said as he opened the cupboard to get another cup. "How about you?"

"Tired." He poured coffee into the cup and then returned the pot to the coffeemaker. He turned and leaned against the counter.

"Are you hungry?" she asked after taking a tentative sip of the hot coffee. "I'm not the world's best cook, but I could manage some eggs, or toast." She moved to stand next to him and set her cup on the smooth granite countertop.

"I could eat," Sean said. "Do you mind if I watch the news?"

"Not at all." She lifted her gaze to his, very aware of his body just inches from hers. "You can watch it in here, or in the living room."

His gaze roamed her over her face and then focused on her forehead. "It didn't bruise too badly."

"I know. Hardly at all. I think the ice helped with that, and with the swelling. Sandy should be able to cover it up for taping today." She rested her hand on his forearm. A current of electricity seemed to telegraph its way from her fingertips straight to her core. *Holy crap,* if she felt this way just touching his arm she couldn't imagine how she'd react if she were to touch him more intimately. She might actually explode. "Thank you," she said, wishing her voice didn't sound quite so breathless. But she couldn't help it. He had that effect on her.

He cocked his head. "For what?"

"For staying here last night." She let go of his arm and then moved past him to the refrigerator. "And for checking on me." She opened the door and pulled out a carton of eggs and a quart of milk. "I vaguely recall not being very polite to you last night." Using her hip, she closed the refrigerator door and turned to find his eyes on her.

"I'd be pissed too if some idiot was waking me up out of a sound sleep."

"You're not an idiot," she said, her smile fading as their eyes locked and held. Her heart skipped a beat and then for some stupid reason her knees started to tremble. "You were making sure I was okay. Not many people would do that."

"You would," he said and then took another sip of his coffee. He lowered his cup from his lips. "You're kind of cute when you blush like that."

"I don't blush," she said and took the eggs and milk to the small granite topped island between the counter and the kitchen table.

Sean's laugh was more of a snort as he rounded the island and picked up the remote from the kitchen table. "Trust me, you blush," he said as stood by the table and turned the television on.

"It's just very warm in here." She pulled open a drawer and pulled out a small mixing bowl, silently cursing herself for being so flustered.

"Whatever you say, sweetheart." He laughed and turned his attention to the television.

As he channel surfed, she stared at his back. He'd

called her sweetheart twice now. And while she was sure he didn't mean it as a term of endearment it still gave her a little thrill.

"How about some scrambled eggs?" she asked as he bypassed the news channel and found ESPN.

He turned and gave her that sexy grin of his. "Sweetheart, I'll eat anything you want me to." His words were innocent, but his eyes weren't. Her face burned as a hot lick of sexual excitement coursed through her. "You're blushing again," he said with a chuckle and then turned his attention back to the sports channel.

Twelve

Shay: What happened to the picture on the table?
Jared: I put it away. Rebecca's gone. You're here now.
Shay: But you wish she was here instead of me, don't you?
Jared: I didn't say that.
Shay: You didn't have to.

BEFORE HEADING TO wardrobe to pick up the clothes she would be wearing for the day's taping, Kayla made a side trip to the studio's break room for another cup of coffee. Her lack of sleep last night was definitely affecting her and while one cup a day was her limit, today was an exception. She needed all the help she could get to stay alert and focused.

As she left the break room with coffee in hand, she almost collided with Rachel in the hallway. "Sorry," she said as she moved aside so Rachel could pass. Not uttering a word, Rachel shot her a disdainful look and then continued down the hall. Kayla watched her retreating back for a few seconds, and then, putting Rachel and her many moods out of her mind, she headed for the wardrobe department.

Twenty minutes later, dressed in one of Shay's tight and cleavage-revealing outfits, she sat on the sofa in her dressing room waiting to be called to the set. On her lap was a stack of fan mail. Since she hadn't had the opportunity to look at the mail over the weekend, she wanted to sort through the envelopes to see if any were from the crazy fan that had been sending her the threatening notes.

She was almost at the bottom of the stack when she saw the small white envelope that was an exact duplicate of the others she'd received. Her stomach knotted with dread as she recognized the precise hand lettering. As with the other three, it was addressed to Shay, and there was no return address. Putting the rest of the mail beside her on the sofa, Kayla grabbed her letter opener but then dropped it immediately. It landed on the multicolored area rug with a dull thud. How could she be so dense? If she opened the letter her fingerprints would be all over it. Gingerly, she moved her finger and thumb so they just touched the corner of the envelope. She rose from the sofa, moved to the desk and opened the top drawer. Inside was a large manila envelope where she kept some head shots. After retrieving it from the drawer, she managed to get it open with one hand and slip the letter inside with no problem.

A sharp knock on the door startled her and sent her heart racing. "Kayla." It was Sean. "They want us on set."

"Come on in," Kayla said, quickly dropping the envelope on the desk before turning toward the door. Sean stuck his head inside. His smile faded as he gaze roamed over her face.

"Are you all right?" he asked, and took couple of steps inside the room. "Is it your head?" He frowned, looking at her with concern. "I knew I shouldn't have let you drive to work this morning."

"I'm fine," she said as the pounding in her temples returned with a vengeance. Kayla didn't like lying to him but for now she didn't want anyone except Lisa to know about the letters. Lisa would be her first call after she was done taping her scenes; Lisa's former boyfriend Luke Slade would be her second. It was time for the LAPD to be notified. Way past time actually; she couldn't shrug this off any longer.

"You don't look fine." He looked skeptical. "You're as white as a sheet."

"I'm just tired."

"Do you have a headache?"

"No. I feel like I have a hangover. But without the fun that usually precedes one," she said, keeping her tone light. "But it's nothing about ten hours of uninterrupted sleep won't cure," she added, moving toward him. "We should go. You know how Bill gets when his actors are late to set."

"I do know. I was just watching Marcus and Rachel. Marcus kept flubbing his lines." Sean backed into the hallway. "They had to do four takes of a two minute scene. Bill's pissed."

"Then we'd better hurry."

"CUT," BILL SAID from behind Sean. "That's a wrap guys. Good job." Bill's production assistant approached him and then the two of them headed for the control room where they would take a look at the day's scenes.

"I'm out of here," Chris, who had been in the scene with Kayla and him, said with a grin. "It's Jenny's birthday. See you tomorrow, buddy." Chris clapped him on the shoulder and then walked off the set.

Sean cast a glance at Kayla, standing on the other

side of the police squad room set where they'd just finished taping. She was talking to Amanda.

For the first time since he'd started working with her, she wasn't fully present in their scenes. He was the cause of that poor night's sleep, and felt bad about it. But he'd done what he had to do to make sure she didn't have a concussion.

Against his better judgment, he'd driven her to his house this morning before work so she could pick up her car. She'd insisted she was fine to drive, so what was he supposed to do? Forbid her? Somehow he didn't think that would have gone over too well.

Earlier, when he'd stopped by her dressing room she'd looked deathly pale. It was probably from lack of sleep, but her face was so wan, he decided right then and there he was either driving her home, or following close behind her in his Jeep to make sure she got home safely.

He heard Amanda tell her to have a nice evening and then she left the set. Kayla turned and headed his way. Letting his gaze wander over her, Sean had to give the wardrobe department major kudos for choosing the clingy red top she was wearing. It was low cut, and emphasized her magnificent breasts. He'd always been a breast man, and knew real breasts when he saw them. And after last night, there was no doubt hers were real.

Before long, wardrobe would be fitting her with a pregnancy pad, and her clothing would no doubt be less sexy, but until then they were still dressing her like every man's wet dream. It was no wonder Matt and his teammates watched the show. If he wasn't on it he'd probably watch it too. Just to get a glimpse of her.

"I'm sorry," she said, halting before him. Her face

was still pale. She'd definitely taken the brunt of their accidental head butt. Other than a slight headache last night, he felt fine. But then, he hadn't fallen and hit the back of his head on the concrete like she had.

"For what?"

"I just wasn't into that last scene at all. I'm glad the last few minutes of it was just you and Chris." She lifted her hand and tucked a strand of dark hair behind her ear. "I can't wait to get home and fall into bed."

Falling into bed sounded good. *Real good.* Especially if he and Kayla happened to fall into bed together.

"Speaking of which." Sean forced the erotic image of their naked bodies entwined on her bed from his mind. "I think you should let me drive you home." He studied her face; her eyes looked tired. "You're too exhausted to drive anywhere."

"I'm really beat," she admitted.

"Then I insist on driving you home."

"You don't have to do that, I…"

He held up his hand, interrupting her. "Sorry, sweetheart, I'm not taking no for an answer. I'll drop you at your house and pick you up tomorrow morning."

Kayla stared at him a few seconds before giving in. "I'm too tired to argue with you."

After they had changed into their own clothes and washed off their stage make-up, Sean followed Kayla out the studio door and into the late afternoon sunshine. As he let go of the door, he heard the sound of a powerful engine revving and Rachel's sports car shot by. Annoyed, he watched her turn left at the corner of the building and then disappear from sight.

Rachel was one of the many people in L.A. who believed traffic laws didn't apply to them. And because she was a soap star and attractive, when she was pulled over—which was quite often—she usually got off with a warning instead of a ticket.

"I guess she's in a hurry," Kayla said, giving him a quick look as they crossed the lot.

"Looks like it."

Kayla glanced at her car. "What the hell?" she exclaimed. Sean's gaze followed hers and he saw what appeared to be spray paint on the passenger side of her car. "Oh, my God," she said as they both stopped in their tracks. "My car. My baby," she said in a low, tremulous voice. She covered her mouth with her hand and stared in wide-eyed disbelief.

Moving around her, Sean felt a flare of anger as he surveyed what some asshole had done. Over the cherry red paint, someone had used black spray paint to write the word SLUT in big bold letters along the side panel of her Mustang.

"That wasn't there this morning. And I haven't left the studio all day." Her voice was angry as she moved to stand beside him. "The lot is gated. We have a security guard. How could this happen?" she asked, gazing up at him.

"We've had fans jump the back wall before," Sean told her, looking around to see if there were any cameras on the building that were directed toward this part of the lot. He didn't see any, but that didn't mean anything. They could be placed out of sight.

Kayla spun around and stalked to the other side of the car. "Damn it," she swore and looked over the top of the car and met his eyes. "They sprayed this side too. It says skank." Her dark eyes glittered with fury. "I think I know who did this."

"Who?" Sean asked as he rounded the car to stand next to her. He looked at the offensive word and wanted to wring the neck of whoever had sprayed the hateful garbage on her car.

"Hang on," she said, reaching into her purse and pulling out her phone. She pressed a couple of buttons on the phone and then put it to her ear while she rubbed her temple with her other hand. "It's me," she said into the phone. "No, I'm not." She stared at the side of her car. "I got another letter."

Another letter? What did that mean?

"I've got it with me. But that's not all. Someone vandalized my car." She paused for several seconds, swinging her gaze to his. "Sean's here. He's offered to drive me home. I'll leave the car here for the night." She was quiet for several seconds, listening to whomever she had called. "Okay, call me after you talk to him. I'm going home."

"What's going on?" Sean asked after Kayla hung up. "Who were you on the phone with?"

"Lisa," she said and then stepped back and took a picture of the side of her car with her cell phone. Circling the car, she took a picture of the other side. She shoved the phone back in her purse and stared at her car, her expression grim.

"Kayla, what the hell is going on?"

She looked him with worried eyes. "Something I've been trying to ignore."

"What do you mean?" Sean asked. "You said to Lisa that you got *another* letter. Is someone threatening you?"

"I'm not sure." She bit her lip. "I didn't think so. I thought it was just some fan who was upset with Shay.

But now…" She looked back at her car. "I'm not sure what to think."

Stunned, he stared at her. "So, you *have* been getting threatening letters?"

"Yes." She nodded. "I'll explain more when we get to my house." She moved to the back of the car and laid her hand gently on the trunk. "I'm sorry someone did this to you," she whispered. She looked up and gave him a rueful smile. "I talk to my car."

"Don't we all? Look, before we leave I'm going to talk to security. There are cameras all over this property. They may be able to see the bastard that did this."

Kayla's eyes narrowed. "I hope so. No one messes with my car and gets away with it."

SITTING ACROSS FROM Sean at her kitchen table, Kayla pressed her index fingers to her temples and wished the splitting headache would go away. An hour after finding her beloved Mustang violated she was still so angry she couldn't see straight.

"How many of these have you received?" Sean asked looking up from the manila envelope in front of her on the table. Neither of them had touched it.

"That's the fourth." Lowering her hands, she rested her forearms on the table. "I threw away the first two thinking they were from some fan upset that Shay was having an affair with Stefan. I thought once Stefan went back to Cassie the letters would stop."

"But they didn't and now someone has vandalized your car." Sean leaned back in his chair. "I noticed you're using your security system. That's smart, but I'm concerned about the garage."

Kayla nodded. "I know. I realized today that anyone

could approach me after I put the car in the garage. I didn't mind the detached garage until now."

"I know you don't want to hear this but you're very vulnerable in this house."

"You're right." She grimaced. "I don't want to hear it. But it's the truth. I have an appointment on Thursday with a representative from my alarm company. Lisa insisted. I was reluctant at first. But now I'm glad I called them."

"I'm glad you did too." His expression was grave. "You look tired."

"I am," she admitted. "But I don't want to go to bed until Lisa calls. She's going to get in touch with a detective she knows and see what he recommends."

"How about something to eat while we wait?" Sean suggested.

"I'm not very hungry."

"Still, you should have something in your stomach."

"I don't have much here to eat," she said, mentally reviewing the contents of her fridge and cupboards and coming up with zilch.

Sean's mouth eased into a grin. "I bet I could find something if I look. I'm good in the kitchen."

He was probably good other places too, Kayla thought as that famous smile of his caused her heart to skip a beat.

He rose from the table and looked down at her. "Just relax. I'll take care of you."

As independent as she was, Kayla liked that sound of that. Right now, having someone fussing over her was kind of nice. Especially if that someone was Sean. "Okay," she said returning his smile before he crossed the short distance to the kitchen.

Was it wrong that she didn't want him to leave? If it was, she didn't care. She liked being with him, she felt safe with him here.

She reached for the remote for the television and hit the power button. The channel was still tuned to the sports channel so she left it on.

"The Dodgers didn't have a game today," Sean commented.

"That's good. The bums probably would've lost."

"Who are you calling bums?" He gave her a mock glare. "At least the Dodgers aren't some wine sipping, hot-tub dipping pansy ass team."

She pointed the remote at him. "Those are fighting words, Barrett. If I was feeling better I'd have a kick-ass comeback. Consider yourself lucky I'm not functioning on all eight cylinders."

He laughed. "Then we'll pick this up when you feel better. I'd hate to crush you at trash talking when you're not a hundred percent."

She regarded him with amusement. "Crush me? Cocky much?"

"Just telling it like it is, sweetheart." He pivoted to open the refrigerator and frowned as he peered inside.

"I told you. It's slim pickings in there. You can check the pantry though. I might have some pasta and marinara sauce. I keep it for emergencies."

Sean met her gaze with raised brows. "Emergencies?"

"Yes. But I might have used it the last time my mom and dad visited." He gave her a *what the hell* look that made her chuckle. "It's quick and easy, and even *I* can't mess up pasta. It's my go-to meal."

"You have a go-to meal?" He shut the refrigerator and opened the pantry door right next to it.

"Of course," she said, turning her attention back to the television where the commentators were discussing the likelihood of the Lakers making it to the NBA championship. As she listened to the latest Kobe versus LeBron debate her cell phone rang. She set the remote on table, reached for the phone, and seeing it was Lisa, hit the speakerphone button.

"What did you find out?" she asked. Sean walked over from the pantry and stood next to her. He hit the mute button on the remote to silence the sportscasters. Kayla glanced up at him, saw the tense expression on his face and then looked back at the phone.

"I spoke briefly with Luke and told him about the situation," Lisa began. "Since you're on television, he's going to have a detective from the LAPD administration office contact you. They have a special unit there that handles people in the public eye. They'll want to see the letters, and they'll also be dusting your car for fingerprints."

Kayla swallowed the sudden lump in her throat. "So he thinks it's serious?"

"He doesn't want to take any chances. You'll want to file a report so this is on record."

"And then what?" Kayla asked.

"It depends on if they find any prints on your car. If we're lucky, the person who did this might have been careless and touched your car. And if they did, hopefully they weren't wearing gloves. And if their prints are on file we can nail them."

"Those are pretty big ifs." Sean said, putting his hands on his lean hips.

"Thanks for driving Kayla home, Sean." Lisa paused. "You're right, those are big ifs. The police may come up with squat. Kayla, you've still got that security guy coming over on Thursday, right?"

"Yes."

"Good. Let him know what's been going on."

"I will."

"And don't go running for a while. Go to the gym instead."

Kayla frowned but didn't protest. As much as she hated it, she had to be smart. Anyone watching her would be able to quickly pick up her routine. "Okay."

"The detective will talk to the security staff at the studio. He'll advise them to beef up the security on the lot and patrol that particular parking area more frequently."

"I talked to them about that before we left the studio," Sean said, "but I think it'll mean more coming from the LAPD."

Leaning forward, Kayla focused her eyes on the phone. "Lisa, I'm supposed to go to that fan event in Van Nuys in a couple of weeks. Should I still go?"

"Yes, but I'd prefer you go with someone. Chris is going. I'll call him and ask him to drive you."

"I'll take her," Sean said. Stunned, Kayla looked up and met his inscrutable gaze. Lisa must have been surprised as well because there was dead silence on the phone for several seconds.

"You said you didn't want to attend that event," Lisa finally said.

"I changed my mind. I enjoyed the luncheon and I don't live that far from Kayla. Chris lives in West Hollywood."

"All right then. I'll contact the organizers and let them know you're attending."

Kayla lowered her gaze to the phone. "Lisa, I'm sorry I didn't tell you about the letters at first."

"You're taking it seriously now, and that's what matters." Lisa's tone turned soft. "You're more than welcome to stay with me for a while until this is settled."

"That's sweet of you."

"Don't ever call me that," Lisa admonished her. Kayla glanced up at Sean and met his amused gaze.

"Sorry." Kayla chuckled. "I know you don't want it to get out that there's a big heart under that steely exterior."

"Damn straight. I have a reputation to uphold," Lisa said sternly.

"Your secret is safe with us," Sean said, putting his hand on Kayla's shoulder. Its warmth through the fabric of her top sent a prickle of awareness through her. The gesture was innocent, yet something about it was almost intimate.

Lisa chuckled. "Kayla, I gave Luke your cell number. He's going to pass it along to the detective in administration. He'll call you tomorrow morning to set up a time to meet with you."

"Sounds good."

"Be careful."

"I will." Kayla nodded. "I'll call you tomorrow and give you an update."

"Okay. And I meant what I said. You can stay with me for as long as you need to."

"Thanks," she said, feeling moisture gather in her eyes.

After Lisa hung up, Kayla stared at the phone until

she felt Sean's fingers squeeze her shoulder gently. She lifted her head and met his gaze, grateful for his presence. If he wasn't here with her, she might very well be a basket case right now.

"I have good news."

"I could use some," she said, suddenly noticing how close he was. The force of his masculinity struck her anew. She wanted to feel his strong arms around her, and not just because she'd had a hell of a day and needed to feel safe. It was so much more than that.

"You have pasta and marinara sauce in your pantry," he said and squeezed her shoulder again. "Why don't you go take a shower while I fix us some dinner?"

She sighed. "That sounds like heaven."

"Then go." Sean lifted his hand from her shoulder and then went back to the pantry. "By the time you're done, dinner will be ready."

Rising from her chair, Kayla moved to the archway that led from the kitchen into the living room. She turned to find Sean intent on opening the glass jar of sauce. She watched him and thought how right it felt having him in her home. How right it felt having him in her life. "Sean." He looked up. Her heart clenched as their eyes met across the room. "Thank you."

"You're welcome." His voice was husky, and between it, and the way his green eyes held hers, Kayla felt goosebumps rise on her arms. For several long seconds their eyes met, and she had to fight the urge to cross the kitchen and fling herself into his arms.

"Go take that shower," Sean said as he set the jar on the counter.

Kayla nodded and turned and left the kitchen.

SEAN HAD JUST found the strainer in Kayla's cupboard when she returned to the kitchen. "How was your shower?" he asked, closing the cupboard door.

"Better than sex," she said moving to the credenza on the other side of the table.

An image of her naked in the shower heightened his pulse. "That must have been some shower."

She pulled open a drawer and then looked at him. "I have a great shower head. It does all sorts of amazing things." Her cheeks turned pink. "You know, like massaging jets, pinpoint spray, that kind of thing."

"Right." He grinned at her. "Dinner's almost ready.

As she put the placemats on the table, he noticed that she'd changed into a pair of dark blue sweatpants that fit her like a glove, and a pink T-shirt that had the logo of a recent breast cancer 10k run emblazoned on the front. Her dark hair was loose, and flowed over her shoulders like silk. In spite of slight bruise on her forehead and her wan complexion, she looked beautiful.

"I'll set the table," she said, moving to join him in the kitchen.

As she opened the cutlery drawer, Sean put the strainer in the sink and turned and reached for the pot on the stove that held the pasta. "Do you have a serving bowl?" he asked, pouring the pasta into the strainer and setting the pot next to the sink

"Behind you. Cupboard next to the stove."

Turning again, Sean opened the cupboard and bent to look inside. "Where?"

"It should be right in front."

"I don't see it."

She moved to stand beside him. "It was there last week." She put her hand on his back and leaned down, her face level with his as they both peered into the cupboard. The clean scent of her soap surrounded him. "There it is. Behind the salad spinner."

"Salad spinner?" he managed to ask. She smelled so good, and her fingers seemed to burn right through his shirt to his skin. He imagined her touching him in other places and instantly felt a tug of arousal in his groin. She was so close he could feel her breath, warm on his cheek. Turning his head, he met her gaze. Her eyes could make a man forget to breathe. Dark, sultry, exotic. What was he looking for again? Whatever it was suddenly ceased to matter when her mouth touched his and lingered. A million dollars could be in that cupboard for all he cared. The kiss was brief, but long enough for him to know he wanted more. A lot more. Her lips were soft and she tasted of peppermint. Toothpaste perhaps? When she pulled back, he opened his eyes, all he could feel was the restless throb of desire in his veins.

"The green thing." A hint of a smile curved her lips.

"Green thing?"

"The salad spinner," she said, patting him on the back and straightening.

Taking a deep breath, he moved the green thing aside and reached for the bowl behind it. Closing the cupboard door he turned to find her setting the table. Oblivious to his scrutiny, she folded one of the napkins into some weird origami shape and then set in the middle of one of the placemats. Unable to take his eyes off of her, Sean couldn't remember ever feeling this comfortable with a woman.

He could get used to this.

SEAN SET HIS fork on his empty plate. "For sauce from a jar, that wasn't half bad." He leaned back in his chair and met Kayla's gaze from across the table. "Did you get enough to eat? There's a little pasta left."

Putting her hand on her stomach, she shook her head. "No, thanks. I'm full."

Letting his gaze linger on her face, he could see she was still pale. And a couple of stifled yawns throughout dinner told him she was exhausted. "I think you should go to bed."

"No. You cooked, I clean." She wiped her mouth with her napkin and set it next to her plate.

"Normally, I'd accept that offer. But not tonight. You've had a rough day."

"Okay, but next time I'm cleaning up." A whisper of smile played over her shapely lips. "In fact, after everything you've done for me, I owe you dinner."

Sean grinned. "Didn't you mention something about not cooking very much?" he asked, pleased to see she was in better spirits than when he'd first brought her home.

"Yes." She paused and her eyes gleamed with amusement. "But I'm really good at ordering take-out." Her smile lit up her face. "In fact, I've been told it's one of my better skills."

"Really?" He wouldn't mind sampling some of her other skills.

"Yes." She nodded. "Trust me, I can order a take-out meal to die for."

"Then how can I resist?"

"You can't," she said, in a voice so soft and low it was almost a caress. Staring into her dark eyes, all he could hear was the sound of his heart as it hammered in his chest. She was right, he couldn't resist. And he didn't want to.

WHEN THE LAST plate was in the dishwasher, Sean wiped down the granite counter top and stainless steel stovetop and then glanced at his watch. It was only eight-thirty yet it felt later. Maybe it was because of the erratic sleep he'd gotten the evening before, or everything that had happened after work, but he was wiped out.

Moving to the window, he opened the blinds to make sure the window was locked and noticed a black coupe cruise slowly in front of the house. It was a convertible, but the top was up and because it was dark outside he couldn't make out the driver. His body tensed and his heart started to pound as he watched the car disappear from sight.

He checked the lock, found it was secure and then closed the blinds. Turning, he spotted the manila envelope lying on the kitchen table. Staring at it, he couldn't tamp down the raw fury that knotted his gut. The letters she'd received and the vandalism to her car was tangible proof that there was some freak out there fixated on her. Now he couldn't help but wonder if that flat tire he'd helped her with was related to the letters and today's vandalism.

Tearing his gaze from the offensive thing, Sean moved to the arched entry to the living room and paused when he saw Kayla asleep on the sofa, still clutching the remote in her hand. She hadn't said one word the whole time he was cleaning up the kitchen, which meant she'd probably gone out like a light the moment she sat down.

If he let her, she'd probably sleep there until morning. But considering what she'd been through the best place for her was bed. Crossing the room, he pulled the remote from her limp fingers and placed it on the oversized trunk that served as a coffee table. Bending his knees, he slid his hands underneath her and lifted her so she was cradled in his arms. Her head lolled against his chest and she made a soft sound but didn't wake up.

Carrying her from the living room, he maneuvered down the hallway until he reached her bedroom. Once inside, he laid her gently on the mattress and then covered her with the quilt folded neatly at the foot of the bed. She'd left the lamp on her nightstand on and its soft glow illuminated her face.

In sleep, her beautiful face was serene. There was no sign of the worried expression he'd seen for a good part of the evening. Her mouth was slightly parted, her lips dewy soft. A lock of dark hair covered her cheek. Reaching out, he brushed it away from her face and couldn't help but caress her cheek. Her skin was like satin, and a hot pang of longing shot through him.

It was no use pretending he didn't want her. Despite all of his well-founded reasons for not becoming involved with her, he couldn't seem to control his growing feelings. He was drawn to her in a way he'd never experienced with any other woman.

Sean gave her cheek a final gentle caress and then turned off the light. He left the bedroom and went to the guest room. She'd be surprised to see him in the morning, but after what had happened today there was no way in hell he was leaving her alone.

Thirteen

Shay: I can help you. I think really fast on my feet and I'm good back-up.
Jared: Forget it. This is police business. Stay put and crochet some booties or something.

LATE THE NEXT afternoon, Kayla stepped out of her dressing room to find Sean leaning against the wall opposite the door. She was surprised to see him. Just as she'd been surprised, touched and more than a little apprehensive to see him making coffee in her kitchen this morning. Why? Because she could get used to having him around, that's why. Meeting his concerned gaze, she felt the familiar flutter in her stomach his presence always seemed to evoke in her.

"How did it go with the detective?" he asked.

"Like I expected," she said, and then doing something she hadn't done since she started working at Lantern Studios, she used her key and locked the deadbolt on her dressing room door. "Unless there are fingerprints on the car, or on the letters, there's no way to know who's doing this to me."

"Did they dust your car for prints?" Sean asked as they walked down the hallway side by side.

"Yes. And they have the letters."

"Have you thought about Lisa's offer?" Sean asked as they rounded the corner. A harried looking production assistant came out of Amanda's office. She held up two envelopes as both Kayla and Sean came to a halt in front of her.

"Script changes for Friday," the P.A. said and then handed one to Kayla. After Sean took his, the assistant gave them a brusque nod, stepped around them and continued down the hall without another word.

"Of course, I've thought about it," Kayla said as she shoved the script into her tote bag. It was all she'd been thinking about. The shock of the letter and the vandalism had worn off. She was no longer afraid, just mad as hell. Someone was toying with her and she wasn't going to play their sick game. Sean wouldn't be happy with her decision, nor would Lisa, but it was her life and she was going to do things her way. "I'm not going to let anyone run me out of my home."

"Are you serious?" Sean exclaimed. He stopped and reached for her arm, pulling her to a halt beside him. He turned toward her, his expression still and serious. "Your car was vandalized. You've received several threatening letters."

"I know that." Anger filled her. Not at Sean, but at the unknown lunatic who was obviously getting off on this little game they were playing. "But the letters have come here to the studio, and this is where my car was vandalized. I doubt this…this…person knows where I live."

"Are you willing to bet your life on that?"

"The alarm company rep is coming tomorrow morning," Kayla reminded him. "I'll be fine for one more night."

"Are you going home now? I'll follow you to make sure you get there safely."

"I appreciate your concern, but I'll be fine. Besides I'm not going straight home, I have an appointment—" she glanced at her watch "—in a half hour at an auto body shop for an estimate on getting my car repainted. They specialize in classic cars. I should get going. I don't want to be late."

Pulling her arm from Sean's grasp, she strode past Amanda's office and headed down the hall. "I don't like this, Kayla," he said, following her.

"Too bad," she said, not sparing him a glance.

"Jesus, you're hard-headed." Sean moved in front of her to open the door. They crossed through the small lobby toward the exit door. Kayla pushed it open and stepped outside with Sean on her heels. "For the record, I think you're being stupid."

Kayla stopped in her tracks and turned to meet his annoyed gaze. "Would you leave *your* house?" she demanded.

"Probably not, but…"

"But you're a man so that's different, right?" She gave an unladylike snort, whirled around and marched toward her car.

"It's not a double standard. The fact is I'm bigger and stronger than you are," Sean said, trailing close behind.

"Yes. You're quite the he-man, and I'm the damsel in distress who needs saving," Kayla snapped. As soon as the words were out of her mouth she regretted them. What was wrong with her? Was she channeling her sister? A sharp barb like that was something Kelly would say. The only difference was Kelly wouldn't regret it.

As they approached her car she saw that someone from studio maintenance had been kind enough to put two removable signs over the offensive words, but knowing her beloved Mustang was still desecrated pissed her off all over again.

"Can you do something for me?" Sean asked, putting a hand on her arm, gently pulling her to stop.

"And what's that?" she asked, looking up at him. The late afternoon picked up the highlights in his golden hair. The ends of it curled carelessly over the collar of his shirt. He looked like a surfer god. They'd kissed twice and there was no way she could deny she wanted more. It would be so easy to let him keep taking care of her, so easy to rely on him. But she couldn't do that. She'd started to trust and depend on Greg and look how that had turned out. Granted, Sean was nothing like Greg, or at least he didn't appear to be. But Greg hadn't shown his true colors until she'd known him a few months. Letting Sean get that close could be disastrous—especially since they worked so closely together.

"Be careful. And don't answer the door." His steady gaze bore into hers. "For anyone."

"I'm not a complete idiot." *Oh, my God.* Why was she being such a shrew? It wasn't Sean's fault someone had targeted her. But still, she didn't like him trying to order her around. She'd lived alone for seven years and wasn't used to anyone telling her what to do.

"I didn't say you were." A frown marred his handsome face. "Pardon me for worrying about you." He let go of her arm and without another word headed for his Jeep.

After she'd stowed her tote bag in the Mustang, Kayla braced her arm on the door frame as Sean backed the Wagoneer out of its space and took off. With a heavy heart, she watched him until he turned the corner and disappeared from sight. A dry sob burned in her throat but she refused to let it out. Instead she climbed into the car and closed the door. *Damn it.* Whoever was behind the letters and the vandalism had been able to do what seven years in Hollywood hadn't. Turn her into a stark-raving bitch.

SITTING ACROSS THE table from Matt at Chi Dynasty, Sean wasn't surprised when the waiter came over with two more beers and said they were compliments of two ladies at the bar. Matt picked up one of the beers and, looking past Sean, gave a nod to the women.

"They're seriously hot," Matt said and then took a long pull from the bottle. "And I do like blondes," he added with a lascivious grin. "Which one do you want?"

"Neither," Sean replied, not bothering to turn around. This was a normal occurrence whenever he and Matt hung out. Women practically came out of the woodwork when Matt was out in public. Most people thought actors got all the women, but the truth was it was professional athletes who were the most besieged by women and groupies. For some of the women it was about scoring with a famous athlete, and for others it was the lure of marrying one and living the good life. Unfortunately, from what Matt told him, a lot of the players were just that—players. They had so many women throwing themselves at them that even the ones who vowed they would never cheat on their wives or girlfriends ended up doing just that.

Matt set the beer down and shrugged. "More for me then," he said, reaching for an egg roll. "Maybe I'll take both of them home."

"I don't think that's a good idea." Sean used his chopsticks to pick up a chunk of orange chicken.

Matt finished chewing. "Why the hell not?"

"Because fucking two women you don't know isn't going to change what happened," he said in a low voice. Matt's expression froze but Sean didn't care. He was tired of tiptoeing around the reason why Matt had done a complete 180 in the past year. Tension hung thick in the air as Matt pinned him with a steely gaze. Sean popped the chicken in his mouth and chewed, wishing that Matt would talk to him. The guy was a time bomb waiting to explode. It was only a matter of when and where.

"You don't know what you're talking about," Matt said with a scowl and then took another swig of his beer.

Sean put his chopsticks down. "Don't I? You've been ejected from more games in the past month and a half than you have in your entire career."

"So?" Matt shrugged. "Guys get tossed all the time. It's not a big deal."

"It *is* a big deal. You're getting a reputation, Matt. And not a good one." He paused as the waiter refilled their water glasses. "If you're not careful the Dodgers will trade you."

Matt let out a bark of laughter. "No, they won't."

"Don't be too sure of that."

"You worry too much." Matt lifted one dark brow and grinned at him. "You need to get laid," he added, looking back at the bar. "It's the cure for what ails you."

Sean pushed his plate back. He'd lost his appetite. Watching his best friend self-destruct and not being able to help him was wearing on him. "Sex won't solve your problems."

Matt winked at the women at the bar and then met his gaze. "I don't have any problems," he said and then reached in his back pocket for his wallet. "I'm just enjoying life. You should try it." He opened his wallet. "Dinner's on me." He pulled out a hundred dollar bill and laid it on the table. "I'm going to the bar and thank the lovely ladies for the beers. Care to join me?"

Sean shook his head. "I'm heading home. I have a script to study." Actually, he didn't. Since he was off tomorrow he had plenty of time to look at his script. But he didn't want to hang out at the bar with two women he didn't know, and didn't want to know. The only woman he wanted to be with was Kayla. The fact that she was home alone while some nut job was fixated on her wasn't sitting well with him.

Matt shrugged and pushed his chair back. "I'm leaving with the team for Philly tomorrow. Meanwhile, I'll be making the most of tonight," he said, then strode to the bar—much to the delight of the two blondes.

A FUNNY THING happened on his way home. Sean took a slight detour—to Atwater Village. He pulled the Jeep up to the curb in front of Kayla's bungalow, cut the engine and the lights and unbuckled his seat belt. Today he'd discovered Kayla was one stubborn woman. As personality traits went, he'd seen worse. But he was just as stubborn and there was no way he was going to sit idly by and leave Kayla alone in that house.

Hell, if he went home all he'd do was worry about her all night anyway. He'd be lucky to get any sleep at all. So why not get no sleep outside her house? At least he would make sure she was safe.

CURLED UP ON the end of her sofa, Kayla sipped her chamomile tea, hoping it would relax her. The meeting with the security consultant wasn't until ten-thirty the next morning so she could sleep in. Sleeping late was a luxury she didn't often indulge in, but tomorrow was going to be an exception. Her cell phone rang, reminding her that she'd forgotten to call Lisa. She leaned forward to pick it up off of the white wicker trunk she'd picked up at a flea market and used for a coffee table.

"Checking up on me?" she asked, not surprised to see Lisa's name on the caller ID. Setting the tea cup on the trunk, she leaned back and got comfortable.

"Are you crazy?" Lisa launched right in, her tone terse. "Why aren't you here at my house?"

"I'll be fine. The alarm is on, the doors and windows are locked, and if it'll make you feel any better I'll sleep with a knife under my pillow."

"Oh, aren't you funny?" Lisa was clearly not amused. "I guess our little talk went in one ear and out the other."

"I called the alarm company, didn't I?"

"A fat lot of good that will do you if that maniac shows up at your house tonight."

"Look, I told Sean this and now I'm telling you. I'm not letting some freak drive me out of my home."

"Some freak who might know where you live."

"I doubt it." Kayla reached for the remote for her stereo system housed in the antique armoire along with the television and hit the power button. Her favorite '80s station came on, Cyndi Lauper singing "Time After Time." Lowering the volume, she tossed the remote on the sofa next to her. "You need to stop worrying about me. Tomorrow I'll have an updated alarm system with all the bells and whistles. The place will be as secure as Fort Knox, or the White House."

"Didn't two idiots crash a White House party a while back?" Lisa paused. "Now that's great security."

"Sarcasm doesn't become you." Kayla grinned. "Isn't it past your bedtime?" she asked, knowing Lisa's penchant for going to bed early so she could get up early to swim.

"You're changing the subject."

"Can't pull one over on you."

"Will you call me tomorrow as soon as the alarm rep leaves?" Lisa asked, finally realizing she was fighting a battle she couldn't win.

"Yes. Now go to bed."

"Fine." Lisa paused. "You know, it might not be such a bad idea to sleep with a knife under your pillow. Just for tonight."

Kayla let out a laugh. "If it'll make you feel better, I'll get the biggest knife I have and keep it with me all night."

"It will. Humor me, all right?"

"Deal."

JUST BEFORE ELEVEN, Kayla stifled a yawn, closed her latest copy of *Entertainment Weekly* and laid it on the trunk. She turned off the stereo and went into the kitchen where she rinsed her tea cup and set it on the stainless steel drain board next to the sink. She was almost out of the kitchen when she remembered her promise to Lisa and returned to the center island where her knives were neatly inserted into a wooden butcher block holder sitting on top of the counter. She selected a knife that looked like it could do the most damage and left the kitchen, turning off the light as she went.

Because she wasn't as blasé about her safety as Sean and Lisa might think, she moved to the front door to double check the alarm. It was activated and the deadbolt was in place. To be on the safe side, she went to the picture window that looked out onto the street, pulled back the floral curtain to check the lock and noticed a familiar vehicle parked at the curb smack dab in front of her house. A mixture of disbelief and anger washed over her.

"Oh, no he *didn't*," she muttered and let the curtain fall.

THE FRANTIC POUNDING on his side window jolted Sean awake. Heart racing like a freight train, he sat up, whipped his head around and saw Kayla's angry face glaring at him through the passenger side window.

Shit. Busted.

He opened his door, slid out of the Jeep, and then rounded the front of the vehicle, stopping short when he noticed the huge carving knife Kayla clutched in her right hand.

"Not happy to see me, I take it." He lifted his gaze from the knife and met her dark eyes. She didn't respond, just stared at him, her posture rigid and her jaw tight. "I hope you don't plan to use that on me." He put his hands up in mock surrender. The moonlight cast tricky shadows across her face; even in this light she was beautiful.

"How long have you been out here?" Kayla asked, obviously not appreciative of his good intentions, or his attempt at humor.

"About an hour," he said, lowering his hands. "Give or take."

"I don't believe this." She spun around and stalked across the grass toward her front door.

As he appreciated the toned and tanned legs on display in the white shorts she wore, he wondered if he should follow her or get back in the Jeep.

"Kayla. Wait," he called to her retreating back and jogged across her manicured lawn. When he reached the porch she tried to slam the door in his face. Quickly, he raised his hand and braced it against the door, preventing her from closing it. "I was worried about you," he said, meeting her furious gaze through the crack between the door and the frame. "I'm not going to apologize for camping out in front of your house."

"What are you? My protector?"

"Tonight, I am," he replied, a little peeved at her attitude. "You know what? Get mad. I really don't care. If I left now and something happened to you I couldn't live with myself, and furthermore Lisa would hunt me down and kill me with her bare hands." An unwilling smile tugged at Kayla's lips but was gone just as quickly.

"Go home, Sean."

"No."

Kayla sighed heavily. "I'm not a child. I don't need a babysitter."

"I stayed in your guest room the past two nights. What's the big deal?"

"The big deal is I don't need you or Lisa trying to run my life." Her chin lifted. A defiant gesture that told him she wasn't going to back down. For some stupid reason she was digging her heels in.

"You're not going to leave, are you?" Her expression plainly said as far was she was concerned he could go to hell.

"Not on your life, sweetheart."

"Then get your ass in here. You can't sleep in that Jeep all night."

KAYLA SLIPPED THE carving knife back into the butcher block holder and turned to find Sean standing under the arched entry to the kitchen. When she'd confronted him outside by his Jeep, he'd tried to humor her, but now his green eyes leveled her with an inscrutable look, and his expression was set in scowl mode.

"You can sleep in the guest room." She put her hands on her hips and glared at him. "But I still think this is unnecessary."

"I disagree," Sean said and then paused, studying her thoughtfully. "What is this really about? You didn't object to me staying here when I thought you had a concussion, or last night after you got the letter and found your car vandalized."

"That was different. I wasn't thinking clearly either night. I don't need anyone taking care of me."

"I didn't know you could be so stubborn."

"There are a lot of things about me you don't know."

"Tell me about it." Sean glanced at his watch. "It's late. What time is your appointment tomorrow?"

"Ten-thirty. But you'll be gone before then." Her tone was harsher than Kayla had intended, but she couldn't seem to help it. Her once orderly life was spinning out of control and she couldn't do a damn thing to stop it.

"Right." His eyes narrowed. "I wouldn't dream of sticking around when you've made it clear you can handle everything by yourself."

Kayla lifted her chin and met Sean's annoyed gaze. "As you said, it's late. You know where the guest room is."

Sean's mouth pressed into a grim line. Kayla knew she ought to apologize for being such a pill but the words wouldn't come. It was like she was twelve years old and in a stand-off with Kelly. Neither of them would ever budge. They were as different as night and day, except they shared a stubborn streak a mile wide. But this wasn't her sister, and she should be grateful to Sean for being concerned about her welfare. Still, the words wouldn't come.

"Good night, Kayla." Sean broke the tense silence, then turned and left the kitchen. She heard his footsteps on the hardwood floor of the hallway and then silence after he closed the guest room door.

AN HOUR LATER, unable to sleep, Kayla padded silently down the hallway, bypassed the living room and entered the kitchen. Light flooded the room as she hit the switch and moved toward the center island. She wasn't prone to insomnia, but whenever it struck, she was always able to get back to sleep if she ate something sweet. It was probably all in her head, but she never questioned it. Why question something that always worked?

The problem was she was pretty sure she didn't have anything sweet in the house. She hadn't been to the store in days and she'd eaten the last Oreo this morning. Just to be sure, she checked the Victorian House cookie jar her mother had given her. Empty. Then she checked the freezer. No ice cream—not even a Popsicle.

Methodically, she pulled open each drawer, hoping she'd stashed a candy bar in one of them in case of an emergency. By the time she'd reached the last drawer she'd given up hope. She rooted around in it and under a stack of take-out menus noticed a familiar photo frame. Pulling it out, she turned it over and studied the picture of Greg she used to display in the living room. Her fingers tightened on the frame as she took in his practiced smile and dark eyes that held no emotion whatsoever.

Unbidden, all the cruel things Greg had said to her during their relationship echoed in her head. He'd criticized her unmercifully, telling her over and over again that, at best, she was a passable actress and that she'd never be taken seriously—especially after the horror films she'd done. His digs were well timed. Usually right after she didn't get a part she'd auditioned for or it had been a while since her agent had called. It wasn't until she'd started to doubt her own abilities that she realized what he was doing: systematically destroying her confidence and her belief in herself.

Thank God she'd figured it out before he'd completely destroyed her.

"You bastard," she whispered, staring at his image as if he were the devil incarnate. Why she'd kept the photo was beyond her. Moving to the sink, she pulled open the cupboard door underneath it and was about to toss the frame in the trash when it slipped from her grasp and fell to the tiled floor with a loud crash, the glass shattering into pieces.

"Damn it." She crouched down, began to pick up the larger fragments and heard the sound of heavy footsteps thundering in the hallway.

"Kayla! Are you all right?" Sean called out, his voice deeply male and edged with concern as he came barreling into the kitchen.

"I'm fine. I just broke a picture frame." Kayla lifted her head to find Sean staring down at her. The sight of him, his jeans riding low on his hips, his shirt unbuttoned, showing off a set of near perfect six-pack abs caused her whole body to flush with heat and desire. "You can go back to bed," she said, hoping he'd do just that so she could cool off. She tore her gaze from his well-defined stomach and dropped the two larger pieces of glass she'd picked up into the garbage can.

"Where's the broom and dust pan?"

"I have a small set in the pantry. On the floor just to the right of the door."

"Don't touch that glass," he warned as he moved to the pantry and opened the door. "You might cut yourself."

Kayla picked up the frame, glanced at Greg's smarmy face and tossed it into the garbage. Then Sean was crouched beside her with the mini broom and dust pan. He was so close, the earthy scent of his cologne invaded her head and made her knees weak. She let her gaze wander over his tanned forearms as he swept the broken bits of glass into the pan. Her body tingled with awareness. She wanted to touch him so badly it was almost a physical ache.

"Who was that picture of?" he asked after he'd dumped the last of the glass into the trash can.

"No one important." She met his eyes, amazed at how in the soft light of the kitchen they glittered like emeralds. "My ex."

"Do you miss him?" He held her gaze with mesmerizing force.

After a long, silent moment, she shook her head.

"No," she whispered and caught a flicker of some indefinable emotion in his eyes.

"We should go to bed," Sean said after several charged seconds.

His words conjured up a lot of things, but none of them had anything to do with sleeping. Suddenly, she couldn't breathe. The air seemed to electrify between them, like an invisible force field, making it impossible for her to move. Every nerve in her body screamed for her to lean forward and press her lips to his. She was just about to give into that instinct when he broke eye contact to close the cupboard door. Kayla let out a breath and brushed her hair back with a shaky hand.

"You're right." She rose and braced her hands on the counter, trying to collect herself. "Thanks for cleaning that up."

"Not a problem," he said, pushing his large frame up and moving to the pantry to return the broom and dust pan. "Try to get some sleep." He didn't spare her so much as a glance before leaving the kitchen.

Get some sleep? Kayla let out a low, mirthless laugh. Like that was going to happen.

SEAN CLOSED THE guest room door and stood there trying to get a rein on his unruly emotions. The sound of breaking glass had jolted him out of what was already a fitful sleep and sent his heartbeat into overdrive. His first thought was that the stalker had broken in; his second thought was he had to protect Kayla.

He'd rushed into the kitchen fearing the worst. But instead of finding Kayla being attacked by the freak who was stalking her, he'd found her crouched over a broken picture frame wearing nothing but a white T-shirt that clung to every voluptuous curve of her body.

Kayla was fine. Sean wished he could say the same for himself. The thought of Kayla mooning over her former boyfriend bothered him. She'd claimed she didn't miss him, but was it the truth? And why did he care? Two kisses didn't mean a damn thing. Not in this day and age.

He looked at the clock on the nightstand. It was late. He needed some sleep, but after being so close to Kayla just now, what he needed even more was a cold shower.

Fourteen

Jared: What the hell are you doing here?
Shay: Following you. What does it look like?
Jared: I told you to stay put at home.
Shay: And I told you I don't like taking orders.

KAYLA CROSSED THE backyard patio holding her cell phone and the script change for Friday. Her yard was small, but she'd planted an array of colorful flowers around the lawn in the brick planter beds, and in the center of the patio there was plenty of room for the round table with a striped blue and white umbrella that shielded her from the sun. There was no swimming pool. The first time she'd set eyes on the bungalow she'd fallen in love with not only the house but the cozy and private backyard. She could live without a pool.

Kayla got comfortable on a cushioned chair at the table, set the script aside and hit the speed-dial button programmed with Lisa's cell phone number.

Lisa answered on the first ring. "How did it go?"

"So far, so good," she said, pulling her sunglasses from atop her head and sliding them on. "They're still here. I told them everything that's happened, along with my concerns, and they came up with some upgrades to my current system. They're in the process of installing everything right now. I came out back to get out of their way."

"What kind of upgrades?"

"Motion lights around the whole house, sensor alarms on all the windows, and security cameras around the perimeter of the house and on the garage." She sighed. "I really hate this."

"You have no idea who this person is, Kayla. You have to take every precaution." Lisa's tone was adamant. "And if you're going to stay in that house for the long term you should have upgraded security anyway."

"I agree," Kayla said and then changed the subject. "What are you doing this weekend? Maybe we can get together."

"This weekend isn't good. I've got a premiere tomorrow night, and a party I have to attend on Saturday. Let's try for next weekend."

"Okay. Have you talked to Sean today?"

"No. Why?"

"Just wondering. Before I went to bed last night, I discovered him parked in front of my house standing guard."

After a lengthy pause Lisa said, "I'm betting *that* didn't go over too well. Did you order him to leave?"

"He refused. He ended up in my guest room and left early this morning. Things were a little tense."

"Well, I, for one, am glad he showed up."

"Of course, you are." Kayla couldn't help but grin. "I'm surprised you didn't come over yourself."

"I thought about it," Lisa retorted. "I'm relieved Sean acted on his impulse. If I'd known he was there I would have gotten a better night's sleep."

"Both of you overreacted."

"Our reactions were normal. Yours, on the other hand, was completely naïve. You should be thanking

Sean instead of being all pissy. Not many men would have done what he did for you last night."

"I'm not being pissy," Kayla said crossly. "Don't you have a meeting or something to go to?"

"Nope." Lisa chuckled. "Did I hit nerve?"

"I have no idea what you're talking about." Kayla tucked a stray lock of hair behind her ear.

"Not all men are like Greg."

"This isn't about Greg," Kayla protested quickly.

"Isn't it?" Lisa asked. "Maybe Sean's getting a little too close and it's scaring you."

Damn Lisa for knowing her so well.

"That's not it at all. I'm not interested in Sean romantically." She flashed back to the two kisses she'd shared with Sean, one of which she'd initiated. But Lisa didn't know about them, or how they'd made her feel. Like her insides had gone all soft and gooey and had her longing for more.

"For such a good actress, you really don't lie all that convincingly."

"I've got to go," Kayla said. She had to stop this conversation before it went any further. Lisa was getting a little too close for comfort. "They want me back in the house."

"Make sure they go over everything with you before they leave," Lisa said. "And call me later."

"I will." Kayla put the phone down and smiled. "Who says I don't lie convincingly?" She picked up the script change for Friday and began to read. Just as she'd speculated with Sean, the writers were having Shay follow Jared on his undercover stakeout. Finally, they were starting to see that Shay had some gumption. She wanted to help Jared, and while following him on the stakeout probably wasn't the best plan, she meant well.

Kayla kept reading, anxious to see how the scene would play out. Would Shay ruin the stakeout, or end up helping Jared? When she got to the end of the scene, her heart began to race. She had to go back and reread it to make sure she'd read it right.

Yes. She'd read it right. It was all there in black and white.

Jared and Shay were going to kiss.

Kayla looked up from the script, dumbfounded. She hadn't expected Jared and Shay to share a kiss so soon. In fact, she'd thought it would be months before they locked lips.

Tossing the script and envelope on the table, she tried—unsuccessfully—to tamp down her emotions. Emotions that had catapulted from excited to extremely nervous. It was ridiculous. She was a professional, and had always acted like one. Plus, she'd kissed dozens of actors in her career and never batted an eye. But Sean wasn't just any actor. He was a man she was intensely attracted to. Even with the crew watching, how could she kiss him and not be affected?

She had to give props to Kenneth Stover and his writing team. They sure knew how to write a cliff-hanger.

EARLY FRIDAY MORNING, Sean walked into Amanda's office. "Got a minute?" he asked as she looked up from some paperwork on her desk.

She took off her glasses and rubbed the bridge of her nose. "What's up?"

"Do you know if the police saw anything on the security cameras on the lot the day Kayla's car was vandalized?"

"I know they looked at the footage but if they saw anything suspicious they didn't share it with anyone here." She frowned and slipped her glasses back on. "According to the security guard at the gate, no one entered the lot that wasn't authorized to be here."

"So then someone had to have jumped the wall." Sean paused, not liking the other possibility. That the stalker was someone they worked with.

"That's what it sounds like." Amanda pointed to several stacks of mail. "That's Kayla's latest batch of fan mail. I took the liberty of looking through it. I didn't see anything that resembled those envelopes but she'll need to open them all to make sure."

He ran a hand through his hair, frustrated that there didn't seem to be any clue as to who was harassing her.

"Sean, everyone here at the studio adores Kayla." Amanda's expression was solemn. "And now that we all know about this wacko, we're keeping a close watch on her mail. Security has been stepped up on the lot. No one can get to her when she's at work."

"I'm sure she'll appreciate that," he said and wondered if that was true. Kayla sure hadn't appreciated *his* efforts to keep her safe. Sean held up his script. "I'd better go. I don't want to be late for rehearsal," he said and turned to leave Amanda's office.

"Better use mouthwash today," she called after him in a cheeky voice.

So Amanda knew about the kissing scene. When he'd read the revised scene last night Sean wasn't surprised that Jared and Shay were going to kiss. The writers weren't stupid. Jared and Shay were catching on, the viewers loved them. It made sense to capitalize on their growing popularity by teasing the audience with a kiss. There was only one problem as far as he could see. How was he supposed to kiss Kayla and not get turned on?

There was always his old standby. Think about baseball. There was only one problem, there weren't enough baseball stats in the world to override his body's response to Kayla Maxwell. Last night, in her kitchen, it was all he could do not to take her right there on the tile floor.

After unlocking his dressing room door, he stepped inside, hit the light switch and turned on the small television he'd bought so he could watch baseball when he wasn't on the set. He tuned it to the sports channel and glanced at his watch. In about ten minutes he and Kayla would start rehearsals for their scenes.

Needing a distraction from his thoughts, he sank down on the recliner in the corner of the room just as the highlights from the Dodgers and Phillies game from the night before came on. The game hadn't been televised so he watched with interest. The Dodgers held a slight lead in the standings over the San Francisco Blaze but it was only the end of May. The season was far from over.

"Shit," he muttered as they showed a clip of Matt charging the mound and going after the Phillies closing pitcher. Sean cringed as he watched Matt throw a vicious punch. Luckily, the pitcher ducked and Matt was swinging at air. But the umpire didn't care and ejected Matt from the game. Leaning back in the chair, Sean watched as Matt argued with the umpire, kicked dirt at him and then stalked off the field. "You're digging your own grave, buddy." He reached for the remote and turned off the television when he heard his name and the directive to report to the set over the studio's loudspeaker.

Just as he stepped out of his dressing room and closed the door, Kayla rounded the corner. He hadn't seen her since he'd left her house yesterday morning. Before he'd left, she'd offered him coffee but they'd barely spoken. Obviously, she was still angry that he'd camped out at her house.

"Hi." He spoke first, letting his gaze roam over her. The bruise on her forehead had faded, and instead of looking pale and tired, she looked fresh and vibrant. Her hair was loose around her shoulders, and she was wearing a pair of snug jeans and a gauzy sheer white blouse with what looked like a tank top underneath it. Unable to resist, he focused on her lips. Heat shot through his body. He was definitely going to have to think about baseball during their kiss or he was in danger of losing every ounce of control he had.

"They just called us on the loudspeaker." If Kayla was still angry at him, she wasn't letting it show. Her voice was pleasant.

"I heard. I was watching the Dodgers highlights."

"I'd tell you I'm sorry they lost, but I'm not. San Francisco is going to win the division," she said with a hint of a smile.

He snorted. "In your dreams."

"You might have a chance if your catcher would get his act together."

"I keep telling Matt if he keeps it up he's going to get traded."

Kayla shot him a surprised glance. "You know Matt Scanlon?"

"He's my best friend," he said as they walked down the hallway together. The tension between them had eased. Perhaps Kayla felt more secure now that she'd had her meeting with the security company. "I've known him since we were kids."

"He's been thrown out of a lot of games this year," she commented as they approached the entrance to the set.

Sean opened the door for her. "I think he's trying to set a record for most ejections during the season."

Kayla stopped at the threshold, turned and lifted her gaze to his. "I owe you an apology."

"For what?"

She bit her bottom lip and her cheeks turned a becoming shade of pink. "For acting like an ungrateful witch when you were only trying to make sure I was safe."

"Ungrateful witch is going a bit too far, don't you think?" he said with a grin.

"No." Kayla laughed huskily and reached up to play with a heart shaped charm she wore on a silver chain around her neck. "And you're just being polite. Admit it. I was kind of bitchy last night."

Sean shook his head. "You admitted it, so why don't we leave it at that."

"Works for me," she said, turning from him to enter the studio.

He followed her through the doorway, letting his gaze linger on the sweet curve of her ass before remembering that he had to squelch any thoughts of her ass, her breasts and her luscious lips. They were on set now, and he had to be professional.

"Hey, guys," Bill said as they stepped on to the set of Jared's house. He was holding his ever-present clipboard, and had a pen tucked behind his ear.

"Hi, Bill," Kayla greeted him cheerily.

"You doing okay?" Bill asked Kayla, concern evident in his eyes.

"I'm not going to let some nut job get the best of me."

"That's my girl." Bill smiled at her with fondness. Amanda was right. Everyone *did* adore Kayla. Even crusty Bill, who rarely took a liking to anyone. "You both got the new scene, right?" Bill asked, looking from Kayla to Sean.

"Yes," Sean said with a nod.

Bill glanced at the clipboard and then at Kayla. "Okay, let's run through the first scene. Kayla, when you come down the stairs, Shay is going to see Jared getting his gun. She's curious, and during the dialogue she becomes annoyed because Jared won't answer her questions about his undercover assignment. When Sean exits I want you to wait a few seconds, grab the prop keys on the credenza just behind the sofa and then follow him."

"Got it."

Bill turned his attention to him. "Sean, start the scene by going to the closet and getting the gun locker down from the top shelf. You know the drill, you've done it before. Just as you put on your holster and check your gun, Kayla will come down the stairs." Bill paused. "Take your marks."

Sean rounded the dark brown sofa that occupied the center of the set and went to stand by the closet door as

Kayla walked up the short flight of steps and ducked from sight. He was relieved they were rehearsing this scene first. That way he could get into character, and maybe—just maybe—when he kissed Kayla, he'd be so in character he wouldn't think twice about who he was kissing.

Yeah, right. Who was he kidding?

SITTING IN HER dressing room, Kayla flipped through the latest copy of *Soap Opera Journal*. Waiting to be called to rehearsal for the last scene was nerve wracking, and as each second ticked by she was getting more and more nervous. The rehearsal of the first scene had gone off without a hitch. Both she and Sean had been prepared and had it down pat the first time they did it.

Bill had been pleased and then said he'd call her back when he wanted to run through the final scene. To pass the time, she'd grabbed the *Soap Opera Journal* from the magazine collection in the break room. She could have stayed on set to watch Sean and Chris rehearse, but decided it would be best for her equilibrium to keep her distance from Sean until the last possible moment.

Looking at photos in the gossip section of the magazine, it suddenly dawned on her that she and Sean were going to have to kiss twice. Once in rehearsal and then again at taping. As her stomach clenched she saw something that immediately took her mind off of Sean. A picture of Greg Alamo.

Kayla gaped at the photo, not only surprised to see him in the soap magazine, but shocked to see him arm in arm with Rachel Hixson at what looked like some red carpet event. They were a striking duo. Greg with his dark good looks, and Rachel with her blonde hair perfectly coiffed and dressed to the nines, were smiling prettily at the camera. Like Rachel, Greg loved attending parties and premieres. He had dragged her to way too many of them when they were together, always saying that the publicity would help their careers. But it was his career he was concerned about, not hers.

The picture was recent, and, thank God, didn't stir any feelings within her other than curiosity. Were Greg and Rachel dating, or was she just another in his long line of starlets? Kayla didn't care for Rachel but she wouldn't wish what Greg had done to her on anyone. He was the worst kind of man: controlling, a pathological liar and a user, or as Lisa called him—a narcissist.

The sudden crackle of the loudspeaker startled her. "Kayla. Report to the set please."

Kayla closed the magazine, rose from the small sofa, took a deep breath, then opened the door and headed for the set.

The dock set was opposite the park set and neither was ever dismantled. They were sets frequently used on the show and therefore it was easier and more cost effective to keep them intact. As she approached, she caught a glimpse of Sean sitting on one of the pier moorings looking extremely hot in his faded jeans and Dodgers T-shirt.

Bill turned from his production assistant and nodded to her before looking over at two day players leaning against the fake wall of the warehouse. The two men smiled at her. They were regulars, and appeared in the background of a lot of scenes at the dock and the parks.

"All right, people. Pay attention." Bill's gaze swung around to encompass everyone on the set. "Sean, I want you over there." He pointed to an alcove that served as a place on the set where people usually stood and eavesdropped on personal conversations that the characters on the show always seemed to have in public places where anyone could hear them. Sean rose from where he was sitting and moved to the alcove. Kayla watched him, unable to slow the frantic beating of her heart. "Kayla, you're off set when the scene starts. You'll come around the corner there." Bill pointed to Sean's right. "Sean, when she gets to the alcove, you'll pull her in and start the dialogue."

Bill turned his attention to the day players. "Guys, you're coming from the opposite direction. You know what line of dialogue is your cue, right?" They nodded in unison. As Kayla walked to her side of the set, the two actors rounded the other side of the set and disappeared. She heard Bill tell one of the cameramen where he wanted the camera when the scene was taped.

Taking her place out of sight from Bill, Kayla felt her pulse racing. "You're Shay," she whispered to herself and shook her arms to loosen up. God, she was tense.

"Okay, let's do this." She heard Bill's voice. "Action."

Stepping around the corner of the set, Kayla moved stealthily, looking around as if she was apprehensive about being on the docks late at night. As she approached the alcove, Sean's hand shot out. He grabbed her arm and pulled her inside with him.

"What the hell are you doing here?" he asked and she relaxed. He was Jared now, just as she was Shay.

She tried to pull her arm from his grasp but he held tight. "Following you. What does it look like?"

"I told you to stay put at home." His tone was exasperated. Jared was exasperated with Shay a lot lately.

"And I told you I don't like taking orders."

He averted his eyes and let go of her arm before looking around with apprehension. "What part of 'I'm on a stakeout' don't you understand?"

"I can help you," she said in a hushed whisper when he looked back at her. She gave him her patented Shay wise-ass smile. He shook his head in disgust, and then Kayla remembered Sean's next line was the cue for the day players to walk by. Her body quivered in anticipation but she didn't break character. "I'm good back-up."

"I have back-up," he said through clenched teeth just as the two actors came around the other corner talking in low voices. "Damn it, Shay," Sean said, and then slipping his hand around her waist, he pulled her roughly against his body and kissed her.

Immediately, everything around her simply faded away. Bill, the crew, the day players—they were gone as if they didn't exist. There was only Sean and the warmth of his body, his spicy masculine scent and the feel of his firm lips on hers. His big hand was splayed against the base of her spine, pinning her against him, holding her upright.

His hot, moist mouth plundering hers caused her knees to buckle. She melted against him, clutching at his shirt with her fingers, returning his searing kiss with a fierceness she didn't know she possessed.

A crackle of raw electricity passed between them, hot and carnal, making her forget everything except how—in this moment—she wanted him more than she had ever wanted any man before in her life.

"Very good." Bill's voice cut through the haze of her desire, forcing her to remember where she was. She pulled back to meet Sean's green eyes, breathless. His eyes flickered briefly with something that looked a lot like what she was feeling—arousal—but it was gone the second he loosened his arm from around her waist. "Now do that at taping and I'll be one happy director."

"I think we can manage that," Sean drawled with a lazy grin and then looked at Bill. "Was that angle all right?"

"Perfect," Bill replied, giving Kayla time to get her bearings. "Good job, you two."

"Thanks," Kayla said, turning from Sean and meeting Bill's approving gaze. He wasn't looking at her strangely so she assumed she looked like she normally did. But she sure didn't feel normal. Her heart was racing and her body felt almost boneless. The only thing she wanted was for Sean to pull her back into his arms and kiss her again.

Excitement curled in her stomach when she remembered that he *would* kiss her again. When they taped the scene later in the day. Her body had almost incinerated from the kiss they'd just shared, she could only imagine what the next one would do.

AS KAYLA WALKED off the set with Bill, Sean couldn't take his eyes off her. Lifting his hand, he touched his lips with his fingertips. What the hell had just happened? And why was he the one so affected while Kayla marched off with Bill like it was just another scene?

Because it wasn't just another scene.

Scrubbing his hand over his jaw, Sean walked off the set. After a late lunch, he left the make-up room and fought a grimace when he saw Rachel heading in his direction.

"Hi, Sean," she said and smiled.

"Rachel." He nodded, intending to pass right by her.

He wasn't in the mood to talk. He had one last scene to tape and kissing Kayla again was the only thing on his mind.

"I had an idea." She put her hand on his arm, causing him to stop. "I think we should go to Ken and tell him we want to work together."

"Why?" Was she joking? Oh, right. She rarely joked about anything, and judging by her confident demeanor, she must really believe he wanted to work with her.

"Because our characters have never been involved and I think we have a good chemistry."

"Ken doesn't take suggestions from the actors, Rachel. You know that."

"He will if both of us approach him." She squeezed his arm, the ends of her long nails dug into his flesh.

"I'm happy with my storyline."

Her eyes flickered with anger when he pulled his arm from her grasp. "You won't even consider it?"

"Ken is the head writer and he already has the story arc written for Jared and Shay. It's not up to you or me."

"I'm sure I could get Ken to do some rewrites. I have more influence over him than you know." She paused and flashed a smug smile. "Just ask Nikki."

"Save it, Rachel. I know you didn't get Nikki fired. She called me while I was at lunch and told me they let her go to free up my character for a new romance." Sean shot her a grin, then delivered a juicy tidbit sure to piss her off. "Oh, and she had good news. She's been cast in the next Ryan Reynolds movie." He managed not to laugh when Rachel's mouth gaped open. "I've got to get to the set," he said, and without another word stepped around her and continued on down the hallway.

When he walked onto the set there were a lot more

people milling around than there had been in the morning. On the far side of the set he saw Kayla talking to Bill. She was in full make-up, and wardrobe had once again found the most cleavage-revealing top to dress her in. She'd worn it during the taping of their first scene and up close he'd been able to see her black bra through the sheer black lace that hugged her body. It was as if the wardrobe staff was torturing him. They probably knew about the kissing scene and decided to find the sexiest thing they had for her to wear. Sean had always suspected that the women in the wardrobe department were sadists—now he knew it was true.

Bill turned from Kayla and strode toward him. "You ready?" he asked, halting in front of him.

"Yes." He watched Kayla disappear around the side of the set to wait for her cue.

"Just do what you did this morning," Bill said, and then gave him a pat on the arm.

Do what he did this morning? He could do that.

"Okay, people. This is our last scene for the day. Let's get this in one take." Bill's tone was upbeat. It always was when Kayla was in a scene. Bill seemed to have developed quite the fatherly affection for her. "Sean, take your mark."

Sean went to the alcove. The lighting was diffused to make it appear like nighttime. The wind machine had been turned on to simulate an evening breeze. The artificial shrubs in planters along the dock ruffled lightly from the air.

"Action." Bill's voice cut through the silence. Sean tried to pretend he was Jared but it wasn't working. All he could think about was in less than two minutes he'd be kissing Kayla again.

Just like this morning, she crept slowly from the corner of the set. As soon as she appeared in his line of sight he reached out, grabbed her arm, and hauled her into the alcove with him. "What the hell are you doing here?" he demanded, and still didn't feel like he was channeling Jared. He held on tight as she tried to pull her arm from his grasp.

"Following you. What does it look like?" she asked with a sarcastic edge to her voice.

"I told you to stay put at home."

"And I told you I don't like taking orders."

He tore his gaze from hers and let go of her arm before looking around. Jared would be concerned that his cover was about to be blown. "What part of 'I'm on a stakeout' don't you understand?"

"I can help you," she whispered when he looked back at her. She shot him the sexy smile she used whenever Shay and Jared were engaged in their friendly and sometimes humorous bickering. He shook his head in disgust, trying to look pissed, but all he could think about was how much he wanted to feel his lips on hers again. "I'm good back-up," she added in a saucy tone.

"I have back-up," he said with a scowl just as the two day players came around the other corner. "Damn it, Shay," he said, and then slipping his hand around her waist, he crushed her to him and did what he'd been dying to do since this morning. He kissed her again.

Under his seeking mouth, her lips were soft and pliant, and it was all he could do not to use his tongue and deepen their kiss. Her breasts were pressed against his chest; she fit against him like they were made for each other. He heard her soft moan and forced himself not to back her up against the alcove wall and devour her. But he wanted to, and his body knew it. Try as he might, he couldn't control the effect she had on him. His heart pounded, his blood thick with desire. He was getting hard, and that hadn't happened during a kissing scene since he was nineteen years old and new to the show. But it was happening now. With Kayla.

"And cut." Bill's voice pierced the erotic vortex he was drowning it. He pulled his lips from Kayla's feeling almost dazed. She opened her eyes and met his. Her dark gaze was sultry, and her full lips were moist and swollen from his kiss. She was as sexy as hell, and he wanted her with an intensity that astounded him.

Realizing he was still holding her, he loosened his grip so she could step back. He heard the sound of cheering and clapping and looked over to see Amanda and Sandy standing at the edge of the set with huge grins on their faces. Kayla turned and laughed, a husky sound that didn't do much to cool him off. "That's how it's done, ladies," she called out, and both Sandy and Amanda made bowing motions in his and Kayla's direction.

Kayla turned back and met his gaze, a smile wreathing her beautiful face. "They're crazy."

Still trying to regain some semblance of control over his body, he didn't answer right away. What the hell was wrong with him? He felt like a horny teenager. He could barely remember his name past the pounding pulse in his groin.

"Sean?" Kayla asked with a puzzled expression.

"What?" He ran a hand through his hair and tried to gather himself.

"You okay?"

"Uh...yeah. I'm good."

"Kayla. Get a move on," Sandy called out. "It's margarita time."

Kayla glanced at Sandy. "I'm coming." She turned back to him. "Sandy, Amanda and I are meeting Lisa for dinner."

"That sounds fun."

She smiled. "Girls night out. We do it every couple of months." She paused. "Well, have a nice evening."

"You too," he said. She turned and headed toward her friends. Without thinking, he called after her. "Wait." Kayla stopped mid-stride to look back at him with inquisitive eyes. "Do you have plans on Sunday?" he asked.

"No."

"I have to go to Pacific Palisades to check on my father's house. Do you want to come along? It's supposed to be a nice day."

What in bloody blazes was he doing? She was an actress, for God's sake. He shouldn't even consider taking things further with her. But the invitation had come out before he could stop himself, and now that it was out there he didn't want to take it back.

After a slight hesitation, she nodded. "That sounds fun. What time?"

"Is eleven too early to pick you up?"

"I'll see you at eleven," she said, her full mouth curving slightly.

Sean stared at her as she left with Sandy and Amanda. Just like last night, he needed a cold shower. Getting turned on and then having to stop was not how nature intended for it to be.

The next time—and there would be a next time—he kissed Kayla it wouldn't be in front of a room full of people. It would be just the two of them. And he sure as hell hoped the next time he kissed her, he wouldn't have to stop.

Fifteen

Shay: You didn't have to kiss me.
Jared: Yes, I did. It was the only way to shut you up.

LOOKING OUT OF her living room window as Sean pulled his Jeep into her driveway, Kayla couldn't suppress the feelings of anticipation and nervousness running rampant through her body. On one hand, she was as excited as a kid on Christmas morning, and on the other, she wondered if she was crazy for ignoring the little voice in her head saying that accepting Sean's invitation was tantamount to admitting her moratorium—as Lance put it—on dating actors was about to go the way of the dinosaur or the cassette tape.

For a moment she tried to rationalize that a Sunday drive to the ocean wasn't a date, but then she gave up and rushed to her bedroom where she grabbed her purse, took one final peek in the mirror and was back in the living room by the time Sean rang the doorbell.

"Hi," she said, after punching in the alarm code and opening the door. Immediately, her pulse spiked. Dressed in jeans and a white knit polo shirt and with his hair charmingly disheveled, he looked every bit the surfer he was—right down to his huarache sandals.

Sean's gaze roamed over her appreciatively. "Good morning." His husky voice sent waves of tingles through her body as she stepped onto the porch to close and lock the door. "Do you want to get something to eat now or later?" he asked as they walked toward his Jeep.

"I can wait until we get there," she replied after he opened the passenger door for her. "I'm sure you know the best places to eat."

"I know the perfect café," Sean said, waiting for her to get settled and buckle her seatbelt. "Your taste buds will never recover."

Kayla laughed. "Sounds like my kind of place."

He smiled, his gaze lingering on her bare legs before he shut the door. As he walked around the front of the jeep, she couldn't take her eyes off of him. The man was seriously hot, and kissed like he knew exactly how to please a woman. Who could blame her for ogling him?

During the short distance to the Santa Monica freeway, Sean asked about her evening with Sandy and Lisa. She didn't tell him how Sandy had kidded her all night about the kissing scene, and how—in Sandy's opinion—Kayla seemed to enjoy kissing Sean a lot more than she enjoyed kissing Marcus. Since it was true, Kayla hadn't bothered to deny it.

"Have you been to Pali before?" Sean asked, casting a quick glance her way before turning his attention back to the road.

"No. I've never been there."

Greg had rented a place in nearby Malibu while they were dating. She'd visited him there, but only a handful of times. The last time had been when she'd broken up with him. He hadn't taken it well, lashing out at her furiously. It turned out that he preferred to be the one who ended a relationship, not the other way around.

"I was thinking after we check on the house we

could go into the village and get something to eat, and then maybe take a walk on the beach."

Kayla looked at him, her curiosity peaked. "Why is it called a village?"

"Pacific Palisades is actually a pretty small community. The locals refer to it as a village, and most of the people who live there have been there for years."

"Like your father?"

He nodded. "From what I've been told, my mother always wanted to live in a house that overlooked the ocean. So he had one built for her."

"That sounds romantic."

"I guess so."

"Did your dad remarry after your mom died?"

"No."

"Maybe he's never gotten over her," Kayla mused.

"I wouldn't know. We don't talk much," Sean said with a hard edge to his voice.

Shifting in her seat, she studied him. The laid back man who had picked her up was gone. His posture was rigid and his grip on the steering wheel was tight. Still, she couldn't stop herself from asking, "How did your mom die?"

"The official diagnosis was a traumatic brain injury. She took a really bad fall," he said, staring out the windshield, the strong line of his jaw tight. "Do you have the new alarm system worked out?" he asked, changing the subject.

"Yes," she said, following his lead. It was pretty clear there was bad blood between Sean and his father. She suspected it was more than James Barrett's disdain for soap operas though.

"I just have to remember that if I want to open a window I have to deactivate the sensor or the alarm company will get an instant notification and send someone out." She hated that she was at the mercy of the unknown lunatic who'd fixated on her. It was creepy and unsettling. "I feel like a prisoner in my own home."

"It's for your protection," he said, hitting his turn signal to change lanes. "You have no clue who you're dealing with. Whoever it is may never come near your house, but it's better to be safe than sorry. And honestly, you needed to upgrade your system anyway."

"So everyone kept telling me," Kayla grumbled as she got her first glimpse of the ocean when Sean pulled on to the Pacific Coast Highway. As always, the sight never failed to impress her.

While she scanned the coastline, Sean slowed the Jeep. The PCH was notorious for its congestion, and the weekend was the worst time to travel on it. Between the beach goers, the tourists, and the residents who lived in the towns along this stretch of coast, there was no shortage of cars, scooters and bicyclists. Pacific Palisades, or Pali, as Sean had called it, was nestled between Santa Monica and Malibu. Many of the homes were built on bluffs that overlooked the Pacific Ocean. Kayla could only imagine the spectacular views they offered.

As they progressed at a snail's pace, Kayla noticed a number of surfers bobbing in the water. Every so often one or two of them would catch a wave and ride it almost effortlessly to shore.

"Did you bring your surfboard?" she asked, turning to look into the back of the Jeep. She didn't see a board, but the cargo area did hold a number of beach towels, and a rubbery looking thing she suspected was a wetsuit.

"No," Sean said, tapping his fingers on the steering wheel in time with the music playing softly on the radio. The tenseness she'd noticed just minutes ago had passed. "I didn't think it would be all that much fun for you to sit on the beach and watch me surf."

"It would be fun if you were giving me a surfing lesson."

He braked as the car in front of them stopped at a light. "Do you really want to learn?" He turned to look at her.

"Yes," she said, meeting his surprised gaze. "My mom has this DVD of a movie she liked when she was young. *Gidget*, with Sandra Dee. We watched it together when I was a kid. After that, all I wanted to do was learn how to surf—just like Gidget."

"That movie started the surfing craze," Sean said. "It wasn't long after that the Beach Boys became popular and Hollywood started making those God-awful surfing movies."

The light turned green and they inched forward with the traffic. "How long have you been surfing?" Kayla asked.

"I got my first board when I was ten."

"Where's your favorite place to ride the waves?"

"Hawaii has the best waves. The Pipeline on Oahu is one of the most dangerous surfing spots in the world."

"What's the Pipeline like?"

"A total rush," he said as they passed a sign welcoming them to Pacific Palisades. "It was like the first time I had sex," he added, shooting her a sidelong glance.

"I'm almost afraid to ask." She couldn't help but

smile. "But I can't resist. Why was it like the first time you had sex?"

His grin was shameless. "Because I couldn't wait to do it again."

"WOW." THERE WAS undisguised awe in Kayla's voice as Sean pulled up to his father's house. It was a Tudor style home with a steeply pitched roof, ornamental timbering on the gables and an arched entryway covered in stone. Although not as sprawling or grandiose as some of the newer estates, it was still impressive.

After cutting off the engine, he got out of the Jeep and rounded it to open the door for Kayla. As she gracefully climbed out, Sean let his gaze linger on her legs. She was wearing a multi-colored sundress in blues and greens that bared her toned arms and shapely legs. Her hair was pulled back in a low pony tail, and the only jewelry she wore was a simple pair of silver hoop earrings. She looked drop-dead gorgeous, and when she'd opened her front door earlier this morning and he'd gotten his first glimpse of her, all he could think about was how she'd felt in his arms, and how much he wanted to kiss her again

"Can you see the ocean from the back of the house?" she asked as they walked side by side to the front door.

"Yes. The view is amazing," Sean said, finding the house key on his key chain.

"I can't wait to see it." Smiling up at him, she pulled off her sunglasses and slipped them into her purse.

He unlocked the door. After they'd crossed the large Travertine tiled foyer, he led her through the formal living room. As they passed the glass curio cabinet just beyond a baby grand piano, she put her hand on his arm, pulling him to a halt.

"That's an Oscar," she said in a hushed tone, leaning closer to the glass. "Best actor in a leading role," she read the inscription and squeezed his arm. "I've never seen a real one before." Sean couldn't help but smile at the reverence in her tone.

"Do you want to hold it?"

"Oh, no, I couldn't," she said with a shake of her head. "If I ever hold one, I want it to be because I earned it. Like your father did. *Faded Glory* was such a great movie, and he was amazing in it. I didn't see it when it first came out because I was too young, but I rented it a few years ago. Your father's performance was powerful."

"It was," Sean agreed. He and his father didn't get along, but there was no denying that James Barrett was a hell of an actor. "He deserved that Oscar."

Kayla looked at him with a hint of surprise in her eyes. "You sound proud of him."

"I can separate who he is as a father from who he is as an actor," he said with a shrug, "and I have the utmost respect for his talent." He looked at the golden statuette. It sat alone on the glass shelf and had been a part of the house for so long that he rarely noticed it anymore. "When I was a kid, my father's friends would come over and play poker once a week." He smiled at the nostalgic memory. "They would sit in the dining room smoking cigars and drinking brandy, or scotch—I'm not sure which. They talked about acting. All of them lived and breathed it. And still do, I'm sure." He looked back at her. "I used to hide behind the couch and listen to them talk for hours. I learned more about acting by eavesdropping on them than I did in any drama class I've ever taken."

"And it shows." Her hand was still on his arm, her warm touch played havoc with his pulse. "Do you remember that eulogy scene you did a few months ago?" At his nod she continued, "You were amazing. There wasn't a dry eye on the set, and it wasn't because we put glycerin drops in them." Her mouth curved in a winsome smile. "It was because you were that good. You were so vulnerable…so raw…that we couldn't help but feel your pain. You were fearless. Absolutely fearless."

"That means a lot coming from you," he said, unexpectedly pleased by her admiration.

"It wasn't just me. It was everyone on the set."

"That's flattering, but your opinion is the only one I care about."

Her eyes widened with surprise. "I…I wanted to tell you after the scene. But I was a little intimidated by you back then." She let go of his arm. He wished she hadn't. He enjoyed her soft touch.

"Intimidated of me?" He couldn't help but grin. "Why? I'm totally not intimidating."

"You're the star of the show, and we'd never been formally introduced. I saw you around the set but I was pretty sure you didn't know who I was."

He grinned. "Trust me, sweetheart. I knew who you were. I just didn't know how good you were until we started working together." Astonishment registered on her expressive face. Was it possible she didn't know how talented she was?

"So are you going to show me that amazing view?" she asked, her eyes sparkling with anticipation. She was so beautiful it almost took his breath away.

Feeling like a damn teenager in the throes of his first crush, he managed to nod. "Come on." Sean put his hand on her elbow and guided her toward the steps that led from the formal living room to the back of the house where the large kitchen and family room were located. "Be prepared to be impressed."

She let out a soft sigh. "I already am."

"It's almost as if we're standing on the edge of a cliff," Kayla said, taking in the sheer magnificence of the view. All she could see was the ocean. From the frothy whitecaps near the shore to the blue-gray waters that seemed to stretch to infinity. It was beautiful and serene, yet at the same time powerful and mysterious.

Standing next to Sean on the expansive deck that jutted out over the bluff, she rested her hands on the top rail, unable to tear her gaze from the grandeur in front of her. A gentle breeze drifted past, carrying the unmistakable scent of the sea, and a hint of the roses she'd glimpsed in James Barrett's garden. The customary coastal fog had burned off early, leaving the sun to caress her bare arms and legs with its gentle warmth.

"I could never get tired of this view," she said.

"I agree." Something in Sean's voice made her turn toward him. Heat suffused her body as she met his brilliant green eyes. The sun played over his handsome face and glinted on his golden hair. It seemed almost criminal that he was so unbelievably handsome. Her heart skipped a beat and then began to pound as their eyes locked. Several charged seconds passed as his gaze lowered to her lips, lingered and then lifted. "You're blushing," he said with a slow, sexy grin that didn't do anything to cool the sudden heat in her body. "You do that a lot." He turned to rest his hip against the railing.

Not about to admit it was because of his effect on her, she shrugged. "It's hereditary. I come from a long line of blushers."

Sean laughed, his eyes crinkling at the corners. A sudden, more powerful breeze ruffled his hair, partially covering his eyes. Without thinking twice, she lifted her hand and gently brushed the strands to his temple.

Spurred on by something she couldn't seem to control, she trailed her fingers to his cheek. Her breath caught in her throat as their eyes met and his laughter faded. Time seemed suspended, and the air grew taut between them. The only sound she heard was the erratic beating of her heart. It was so loud she was sure he had to hear it.

Lowering her hand, she couldn't seem to look away from his mesmerizing gaze. The cool sea air whispered across the heated flush of her body, and the subtle scent of his cologne made her feel almost lightheaded. Could he see how much she wanted him? Because she did. She wanted him desperately and didn't want to hide it anymore. For the past six months, she'd been playing it safe. Maybe it was time to throw caution to the wind and see what happened.

"Did I tell you you look beautiful?" His voice was husky, his eyes so intense she could almost feel the touch of his lips on hers by the look in them. She ached for him to kiss her. He lifted his hand and brushed her cheek with his fingertips; his gentle caress caused her knees to tremble. "Because you are," he said in a husky whisper that sent a prickle of excitement across her skin.

He traced his fingers to her jaw and when he feathered his way down to the pulsing hollow of her throat, her breath hitched. He noticed, and with just the hint of a smile, he lowered his head until she felt the moist heat of his mouth against hers.

At first their kiss was gentle, as if they were savoring the taste of each other. Then everything changed. His lips coaxed hers open and the first touch of his tongue against hers almost stole her breath away. She felt his hand skim down her back, and then she was hauled up against his body, pressed so tightly to him that she could feel every inch of him.

Their kiss turned wet, deep and so passionate that she couldn't contain her soft moan of pleasure. Sliding her hands up his broad shoulders to his neck, she sifted her fingers through his hair; it was soft to her touch. At the moment it was the only soft thing about him.

His hands roamed over her back and seemed to burn right through the fabric of her dress. Her breasts felt heavy, and between her legs her muscles tightened as hot desire pooled at her core.

Lost in their kiss, she arched against him, relishing the feel of his muscular chest against the softness of her breasts. It was as if she couldn't get close enough and silently cursed the barrier of their clothes.

Seconds later, she felt his hands spanning her waist and then—almost reluctantly—he pulled his lips from hers. Opening her eyes, she drew a ragged breath and felt her lower body clench with need when she saw unspoken desire smoldering in his gaze.

"It was all I could do not to kiss you like that on the set." His voice was low and gravelly. He made no move to loosen his hold on her, which was fine with her. A wolfish grin tugged at his lips. "I came pretty close to breaking my no tongue rule on Friday." His admission sent a delicious thrill through her.

"A no tongue rule," she mused. "That's very gentlemanly of you." Resting her hands on his shoulders, she was extremely aware of his muscular thighs pressed against hers.

Sean's eyes gleamed mischievously. "I'll bet you wish Marcus had that rule."

"God, yes." She wrinkled her nose in distaste. "But after one good bite I think he learned his lesson."

Sean's eyes widened. "You didn't?"

Kayla couldn't help but grin as she nodded. "I did."

"I'll have to remember that," he said with a smile. "I'd hate to suffer the same fate."

Playing with the collar of his shirt, she returned his smile. "Don't worry, you won't."

His eyes flickered with amusement. "Have I just been given the okay to break my no tongue rule at work?"

With the way she was feeling, Kayla would let him break any rule he wanted. As many times as he wanted. "How about you break it right now?" she whispered.

"I can do that," he said, lowering his mouth gently to hers. She reacted immediately to the smooth warm demand of his lips. Heat simmered in her lower body, and her pulse danced with excitement as his mouth opened against hers. The touch of his tongue against hers was electric. Moaning softly, she caressed his nape and was vaguely aware of his hands gently cupping her buttocks, pulling her even closer to his hard body. God, he felt good. And what he was doing to her felt even better.

She didn't want him to stop. *Ever.*

But seconds later he did just that. He pulled his lips from her and when she opened her eyes and met his she felt dazed, and her heart raced as if she'd just finished running a marathon.

"I think I like breaking the rules," he said and gave her a roguish grin that heightened the beat of her pulse. His hands slid up to the small of her back and rested just above the curve of her butt. "And I might break a few more if we don't go into the village and have brunch."

She didn't have to ask what he meant. She'd felt the hard ridge of his erection against her abdomen. He was just as turned on as she was. And knowing that she was the cause of his arousal filled her with a certain sense of womanly satisfaction.

Tilting her head, she smiled up at him. "Aren't rules meant to be broken?"

Letting her gaze roam over his handsome face, she had a strong feeling that even if she wanted to resist him, she wouldn't be able to. His kisses had been the appetizer, now she was ready for the main course.

"Isn't that half the fun?"

Loosening his hold on her, he stepped back but kept his arm around her waist as together they gazed out at the ocean. Her body, like the sea, churned restlessly with the desire he'd evoked in her.

"Thank you for bringing me here. This has to be the most beautiful spot on earth."

"I should thank you."

She turned her head and met his solemn gaze. "Why?"

"I've taken this place for granted my whole life. Seeing it through your eyes makes me realize how special it really is. It's human nature, I guess. But then, sometimes we're lucky enough to get a wake-up call. Like I did today."

Sean's words filled her with a warm glow that had nothing to do with sex. His voice, like his eyes, was tender. If it was possible to fall even deeper under his spell, she'd just fallen.

"I'm glad I could be your wake-up call."

Sixteen

Jared: Do you think about Stefan much anymore?
Shay: No. Not so much.
Jared: That's good.
Shay: Why is that good?
Jared: It just is. What is this? The grand inquisition?

THE AIR WAS filled with a mixture of salt water and suntan lotion. Walking beside Sean as they strolled barefoot along the wet sand near the water's edge, Kayla was more aware of him than ever. Working and living in L.A., she'd grown used to being around attractive men. They were a dime a dozen, most of them as shallow as a toddler's wading pool. But there was something about Sean that affected her as no man ever had.

She could say it was his lethal good looks, or even that sexy as hell grin that caused her heart to pound. But it was more than that. There was a depth and an inherent decency in Sean that she couldn't help but be drawn to.

It also didn't hurt that his kisses made her tremble with need, and ignited a fire inside of her that burned so fierce she thought she might explode. At Café Vida, where Sean had taken her for a late breakfast, all she could think about were the searing kisses they'd shared on the deck overlooking the ocean. Those hot kisses had whetted her appetite for more.

"What made you choose acting as a profession?" he asked, forcing her from her increasingly erotic thoughts.

"It chose me," she said as they passed by two young boys building a castle with the wet moldable sand. Engrossed in their task, the boys didn't even look up. "When I was a freshman in high school, the elective I wanted to take was filled so I had to pick another one."

"And you chose drama?"

"It was the only other elective available," she said, watching him as he reached up to brush his hair back. Her gaze lingered on his muscular forearm, and, unbidden, the memory of him holding her in his arms flashed through her mind, reminding her of the feel of his hard body against hers. "I was scared to death," she said, averting her eyes before her wayward thoughts got the better of her. "I was very shy, and deathly afraid of public speaking."

"Obviously you overcame that."

"It took a while," she said, remembering the horrible bout of nerves she'd endured before each class.

"How do you do it? Disappear into your character so easily?"

"I don't know," she said with a shrug. "It was weird the first time it happened. I felt like I'd gone into some sort of trance. I knew what was happening around me, and I was engaged in the process, but suddenly I wasn't me anymore. I was Juliet."

He lifted his hand to brush his hair out his eyes. "I see *Romeo and Juliet* is a high school staple up north too."

"I think it's a state law that every high school has to

perform it," she said with a smile as she stepped over a small piece of driftwood. "Why did you choose acting? Because of your father?"

"In spite of him."

"What do you mean, in spite of him?"

"As I'm sure you've figured out. My father and I don't get along. Following in his footsteps was the last thing I wanted to do because it's what he does. But I guess acting is in my blood. When he found out I was into it he tried to tell me what I should and shouldn't do."

"Did he give you advice?"

"No. But there were very specific guidelines he tried to get me to adhere to. He didn't want me to do television. He said it was beneath me. When I told him I was auditioning for a part on a soap opera he ordered me not to do it." His voice was grim. "And you can see how that turned out."

"Did you accept the role because you really wanted it, or to thumb your nose at your father?" A few weeks ago she wouldn't have dared to ask him such a question, but things were different now. He'd mentioned his father to her several times. Maybe he was beginning to trust her.

"I wanted the job. But if I'm being honest, I think the main reason was because I knew my father would hate it," he said after a brief silence. Stopping, he turned toward her, his gaze thoughtful. "I've never told anyone that before," he added as she halted next to him.

"I won't tell a soul." Touched that he'd confided in her, she gave him a reassuring smile. "I mean it. *TMZ* could torture me and I still wouldn't talk."

Amusement flickered briefly in his eyes. "Why is

it I can tell you things I've never said to anyone else?" The intimate sound of his voice reverberated through her like a lingering caress. Her skin prickled with excitement.

Good Lord, even his voice turned her on.

"I've been told I'm a good listener," she said, trying hard not to be affected by his blatant masculinity. She wasn't trying hard enough. Every nerve in her body was on full alert.

A hint of a smile played on his firm lips. Lifting his hand, he brushed his fingers over her cheek. His touch was gentle, yet its effect was potent; a bolt of fire lanced through her. The air grew taut between them and the smoldering look in his eyes caused her breath to catch in her throat.

"I think it's more than that," he said, trailing his hand to her neck and cupping her nape. "Much more," he added huskily and then, not breaking eye contact, he lowered his head and captured her mouth with his.

Instantly, his demanding lips set her body aflame with desire. She melted against him, not caring that they were on a public beach, and that anyone in the immediate vicinity could be watching them. Parting her mouth, she returned his deep, soulful kiss with a longing unlike anything she'd ever felt or imagined. She wanted him, of that there was no doubt. And if they were anywhere else she would let him do anything he wanted to her and love every second of it.

But they were in a public place, and Sean suddenly seemed to remember that. He dragged his mouth from hers and took a ragged breath. Dazed, Kayla opened her eyes, saw the heat in his and trembled at its intensity.

"It looks like I'm breaking *all* the rules today," he

said with a wry grin. She felt his fingers on her ponytail and then he pulled the elastic band from it. Her hair, released from the band, cascaded over her shoulders and back. "I like your hair down."

Still pressed up against him, she could feel his erection straining against his jeans. His other arm was wrapped tightly around her. She'd been so lost in his kiss, she hadn't been aware of anything else.

"We should probably go," he said, but made no move to loosen his hold on her. She could feel every inch of him and it didn't do a damn thing to cool her arousal. Her body was primed and ready to go. "Except everyone on this damn beach is going to be able to see how much I want you." His grin was so sinful she felt her cheeks start to burn. "You're blushing again, sweetheart," he said.

She nodded, not bothering to deny it. "It's a curse."

"It's actually kind of cute, and it makes me wonder..." He trailed off as his eyes roamed over her face.

"Wonder what?"

"Do you blush all over?".

Distinct warmth pooled between her legs at the implication of his words. "You'll have to find out for yourself," she said and smiled.

A wicked gleam lit Sean's eyes. Butterflies danced wildly in Kayla's stomach, leaving her almost breathless.

"Trust me, sweetheart. I intend to."

DRIVING NORTH ON Hillhurst, Sean found himself thinking about what was going to happen when he and Kayla arrived at her house. Despite their scorching kisses on the deck above the ocean, and then on the beach, he'd learned a long time ago not to assume anything when it came to women. They were as unpredictable as the weather, and just when he thought he'd figured them out, something would happen that made him realize he didn't understand them at all.

But there was one thing he did know. Kayla wanted him every bit as much as he wanted her. The physical attraction between them was intense. Too intense for either of them to ignore for much longer.

The sun would be setting in less than an hour. The day was ending, the night just beginning. With every fiber of his being, Sean wanted to spend the night with her.

But despite her passionate kisses and sexy banter, he wasn't sure she was ready to take things to the next level.

He, on the other hand, was more than ready. As each day passed, his need for her grew stronger and more powerful—he wanted her so badly he ached from it. But whatever happened tonight would be up to her. He could take a few more cold showers if he had to.

Stopping at a red light, he felt the weight of Kayla's gaze on him and turned toward her. Just looking at her took his breath away. She had eyes a man could drown in, and her lustrous dark hair flowed over her shoulders like a silken waterfall. It felt as soft as it looked; he'd discovered that today on the beach.

"Are you hungry?" she asked.

"I could eat," he replied. "It's been a while since brunch."

"Cheech's is on the next block. We could pick up a pizza and take it back to my house."

He held her gaze, knowing he wasn't imagining the

crackle of awareness between them. A spike of heat caught him low in his gut, and it wasn't until the car behind him honked that he realized that the light had turned green.

God, how he wanted her.

Spotting an open spot near Cheech's, he pulled into it and reminded himself that being invited in for pizza didn't automatically mean they would end up in Kayla's bed. But if they didn't then tonight he'd be taking the longest—and coldest—shower of his life.

SITTING NEXT TO Sean on the sofa in her living room, Kayla almost felt bad for him as they watched the sports channel's coverage of the Dodgers' loss to Philadelphia. But, as a true Blaze fan, she found it hard to muster up any sympathy for her team's most hated rivals.

"Don't say it," Sean said as he crumpled up his napkin and tossed it on the empty pizza carton on the coffee table.

"Did I say anything?" She tried her best not to sound too happy. The Dodgers loss, combined with a Blaze victory had edged San Francisco into second place in the standings. They were one game behind the Dodgers but Kayla was confident her team would overtake his before too long.

"No, but you want to," he said with a slight grin as he leaned back against the sofa. "At least Matt didn't get thrown out of the game. It's looking more and more like he might be traded. And if that happens, I'm afraid it may send him completely over the edge."

"You know I'm not a Dodgers fan." Kayla shifted sideways, adjusting the hem of her dress so she could curl her bare feet underneath her. "But I'd have to be living under a rock not to have seen the change in him. Two years ago he was the National League MVP, and now every time I see him in a highlight reel he's getting into a fight or being ejected from a game."

"I've known Matt since we were kids. He's like a brother to me, and I have no idea how to help him. He suffered a terrible loss last year. It's something that's been kept out of the press, thank God, because he doesn't want anyone to know about it." Sean looked at her; it wasn't hard to see the worry in his eyes. "I've tried to talk to him but he won't even admit he's hurting."

"Maybe he's not ready," she said, thinking of Kelly and the issues she'd faced several years ago. It wasn't until her sister admitted she had a problem that she would let anyone help her. Moving her hand to his shoulder, she squeezed it gently. "Just be there for him when he needs you. That's all you can do until he's able to face whatever it is that's troubling him."

Sean grimaced. "In theory, I know you're right. But it's hard watching him throw away everything he's worked for."

"You can't help someone who doesn't want to be helped," she said. "I know that's not what you want to hear, but it's the truth. He knows you're his friend, he'll find you when he needs you."

"So just wait." Sean sighed. "Is that what you're telling me? I'm not very patient." His gaze lowered to her lips, lingering long enough to send a lurch of excitement through her body. "When I want something, I'm not fond of waiting for it." His gaze lifted to hers. The blazing intensity in them sent her heart racing.

"We're not talking about Matt anymore, are we?"

Kayla asked. Ever since they'd left Pacific Palisades, her thoughts had been focused solely on this moment, when they would be totally alone and able to give in to their desire.

And she *so* wanted to give in.

Turning, he moved closer. Their eyes locked. "No, we're not," he said, making no move to touch her, "I want you, Kayla." The husky tone of his voice sent a delicious shiver up her spine. "And I'm not telling you something you don't already know."

"It was kind of hard not to miss." She cast a quick glance at his lap, unable to keep from smiling.

"I tried thinking about baseball, but—" he shrugged "—it didn't work. All I could think about was you."

Her smile faded and her heart started to pound when she saw naked hunger flicker in his eyes. Aching to feel the heat of his body against hers, she leaned forward. "I must be doing something right if I beat out baseball," she said softly.

"Sweetheart, you're doing everything right," he said just before he pressed his lips to hers and kissed her with a tenderness that made her whole body quiver. Sliding her hand down his shoulder to his strong biceps, she leaned into him. He deepened the kiss, his mouth demanding a response. She gave it to him, holding nothing back as the blood in her veins ran hot and molten.

Long seconds later, stunned by the primal feelings he'd evoked within her, she tore her lips from his. Taking a deep breath, she met his heated gaze. He put his hands on her shoulders, his warm touch raised goosebumps on her flesh. "We don't have to do this if you're not ready." Sean's voice was gentle, which was amazing considering the ferocity of their kiss.

"I've been ready all day," she blurted out before she could stop herself and then snapped her mouth shut and felt her cheeks start to burn when he grinned with masculine satisfaction. "Don't say it," she said. "I know I'm blushing."

"I won't say it. But I will say that I'm fine with whatever you want to do. If you want me to leave, I'll leave." He squeezed her shoulders gently. "And if you want me to stay, I'll stay. It's totally up to you."

"I want you to stay," she whispered.

"I was hoping you'd say that," he said huskily, and then, lifting a hand to her chin, he tilted her head up and leaned forward to press his mouth to hers. His kiss was light—teasing almost—as he brushed his firm, sensual lips over hers. He slid his hand to her nape. She shivered at the light touch and swayed toward him, longing to be in his arms again.

His lips grew more insistent, and then, without warning, he pulled back and uttered a muffled curse. "What's wrong?" she asked when she opened her eyes and saw his dark expression.

"I don't have any condoms," he said in strained voice.

She stared at him more than a little surprised. "Not even one?" She thought all men carried at least one in their wallet, just in case they got lucky some place other than their own bedroom.

He shook his head. "But if I did, you'd probably think I planned for this to happen."

"Probably," she said and then smiled. "I kind of like that you didn't expect this."

"I expected it." Sean's grin was cocky. "Just not tonight."

"Confident much?"

"Sweetheart, our chemistry is off the charts. And not just in front of the cameras." His eyes lowered to her lips and lingered. "I've been thinking about making love to you for weeks." His lifted his eyes and held her gaze. "But I can wait until we have protection. You're worth waiting for."

Kayla's chest tightened at the tenderness in his gaze. She was on birth control so pregnancy wasn't an issue, but after Greg, and his numerous affairs when they were together, she swore to never have sex without a condom unless she was in a committed relationship and the man she was with had a clean bill of health.

"Come with me," she ordered, unfurling her legs and rising from the sofa. She reached for his hand.

"Where are we going?" he asked, getting to his feet.

"To the kitchen." He didn't say a word as she led him into the kitchen and around the granite island to a row of drawers. Letting go of his hand, she reached for the handle of the one she called her "junk" drawer and pulled it open. "I went to an AIDS awareness benefit with Lance a couple of months ago," she said retrieving a multicolored plastic bag from within. "They were giving out goodie bags." She closed the drawer, held the bag up and smiled. "One of their goals is promoting safe sex."

Sean grabbed the bag from her outstretched hand and opened it. "Jesus, they're not only promoting safe sex, but a *lot* of safe sex," he muttered, peering into the bag. "There's every brand of condom known to mankind in here." He looked up, his grin wolfish. "We never have to leave your house again."

Kayla couldn't contain her burst of laughter. "I hate

to break it to you, but we have to be at work by seven tomorrow morning."

"Then it's a good thing I've already memorized my lines." He set the bag on the countertop and slipped his arms around her waist.

"Why's that?" She smiled up at him.

"Because I plan to be very busy tonight," he said, his voice low, suggestive. "All night."

Her heart skipped a beat. "All night?" she echoed.

He nodded solemnly. "And maybe in the morning too." He paused, tilting his head. "If you're okay with that?"

If she was okay with that? Yes, she was definitely okay with that.

He dipped his head and covered her mouth with his. She opened her mouth, eager for the feel of his tongue stroking hers. As if sensing her need, he dove in. Their tongues met and then tangled in a sensuous duel that sent a jolt of sexual need straight to her core.

As their mouths mated hotly, luscious anticipation curled through her. Lifting her arms, she wound them around his neck and arched against him. She felt his hands slide down to her buttocks. His fingers dug into her soft flesh and he ground her against his hips. His erection pressed into her, letting her know that he was every bit was turned on as she was.

Pulling his mouth from hers, he trailed his warm lips to her cheek, and then to her jaw. Tilting her head back, she gave him access to her neck. He took full advantage of it, finding a sensitive spot near her collarbone and then sucking on it. The effect was instantaneous; every nerve ending on her body tingled with awareness and her mind went blank. All she wanted was Sean. Nothing else mattered.

"Let's go to your bedroom," he whispered against her throat. Before she could utter a word, he lifted her effortlessly, sliding his hands underneath her so she was cradled in his strong arms. Stunned by his quick move, she hung on to his neck. "We can save the counter for later," he added with a wicked glint in his eyes.

Glancing at the smooth granite, Kayla imagined what Sean could do to her on it. Arousal coiled in her core as several different scenarios came to mind.

"Wait," she exclaimed as he turned toward the living room. He stopped and gave her a confused look. "We forgot the condoms."

Relief flickered in his eyes as he pivoted back to the counter. "Can you grab them? My hands are kind of full right now," he said with a brash grin.

Unclasping her fingers, she reached for the bag with one hand and held on to his neck with the other. As soon as she had the bag, he swung around and carried her out of the kitchen. As he strode down the hallway, her heart felt like it was beating out of her chest.

After carrying her into the bedroom, Sean gently eased her from his arms. The minute her feet touched the floor his hands spanned her waist and he pulled her against his body. The bag slipped from her grasp as he crushed his mouth to hers. Her body was on fire, and there was only one person who could douse the four alarm blaze burning inside her. The man who started it.

When his lips left hers and seared a scorching path from her jaw to her neck, Kayla was breathless. As he kissed the throbbing pulse at the base of her throat, she felt his hand tugging on her zipper, pulling it down.

Her dress loosened. When he lifted his head, their eyes locked as he hooked his thumbs under the straps of her sundress and pulled them over her shoulders. The dress slid down her body and pooled around her ankles.

Her heart leaped in excitement as his eyes boldly raked over her. She wasn't completely naked. Not yet. She stood before him in her lacy blue bra, matching thong and her sandals. Her nipples were taut, straining against the sheer fabric of her bra, and between her legs, her sex pulsed.

Needing to feel his lips on hers again, she reached out, clutched his shirt with her fingers and pulled him toward her. His eyes widened in surprise, and then his lips found hers once again. She kissed him hungrily, lost in a vortex of passion she might never emerge from. As their ravenous kiss continued, she felt his hand slip up her spine to the nape of her neck. Grabbing a fistful of her hair, he took possession of her mouth, and nothing that had come before prepared her for the ravishing onslaught of his lips.

This was no gentle kiss. It was raw, blistering and so hot it was all she could do to keep her knees from buckling. The desire she'd been suppressing for most of the day exploded; her body practically convulsed with it. Blindly, she reached for the hem of his shirt and moaned against his mouth when she slid her hands under it and touched his bare skin.

She'd wondered if his skin would be warm to her touch. It was. She'd also wondered if his muscles would feel as hard and solid as she imagined them to be. They were. So far, everything about him had exceeded her expectations.

There was only one problem. He was still wearing his clothes.

Breaking their kiss, she tugged his shirt upward. Releasing her, he lifted his arms so she could pull it over his head. She flung it to the floor and let her gaze wander over his sculpted chest. Except for a light coating of fine blond hair, it was smooth and tapered down to a tight waist with rock hard abs. His jeans rode low on his hips and she noticed another smattering of fine golden hair trailing down from his belly button to disappear under the waistband of his jeans. She imagined following that trail with her lips, and when she noticed the bulge between his legs, she felt a hot blush spread over her face. Jerking her head up, she met Sean's fiery gaze.

"My turn," he said, lifting his hand to front clasp of her bra. Deftly, he opened it with his fingers. It loosened and he slid it off of her shoulders. She let it fall to the floor behind her. "God, you're beautiful," he said as his hands rose to her breasts. His fingers brushed lightly over her taut nipples, electrifying her. "I wanted you the second I saw you."

"You did?" she whispered, stunned that he'd even noticed her back then.

"Yes." His gaze lowered to her breasts.

"I have a confession," she said without thinking. "I had a huge crush on you in high school."

He looked up, his brow lifting in surprise. "Really?"

"Yes. Back then my schoolgirl fantasies never got this far. I just wanted you to take me to the senior prom." She paused, nervously biting her lower lip. She couldn't believe she'd just told him that.

He leaned in and planted a searing kiss on her mouth. Within seconds she was reduced to a quivering mass of gelatin. *Damn, the man can kiss.* His tongue was hot and smooth as it stroked hers. She'd certainly never imagined this in any of her high school fantasies. "I want you," he muttered against her lips.

"I want you too," she whispered, lifting her hands to twine her fingers in his soft hair. Their lips fused hotly and she forgot everything except her raging desire for him. His hands spanned her waist and he pulled her against him. The hard ridge of his shaft pressed into the juncture of her thighs, filling her with unbridled anticipation.

So wrapped up in the sensations that were flooding her body, she was surprised when she felt the edge of the bed against her knees. Sean lifted his lips from hers. "Sit," he said in a low voice.

With her heart beating wildly, Kayla sank down on the bed. Sean crouched down in front of her, and after removing one sandal from her foot, he reached for the other foot and did the same thing. Shifting his weight to his knees, he put his hands on the bed on either side of her hips. His face was level with hers and when their eyes met, she felt a surge of longing so powerful it took her breath away.

"Whatever you want," he said. The silky cadence of his voice caused a lurch of excitement to flow through her body but all she could do was stare mutely at him. "I'll do whatever you want," he said and then lowered his mouth to her breast. His lips closed over her nipple, gently sucking it until she gasped in pleasure. Then he moved to the other one, continuing the sweet torture until she had to lift her hands to his shoulders to keep from falling back on the bed in a boneless heap.

After paying homage to her breasts for a number

of pleasurable seconds, he pulled back, slid his hands to her hips and hooked his fingers in the waistband of her thong. Grasping his shoulders, she eased up so he could pull it off.

The thong hadn't even hit the floor before he returned his attention to her breasts. He caressed them with his hands, kissed them with his lips and teased her nipples with his tongue. She'd never realized her breasts were so sensitive, but under Sean's talented mouth she was becoming more aroused by the second. Liquid warmth pooled between her legs, and her body throbbed with a need only he could satisfy.

He looked up at her, and when she met his sizzling gaze, all she could hear was the primitive beating of her heart. It echoed in her head, urging her to give in to her most basic instincts. And when his hands moved to her knees, she did. She didn't resist when he gently spread her legs.

"Do you know how painful it is walking around all day long with a hard-on you can't do anything about?" The cadence of his voice was low, his touch delicious.

"I'm afraid I don't," she said, lowering her hands and bracing them behind her on the bed.

"It's frustrating as hell," he said, sliding his hands over her soft skin. He stopped just before the juncture of her thighs. He didn't touch her, but he was so close her sex clenched and throbbed.

Suddenly, *she* was the one feeling the frustration.

Leaning forward, he closed his firm wet mouth over her breast. He drew on her nipple, suckling and teasing her until her breath caught in her throat and she arched in pleasure, offering him her breasts. Seconds later, he turned his attention to her other nipple. The sensation of his lips on her taut peak was incredibly arousing; every wet rasp of his tongue sent a current of electricity straight to her core.

She felt like a voyeur as he trailed his lips to her midriff but she couldn't seem to help herself. Watching him was erotic; she couldn't look away. As he moved lower, she spread her legs wider, amazed at how wanton she'd become.

Grasping the chenille bedspread with her hands, all she wanted was for him to touch her intimately, but instead he pressed a tantalizing kiss on the inside of one thigh and then the other. And then maddeningly, he trailed his fingers over the tops of her thighs. Her skin prickled and her nipples grew taut. She was beginning to think he was torturing her on purpose.

Slowly, his lips moved closer. Desire clawed at her, hot and sharp. Biting her lip, she whimpered with relief and pleasure when his tongue finally dove into her feminine folds. He gave her a long lick that sent a slow throb of desire pulsing through her body. He did it again, but this time he found her clitoris. Her hips jerked in pleasure not only because of what he was doing to her, but because she was watching him do it.

It didn't take long for her hips to undulate under his rhythmic ministrations. Closing her eyes, she got lost in the pleasure of it all. Her clit felt engorged and her lower body, especially her sex, felt heavy and warm. "Sean…" she whispered his name. Kayla heard his low growl, and then he plunged his tongue into her opening. Her passion hit the roof and a shuddering moan slipped from her lips. As Sean continued his erotic assault on her, a shot of something steamy coursed through her body. Every feeling she had was centered between her legs, and that became clearly evident when he withdrew his tongue from her and moved up to suckle her clit. It was so intense she almost screamed. She thrust her hips against his face, her orgasm teetering on the edge.

As if he knew that, Sean slid his hand up to her hips. Digging his fingers into her, he pulled her roughly against his mouth and kissed her burning flesh with a voraciousness that thrilled her. Closing her eyes, she couldn't stop her soft moans of pleasure. He was too thorough, and she was too far gone. He found her clit again, and that's when it happened. Her body exploded into a million tiny pieces. Exquisite pleasure washed over her in waves as his mouth stayed fused to her throbbing sex, drawing out her pleasure and then easing her down as her body calmed.

Her breathing was labored, and her body felt hot and slick with perspiration. Opening her eyes, she met Sean's satisfied gaze in complete and utter astonishment. She wasn't a demure virgin, by any means, but she'd never felt anything like that before. Ever.

Sean stroked her thighs. His touch as gentle as a feather against her ultra-sensitive skin. "That was hot."

Kayla totally agreed, but as Sean stood up to unbutton and unzip his fly, she couldn't seem to formulate a coherent sentence. Mutely, she watched him kick off his shoes, drag both his jeans and briefs down over his hips and step out of them. When he straightened, Kayla marveled at his masculine perfection.

Not only was he the hottest man she'd ever laid eyes on, his body was solid muscle. There wasn't an ounce of fat anywhere. Unable to resist, she lowered her gaze. Between those powerful thighs of his, he was fully aroused and very impressive.

As he bent to retrieve the bag she'd dropped on the floor, she was treated to an amazing view of his ass. It was perfect, just like the rest of him. Sliding back on the bed, she stretched out on the soft bedspread to watch him—her heart pounding in anticipation—while he rummaged through the plastic bag and pulled out a condom. "They have my brand," he said with a grin and moved toward the bed.

Dropping the bag and the condom on the nightstand, he climbed on the bed and lay down next to her, his clean male scent surrounding her. Their eyes locked when he hooked his leg over hers, slid his warm hand down the curve of her back and eased her body closer to his.

Finally, it was skin against skin, the softness of her body against the hardness of his. As her heart pounded a primal beat, Kayla felt as if she were drowning in Sean's smoldering green eyes. Unable to resist, she pressed her mouth to his and their lips tangled in another scorching kiss.

With the freedom to touch him wherever she wanted, she did just that. Tracing her fingertips along the smooth skin of his back, she marveled at the sheer strength of his body. She wasn't petite, but next to him she felt as if she was.

Feeling his erection press into her, she slid her hand between them and slipped her fingers around his hard shaft. He pulled his lips from hers with a gasp. "Sweetheart, you're playing with fire."

"I know." She squeezed him gently. "But turnabout is fair play."

"Tempting." He grinned. "But I need to be inside you." Raw sexual heat flared in his eyes. "Now."

Quickly, he rolled away and reached for the condom. He tore open the foil wrapper but before he could do more she snatched it from his hands. "Let me," she said, and after removing the condom, tossed the wrapper on the nightstand. "On your back," she ordered.

"I have to say. I like this side of you," he said as he obeyed. Sitting up, she crawled over him and slid the condom over his hard shaft. She closed her hand around him and gave him a gentle squeeze. "Not so fast, sweetheart," he said, clamping his fingers around her wrist. The next thing she knew she was on her back staring up at the ceiling, spreading her legs as he climbed over her.

Sean leveraged himself above her, his hands braced on either side of her. His eyes were filled with arousal and his breath hitched when she shifted slightly beneath him, rubbing against him.

"You're killing me. You know that, don't you?" His voice was husky yet amused.

Lifting her hands to caress his broad shoulders, she smiled. "I'm sorry."

"No you're not." He grinned sexily. "You enjoy torturing me."

"Like you didn't just torture me," she said with a laugh. "But I'll admit to enjoying every minute of it."

"I could tell," he said, and then slowly slid his thick shaft into her. She gasped in pleasure as he filled her. "All that moaning gave you away," he added after he was completely imbedded inside her. And if she wasn't already hot, Kayla knew she would feel her cheeks burning. "You feel good," he said in a husky whisper and then began to move.

His thrusts were slow and controlled. At first. But soon his tempo increased, and with each thrust she, again, felt the sweet tension building inside her. Moving her hips in rhythm with his, she ran her palms over his ribcage to caress his back. His skin was hot and slick with moisture, just as hers was.

Lowering his head, he kissed her as they rocked together on the bed. His kiss was soft and tender. Kayla's mind reeled. They were connected in the most intimate of ways, and as crazy as it might sound to anyone else, she felt like she'd come home.

"Kayla," he whispered huskily against her mouth and began to move faster. Each sensuous stroke seemed to stimulate her even more. Sliding her hands down his back, she dug her fingers into his buttocks and arched her body up to meet his, seeking the same sweet release she'd found just minutes ago.

Tearing his lips from her, he held her eyes with such intensity it almost took her breath away. He drove into her hard, triggering her orgasm. She gasped in pleasure as it ripped through her body like a tidal wave.

Sean wasn't far behind. He thrust into her wildly before tensing and letting out a low, shuddering moan. Wrapping her legs around him, she ground against him until he collapsed on top of her and buried his face in the crook of her neck.

"Am I crushing you?" he asked, lifting his head to look at her.

"I'm fine," she said, relaxing her legs. Pulling her arm from under his, she reached up to brush his hair from his brow. She liked the feel of his weight on her.

"That was amazing," he said, and then pressed his lips to hers. Her heart clenched at the gentle sweetness of his kiss. "*You're* amazing," he said, trailing his lips to her jaw and then to her neck. She shivered when he found a sensitive spot at the base of her throat.

"So are you," she whispered, and had a strong feeling that if he had a mind to, Sean could rekindle her desire with no problem whatsoever.

Retracing the path back to her mouth, he kissed her again. "Guess what?" he asked when he raised his head.

"What?" she asked warily, noting the mischievous sparkle in his eyes.

The smile he gave her was made of pure sin. "You do blush all over."

Seventeen

Shay: I've never stayed in one place for very long. But I think I could stay here.
Jared: Why?
Shay: Because it feels like home.

KAYLA PULLED HER lips from Sean's. Her dark eyes were filled with heat. "What the hell was that?" she, or rather Shay, asked Jared. "You didn't have to kiss me."

"Yes, I did," Sean said, wishing he could kiss her again. But they were on the set and it wasn't in the script. "It was the only way to shut you up."

"I was just trying to help."

"You're a civilian, Shay." He ran his hand through his hair, feeling a lot like the time he'd been caught in the undertow when he'd been surfing. Fighting it had been in vain, so he'd just given in to it. "Go home. Now."

"But..."

"Now. We'll talk when I get home."

"Fine," she said and shot him a hostile glare before stepping around him and stalking off.

"Good job, guys." Bill's voice boomed across the set.

Sean wondered if anyone else could feel the sexual undercurrent simmering between them. He certainly felt it, and as the morning progressed, the tight control he'd kept on his body was starting to slip.

He wanted her. And if he didn't have her again soon he just might explode.

But they were at the studio, and like at any other workplace, people gossiped. In Hollywood however, gossip was practically an Olympic sport. If there was any indication that he and Kayla were more than co-workers the news would be all over the studio—and on the internet—before nightfall.

Right now their relationship was private and he wanted it to stay that way. He didn't know where it was going or what would happen in the future, but he couldn't stop thinking about her.

"Sean." Bill walked toward him clutching his clipboard. "I liked the way you played that scene. The kiss has affected Jared more than he wants to admit." Bill smiled. "I really felt that. Bring that to taping this afternoon."

"No problem." And it wouldn't be. Reprising their on-screen kiss from Friday reminded him of their hot encounter the night before. He didn't have to fake being affected by Kayla.

"I'll see you after lunch," Bill said, and then walked off the set to consult with his assistant who'd been hovering nearby.

As two of the lighting techs began to set up the lights for the taping, Kayla grabbed her coffee from an oblong table near the front door of the set and headed toward him. She dressed as she normally did for rehearsal. Casually. Her hair was up in a loose ponytail, and she wore no make-up. She looked just as beautiful as she had when, just after dawn, he'd woken up next to her.

"You broke your no tongue rule." She smiled before taking a sip of her coffee.

"I know. Not very professional of me, was it?" Grinning, he shoved his hands into his pockets so he wouldn't touch her. The techs were busy adjusting the lights, but they weren't blind.

"No, it wasn't." A wicked gleam made her eyes sparkle. "You know, the dialogue in our last scene is a bit tricky," she said, glancing from him to the techs. "Would you mind going over it again with me?" She looked back at him. "We could use my dressing room."

She was full of shit and they both knew it. She'd nailed her dialogue in rehearsal just like he had. "Sure." He nodded, aching to be alone with her. "I'd be happy to help you out."

Her smile was far from innocent. "I thought you would."

There wasn't a pore in his body that wasn't aware of her as they left the set. As he walked beside her toward her dressing room, Kayla's softly scented perfume filled his senses, increasing his desire for her. Several studio employees passed them in the corridor, and other than a nod hello, no one gave them a second look. After all, they'd rehearsed in Kayla's dressing room in the past. It wasn't all that unusual for him to be there.

After she unlocked the door, he followed her in. Closing the door behind him, he watched her as she tossed her cup in a small wastebasket and set her keys on the desk. She wore black sweats or as she'd called them this morning…leggings. They clung to her like a second skin. Her top wasn't as snug. In fact it was more like a tunic. He'd noticed that instead of deliberately showcasing her amazing body, she preferred to dress comfortably. But it wouldn't matter what she wore, she could wear a potato sack and still look stunning.

When she turned, their eyes locked. The heat in her gaze caused a rush of something more than physical desire to swamp his body, but he had no idea what it was because he couldn't remember ever feeling it before. Taking a breath, he tried to slow the rapid beating in his chest, but the effort was futile. His heart was pounding like a jackhammer.

"Lock the door," she said, and without tearing his gaze from hers, he reached behind him and turned the deadbolt. Lifting a hand to her hair, she pulled the band from it and it fell loose around her shoulders. She slipped the band around her wrist. "It's probably a good thing that Jared and Shay won't share another kiss for a while," she said, moving toward him.

"Why is that a good thing?"

"Because—" she halted in front of him "—if you kiss me like that again everyone's going to figure out we're more than just co-workers." She lifted her hands to his chest. Her light touch over his Dodgers T-shirt sent an arrow of heat straight to his groin. "For a few seconds I forgot we were at work."

Unable to resist the primitive force inside that demanded he reach for her, he slipped his hands to her waist and pulled her against him. Her body felt soft and pliant against his, reminding him of last night. When he made love to her he'd felt every quiver, and heard every soft moan. She held nothing back, and this morning he wanted her again—desperately. But they'd overslept, and because he'd had to go back to his house to shower and change he barely got a chance to kiss her, let alone make love to her again. "What are you doing after work?" he asked.

"I'm dropping my car off at the body shop where I

got the estimate the other day." Sliding her hands up from his chest, she wound her arms around his neck. The move caused her body to press even more intimately to his and did nothing to ease the urgent demands his body was making.

"Do you need a ride home?" he asked, letting his gaze linger for several seconds on her full lips.

"As much as I'd like that, they're arranging a rental car for me."

"How about dinner, then? We could go out or…" He trailed off and grinned.

"Or what?" she asked, her eyes lighting up with amusement.

"Or you can impress me with those take-out ordering skills you were bragging about."

Her laugh was warm and husky, making it difficult for him to concentrate.

"And we could run lines for tomorrow's show," he added, hoping it would help his case.

"We only have two scenes tomorrow," she said caressing his nape. Her touch was light but, nonetheless, a punch of arousal shot through his body. "It shouldn't take long to memorize our lines."

"No, it shouldn't." Lowering his head, he planted a kiss at the base of her throat and then worked his way up her neck.

"What will we do with all that extra time?" she whispered and then shivered when he pressed his lips just under her jaw.

"I'm sure we'll think of something," he said and then sought her lips with his. She responded immediately, returning his kiss with such fierceness that all coherent thought left his brain. And he was fine with that. Thinking was overrated anyway. All he wanted to do was feel, and what he felt was the silkiness of her tongue, and the warmth of her lips. She sighed against his mouth. The soft sound enticed him to deepen their kiss and slide his hands down to the curve of her ass where he pulled her against him in such a way that she would have no doubt about how much he wanted her.

And he wanted her. So badly he didn't hear the ringing of his cell phone until she spoke, "Whoever that is has rotten timing," she murmured against his lips.

"Ignore it," he said kneading her buttocks and grinding her against his cock. Whoever was calling couldn't be as important as what they were about to do.

The damn phone kept ringing. Kayla pulled away from his lips. "It might be important," she said, unclasping her hands from around his neck.

"I doubt it," he said with an exasperated sigh. Reluctantly letting her go, he reached into his back pocket for his phone. He glanced at the caller ID. "This had better be good." He hit the speakerphone button. "What's up, Lisa?" he asked, trying to keep the frustration out of his voice.

"Did you and Kayla enjoy the beach yesterday?" Lisa's tone was cool.

He met Kayla's eyes. She looked as surprised as he was. "How did you know we were at the beach?" he asked.

"Because pictures of your romantic stroll, not to mention a pretty hot looking lip-lock, are burning up the internet this morning."

"What?" Kayla exclaimed, her face paling.

"Good morning, Kayla." Lisa's voice was still chilly. "You were my next call. I don't like surprises like this.

Luckily, I was informed about the photos before my phone started ringing off the hook."

"Who took them?" Sean asked. He hadn't seen any paparazzi but that didn't mean anything. The bastards were very adept at hiding in plain sight.

"Does it matter? Anyone with a cell phone could have taken those shots." Lisa's sigh was laced with disappointment. "Both of you know better."

"We weren't thinking," Kayla said. She moved to the sofa and sank down on it.

"That's obvious. Look, personally, I have no problem with this. You're consenting adults and what you do is your business."

"That's right, it is," Sean snapped, not angry at Lisa, but at himself for forgetting that his and Kayla's personal lives were something a portion of the population was interested in. It was the one thing he didn't like about his profession; the invasion of privacy. "I'm sorry," he said after a tense silence. "I'm not mad at you."

"We need to talk about what you want me to say," Lisa continued. "And what *you're* going to say. Remember, you have that fan event in Van Nuys on Saturday. Be prepared to deal with questions from your fans about those pictures. They're going to want to know if you two are dating."

"Can you say no comment until Sean and I talk about it?" Kayla asked.

"Of course. And I can continue to say that if that's what you want. It's your call, but in my experience the more you deny something the more curious people will become. It's better to be upfront."

Sean ran a hand through his hair and moved to join

Kayla on the small sofa. He was pissed that they had to go public so quickly. "Can we get back to you?" he asked, setting the phone on the table in front of him.

"Yes. I've got several appointments today but if you leave a message I'll call you when I'm available."

"Thanks, Lisa," Kayla said. "I'm sorry you were blindsided."

"We'll handle it," Lisa replied in gentler tone and then hung up.

Shifting on the sofa, Sean met Kayla's gaze. "That really killed the mood, didn't it?" she said with a rueful smile.

"I'm sorry." He reached for her hand.

"It's not your fault. The fact is we're on television, and in the public eye. We forgot that yesterday."

"What do you want to do?" he asked.

"I don't know. I'm not ready to define what we are to each other. We don't even know that ourselves yet."

"Lisa has a point though. Saying nothing will only fuel the fans and the media's desire to know more."

"That's true. We could say we're just friends," Kayla suggested.

"No one will believe that." He squeezed her hand gently. "I wasn't kissing you like a friend. Why don't we just say we're dating and leave it at that? After all, I want to keep seeing you."

Her eyes softened. "And I want to keep seeing you."

"Then that's what we'll do." He leaned forward and pressed his lips to hers. "I should go," he said, pulling back even though he wanted to stay and pick up where they'd left off. Lisa's call had been like stepping into a cold shower but it wouldn't take much for him to get hard again. "If Lisa knows about those pictures it won't take long for the whole studio to find out. So, unless we want to provide more grist for the rumor mill we probably shouldn't stay in here too long with the door closed."

"You're right. I was in a relationship with an actor a couple of years ago. He cheated on me with a number of other actresses. I've been the subject of gossip before. As much as I hate it, I can handle it."

"So can I," he said, hating that they'd been found out a lot sooner than he'd anticipated. But it didn't change a thing. The whole world could gossip about them for all he cared, he wasn't going to stop seeing her.

SEATED A FEW feet from Sean in the ballroom of the Airtel Hotel in Van Nuys, Kayla was astounded at the number of *A New Dawn* fans lined up to see their favorite stars. But what was more astonishing was the number of fans who were wearing T-shirts with her and Sean's pictures on them.

She'd just signed an autograph for the fan who was now talking to Sean when she recognized the attractive blonde next in line. "Hi, Stephanie," she said, happy to see a familiar face.

"Hi, Kayla," Stephanie grinned and pointed to her chest. "Do you like the T-shirt? A bunch of us on the website had them made to support JaShay."

"JaShay?" Kayla echoed.

"It's Jared and Shay smushed together. All the great soap couples have their own name." Reaching into her denim tote bag, she pulled a blue folder from inside and set it on the table. "I brought along the fan club stuff we talked about at the luncheon."

Kayla reached for the folder and slid it toward her.

"I'll take a look at it when I get home. How's the job search coming?"

Stephanie's eyes lit up. "I have a second interview tomorrow. It's an administrative assistant position at an advertising agency. Donna got a job last week." Stephanie beamed. "She couldn't make it today. She went to Vegas with her boyfriend to celebrate."

"It sounds like things are turning around for both of you."

"And not a minute too soon. I think I have a good shot at getting the admin assistant job. The first interview went really well. Oh, I forgot." Stephanie reached into her tote again. "I have T-shirts for you and Sean." She pulled out the shirts and set them on the table. "You should check out our website. It's called Fated Hearts. Donna and I started it after the fan club luncheon. We already have over four hundred members and our fan fiction section is getting some really good stories."

"Fan fiction?"

Stephanie nodded. "Yeah, a lot of your fans are really good writers. They write stories about Shay and Jared."

"I'll have to check it out."

"I have to warn you," Stephanie leaned forward, lowering her voice. "Some of the stories are pretty racy."

"Racy?"

"Sexually explicit." Stephanie winked. "And not for the faint of heart."

"Oh." Kayla glanced at Sean. He was engrossed in a conversation with another fan. "Thanks for the warning."

Stephanie tilted her head and grimaced. "I guess it would be kind of weird reading stuff like that. Especially when it's written about your character. It just goes to show that Shay and Jared have a lot of fans who want them to get together."

"Evidently," Kayla said, hoping her mom hadn't found the website. The thought of her mother reading sexually explicit stories about her and Sean's characters was a bit horrifying.

"I'm holding up the line," Stephanie said. "Let me know what you think about the fan club stuff. Even if I get the job, I still want to do it." She paused. "But only if you really want a fan club. I'll totally understand if you don't."

"Let me think about it. I'll let you know one way or the other." Kayla reached for the shirts. "Thanks for these."

"You're welcome. Enjoy the rest of your weekend."

"Good luck on the interview," Kayla called after her and figured Stephanie must not have seen the pictures of her and Sean. Unlike every other fan she'd spoken to, Stephanie hadn't asked her if she and Sean were an item. Here, like at the studio, she'd perfected the line that they were just dating. She didn't elaborate and neither did Sean. So far, everyone was fine with the brief explanation. Amanda and Sandy said they weren't surprised, and when Lance called her after seeing the photos on the internet, he'd let out an even more girlish squeal than her mother had. The only person who seemed perturbed by the news was Rachel. Her blue eyes had been icy and her expression dour every time they crossed paths at the studio. But not one word had passed her lips and Kayla was extremely grateful for that.

As the next fan approached, Kayla had the strangest feeling she was being watched. Looking around the room, she didn't see anyone in particular staring at her. The fans were lined up in front of whichever star they wanted to talk to, and most of them were laughing and smiling as they chatted with one another. No matter which character was their favorite, they shared a common love for the show. Kayla had never met nicer or more loyal fans in her life and was grateful for the support they'd given her.

From the corner of her eye, she noticed a vaguely familiar face in the crowd in front of her. Craning her neck to get a better look, the woman turned her way and their eyes clashed. Startled at the hostility in the older woman's gaze, it didn't take but a moment for her to remember where she'd seen her—in the grocery store produce section two months ago. The woman wore a purple jogging outfit with metallic beading instead of the hot pink number she'd sported in the grocery store, but there was no doubt in Kayla's mind that it was her.

The woman held her gaze and then mouthed the word *slut* before moving forward in the line. *Rachel's line*. Forcing her attention back to the fan in front of her, Kayla's mind reeled with the possibility that the woman from the grocery store was the person who'd been writing the threatening letters.

Rising from her chair, she smiled apologetically at the woman in front of her. "Do you mind if I use the restroom? I'll be right back."

"No problem." The fan smiled. "I don't mind waiting."

"Thanks," Kayla said and skirted the table. As she headed for Rachel's table, purple jogging suit woman saw her coming. Her eyes grew round with alarm and she bolted from the line and headed for the ballroom's double doors.

Keeping her eyes on the woman, Kayla cut through a swath of people hoping to get to the door before the older woman. Unfortunately, several fans grabbed her arm to say hello, slowing her progress. By the time she got to the door and into the large foyer outside, the woman had disappeared.

"Damn it," she muttered, and then almost jumped a foot when a strong hand wrapped around her arm. She whirled around and met Sean's concerned gaze.

"What's wrong?" he asked. "Why did you run out of the ballroom?"

"I think I might know who the stalker is."

Sean's eyes flickered with surprise. "Who?" He let go of her arm.

"A couple of months ago, I was in the grocery store and a lady came right up to me in the produce section and called me a slut. She berated me for sleeping with Stefan. She thought I was Shay."

"Was she here?" Sean looked around the foyer.

"Yes. I got up to confront her and she ran out of the ballroom."

"I'll check the parking lot. What's she wearing?"

"A purple jogging suit with metallic beading all over it."

Sean's eyes widened. "A *what*?"

She opened her mouth to explain. "Never mind. I'll find her," Sean said and then turned and took off. After he disappeared from sight, Kayla prayed he would find her and hoped the woman was their suspect. If so, then she wouldn't have to keep looking over her shoulder, afraid that her mysterious stalker would show up at her door.

Knowing she couldn't do anything more, she returned to the ballroom and thanked the fan who'd been waiting for being so patient. Ten minutes later, she saw Sean weaving his way through the still-packed ballroom. He took his place next to her.

"Did you talk to her?" Kayla asked after signing a photo for a very excited teenage girl.

"No, but I got the license plate number of her car," he replied. "I called Lisa and gave her the plate number. She's going to call Detective Shelton and give it to him. Hopefully he can track her down and question her." His gaze held hers for several seconds before an elderly fan in a wheelchair rolled up to him.

THREE HOURS LATER, Kayla sat next to Sean on the leather sofa in his living room and wished she could concentrate on the baseball game they were watching. But she couldn't. She'd been so sure the woman from the grocery store was the stalker that when Detective Shelton called to say that he'd talked to the woman at length and could neither confirm nor deny that she was the stalker, Kayla wanted to scream in frustration.

According to the detective, the woman didn't have any qualms about admitting her hatred for the character of Shay McKade but swore up and down that she didn't write the letters, or vandalize the Mustang. And since there were no fingerprints on the letters, or the car, there was no way to prove if she was telling the truth or lying through her teeth.

"Are you hungry?" Sean asked, reaching for the remote and hitting the mute button.

"Not really." She stared at the now silent television and saw that his Dodgers were up a run in the ninth inning. She hadn't even noticed. That's how distracted she'd been.

"I know you wanted it to be her." He tossed the remote on the coffee table. It landed with a soft thud on top of a sports magazine.

She turned to look at him. "Amanda gave me another stack of fan mail and I couldn't bring myself to look at it." It was sitting on her kitchen table untouched.

"They're checking it for similar envelopes and handwriting, right?"

"Amanda said there was nothing suspicious in this batch, but I still don't want to open any of it." She was feeling sorry for herself and knew it. She was at the mercy of some unknown person and there was nothing she could do about it.

"Come here," Sean said softly. He put his arm around her and pulled her against him. She snuggled against his chest, grateful she didn't have to go back to the house she used to love. A house with a state of the art security system that made her feel like a prisoner. She couldn't even open a window without entering codes on the new keypad. "This won't last forever," he said, gently stroking her arm.

"I know," she said and decided to change the subject. She'd been wallowing in self-pity ever since the detective called. "Kelly will be here in a couple of weeks. She's traveling with the Blaze when they come down for their series with the Dodgers." Her mood lightened at the thought of spending time with her sister.

"Is she staying with you?"

"Yes, and I can't wait. I haven't seen her since Christmas." She glanced up at him. "She always gets tickets to the games. Maybe you could join us and meet her."

"I'd like that." He looked back at the television and grinned. "Game's over. Dodgers won."

"Don't rub it in."

"Don't get mad at me because my team won and yours lost. I can't help it if your team sucks."

"Hey." She sat up and lightly punched his arm. "Take that back," she demanded. Sean rubbed his arm and grinned, clearly amused. "My team does not suck. They won three in a row before today."

"And yet they still trail the Dodgers in the standings," Sean said with a smirk.

"Now you're just being ugly," she said and got up from the sofa. "I could go for a beer. Is there some in the fridge?"

His eyes crinkled at the corners as he grinned. "Are the Dodgers in first place? Is the Pope Catholic? Does a bear—"

"You're making me mad," she interrupted, trying not to laugh. It was hard though. That smile of his was irresistible. "And you don't want to make me mad."

His brows rose. "Really? What happens when you get mad?" His lips twitched in amusement. "Should I be scared?"

"It's not pretty," she retorted, as she turned and marched into the kitchen. She opened the refrigerator, grabbed two bottles and closed the door.

Sean sauntered into the kitchen; Kayla handed him a bottle. "Thanks," he said, twisting off the top and tossing it on the countertop. She did the same and took a sip of her beer. "You're not really mad, are you?" He leaned against the counter and took a long pull from his bottle.

Meeting his gaze, she narrowed her eyes. "I will be if you keep talking smack about my team."

He shrugged. "I was just stating a fact, sweetheart. The Dodgers are in first place."

"Not for long," she shot back and let her gaze roam over his powerful body. They hadn't spent any time together since Sunday night but it wasn't for lack of trying. On Monday, at the body shop, there had been a snafu with her rental car and she'd had to wait two hours. By the time she'd gotten home it was after ten. On Tuesday, she'd had plans with Sandy to attend a concert, and on Wednesday evening she and Lance had had their monthly movie date. On Thursday, they'd made dinner plans but then Sean had to cancel after getting an emergency call from the housekeeper at his father's house. A pipe had busted and Sean had had to drive out to Pacific Palisades to deal with the plumber. Then he'd had to go back the next afternoon because the plumber wasn't able to finish the repairs in one day.

"You sound pretty sure about that," Sean said, setting his bottle on the counter behind him. "I'll bet you a hundred bucks that the Dodgers, not the Blaze, win the Western Division."

"I'll take that bet." She held out her hand.

He reached for her hand but instead of shaking it, pulled her toward him. "Let's kiss on it instead," he said huskily. His hand slid around her waist, anchoring her against his hard body. The contact was electric, and as his lips met hers she blindly set her bottle on the counter behind him so it wouldn't slip from her fingers and drop to the floor.

His kiss wasn't gentle. It was forceful, demanding, and so damn hot she could already feel desire throbbing in her veins. She wasn't surprised. Ever since the night they'd made love all she'd done was think about how amazing it was, and how much she wanted it to happen again.

"This has been the longest week of my life," he said as his mouth moved down her throat, his tongue hot and wet. Slipping her hands under his shirt, she touched his bare skin and shivered when his lips found the sensitive spot at the base of her neck. "All I wanted was to see you and it seemed like everything conspired against us," he murmured against her skin. Cupping her butt, he pulled her even closer. She felt the hard ridge of erection and it sent a shiver of excitement through her.

"Not to mention everyone at the studio watching our every move," she whispered. "I felt like a bug under a microscope."

"Tell me about it." Lifting his head, he slid his hand up her back to fist his fingers in her hair. "It's my fault. I shouldn't have kissed you on the beach."

"I liked kissing you on the beach. I wouldn't change a thing about that day—" she met his hot gaze "—or that night."

"I really want you right now." His voice was husky, her body throbbed in response.

"I want you too," she said, stroking the warm skin of his back. "But there's only one problem."

His brow furrowed. "What?"

"I left the bag of condoms at home."

A slow, wicked smile curved his lips. "Don't worry, sweetheart. I've got it covered."

Eighteen

Shay: Feel this.
Jared. Wow. Our baby is kicking up a storm.
Shay: Our baby?
Jared: I think of her as mine. Is that okay?
Shay: It's more than okay.

KAYLA LET THE hot water sluice over her skin and closing her eyes, enjoyed the feel of Sean rubbing the slick bar of soap over her back. His walk-in shower was huge, with showerheads on both sides of the enclosure. They were only using one and that was because he said if she used the other one she would be too far away.

"That feels good," she murmured as he slid the soap over her shoulder blades, then down to the small of her back and the curve of her buttocks.

"That's the plan," he whispered and then pressed his lips to her shoulder and kissed her wet skin. She sighed as he ran the soap down her left arm, and then her right. He pulled her toward him and then circled her with his arms and began to slide the soap over her breasts. Her breath hitched in her throat as a little ball of need burst to life in her lower body. She leaned against him as he continued to leisurely soap her breasts. Each pass of the soap over her taut nipples sent frissons of fire up and down her spine. And when his hand lowered to her stomach, Kayla couldn't help but sag against him.

Her limbs felt like rubber, and when his hand slipped between her legs and he used the soap to massage her mound she was sure she would collapse to the shower floor if his strong arms weren't supporting her.

For a solid week she'd thought about being with him again. And as each day passed with something new getting in the way of their being together, her desire had increased exponentially. At the studio, they played it cool. There were no public displays of affection, but the hot look in his eyes as they rehearsed was enough to set her body on fire. And other than a few very hot kisses as they left work each day, he hadn't touched her the way she was dying for him to.

The way he was touching her now.

When he dropped the soap and slid his finger into her wet heat, she couldn't stop the soft gasp of pleasure that spilled from her lips. He stroked her slowly, expertly, intensifying her need. She leaned her head back against his shoulder as he tortured her deliciously between her legs while his other hand palmed her breast. Hot water slid over them, steaming up the bathroom like a sauna. It was as if they were in their own private paradise where nothing and no one else existed.

Her desire heightening, Kayla began to move her hips in rhythm with the sensuous strokes of his finger. His penis was hard against her buttocks. She could feel how what he was doing to her turned him on, and it only added to her own pleasure. "Oh, God," she moaned and bit her lip when his finger found her clit and massaged it gently. Her body quivered in response, and the sweet tension inside curled even tighter.

"Let go, sweetheart," he whispered hypnotically in her ear. "Come for me. You know you want to."

Hell yes, she wanted to.

"Tell me what you want," he commanded.

"I want to come," she murmured and then moaned again when he gently massaged her sensitive bud. "Oh, God," she whispered breathlessly. "Oh, my God." Her body was on fire, and her sex felt heavy and aching for release. She bucked against his hand, seeking it, dying for it. "Make me come," she commanded in a taut voice that didn't sound like her at all.

"Be happy to," he said with satisfaction, and then he circled her clit teasingly until the pent up desire exploded inside her in wave after wave of mind-blowing ecstasy.

Sean's hand slipped from between her legs and then she felt his hands on her shoulders. As he turned her around, she opened her eyes and met his hot gaze. "I want you," he said in a raw, hoarse voice. "Right now."

"Then take me," she whispered, thrilled at the way his eyes darkened with raw need. Tearing his gaze from hers, he reached for something on the top of the shower stall. She smiled when she saw the foil wrapped condom in his hand. "You planned this?" she asked with a smile as he tore at the wrapper and pulled out the condom.

"All week," he said as he rolled on the condom and then backed her up against the wet tile. The water had started to cool. That was okay though, her body was hot and it felt good. Sliding his hands to her hips, he cupped her butt and lifted her. "Wrap your legs around me," he ordered, and as she did he entered her with one smooth stroke. "Oh, yeah," he murmured huskily. His eyes glittered with desire as he thrust into her and she couldn't look away.

Reaching out with her hands, she braced them

against the tile, trusting he would support her. He did, cupping her buttocks as he continued to slide into her heated center. "Am I hurting you?" he asked as his thrusts became more powerful.

"No," she whispered. The pressure against her clit each time he slid into her was amazingly erotic and extremely pleasurable. "I think I'm going to come again," she said in amazement and cried out as she came for the second time.

"Kayla," Sean's eyes burned into hers as pleasure shook her body. "You are *so* damn beautiful." He let out a hoarse moan and then pulled her closer. He sought her mouth with his as he ground into her. She felt his muscular body shudder and then heard his soft groan of pleasure as his orgasm overtook him. Slipping her arms around his neck, she held him tightly, overwhelmed with emotion. Against her chest she could feel the pounding of his heart and a feeling of peace settled over her. A beat later, he pulled his lips from hers. Their eyes met intimately. "That is—hands down—the best shower I've ever had in my life," he said with a sexy grin.

"IT WORKED, YOU know."

"What worked?" Sean asked. Lying next to him on his bed, Kayla was tucked in his arms. She snuggled closer, trailing her fingertips lazily over his chest. Her touch was a feather light caress, yet he was achingly aware of her with every pore of his body—her nearness, the scent of her body, the heat of her skin.

"Your plan to distract me."

"Plan? I know of no such plan."

"Don't pretend you don't know what I'm talking about."

He glanced down to find her gazing up at him. "The only plan I had tonight was to get you naked." He grinned. "And it worked."

"What worked is that I feel safe with you. And for a little while I forgot about…" she broke off, biting her lip "…about whoever's doing this to me."

The haunted look in her eyes slayed him. At the studio she was pretty good at hiding her feelings, but behind her smile and easygoing manner there was a wariness that hadn't been there before. It pissed him off that some sick bastard had turned her life upside down.

He wanted to keep her safe. Hell, if he thought she'd agree to it he'd ask her to move in with him so he could make sure the nut job stalking her couldn't get to her.

Move in with you? Where did that come from?

Her hand stilled on his chest. "Sean? What's wrong?"

"Nothing," he said quickly.

"You zoned out there for a second." Amusement danced in her eyes. "What were you thinking about?"

Sliding his hand down the curve of her hip, he pulled her closer. She felt like hot silk in his arms. His pulse leapt when her eyes darkened with unspoken desire. "I was thinking of another way to distract you."

"Hmm… I think we're on the same wavelength," she whispered huskily. Her hand inched down to his stomach, and then even lower. He sucked in a breath when she wrapped her fingers around his cock. Her lips curved in a suggestive smile that hinted at all sorts of erotic things. "In fact, I can read your mind."

"Really? What am I thinking?" He lowered his gaze to the lusciousness of her full lips. "Tell me."

"I'd rather show you."

And moments later, when she was using her lips and her tongue to drive him out of his mind with pleasure, he had only one coherent thought…she really could read his mind.

TWO WEEKS LATER, Kayla was thrilled to see her sister pull her rental car into the driveway. Rushing from the kitchen window to the front entry, she punched in the security code to deactivate the alarm and opened the door. As Kelly climbed out of the car, Kayla cut across the lawn to greet her.

"Hey, Sis." Kelly's smile was wide as they embraced by the side of the car.

"It's so good to see you," Kayla said, pulling back and surveying her sister. Within seconds, her fear that Kelly might have relapsed were put to rest. Her sister looked healthy and happy. "How was your flight?"

A slight frown crossed Kelly's face. "Tense. The guys are keyed up about the series with the Dodgers," she said, closing the car door. Kayla followed her to the back of the car. "No one wants to say it, but we've got a lot riding on these games." Kelly popped open the trunk.

"Let me get that," Kayla said, reaching in to pull out her sister's suitcase. "If the Blaze sweep the series they'll be in first place." Kelly closed the trunk and together they walked toward the house.

"Exactly. Not to mention the fact that our rivalry with the Dodgers is one of the most contentious in the league," Kelly said as they walked into the house. Kayla set the suitcase on the entryway floor and after closing and locking the door, punched in the alarm code.

If Kelly had noticed the alarm pad was new she didn't say anything.

"Management specifically requested someone from media relations be down here for all four games," she continued. "I just hope the guys keep their cool. The last thing I need is one of them going off half-cocked like Matt Scanlon does on a regular basis." Kelly shook her head in disgust. "The jerk got booted again two days ago in San Diego."

"I saw that," Kayla said as she and Kelly moved into the kitchen. She'd watched the game with Sean and seen firsthand the frustration on his face as Matt argued with the umpire about a play at the plate and then launched into a heated tirade that finally got him ejected.

"Let's not talk about baseball." Kelly's frown disappeared and a sly smile lit her face. "I want to know what's going on with you." Her sister's eyes twinkled devilishly. "How's Sean?"

"How about some iced tea?" Kayla asked, not sure if she was ready for the third degree about Sean.

"Don't change the subject. You don't have to give me a blow by blow." Kelly's gaze softened. "I just want to know if you're happy."

"I am," she admitted. "I didn't know it could be like this."

"That's because you were with that asshole, Greg." Kelly's dark brows drew together. "The guy blew a gasket if another man looked twice at you, but thought it was a-okay for *him* to screw anything with a pulse."

"I almost didn't give Sean a chance because of him."

Kelly's expression brightened. "So was it those killer green eyes or the rockin' bod that changed your mind?"

"Both," Kayla said with a smile and let out a soft sigh.

"Uh-oh." Kelly grinned. "Someone's got it bad."

Kayla walked around the island while Kelly leaned against the counter. She could feel her sister's penetrating gaze on her as she opened the cupboard door and retrieved two glasses.

"Are things getting serious between you and Sean?" Kelly asked, tucking a lock of hair behind her ear.

She set the glasses on the counter. "I thought you didn't want a blow by blow."

"I don't. But I've never seen you like this with any other guy. You're practically glowing. *And* you're turning red."

Kayla looked up in dismay. Kelly's expression was almost gleeful.

"Oh, yeah." Kelly reached for a glass and flashed a wide smile. "You've got it *real* bad."

SITTING BESIDE KAYLA at The Sky Room in Long Beach, Sean glanced at his watch and wondered where the hell Matt was. Until recently, Matt was the most punctual person he'd ever met. Matt's philosophy had always been that everyone's time was valuable and keeping people waiting was rude and disrespectful. But now Matt was the one who showed up late, if at all. It seemed as if his friend was falling deeper and deeper into a dark abyss he might never emerge from. And it scared Sean to death.

Across from him, Kayla's sister Kelly gazed out the window. They were seated by a window with a beautiful view of Long Beach Harbor in front of them.

Looking at Kayla and her sister, it was easy to see they were related. Kelly had the same heart-shaped face as Kayla and they shared the same features, but where

Kayla's hair and eyes were a dark brown, Kelly's eyes were whiskey colored and her hair light brown and streaked with blonde highlights. She was taller than Kayla by a good four inches and her body was more athletic. Kayla had told him Kelly played softball in high school and college but even if she hadn't mentioned it he would have known it by looking at her. The way she carried herself reminded him of Matt. A strong and confident athlete.

Kayla glanced at him. "Should we wait, or go ahead and order?"

"Wait for what?" Kelly asked, turning from the view.

"I invited my friend Matt to join us." Sean reached for his glass of Pinot Grigio their waiter had recommended. "But he probably had some media obligations after the game. I'm sure he'll be here shortly though." He took a sip. Athough he preferred beer, the wine was very good.

"Media?" Kelly's brows rose and then realization dawned in her eyes. "Is your friend Matt Scanlon?"

"Yes." He set his glass on the table.

Kelly's lips pressed together in a grim line, but she didn't say a word. She didn't have to. Anyone in Kelly's profession would undoubtedly know all about Matt and his downward spiral. And if the trade rumors were true, Kelly had to be afraid that Matt might be traded to the Blaze. And then Matt, and his on and off the field antics, would become her headache instead of the Dodgers'.

Sean heard the noise level in the room heightened over the soft strains of the jazz band playing on the other side of the restaurant. Sean looked up to see Matt standing next to the hostess. He was gazing down at her, his megawatt smile out in full force. The petite blonde was eating it up. Sean was sure that before Matt left the restaurant the hostess would make sure he had her phone number.

"He's here," Sean said as Matt tore himself away from the hostess and sauntered across the restaurant as if he were Moses parting the Red Sea. Along the way, women stared at him with undisguised lust, and the men with admiration and envy. It had always been that way, but until recently Matt hadn't believed his own hype. He'd been humble and hardworking, a model ball player. Now his ego was as big as the Pacific Ocean. The man Sean had known practically all of his life was becoming a stranger to him.

"Sorry I'm late," Matt said when he reached the table. His gaze went immediately to Kayla and the frank appreciation in his eyes irritated Sean. Lifting his arm, he draped it over Kayla's shoulders possessively. "It's nice to finally meet you, Kayla," Matt said smoothly as he pulled his chair out and sat down next to Kelly without even looking at her. Kelly's eyes flickered with annoyance as she shifted in her chair, leaning slightly away from him. "I'm a big fan of your work," Matt added with a suggestive smile that made Sean want to punch him.

"Thank you," Kayla replied politely before glancing at her sister. "This is my sister, Kelly."

Matt turned and gave Kelly a nod. "Nice to meet you." His tone was perfunctory, dismissive even. Kelly's eyes flashed even as she pasted a fake smile on her face and murmured a similar response. Matt swung his gaze back to Kayla. "Did you enjoy the game?"

"Yes. We had great seats right behind the dugout."

Kelly picked up her wine glass. "And our team won. It doesn't get much better than that," she said with a slight curve of her lips before delicately sipping her wine.

Matt's eyes widened as he turned toward Kelly. "You're Blaze fans?" he asked with a scowl.

"Since birth," Kelly said as she set her glass back on the table. "Right, Kay?" she asked her sister. Kayla nodded as Kelly looked back at Matt. "One down, three to go."

"You're not sweeping us." Matt leaned back in his chair and fixed Kelly with his patented stink eye. "You got lucky today."

Kelly shrugged. "Rizzo's pitching tomorrow. And as I recall, you struck out three times the last time you faced him."

Matt's scowl deepened. "Rizzo's an overrated punk."

"Dave Rizzo's won the Cy Young award two times," Kelly countered. "And when the phrase overrated punk is used, he's not the man who comes to mind." The air became thick with tension as their eyes clashed. Sean felt Kayla's gaze on him but he couldn't look away from Matt and Kelly. He'd never seen Matt do anything other than charm women. This was a first.

"The band is amazing," Kayla said, breaking the taut silence. "There aren't many restaurants like this anymore." She looked at the couples dancing on the parquet dance floor and sighed. "And with this Art Deco décor it's almost like we've stepped back in time."

Sean ran his gaze from her upswept hair down to the graceful curve of her neck. After the game, she and Kelly had gone back to Kayla's house to change clothes. She was wearing a light blue dress that hugged her body like a glove. She looked stunning. "Would you like to dance?" he asked. He liked Kelly but she'd been with them all day. He needed some alone time with Kayla.

Her dark eyes lit up. "I'd love to." She looked at Kelly and then Matt. "You don't mind if we leave you for a few minutes, do you?"

"No." Kelly's voice was strained. She gave Matt a cursory glance. "We'll be fine."

Sean noticed Matt's dark expression and hoped his friend would play nice while they were gone. He pushed back his chair, and then reaching for Kayla's hand he pulled her to her feet and led her across the restaurant to the dance floor.

When they stepped onto the dance floor, he slipped his arm around her waist and pulled her close. She rested her hand on his shoulder and met his gaze with worried eyes. "Maybe we shouldn't have left them alone," she said as they began to move to the slow bluesy song.

"They're adults. I think they can handle being alone together for five minutes."

"My sister can be…" she bit her lip "…well, let's just say, she can curse like a sailor and isn't afraid to speak her mind. Especially when provoked."

"Matt's used to women fawning all over him."

"Kelly doesn't fawn over any man."

"Really? I hadn't noticed."

Kayla laughed softly. "She's a lot like Lisa."

"That's scary."

"Stop it," she said, playfully slapping his shoulder.

Sean glanced at the other couples on the small dance floor. Not far from them, an older couple swayed slowly to the music, staring deeply into each other's eyes. Kayla followed his gaze.

"They look happy, don't they?"

"Yeah." He looked from the couple to Kayla. "You look amazing," he said. He slid his hand down the silky fabric of her dress to rest on her lower back. She was wearing that light vanilla-scented perfume again—it was intoxicating. *She* was intoxicating.

"Thank you. So do you." She moved her hand to the lapel of his suit jacket. "This is how people dressed back in the old days when they went out for dinner."

"This was a celebrity hangout back in the day," Sean said. "Elizabeth Taylor, John Wayne and Cary Grant were regulars." He paused. "My mother and father used to come here," he said. "When I was really young I used to watch her get ready to go out." A memory of her putting on her favorite earrings flashed in his mind. "She looked a lot like Grace Kelly."

He saw the curiosity in her eyes but didn't elaborate. Thinking about the past was futile; it didn't change anything. Not the fact that his mom was dead or that he could have prevented it. "There's a bar above the restaurant," he said. "The Up Lounge."

"I'll bet the view is spectacular."

"It is." He let his gaze wander over her face. "But I think the view right here is even better."

"Yes. It certainly is," she said in a husky whisper that affected him just as if she'd kissed him. Awareness thickened his blood and, instinctively, he pulled her closer. She laid her cheek against his shoulder and they moved in unison to the sultry music. Closing his eyes, the only thing he was aware of was the sweet smell of her hair and the warm softness of her body against his. She fit against him perfectly, as if she'd been made just for him.

Lost in the woman he held in his arms, Sean didn't notice the music had stopped until he heard the light applause from the patrons in the restaurant and on the dance floor. Kayla lifted her head and looked up at him. His breath caught in his throat and his heart started to pound when his eyes met hers. They were dark and luminous.

Suddenly, he couldn't breathe. Or speak. Or look away.

He wasn't sure how much time passed. It could have been seconds, or minutes. And it wasn't until the band started to play another more up-tempo number that the spell between them was broken.

"Thank you for the dance," she said in a voice that sounded pretty normal.

How could that be? He felt like one of the Pipeline's giant waves had just crashed over him and sent him hurtling to the ocean floor.

"We should probably go check on Matt and Kelly," she said. Reluctantly, he let her go and when they walked off the dance floor he still hadn't said one damn word.

His mood shifted dramatically when they approached the table and saw Matt and Kelly staring at each other like two gunslingers about to shoot each other dead.

Kelly stood up, her eyes blazing as she looked at Kayla. "I'm going to the ladies' room." Picking up her purse, she gave Matt a withering glare and then marched stiffly away from the table.

"I think I'll go too," Kayla murmured and took off after her sister.

Sean watched her disappear and then sat down across from Matt. "We were gone less than ten minutes. What the hell did you do?" he asked.

Matt gave him a wounded look. "What did *I* do?" He shook his head in disgust. "That, my friend, is a first class bitch."

"You're just pissed because she didn't immediately bow down and offer to suck your dick like most of the women in this town do."

"She's a fucking Amazon." Matt scowled. "I wouldn't let her anywhere near my dick."

"Is that how you talked to her?" Sean asked. "Because if you did, I don't blame her for anything she said."

"How about how she talked to me?" Matt's expression was incredulous. He really believed he was the injured party. "And she's a fucking Blaze fan to boot."

"So is Kayla," Sean pointed out. "And Kelly's not only a fan, she works for the Blaze."

"Doing what?"

"Public relations."

Matt snorted. "Figures."

"I spent most of the afternoon with Kelly," Sean said, meeting Matt's scornful gaze. "And I like her. But more than that, she's Kayla's sister, and Kayla's important to me, so back off or—"

"Or what?" Matt's eyes narrowed.

"Or get the hell out of here," Sean said, keeping his voice low. Their fellow patrons were already paying attention to their table because the Dodgers' star catcher was sitting at it. They didn't need to invite more attention by arguing in public. He leaned forward. "I know you went through hell, but this has got to stop. You're out of control."

Matt's eyes blazed with anger. "Don't analyze me. You're not a shrink."

"You're right, I'm not. But you sure as hell need one."

"And you don't?" Matt asked. "When's the last time you talked to your father?"

Sean tensed. "My father is none of your business. Don't turn this around on me." He leaned back as Matt rose from his chair and stared down at him with steely eyes.

"I'm sick of this." Matt's mouth curled with contempt. "I'm outta here."

"WHAT A PRICK!"

Knowing Kelly's salty vocabulary as well as she did, Kayla knew Kelly was being kind. Looking at her sister's flushed face in the mirror she couldn't remember ever seeing her so worked up over a man.

"Are you okay?" she asked as they washed their hands at the double sink.

"I'm fine," Kelly said as she pulled a paper towel from the dispenser next to her.

"What happened? What did he say to you?

"I don't want to talk about it." Kelly dried her hands and tossed the paper towel into the trash. She opened her purse and pulled out a tube of lipstick. Meeting Kayla's eyes in the mirror she said in a controlled voice, "But I'll say this. Matt Scanlon and his gigantic ego didn't affect me in the slightest."

Kayla almost believed her. Right up until the moment they left the restroom and found Matt striding toward them. He greeted a several fans with his killer smile, but when he reached them his cocky grin faded and his almost black eyes fixed Kelly with a stare so glacial that Kayla shivered. She glanced at Kelly and saw the same frosty edge in her eyes. Her posture was rigid and her fingers were like talons digging into her purse.

Neither of them spoke, they just stared at each other for what seemed like an eternity. And then Kayla realized they were having what amounted to a staring contest, just like she and Kelly used to have when they were kids. Kelly always won.

And she won this time. Matt finally looked away and at her. “Goodnight, Kayla. It was nice meeting you.”

Before she could reply he brushed past them and both she and Kelly watched as he walked over to the blonde hostess and started chatting her up.

“Jackass,” Kelly muttered and then turned to her. Her face was still flushed and her dark amber eyes still glittered with anger. “I need a drink.”

If this was Kelly unaffected Kayla didn’t want to be around her when she *was* affected. Following her sister to the table, she hoped Matt and Kelly didn’t cross paths again. If they did, there was a good chance neither of them would survive.

Nineteen

Shay: It occurred to me today that I've never thanked you for helping me.
Jared: You don't have to thank me.
Shay: Yes, I do. I can honestly say that you're the best man I've ever known.

THREE DAYS AFTER the incident with Matt in the restaurant, Kayla walked Kelly to her rental car, wishing her sister could stay longer but grateful for the time they had been able to spend together. Every night they'd stayed up talking and giggling just as they had when they lived at home. Lisa and Lance had joined them one night and they'd stayed up half the night drinking wine and discussing almost every topic under the sun. Lance was particularly entertaining, and had them in stitches as he regaled them with what he assured them were true stories about the celebrity clients that visited his salon.

After Kelly stowed her suitcase in the trunk, she closed it and looked at Kayla with concern. "You'll be careful?"

"Yes." Kayla nodded. She'd finally told Kelly about the letters and the vandalism of her car. "You saw my new security system," she said and pointed to the cameras now installed in strategic spots on the roof, "and my cameras. It's like a fortress. In fact, I'm thinking a moat and a drawbridge might be in order."

"You goof." Kelly gave her a hug. She held on to her tightly and then pulled back. "I don't feel right keeping this from mom and dad."

"They'll only worry."

"They're parents. They worry about everything." Kelly grinned. "But I'll respect your wishes. Just as you've always respected mine." She was referring to the darker side of her eating disorder and just how much despair she'd been in at the time. "Have I ever thanked you for that?" Kelly asked, her eyes suddenly moist.

"Thanks aren't necessary. We're sisters and friends. I'm here for you always."

"Same here, Sis." Kelly blinked the moisture away and then grinned. "We swept the Dodgers," she said with a triumphant gleam in her eyes. "And the icing on the cake was when Scanlon got ejected in yesterday's game."

Kayla couldn't share her sister's glee. Granted, Matt had acted like an ass at dinner, but she knew how worried Sean was about him, and there was no joy to be had in celebrating Matt's meltdown. Trade rumors were flying fast and furiously and, according to all the baseball analysts, Matt was days away from being traded. According to Sean, Matt could very well lose it if he was traded from the team he'd loved since he was a kid. "Don't gloat," Kayla warned. "Matt could end up being traded to San Francisco."

Kelly's grin faded. "Doug would never allow it." Doug was the team's general manager and had to approve all trades and player acquisitions. "Besides, we've got two catchers, one of which will undoubtedly win rookie of the year. We don't need a third. Especially one with baggage."

"You're probably right," Kayla said as Kelly opened the car door. "But what would you do if it happened?"

Kelly grimaced. "Lose my mind, of course. But, thankfully, San Francisco is one team that doesn't need a back-up catcher. So I'm not going waste my time worrying about it. Besides, even one thought about Matt Scanlon is one thought too many. The man is a Neanderthal."

"But a very hot one," Kayla said, and watched as Kelly's cheeks turned a light shade of pink. "Don't you think?"

"No," Kelly said with disdain and slid into the car. She started the ignition. "I'm not into men with dark hair and obsidian eyes."

Obsidian eyes?

"Whatever you say, Kel," Kayla said, thinking her sister had protested just a bit too much.

As Kelly backed out of the driveway, a brown delivery truck pulled up to the curb. Kelly waved and then disappeared down the street. The driver climbed out of the truck and trudged up the driveway carrying a package the size of a shoebox.

Per Lisa's instructions, Kayla hadn't ordered anything for herself online in a few years. While she wasn't a major star, she was still in the public eye and Lisa had been concerned her credit card and personal information could be compromised. So whenever she saw something online, Lisa ordered it for her and Kayla paid her back. Lisa had ordered the sandals just two days ago. The company's promise of fast delivery at a low cost was obviously no joke. After signing for the package, she crossed the yard eager to see if the sandals were as cute as they'd looked online.

Once inside the house, she activated the alarm and went to the kitchen. Setting the box on the granite countertop, she found her box cutter in the junk drawer and cut through the tape at each end of the box. She set the cutter aside and lifted the lid.

Immediately a foul smell filled the air and when she pulled the tissue paper from the box and saw what looked like a dead rat inside her blood turned to ice and her body started to shake. Forcing herself not to retch, she quickly replaced the lid, and for the first time noticed the precise block lettering on the label. It had Shay's name on it, but her address.

The stalker knew where she lived.

Her cell phone was on the counter. She reached for it with a trembling hand. Sean answered after one ring. "Hi, sweetheart." His voice was warm and solid, and for a moment that gave her comfort.

"I got a package from the stalker."

"What? When?"

"Just now. I was outside saying goodbye to Kelly when the delivery guy drove up. When I signed for it I didn't notice that the label had Shay's name on it. I just took it into the house."

"Did you open it?"

She took in a deep gulp of air, trying to stop herself from freaking out. "There was a dead rat inside."

Sean swore softly. "Call Detective Shelton right away." Sean paused for several seconds. "Damn it, they just called me for rehearsal. Call him now, Kayla. This is the last scene before lunch. I'll be there as quickly as I can."

"I'll call him as soon as I hang up," she promised, not able to control the sudden shaking of her knees.

Naively, she'd thought that maybe the stalker had been the woman at the grocery store and had been spooked by Detective Shelton's visit. But obviously, whoever it was had just been lying low for a while. "I activated my alarm," she said anticipating his next question.

"That's good." Sean's voice was calm and she was grateful. She felt anything but calm. "I'll be there as soon as I can. Kayla, it's going to be all right."

"I hope so," she said in a shaky voice.

After their conversation, Kayla went back to the kitchen and giving the box a wide berth found the card Detective Shelton had given her in her purse. Staring at the box, she placed the call and prayed he or someone from the LAPD would find something in or on the box that would lead them to the sick person tormenting her.

AFTER BREAKING EVERY traffic ordinance in L.A., Sean pulled the Jeep into Kayla's driveway and parked in front of her garage. He'd hoped that whoever it was that was sending the letters had decided to stop. But evidently the person had decided to play an even sicker game. The stalker was letting her know he knew where she lived.

When he got to the front door and she opened it his gut clenched at the haunted look in her dark eyes. She didn't say a word. She just closed the door behind him, punched in the alarm code on the keypad and then turned and stepped into his arms. Holding her, he felt her body shake with quiet sobs and it almost destroyed him. He felt absolutely helpless, something he wasn't used to feeling.

"I'm sorry," she murmured against his chest.

"Don't be." He stroked her back and wished he could

wring the son of a bitch's neck. He'd been useless at the studio, and for the first time since he'd started on the show, he'd phoned in his performance. He'd gone through the motions, reciting his lines as quickly as he could. Bill wasn't happy, but Sean didn't care. All he could think about was getting to Kayla.

"Detective Shelton left about ten minutes ago," Kayla said, lifting her head and meeting his gaze. Wet tears clung to her eyelashes and dampened her cheeks. "He took the box and said he would call me after they've checked it out. They're also trying to track it through the delivery company."

Sean doubted that the sender would have been dumb enough to use a legitimate return address, but then again, some people who thought they were clever turned out not to be that bright. He hoped this person was one of them. "Do you want to come and stay with me?" he asked, wanting to do something—anything—to erase the fear he saw in her eyes.

Her smile was tremulous. "Part of me would like nothing better," she said and then she pressed her lips together and shook her head, "but if I do that then whoever is doing this wins. They'll have driven me from my home." Her eyes hardened. "I can't let that happen."

"I understand. Hey, I have an idea. We're both off tomorrow. Why don't we drive out to my father's house tonight? We can stay in the guest cottage and then do whatever we want tomorrow."

"You're trying to distract me again, aren't you?"

"Guilty as charged. But I do have to check the house." He paused and grinned. "And I think it's time for that surfing lesson I promised you."

"I know what you're trying to do," she said softly, "and I think it's sweet."

"Sweet?" he scoffed but his heart turned over at the tender look in her eyes. "I am *not* sweet."

"Yes, you are," she said with a smile. "And I'd love to go to Pacific Palisades with you. But you may regret it after one surfing lesson. I might end up drowning you."

He stared into her dark as midnight eyes. He was already in danger of drowning.

But it wasn't in the ocean.

THE FAINT SOUND of gulls woke her. Opening her eyes, Kayla felt disoriented but then she remembered. She was in Pacific Palisades. With Sean. Although alone in the king-size bed, she wasn't alarmed. Sean was an even earlier riser than she was. Slipping out of bed, she padded to the small bathroom and after using it she washed her hands and brushed her teeth.

The cottage was self-contained and beautifully decorated with antique furniture and eggplant-colored linens. Opposite the bed was a large window covered by wooden shutters. When they were open, the view of the ocean was just as grand and breathtaking as it was from the deck outside. But they were closed now and the room was dim.

Last night, she and Sean had sat on the chairs on the deck and watched the sunset. Kayla had never seen such a beautiful sight. As the sun dipped below the horizon, the sky became colored with ribbons of pinks and oranges that took her breath away. Watching it with Sean holding her hand had made it even more special. As each day passed her feelings for him were growing stronger, filling her heart with a happiness she'd never known before.

Moving to the door, she stepped out on the deck and found Sean sitting in one of the deck chairs wearing his favorite Dodgers T-shirt and a pair of navy blue sweats. He was staring out at the ocean so intently he didn't even turn when she closed the door behind her.

"Good morning," she said and shivered. The coastal fog wouldn't burn off until around noon and her skimpy sleepwear wasn't enough to ward of the chilly morning air. Sean looked up at her as she halted beside him. He smiled but the smile didn't reach his eyes. "What's wrong?" she asked.

Sean reached for her hand and pulled her to his lap. She settled atop his rock hard thighs as his arms circled around her and held her tightly. "I had a message from Matt on my phone this morning." He sighed and continued, "The Dodgers told him yesterday after the game that they're shopping his contract around. They're trading him."

"Oh, no," Kayla whispered, not all that shocked at the news. "I'm so sorry to hear that. How's he taking it?"

"Not well. He was drunk when he left the message and when I tried to call him this morning he didn't pick up."

"Maybe you should go see him. Didn't you tell me he lives in Santa Monica? That's not far from here." Kayla saw Sean's jaw clench and knew that if he didn't check on Matt he'd worry about his friend all day. "I saw a few books in the cottage. I can sit on the deck and read until you get back."

"Are you sure?"

"Positive."

"Thank you for understanding. I'll wait a bit before leaving. It's still early. We seem to get up at the crack of dawn, don't we?"

"You can blame our hours at the studio," Kayla replied with a smile. "But I've found I like early mornings. Everything is new. It's quiet. You can hear yourself think."

Sean searched her face. "Do you know that one of the first things I noticed about you was your smile?" Surprised, she shook her head and he continued, "You always seemed so happy. Everyone at the studio loves you…"

"Everyone except Rachel," Kayla interrupted, unable to suppress a wry grin.

"She doesn't count," Sean said, lifting a hand to brush her hair back behind her ear. He trailed his fingertips to her cheek to caress her skin. His intimate touch and the tender look in his eyes caused her heart to turn over. "How do you do it? How do you stay so normal in this crazy business?" he asked. "And how is that even this early in the morning you're so damn beautiful it hurts?"

"My parents," Kayla said softly, snuggling against him. His body was warm, warding off the early morning chill. "They raised me, so they get the credit. As for my looks, well, that's not my doing either. I guess Kelly and I are lucky our parents are attractive."

"I'm the lucky one," Sean said huskily. "Because I met you." As their eyes locked, Kayla could no longer deny the depth of her feelings for him. The truth had been staring her in the face for a couple of weeks but for whatever reason she'd chosen not to acknowledge it.

She was completely and totally in love with Sean Barrett and it felt like the most natural thing in the world. Reeling from her realization, she stared at him mutely. She wanted to tell him how she felt and yet something stopped her. She knew exactly what it was. It was the fear of giving her heart to a man who might not feel the same way about her.

"I have an idea," Sean said, his smile finally reaching his eyes.

"Okay, what great idea do you have now?" She returned his smile and noticed the slight stubble on his jaw and how sexy his tousled hair looked in the morning. He always looked gorgeous but there was something about him the morning, an earthiness that stirred her as no other man ever had.

"Let's go back to bed for a while."

"Are you still tired?"

"No." His gaze lowered to her lips. "But I'd like to make love to you." Her heart pounded as he lifted his eyes and met hers. The dark heat in them was mesmerizing. "If you'll let me."

Kayla pressed her lips gently to his. "I'll let you," she murmured as Sean took possession of her mouth just as masterfully as he'd taken possession of her heart.

WHEN MATT OPENED the front door of his beach house, Sean wasn't surprised to see that his friend looked like hell. His eyes were bloodshot, dark stubble shadowed his jaw, and his jeans and polo shirt were rumpled and wrinkled from passing out in a drunken stupor the night before.

"I got your message," Sean said as Matt eyed him warily, hanging on to the door as if it were a lifeline.

"What message?" Matt asked, scrubbing a hand over his jaw.

"Can I come in?"

Matt pulled the door open. "Suit yourself," he said and turned and shuffled into the living room where he collapsed on the sectional sofa in front of the large picture window that looked out onto the beach and the ocean beyond. Closing the door, Sean followed him into the room and saw the empty bottle of Jack Daniels sitting on the coffee table next to a slightly scuffed baseball. No wonder Matt looked like shit. He'd bypassed his usual beer and gone for the hard stuff. "I don't remember leaving you a message." Matt leaned his head back on the sofa and stared up at the ceiling. "What did I say?"

"That the Dodgers are trading you." Sean walked to the window and stared out at the ocean. It was gray just like the clouds above it. The fog had yet to burn off.

"Well, you must be thrilled." Matt's tone was terse. "I mean, you predicted this, right?"

Sean's heart was heavy. Seeing his best friend in so much pain was tough to watch. "I'm not thrilled at all." He turned from the window and folded his arms over his chest. "I'm pissed."

"Join the club," Matt said, lifting his head from the sofa. "Fucking Dodgers."

"I'm not pissed at them, I'm pissed at you."

Matt's red rimmed eyes widened. "So we're back to that?"

"Yes. We're back to that. And if this isn't a wake-up call for you I don't know what is."

"Why'd you come here?"

"You're my friend. I'm worried about you."

Matt let out a loud snort. "Worry about yourself, buddy. I'm fine."

"You don't look fine. You look like shit." Sean felt his anger rising and tried to temper it. Yelling at Matt wouldn't help his cause any. "You've been kicked out of thirteen games and it isn't even the All-Star break yet. You're partying and picking up strange women left and right, and the way you treated Kelly Maxwell the other night was outright rude. You never used to be like this, Matt." Matt stared at him and for a split second Sean saw a flicker of pain in his friend's eyes, but it was gone in a flash and Matt's eyes once again became as hard as granite. "Please get some help," Sean implored him. "Before you lose everything."

"It's too late." Matt's mouth twisted in a painful grimace. "I lost what was most important to me a year ago yesterday." Sean's heart dropped like a stone. He'd been so worried about Kayla that he'd forgotten what day it was. Matt leaned forward to pick up the baseball resting next to the empty liquor bottle. He stared at it with haunted eyes and it was then that Sean noticed the colorful crayon markings on it. "And the only one who remembered was me," he whispered as he squeezed his eyes shut and bowed his head.

Crossing the room, Sean rounded the coffee table and sat down next to his friend. The friend he'd known since they were in first grade. The friend who had always had his back, and because of his own dysfunctional family, was the only one who understood what Sean had gone through when his mother died, and why that day had changed everything between him and his father. Hell, if it hadn't been for Matt, he wasn't sure he would have had any good times at all back then.

“I remember,” Sean said and put his hand on Matt’s back. Matt looked up and turned his head. His face was a mask of misery. He looked broken and it tore at Sean’s gut because until a year ago Matt had been the strongest person he’d ever known. “And if you’re ready to talk. I’ll listen.”

Twenty

Shay: This whole town thinks you're crazy for marrying me.
Jared: I don't care what they say. I don't regret marrying you.
Shay: Wait another month when I'm as big as a house and very, very cranky.
Jared: You'll still be beautiful.

WHEN THE MORNING fog finally burned off, the weather was absolutely beautiful. So beautiful that Kayla had almost forgotten about the dead rat incident until Detective Shelton called to tell her there were no identifiable prints on the box, and the return address provided to the delivery company didn't exist. There was a note inside the box and after the detective had read it to her, Kayla was more angry than frightened. It was the same garbage. The letter writer called her a slut and a whore and told her if she knew what was good for her she'd leave town.

Wearing a pair of fleece sweatpants, T-shirt and a hoodie, Kayla sat on one of the Adirondack chairs on the deck with a book face down on her lap. It was a mystery and interesting, but it was hard to ignore the majestic view in front of her. After every chapter she couldn't help but put the book down to gaze at the white capped waters of the Pacific Ocean.

Sean had been gone for several hours, but before he left to see Matt he'd made love to her with such tenderness that it had taken her breath away. She wasn't sure if it was because of her newly acknowledged feelings for him or not, but this morning the connection between them had seemed more intense than ever before.

Hearing steps on the stone pathway that led from the house, Kayla turned in the chair expecting to see Sean. But it wasn't him, and when she recognized the man that rounded the cottage her jaw dropped.

"Well, this is an intriguing surprise." James Barrett put his hands on his hips and stared at her with undisguised amusement.

Shocked, Kayla grabbed the book and pushed herself up from the chair. "Mr. Barrett," she said, taken aback by his arrival. Sean hadn't said a word about his father returning from New York. "I can explain," she began but then snapped her mouth shut when he lifted his hand and gave her a good humored smile.

"No need, Ms. Maxwell, I know who you are."

"You do?"

James Barrett smiled, and when he did Kayla could see where Sean got his good looks from. He had his mother's blonde hair and green eyes, but other than that he looked much like his father. The man was close to sixty, but he was still extremely attractive.

"You're Kayla Maxwell, and you're currently costarring with my son on *A New Dawn*." James moved toward her.

"You watch the show?" Kayla asked, clutching the book tightly in her hands.

"Please," James motioned to her chair, "sit down. Do you mind if I sit with you for a bit?"

"No," Kayla said, sinking to the chair. "This is your house after all."

James Barrett settled in the chair next to her and Kayla could hardly believe it. Other than her audition with Steven Spielberg, she had never been one to get star struck. But she was now. How could she not be? The man sitting next to her was as revered as DeNiro, Pacino and Hanks.

"I didn't see Sean's Jeep in the driveway," James commented. His eyes were blue. A piercing blue that seemed to see right through her.

"He went to see his friend Matt." Kayla sat primly in her chair, holding the book securely on her lap. "He should be back soon."

James shook his head. "I heard the news. Matt must be devastated. Both he and Sean have been Dodgers' fans since they were kids." Lifting his leg, he rested his ankle on his knee. He was dressed in jeans and a deep blue cotton shirt. He seemed relaxed and not what she expected. From how Sean described him she thought he would be austere, distant and not friendly at all. "May I call you Kayla?" James asked.

"Of course."

"Kayla, I think you have a tremendous amount of talent."

Stunned, Kayla stared at him. "Thank you." She looked around suspiciously. "Am I on *Punk'd*?" she asked. This was just too surreal to be happening.

James looked confused. "I'm not sure what that is."

"It's kind of like that old show *Candid Camera*," Kayla explained. "Only with celebrities."

"Oh." James' lips curved. "I see. Well, suffice it to say, the only cameras on the estate are security cameras." He paused, assessing her with his startling blue eyes. "How long have you been acting?"

"Since high school."

"Your technique is effortless. And you listen." James rested his elbows on the arms of the chair. "That's a very important skill. Sean has that gift as well."

"I know. I love working with him. He's a very giving actor." Kayla paused and wasn't sure if she should ask the question she was dying to ask. "Do you really watch the show?"

"Of course. My son is on it so I make it a point to catch it when I can."

"Why do you let him believe you don't watch it?" Kayla asked, brushing back a lock of windswept hair from her forehead hoping she wasn't being too forward. "He thinks you're embarrassed that he's on a soap."

"Acting is acting," James replied with a shrug. "And I would never begrudge anyone in my field a job. They're hard to come by. But I happen to believe that Sean hasn't even come close to realizing his full potential." James sighed. "Sean is a natural actor. I had to learn my craft. But for Sean it comes easily, just as I suspect it does for you."

"I don't know about that," Kayla protested and then realized what he was doing. "You didn't answer my question."

James tilted his head. "What question was that?"

"Why do you let Sean believe you don't watch *A New Dawn?*"

"My son and I have a very complicated relationship," James replied after several seconds. "Which I'm sure you know since you're involved with him."

"How do you know we're involved?"

"You're here, aren't you? Sean has never brought a woman to this house." He smiled. "But even if he hadn't, the heat between the two of you practically ignites the screen. Sparks like that don't fly unless there's an intense attraction."

Kayla felt her cheeks start to warm. "I can't believe you picked up on that."

James chuckled. "Everyone's picked up on it, Kayla. My assistant watches the show and she tells me you and Sean are the hottest couple in the daytime world right now."

"Our characters have caught on," Kayla acknowledged. "You still didn't answer my question." He seemed to be an expert at changing the subject.

"I know, and I'm not going to." His smile faded. Suddenly he looked much older and somewhat vulnerable. "The person I should be talking to is Sean. There are some things we need discuss." James shifted his gaze to the ocean, his expression filled with sadness. "And it's a discussion that's long overdue."

SEAN GOT A bad feeling the moment he pulled the Jeep into the circular driveway and saw his father's Mercedes SUV parked in front of the garage. He knew for a fact his father had taken it to the airport. He did that when he was flying private, not commercial. And these days James Barrett always flew private.

After parking the Jeep, he decided to go through the house instead of around the back. He'd have to see his father eventually, so it was probably best get it over with as quickly as possible. Using his key, he unlocked the door and entered the foyer. As he closed the door, he heard the sound of laughter. Feminine laughter. Familiar feminine laughter.

He crossed the foyer and made his way through the formal living room but stopped just before entering the kitchen when he heard Kayla's voice.

"What happened after you saw the movie?"

"I told Steven that I forgave him for not casting me as Indy. Harrison was perfect in the role. I can't imagine the film without him in it."

"It's one of my favorite movies."

"Mine too," his father replied.

"I auditioned for Mr. Spielberg once," Kayla said. Sean gritted his teeth. Why the hell was she being so chummy with his father? "I was a nervous wreck and didn't get the part."

"He's actually a very nice person," his father said. "Steven is quite fond of Sean. In fact, just a few months ago he was interested in Sean for a role in a mini-series he's producing for HBO."

Okay, that was it. He'd heard enough. Clenching his fists, he strode into the kitchen. Kayla and his father were sitting at stools on the far side of the marble covered island in the middle of the room and both looked at him with surprise when he walked in.

Kayla spoke first. "How's Matt?"

"Better than he was last night," Sean replied looking from her to his father. "When did you get home?"

"A couple of hours ago."

"I thought the play ran through August." Sean crossed his arms over his chest and studied his father. He hadn't seen him since Christmas. He looked older than he remembered. His light brown hair was now almost completely gray, but on him it looked good.

"The producers decided to go dark for two weeks. When I go back to New York the run will be extended through September." James's penetrating eyes held his. "I thought I'd use the time off to spend some time here at the house. I was hoping to talk to you."

"I can't imagine what you and I have to discuss," Sean said and heard Kayla's soft gasp. She probably thought he was being rude. But he didn't care. James Barrett wasn't *her* father, she had no clue what his life had been like in this house after his mother had died.

"More than you think," his father replied cryptically. "But now's not the time."

Mentally drained from his talk with Matt, Sean looked back at Kayla. "Go get your things, we're leaving."

"But…" she began.

"We're leaving," he interrupted her in a tone much harsher than he intended. Kayla dark eyes flashed with annoyance, but she slid off the stool and left the kitchen through the back door.

"For Christ's sake, Sean, don't take it out on the poor girl for having a conversation with me. She was just being polite."

"Don't tell me what to do," Sean looked back at his father. "And don't think that you can get to me through her."

"I wouldn't do that," James looked at him with a wounded expression. "You really must hate me."

Unmoved, Sean stared at him. "Hate requires emotion. And I don't have enough emotion for you to feel hatred, or anything else." Taking a deep breath, he tried to calm himself. "The plumbing issue was resolved. The refrigerator is pretty bare. You might want to go into the village if you want to eat tonight."

"Thank you for looking after the house."

"Mom loved this place. I did it for her, not you," he said, dying to get away from the house now that his father was back. "I'll wait out front for Kayla." Turning, he moved toward living room.

"Sean, hold it right there." Surprised at his father's brusque tone, he stopped in his tracks and turned to face him. "We're going to talk. It won't be tonight because Kayla isn't a part of this, but before I go back to New York, we're going to hash this thing out."

"What thing?"

"You and me."

"There is no you and me," Sean said sadly. "There hasn't been since Mom died."

FOR THE FIRST time since she'd met Sean the silence between them was uncomfortable. He'd barely spoken a word since they'd left his father's house and that bothered her. In her family they talked things out when they were angry or upset. Her parents' motto was never go to bed mad and she'd always tried to live by their example.

"Are you okay?" she asked, finally breaking the silence.

"I'm fine," he replied, not taking his eyes off the road. They were on the Santa Monica freeway heading back to their side of town.

"Are you angry that I was talking to your father?"

"It's a free country." He shot her a cursory glance. "Talk to whomever you want."

"He was very nice," she tried again. She thought about telling him that his father watched the show and had for ten years. But that was between James and Sean. They had issues to work out. It seemed like his father wanted to try, but Sean didn't.

"Good for you," Sean said. "The great James Barrett actually talked to you. Did you get his autograph too?"

"If you're implying that I'm some sort of star struck groupie you couldn't be more wrong." Staring at his rigid profile, Kayla felt anger start to simmer inside of her. "You're not going to give him a chance, are you?"

Sean jerked his head around and met her gaze. His eyes were as hard as diamonds. "He doesn't deserve a chance. You met him for the first time today. I've known him for thirty years." He looked back at the road. "You need to stay out of it. You have no clue what you're talking about."

"Fine," she said and stared at the car in front of them. "But you only have one father, Sean. He's not going to live forever and when he's gone you may regret not trying to bridge the gap between you. And furthermore, I believe in second chances."

"Let it go," Sean said in a low and controlled voice. "Please."

"Whatever you want," she said curtly and they rode in silence all the way to Atwater Village.

The minute he pulled to a stop in her driveway, she unbuckled her seatbelt and opened the door. "Don't get out," she said and climbed out. "I'll see you at the studio on Monday," she added and moved to close the door.

"Kayla. Wait," he said just as the door shut. Knowing she was being childish, she hurried to her front door and pulled her key from her purse. She heard his door open but didn't look back. Instead she unlocked the door and stepped inside. After disarming the alarm, she went to close the door and found him standing on the threshold.

"May I come in?" he asked. Seeing the tension etched on his face, she softened and nodded. "Thank you," he said as he came inside.

"Would you like some water?" she asked after she closed the door and reset the alarm. "I'm thirsty."

"Sure," he said and followed her to the kitchen. After flipping on the light, she put her purse on the counter and retrieved two bottles of water from the fridge. "Thanks." He twisted the cap off and took a long drink. Opening her bottle, she took a sip and met his contrite gaze over the top of her bottle. "I'm sorry," he said, leaning against the island countertop. "I've been acting like a jerk ever since I got back from Matt's."

"Was he in bad shape?" she asked, forgetting his father for the moment.

"Yes, but for the first time in a year he opened up and talked to me."

"That's encouraging." Kayla took another sip of water. Sean set his water on the counter and reached up to rub his eyes with his forefinger and thumb. He looked tired, and she tried to put herself in his shoes. He'd just had an emotional scene with Matt, and then came back to the house to find his father had unexpectedly returned home. The father he didn't get along with.

"I'm sorry too," she said. "For pushing you about your father. It's not my place. What happens between you and your father is between the two of you."

Sean lowered his hand and met her eyes. "I know you mean well, and I really do appreciate that."

She picked at the plastic wrapper on her bottle. "I guess we just had our first official fight."

The corners of his mouth tilted upward. "And we survived it."

"Actually, it was more of a tiff than a fight."

"Damn, I was hoping for some make-up sex," he said with a roguish grin.

That sexy grin of his got to her every time. She smiled back at him. "You're too tired for make-up sex."

"Maybe, but I won't be tomorrow morning," he said and moved to take the bottle from her hand. He set it on the counter and then reached for her hand. The sexy grin was gone, and in its place was the same vulnerable look she'd seen on his father's face earlier in the day. It tugged at her heart.

"I'm not proud of how I behaved tonight. I'm sorry you had to witness it." He rubbed his thumb gently over the back of her hand. "My father and I have a very complicated relationship."

"It's more than just him disapproving of you being on a soap opera, isn't it?

His eyes flickered with surprise. "Yes. Much more."

"Have you ever talked to him about it?" she asked, remembering James Barrett's cryptic words.

"There's nothing to discuss."

Kayla suspected it had something to do with his mother, but she wouldn't press him. Sean's eyes softened. "I know I don't deserve it after the way I've acted, but can I stay with you tonight?"

She nodded, knowing she couldn't send him away. "Yes."

"Thank you," he said huskily and then pulling her close, he held her tightly. "I need you," he whispered.

THE FOLLOWING TUESDAY, Kayla was in her dressing room waiting to be called for taping when the familiar strains of "Who Can it Be Now" played on her cell phone. Picking it up from the desk, she glanced at the number before answering.

"Hi, Kel," she said, putting aside the book she'd been reading.

"I have bad news," Kelly said, took a deep breath and then continued, "Rick Taylor was riding his damn motorcycle—the one he was told not to, by the way—and was hit by a drunk driver on the Bay Bridge."

"Oh, my God. Is he all right?"

"He's got a broken leg, several cracked ribs, and a broken collarbone. He's lucky to be alive." Kelly's sigh was heavy. "He's out for the rest of the season."

"But he'll be back next year, right?"

"The doctors don't see why not. He's young and in excellent physical condition. If he follows their orders he should be back for spring training."

"That's good news."

"For him. But not for us," Kelly's tone was ominous. "I think the team is going to pick up Matt Scanlon's contract."

"Do you know that for sure?"

"No, but that's the rumor. With Taylor out for the year, we need another catcher. And he's available." There was a long pause. "Kay, the man is not only a jerk, he's disruptive in the clubhouse. As much as we need a catcher, having him on the team isn't going to help us."

"It's not a done deal yet."

"I know. Damn it, my desk phone is ringing. I'd better answer it. It could be Doug calling. I'll keep you posted. Love you."

"Love you too," Kayla said and was about to put

her phone down when it rang again. This time it was her normal ring tone so she knew it wasn't family. She glanced at the caller ID and saw it was her agent. As she was about to answer it, she heard her name on the loudspeaker and didn't take the call. Bill was in a testy mood today and she as sure as hell didn't want to make it worse by being late to the set. Bill on a rampage was never a good thing—for anyone.

IT WAS RARE for Sean to have a Tuesday off, and even more rare for Matt to have one too. But it was the All-Star break and with no regularly scheduled games for any team in the league, his friend had several days off. Another thing that was rare. Matt had been voted into the All Star game every year since his rookie year. It seemed his bad behavior wasn't going unnoticed by his fans.

As he pulled the Jeep into an empty parking space near the beach, he thought it odd that Matt had called to invite him to Huntington Beach to catch a few waves. Odd because when he'd left Matt at his beach house after their talk, Sean wasn't sure if Matt had hit rock bottom, or if his downhill slide wasn't quite complete. Maybe he'd find that out today.

After slipping on his wetsuit, he carried his board to the beach and was soon paddling out past the breakers. There were several surfers spread out evenly in the water but Sean recognized his friend right away and headed for him. Drawing even with Matt, he maneuvered around so that he was facing the shore and then sat up and straddled his board.

"I wasn't sure you'd come," Matt said, staring at the

beach. "I haven't been very good company for a pretty long time."

Sean didn't contradict him. Matt was right. Being around him for the past year had been tough.

"Thank you for checking on me last weekend."

"You'd do the same for me." Sean braced his hands on his board as a large swell wobbled it.

"The Blaze are picking up my contract. I'm going to San Francisco after the All-Star break." Matt turned and met his stunned gaze. "I've played my last game in a Dodgers uniform."

Sean wasn't quite sure what to say. He hated the thought of Matt not being a Dodger. And to be traded to a team both of them had despised since they were kids was like adding insult to injury. But on the other hand, he'd still get to play ball. "I'm sorry, man."

"Don't be. I brought it on myself."

"When did you find out?"

"When I was driving over here. My agent called and gave me the news." Matt trailed his hand in the water and then used it to slick back his hair. "Rick Taylor was in a motorcycle accident last night. He's out the rest of the season. The Blaze need another catcher. They can't finish the season with just their number two guy."

"That sucks. Taylor was a shoe-in for rookie of the year. He's a helluva a catcher. He reminds me of you your first year."

"Yeah. He's that good." Matt grinned.

Sean laughed. "Still modest, I see."

"I leave the day after tomorrow." Matt's expression turned somber. "I think this may be for the best. I need to be away from L.A. for a while. The memories here are still pretty raw."

Sean breathed a sigh of relief. Maybe, just maybe, Matt was ready to turn things around.

"You'll keep in touch, right?"

"Of course." Matt held his gaze. "You're my best friend. I'm sorry for the shit I put you through this past year. You didn't deserve it."

The silence between them was filled with unspoken emotions. The bond between them had been strained but it hadn't broken. "I'm still rooting for the Dodgers," Sean finally said.

Matt's laugh was booming, and for the first time in a year, Sean knew his friend was going to be all right.

Twenty-One

Shay: You think I'm beautiful?
Jared: Yes.
Shay: You're not so bad yourself.
Jared: I get that a lot.

BEFORE LEAVING THE studio for the day, Kayla stuck her head inside Amanda's office. "You wanted to see me?"

Amanda turned from her computer screen and nodded. "I want to update you on the activities at Fab Fan Weekend."

"I can't wait to go to Savannah," Kayla said, stepping inside her office.

Swiveling her chair around, Amanda said, "Great, because I think you and Sean both being there has increased ticket sales. Not only do the viewers love your characters together, they're thrilled you're dating in real life."

"I'm pretty thrilled about that myself."

Amanda's brows rose and she smiled. "Really? I never would have guessed."

"Funny." Kayla grinned. "What's the plan for Savannah?"

"You leave a week from tomorrow." Amanda picked up a sheet of paper on her desk and glanced at it. "The airfare and lodging have been paid for by the network. On Friday you have the morning free, but then there's a luncheon with the contest winners from *Soap Opera Journal*. Friday evening there's an informal dinner and Q&A session for all the actors invited to the event."

"That sounds fun." She glanced at the clock on the wall. She still had plenty of time before meeting Sean at Cheech's. "What about Saturday?"

"The morning and afternoon are set aside for fan events. They're meet and greets like that one you went to in Van Nuys. Saturday night is the formal dinner. Several awards will be given out." Amanda looked up. "You've won three of them."

"What? You're kidding!"

"Nope. The readers of both *Soap Opera Journal* and its sister publication *Soap Scoop* are sponsors along with the network. They opened an online poll two months ago that closed last week. You won for best newcomer, best actress, and both you and Sean won for best couple."

"Wow. That's amazing considering the writers are taking things pretty slowly."

"The audience knows it's coming and judging by the responses on the viewer comment line they can't wait for Jared and Shay to get together. I'm glad Ken's not rushing it." Amanda's lips twitched with amusement. "By the time Jared and Shay admit they're in love with each other the viewers will be so excited they'll have a spontaneous orgasm."

Kayla burst out laughing, and after Amanda finished updating her about the event and handed her an itinerary she left the studio. Walking across the parking lot, she saw Rachel about to get into her sports car. It was parked next to her Mustang, which had been repainted. The body shop had done an excellent job. The hateful words were gone and the new paint gleamed in the afternoon sun.

"How'd you do it?" Rachel stared at her over the roof of her car. "How did you rig the voting for the awards you won?"

"Are you serious?" Kayla halted behind her car. "I didn't rig anything."

Rachel rolled her eyes. "Don't play Miss Innocent with me. There's no way you could beat me in any category unless the voting was rigged."

Good Lord, the woman's ego was huge.

"You're out of your mind." Kayla moved to the side of her car, digging her keys out of her purse.

"You think you're better than me, don't you?"

Looking up from her purse, Kayla saw malice in Rachel's blue eyes. "No. I don't," she said, unlocking her car.

"You won't be around long," Rachel snapped. "I've been on *A New Dawn* for six years. I have more experience, and more talent than you'll ever have."

"If you say so." Kayla opened the door and tossed her purse and the folder Amanda gave her inside.

Rachel's mouth twisted in an ugly grimace. "And furthermore, once Sean is done with you, he'll turn to me so fast it'll make your head spin."

Bracing her hand on the door frame, Kayla met Rachel's frigid stare. "Jealousy isn't a very attractive quality, Rachel."

Rachel's mouth gaped open. "Me? Jealous? Of you?" She let out a loud snort. "And you call *me* crazy?"

Deciding to not give Rachel what she wanted—a reaction—she feigned a smile. "I'd love to stay and chat but I'm meeting Sean for dinner. Have a nice evening," she said and got into the car. Driving away, she looked in the rear view mirror to find Rachel watching her drive away.

Turning the corner, Kayla couldn't help but think that her life was becoming one big soap opera. She had a stalker, *and* a jealous co-worker.

What was next? Amnesia?

AN HOUR LATER, Kayla sat at a table at Cheech's. Sean sat across from her, and in between them was a large pepperoni pizza.

"Matt's been traded to San Francisco," Sean said before taking the last bite of his first slice.

"It's a done deal?" she asked. "I haven't heard a peep out of Kelly."

"He found out this morning."

"How's he taking it?"

"Better than I thought."

"I'm sure Kelly's not. I'll call her before I go to bed. She's going to need someone to vent to." She was about to pick up her pizza when her cell phone rang. Pulling it from the side pocket of her purse, she looked at the screen. "Oh damn. I forgot to call Donald." She looked up. "My agent." The phone rang again. "Do you mind?"

Sean shook his head and reached for another piece of pizza.

"Donald," she said putting the phone to her ear. "I'm so sorry. I saw you called right before rehearsal and then forgot to call you back. What's up?"

"Not a problem, Kayla. I had meetings with clients most of the day." Donald Carter had been her agent since she'd moved to Los Angeles. "I got a call from a casting agent working with Amblin."

"Amblin? That's Steven Spielberg's production company," she said and met Sean's curious gaze. "This sounds like good news."

"It is," Donald said with the same upbeat enthusiasm that had convinced her to sign with him seven years ago. "They'd like you to come in for an audition. The actress they originally went with has been let go. The details are sketchy. I heard something about rehab." Donald paused. "Anyway, someone over there has seen you on the soap and wants you to come in. Are you interested?"

"Am I interested?" Kayla asked and then laughed. "What do you know about the part?" She gave Sean a thumb's up sign and grinned.

"The character's an Army nurse. That's all I know. The project's a twelve part mini-series about Pearl Harbor. It'll be on HBO."

"When's the audition?"

"Friday. Will that be a problem?"

"Not at all. I'm off on Friday."

"That's a good omen." Donald was very superstitious. "I can send over a courier with the audition script tonight, or first thing tomorrow morning. What works best for you?"

"You can send the script over in the morning. I'll be at the studio at seven," Kayla said, excitement coursing through her body. A role in a Steven Spielberg production was a huge deal.

After Donald said his goodbyes, Kayla shoved her phone in her purse. "I have an audition on Friday."

Sean set his half-eaten pizza on his plate. "So I heard. For Amblin, right?"

"Yes." She pumped her fist in the air. "This is so exciting."

"That's interesting." He leaned back in his chair and pinned her with a hard stare. "Right after meeting my father you land an audition for one of his best friends' projects."

Kayla frowned. "What's your point?"

"The timing's a little suspect." His eyes narrowed. "Don't you think?"

"The other actress was fired."

"Isn't that convenient?"

"Donald said someone over at Amblin has seen me on the show and wants me to audition. They haven't offered me the role. It's just a reading."

"Oh, you'll get it. Don't you see? My father is using you."

"How would your father benefit from me being cast in—"

Sean slapped his hand on the table. She flinched as the glasses shook and the silverware rattled. "To get to me!"

"What the...?" She stared at him. "You're being paranoid."

"And you're being naïve," he shot back. "You're a damn fool if you take this audition."

"You can't be...Sean." Her blood turned cold. "This is the chance of a—"

"It's a set-up." His voice was flat, his green eyes unyielding. "Rachel would kill for this."

"What does *that* mean?"

"My father's connections...she'd do it in a heartbeat."

"I'm not Rachel!"

"Then prove it."

Furious at his demand as well as the unflattering comparison to Rachel, Kayla fumbled for the strap of her purse. "Are you so filled with…with resentment that you would ask—*no demand*—that I sacrifice my dreams on the off chance that your father may have put in a good word for me?"

"So you do believe he recommended you."

"No, but if he did maybe it's because he believes I'm talented. Did you ever think of that?"

"My father doesn't know you. You're just one of hundreds of actresses in this town." Sean's words were cutting. "I doubt he's seen *Halloween Hell*, and he wouldn't be caught dead watching *A New Dawn*."

Rising from the table, she stared down at him. "Your father knows exactly who I am. He watches the show."

Sean's eyes widened and then narrowed. "That's bullshit."

"Ask him." Throwing down her napkin, she held his irate gaze. "Oh, and by the way. Not everything is about you," she said and turned and, without a backward glance, stalked toward her car.

Not everything is about you.

Pacing back and forth in his dressing room holding his script, Sean replayed Kayla's angry words over and over in his head.

It was so damn obvious what his father's intentions were. How could Kayla be so unaware? For years his father had been trying to get back into his life and control him. The minute James Barrett had met Kayla he saw his chance to worm his way back in. Well, it wasn't going to happen. Not in this lifetime.

Sean slapped his script down on the desk in the corner and scrubbed a hand over his jaw. His father wasn't stupid—he'd give him that. If anyone could have convinced him to give his father a chance, it was Kayla.

A soft knock at the door startled him. He turned and crossed the small room. Opening the door, he found Kayla on the other side.

"We need to talk," she said. She looked fresh and beautiful. Obviously their argument hadn't prevented her from getting a good night's sleep. Unlike him.

"You're right," he said, stepping aside so she could enter, "we do." After closing the door he turned to face her. "Are you here to tell me you're not going to the audition on Friday?"

"Actually." Her chin angled up and she met his gaze. "I was hoping we could have a rational discussion about the matter."

"Are you implying I wasn't rational last night?" he asked, putting his hands on his hips, glowering at her. "I know my father a lot better than you do. For the past ten years he's tried his best to insinuate himself into my life. He couldn't bother with me after my mom died and then he decided to start playing dear old dad." Sean ran a frustrated hand through his hair. "But it was too late. I took the job on the soap, left his house, and never looked back."

Kayla met his gaze unflinchingly. "Oh, you looked back."

"What the hell does that mean?"

"You told me yourself you've spent holidays with him. You looked after his house, and even took care of his plumbing problem last week. You didn't cut him out of your life. Underneath all the anger and resentment you're carrying around there's a part of you that cares about him."

"Are you analyzing me?" Clenching his fists, he moved to stand in front of her. "Sweetheart, you have no idea what you're talking about."

"I know that if you hated your father as much as you want me to believe, you wouldn't acknowledge him at all."

Her words stung, and hit closer to home than he wanted to admit. Instinctively, he struck back. "I should have known you were too good to be true." Hurt flickered in her eyes but he went on, driven by a force beyond his control. "You're an amazing actress, Kayla. And I bought it hook, line and sinker."

Her brow furrowed. "Bought what?"

"That sweet innocent 'girl next door' persona you've got down pat," he said. "You played me like a fiddle." He paused. "Tell me, did you write those letters and send them to yourself?"

"What?"

"Is there really a stalker? Or did you make it all up?" She stared at him wordlessly. Leaning forward, he went for the jugular. "Did you fuck me to get to my father? Was that your end game?" Her face blanched. He quickly banished the voice inside of his head that was telling him he was going too far. "Are you going to fuck him too?"

"How dare you!"

Her hand blurred toward his face in a stinging slap. Her eyes were black with rage—he never imagined he would see her like that.

"I'm done."

"Kayla—"

"No one talks to me like that. Not anymore. Not ever again." She brushed past him toward the door, but turned back. "Obviously Matt isn't the only one with issues," she said in a cold flat voice. "You might want to think about that. Before it's too late."

"What the hell does that mean?"

She didn't say a word. Instead she opened the door and then slammed it behind her when she walked out. The sound reverberated painfully in his heart and he was left alone in the sudden overwhelming silence of the dressing room.

ON FRIDAY MORNING, Kayla sat clutching her script in her hands as she waited to be called in for her audition. Across from her, the receptionist was on the phone calling agents and politely telling them that their clients didn't get whatever role they had auditioned for. She hoped Donald wouldn't be getting one of those regret calls after *her* audition.

"That must be tough," Kayla said when the receptionist finished with her last call.

"It was hard at first." The redhead smiled. "I feel bad for the agents. They're the ones who have to break it to their clients." She paused. "If you get the part will you leave *A New Dawn*?"

"You watch the show?"

"I love it. Is Sean Barrett as hot in person as he is on TV?"

Kayla's heart squeezed painfully. She didn't want to think about Sean but he was all she'd been thinking about since their heated argument. Yesterday they'd had a scene together and she could barely get her lines out. Bill had looked at her with concern and after Sean walked off the set when the scene was over she'd barely been able to contain her tears.

She noticed the receptionist staring at her expectantly. "Yes," she said. "He's very hot."

The phone buzzed and the receptionist picked it up. The call was short. She hung up and pointed to a door to Kayla's left. "They're ready for you." She smiled. "Good luck. I'm rooting for you."

"Thank you." Kayla stood up and smoothed a hand down the front of her dress. Taking a deep breath, she turned and opened the door.

Thirty minutes later, Kayla uttered her last line and waited. There was silence in the room and then the casting director leaned to his left and whispered something to the woman sitting next to him.

"Nice touch with the hair," he said after they were done conferring. "And the dress."

She lifted her hand to her hair. Lance had set it in a popular style from the late '30s. She'd found the dress at a vintage store and thought it looked like something an Army nurse would wear when she was off duty in Honolulu.

"You gave an excellent reading," he continued. "We're very impressed."

"Thank you." She smiled at them. "And thank you for the opportunity."

The woman shifted in her chair and then said, "If we were to cast you would there be a conflict with *A New Dawn*?"

"I spoke to the executive producer and she said if I got the part they would work around your shooting schedule."

The woman smiled. "Good to know."

"We'll be calling your agent with our decision." The casting director got up from his chair and moved toward her. "And we really appreciate you coming in on such short notice." He escorted her to the door. He put his hand on her arm. "I meant what I said. We were impressed." He opened the door and winked. "See you soon."

When the door closed behind her, Kayla gave a farewell wave to the receptionist—who was on the phone again—and then rushed out of the office, her heart pounding with excitement. Once outside, she pulled her phone out of her purse and scrolled through her contact list until she got to Sean's name. She was about to press the call button when moisture welled in her eyes. She couldn't call him. He didn't want to talk to her. He thought she was using him to get to his father. Shoving her phone back into her purse, she walked to her car, not bothering to wipe the tears from her cheeks.

THE NIGHT BEFORE she was leaving for Savannah, Kayla was packing her suitcase when her cell phone rang. The melodious sounds indicated it was a member of her family. She hoped it wasn't her mom.

Picking the phone up off of the nightstand she breathed a little easier when she saw it was her sister. "Hi, Kel," she said, sinking to the bed and leaning back against the soft pillows piled against the headboard.

"I just wanted to call before you left for Savannah. How are you?"

"Hanging in there."

"Did you tell Mom about you and Sean?"

"Nope. I can't go there yet. I'll tell her when I get

back." She paused. "I was just starting to pack. How's everything with you?"

"Just peachy." Kelly's tone indicated anything but.

"What's going on?"

"Well, as you can imagine, the media is going crazy over the fact that the Blaze have acquired Matt Scanlon." Kelly sighed. "I was assigned the task of scheduling interviews for him but he's being difficult. He told me point blank he's not doing any interviews. His exact words were 'I'm here to play ball, not spill my guts to a bunch of reporters.'"

"Did he say anything about what happened at the restaurant?"

"No, and I doubt he will. The guy's a first class jerk." Kelly paused. "Let's not talk about him. It just makes me angry. Have you talked to Sean?"

"We had a few scenes this week, but we haven't talked other than that." Kayla stared up at the ceiling.

"He hasn't apologized for what he said to you?"

"No. Obviously he feels he has nothing to apologize for." Remembering his hurtful words, Kayla's heart clenched with pain. "I can't believe he thinks I would fake having a stalker. Or that I would sleep with him to get to his father."

"I don't think he really believes that. He has to make you the bad guy because he can't deal with whatever his issues are with his dad."

"You sound like a shrink," Kayla said with a smile.

Kelly chuckled. "You think?" She paused. "Is it really over between you two?"

"It appears to be. Other than rehearsal and taping he's avoiding me."

"Men are such babies."

"To be honest, I've been avoiding him too. When we have scenes I can barely look at him."

"Because it hurts too much?"

"No. Because when I look at him all I can think about are new and creative ways to kill him."

Kelly let out a bark of laughter. "Join the club. That's how I feel when I look at Matt Scanlon."

"At least Matt didn't call you a whore." After a long silence, Kayla said, "Kel?"

"Sorry. I took a sip of water," Kelly said, clearing her throat. "Maybe you two can talk while you're in Savannah. I don't like what Sean said either, but it was in the heat of the moment. Things between you may be salvageable."

"I doubt it," Kayla said glumly. "I don't think there's any way to come back from being called a whore."

MUCH TOO EARLY the next morning, Kayla followed the driver of the black Town Car to the curb stifling a yawn and clutching a cup of desperately needed coffee.

There would be no thinking about Sean today. In fact, it was going to be Sean free day starting the second she got in the car. She smiled at the driver as he opened the door.

"Surprise!"

Kayla almost dropped her coffee. There was Lisa tucked into the back seat, grinning at her.

"Oh, my God." She cocked her head and blinked. "Lisa?"

"Guess who's going to Savannah with you?"

Stunned, but in a good way, Kayla slid into the back seat next to Lisa and put her coffee in the cup holder. "Why didn't you tell me?" she asked, buckling her seat belt. The driver closed the door and then moved to the back of the car to stow her suitcase in the trunk.

"Because I wasn't sure until the last minute that I could get away." As usual, Lisa looked very chic. Her blond hair was pulled back in sleek chignon, and although dressed comfortably for travel, she still looked like a supermodel. "But I rearranged a few commitments and here I am."

"Does Sean know you're coming?"

"No, I didn't tell him," Lisa said. "I'm going to Savannah as your friend, not as a publicist."

Kayla leaned back against the sleek leather seat, feeling a lot better than she did five minutes ago. With Lisa in Savannah with her, the trip just might be bearable. Plus, she would be almost three thousand miles away from her stalker. For the first time in weeks she could breathe easy.

Twenty-Two

Jared: Where are you going?
Shay: I'm leaving. I can't stay here anymore.
Jared: Why?
Shay: Because I'm in love with you, and we both know that your heart will always belong to Rebecca.

SEAN WAS CROSSING the atrium lobby of the Riverfront Marriott after taking an early morning run along the Riverwalk when he saw Kayla and Lisa emerge from one of the elevators. He couldn't take his eyes off of Kayla. Even dressed in shorts and a tank top she looked breathtaking. Her hair was pulled back in a loose ponytail and a pair of sunglasses were perched on the top of her head. She looked relaxed. Much more so than he was.

The minute Kayla saw him her smile faded and her expressive face changed, becoming taut and strained. Beside her, Lisa fixed him with her steely blue eyes. He'd talked with her two days ago about a charity event. She'd been professional but on the chilly side. It was clear she hadn't thawed.

"Hello, Sean," Lisa said as she and Kayla halted in front of him.

"Good morning," he said, meeting her gaze and then glancing at Kayla. "Where are you two off to?"

"Tybee Island Lighthouse," Lisa said while Kayla remained silent. "We're getting an early start so we can be back in time for the luncheon."

"You'll be at the lunch? I thought it was just for the actors and the contest winners," he said as Kayla's cell phone rang. She pulled it out of her purse and looked at it.

"It's Donald," she said to Lisa. "Excuse me." She gave him a stony look and then stepped away to take the call.

"I'm attending the luncheon, but not in my capacity as publicist," Lisa answered his question. "I thought Kayla could use a friend right now." She looked at him pointedly. "Since you're being such a jerk."

"I knew you'd take her side."

Lisa's eyes narrowed. "She's also still in danger from that lunatic who's stalking her. I'm here to protect her."

"We're three thousand miles from danger," he shot back. Lisa frowned but before she could say anything Kayla rejoined them.

"Donald got a call from the casting director at Amblin," she said to Lisa, ignoring him. "I got the part."

"I'm sure my father saw to that," Sean said, unable to stop himself.

Kayla turned to him. Anger flashed in her dark eyes. "I guess it's easier for you to believe that than to admit I got the part because of my talent."

"I never said that."

"No. You just called me a whore."

"Now wait a damn minute, I—"

"No, *you* wait," Kayla interrupted and poked a finger into his chest. "I've never slept with anyone to get a part. Ever. And I sure as hell didn't sleep with you to get to your father." She paused. "I cared about you. You…you ass."

Cared. She'd used the past tense. His stomach churned sickeningly.

Lisa put her hand on Kayla's shoulder. "We should go. The lobby is not the place for a scene."

Kayla expelled a long breath. "Lisa's right," she said, pinning him with a dark glare. "We're done anyway," she said and turned and stalked toward the lobby doors.

After she disappeared from sight, Sean turned to find Lisa looking at him. "You're an idiot," she said, and with a sad shake of her head left him standing in the lobby feeling like a first class jerk, and in addition to that, more alone than he'd ever felt in his entire life.

AN HOUR LATER, Sean sat at an outside table at a small café along the river trying to enjoy his breakfast. The restaurant had been highly recommended by the hotel concierge but just like everything he'd eaten for the past week, it tasted like cardboard.

"Excuse me." He looked up from his plate to see a woman—probably in her late fifties—smiling down at him. "You're Sean Barrett, aren't you?"

"Guilty as charged." He put his fork down and returned her smile. She was the friendliest face he seen all morning.

"I hope you don't think I'm rude, but I was wondering if I could get your autograph."

"Of course." He leaned back in his chair as she rummaged through her purse and then pulled out an autograph book. "What's your name?" he asked after he took the book and a pen from her.

"Rita. Are you enjoying Savannah?" she asked as he opened the book and started to write.

"So far." It was a lie, but it wasn't like he could tell her the truth.

"It's a charming city," Rita went on. "Very romantic."

"I've always heard that." He signed his name underneath the short inscription he'd written and handed her back the book and the pen.

"I read that you and Kayla Maxwell are dating." She paused and, to his surprise, winked. "This is the perfect place for two people in love. I hope you'll both enjoy your stay here." Returning the book and pen to her purse, she gave him a wide smile. "Thanks for the autograph," she said before walking into the café.

Yes. Savannah *was* charming and romantic. Kayla had been so excited about the trip and they'd made plans to explore it together. And now here he was…alone.

Wasn't that just fucking perfect?

The ringing of his cell phone interrupted his thoughts. He picked it up and frowned. As always, his father's timing was impeccable. The man always seemed to call just when Sean least wanted to hear from him. James had called three times since the day he'd returned from New York, and each time Sean let the call go to voice mail. His father's messages had been the same each time. He wanted to talk.

"Go to hell," Sean muttered and stared at the phone until it went silent. There would be no talking. As far as he was concerned there was nothing more to talk about.

He put the phone down and picked up his coffee. After taking a sip, he was surprised to see Rachel walk out of the restaurant with a man who looked vaguely familiar. They stood near the entrance talking intently. The man lifted his hand and caressed Rachel's cheek. Rachel didn't look Sean's way and he was fine with that. He had no desire to make small talk with her.

Studying the man's profile, Sean tried like hell to remember where he'd seen the guy before. He was average height with dark hair and eyes. There were several actors from the network's other two soaps attending the event; he could very well be from another show.

After Rachel and her companion left, Sean managed to choke down his breakfast but it still bothered him that he'd seen the man with Rachel before and couldn't place him. He knew it would come to him eventually if he would just stop trying to figure it out. And it wasn't like the guy was anyone of consequence anyway. Probably just another in Rachel's long line of conquests.

KAYLA SETTLED INTO the cozy chair with the latest issue of her favorite fashion magazine for some downtime before the banquet. When a knock sounded at the door, she glanced at the clock on the dresser, tossed the magazine aside, then crossed the spacious room and pulled open the door. "Okay, Lisa. You said to be ready early but this is..."

It wasn't Lisa.

Sean stood in the hallway, his tailored jacket unbuttoned and his hands tucked into the pockets of his pants. "Hi."

"H-hi."

"May I come in?"

Slam it. Slam the door in his face. He deserves it. Do it!

She stepped back so he could come in without touching her. She caught a whiff of his woodsy cologne and fought the memories it evoked. She closed the door and turned to face him.

He searched her face and for a fleeting moment she saw something that looked like hurt underneath his polished veneer.

Good.

"You…you look…absolutely stunning."

"Thank you." She clasped her hands in front of her to keep them from trembling. They hadn't been alone together for the past week. It was hard to be this close to him and not remember the way he'd made love to her, the way her body responded to his touch. "Why are you here?"

"I've been thinking about what you said yesterday morning in the lobby. And I want to apologize for insinuating that you would use sex to get a part." He ran a hand through his sun streaked hair. "I know you wouldn't do that."

"Then why'd you say it?"

"Because I was angry. I honestly believe my father is behind your audition and probably strongly suggested that you be cast."

"So you still don't believe I got the part on my own merit?"

"You're extremely talented, Kayla. I've always thought so."

"But not talented enough to land a role in a Steven Spielberg production?"

"It's not about your talent. It's about my father manipulating the situation. Why can't you see that?"

"Because I don't think the worst of people, Sean." Kayla sighed. "I wasn't brought up that way. You see some sort of nefarious plot and I see that because of the hard work I've done on the show, I'm finally getting recognized as a serious actress. Not just some slasher flick bimbo." She paused. "I want more for myself. As much as I love *A New Dawn,* I don't want it to be my career. And I find it hard to believe that you'd find it challenging to work on a soap for the rest of your life. It's like you're determined not to give your father the satisfaction of being right."

"Right about what?" Sean asked, his green eyes narrowing.

"That you're too talented to play the same character for the rest of your life."

"I'm happy on the show." His response was automatic and his eyes bleak. It saddened her. He had so much potential but was so stuck in the past he couldn't see that he was holding himself back. "And I refuse to trade on my father's name," he added harshly.

"Your father's name might get you in the door. But after that it's up to you. Your father has influential friends, but you know as well as I do that in Hollywood it's all about box office receipts. Not one of his friends would cast you if you couldn't act. They wouldn't take the chance their movie would tank."

Sean stared at her for several tense seconds. "Did you accept the role?"

"Yes."

"Well, I guess there's nothing more to say." His expression became shuttered. He would settle for nothing less than her turning down the part in the mini-series. Something she wasn't willing to do. "I hope it works out for you," he said in a voice devoid of emotion.

"Thank you." Moisture gathered in her eyes. Blinking, she followed him to the door.

"Goodbye, Kayla." He opened the door. "Enjoy the evening," he said and then left the room without a backward glance.

STRIDING DOWN THE carpeted hallway toward the elevator, Sean almost wished he hadn't gone to Kayla's room. When she'd opened the door, he could barely speak. She'd looked so damn beautiful it was all he could do not to pull her into his arms and kiss her senseless.

He'd thought maybe he could salvage things between them. But the moment she started playing shrink—analyzing him and his relationship with his father—he knew she would never understand what it meant to be James Barrett's son. Nor did she understand the kind of power his father wielded in Hollywood.

Somehow in the brief exchange she'd had with his father, Kayla had sympathized with him. The old man had probably played the poor misunderstood father card and then turned on the Barrett charm. And Kayla had bought it. Now *he* was the bad guy who had turned his back on the father who had always loved him.

What a crock of shit.

Reaching the elevator, he pressed the call button. When the elevator arrived and the doors slid open, he moved to step into it and almost collided with the man exiting. "Excuse me," he said and immediately recognized him. It was the same dark-haired man he'd seen with Rachel outside the restaurant. Again, he felt that he'd either met the guy, or seen him somewhere before. As he stepped aside, the man gave him a nod but didn't speak. He quickly brushed past him and into the hallway.

Watching him walk away, Sean still had no clue why the guy looked so familiar. Knowing he'd figure it out eventually, he moved into the elevator and hit the button for his floor. He still had some time to kill before the awards dinner started and he didn't feel like making polite chit chat with anyone. Getting blind stinking drunk sounded a hell of a lot better. Maybe then he could stop thinking about Kayla and how much he missed her.

When he got off of the elevator, he fished his card key from the pocket of his suit jacket and headed for his room. After rounding the corner of the corridor, he stopped in stunned surprise when he saw who was standing in the hallway. "What are you doing here?" he asked.

James Barrett's blue eyes assessed him coolly. "You know exactly why I'm here, Sean. You may not want to talk to me, but you're damn well going to listen to what I have to say. Now, do you want me to say my piece here in the hallway, or are you going to invite me in?"

STARING AT HER reflection in the mirror, Kayla dabbed at her tearstained cheeks with a tissue. The thought of attending the awards banquet almost sickened her. She and Lisa would be seated at the same table with Sean and several of their co-stars. And not only would she have to pretend to have a good time, she would have to get up and accept three awards. One of them with Sean. She pressed a hand to her queasy stomach. *Is it too late to say I ate some bad sushi and pull a disappearing act?* Forget that idea. For one thing it was a documented fact that she hated sushi, and for another, she could never disappoint the fans that might have come to see her.

Opening the small clutch she was using for the evening, she pulled out a tube of her favorite red lipstick and touched up her lips. She might feel like hell on the inside, but at least she looked presentable on the outside.

A sharp knock sounded on the door; her pulse started to race. It was still too early for Lisa to arrive. Maybe Sean has come back, she thought, unable to tamp down the frisson of hope that ignited inside of her. Dropping the lipstick case next to her purse on the vanity, she left the bathroom and hurried to the door. Pulling it open, her heart plummeted to her stomach as stared at the last person on earth she had ever expected to see in Savannah.

"What the hell are *you* doing here?"

SEAN UNBUTTONED HIS jacket and turned to face his father. He didn't like surprises, and his father showing up unannounced in Savannah qualified as a big one. "You wanted to talk. So talk."

"Do you mind if I sit down?" James motioned to the upholstered chair next to a round table in the corner of the room. "It's been a long day. My connecting flight in Kansas City was delayed for about two hours."

"You flew commercial?" he asked as his father moved to the chair and eased himself on to it. Looking at him, Sean could see the tiredness etched on his face, and again realized his father was getting older. Tonight though, he seemed particularly vulnerable. A trait Sean had never associated with his father.

"I couldn't arrange for a private jet on such short notice."

Sean gave a hollow laugh. "And here I thought the great James Barrett could get anything he wanted just by snapping his fingers."

"I don't wield as much power as you obviously think I do." James settled back in the chair and met his gaze with enigmatic eyes.

"But you got Kayla the part in that Pearl Harbor mini-series. You called Spielberg and had him call his casting people, didn't you?"

James shook his head. "I haven't talked to Steven in several weeks."

"I don't believe you."

"Believe what you want. The last time I talked to Steven he told me there was a part in the project he thought you'd be perfect for. You weren't interested, remember?"

"So you're telling me you had nothing to do with Kayla getting the part?"

"Yes, that's exactly what I'm telling you. I didn't pull any strings, but I'm happy to hear she landed the role." James smiled. "She's a very talented actress."

"How would you know anything about Kayla? You just met her."

"I've seen her work. On your show." Sean remembered Kayla saying that his father watched the show, and just like then, he was having trouble believing it. "I can see you're surprised," James continued. "But it's the truth. I've watched *A New Dawn.* Not regularly, but enough to see that you're too talented to stay there. There's so much more you could do."

"I find it odd that in all these years you've never

mentioned it," Sean said. "You've spent the last ten years trying to get me to leave the show because you're embarrassed I'm on it."

"I've never been embarrassed by you, Sean. But I can see why you might believe that. I've never told you how proud I am of you." The corners of his mouth lifted in a wry smile. "I find it far easier to express myself when I'm saying words someone else has written for me."

For a moment, Sean was speechless. His father was proud of him. It shouldn't matter, not after everything that had happened, but still, the part of him that had always longed for his father's approval was gratified. Quickly, he squelched the feeling and got back to the matter at hand.

"What's so important that you had to fly across the country to talk to me?"

"Your mother."

"Mom?" Sean's heart began to pound. "No way. I'm not talking about her with you."

James put his hands on the armrest of the chair and leaned forward, his expression somber. "Then just listen. It wasn't your fault, Sean."

Sean searched his father's face, unable to believe what he'd just heard. He'd longed to hear those words for so long and had given up hope they would ever be spoken. Or if they were that it would make a difference.

"That's not what you said at the hospital."

"I know what I said," his father said, holding his gaze. "And if I could take back those words I'd do it in a heartbeat." James looked down at the carpet. Several tense seconds elapsed before he looked up. "Laura wanted me to change the battery in the smoke alarm before I left for the studio that day. I was running late and didn't feel like dragging out the ladder so I told her I'd do it when I got home." His father leaned back in the chair, looking even older than he had a few minutes ago.

"She asked me to do it but I blew her off," Sean said. "I told her I'd do it when I got back from the beach." Sean closed his eyes and remembered coming home to find his mother lying in a lifeless heap on the tile floor in the foyer next to the ladder. For months afterward, he couldn't get that image out of his mind. "I called 911," he said, opening his eyes and meeting his father's sad gaze. "And then I called you but all I got was your voice mail. I kept calling and calling but you never answered."

"The phone was in my trailer. The second I listened to your messages I left for the hospital. When I got there…"

"She was dead," Sean finished for him. "And you said it was my fault." He paused, the memories of his father's accusations, even after all these years were like dagger blows to his heart. "I was surfing, just like I did every day," Sean said through clenched teeth. "I didn't *know*."

"I was out of my mind with grief." James's eyes welled up. "But instead of comforting you, I lashed out at you. I was so overwhelmed with guilt that I couldn't see past it. And when I did, it was too late. I'd alienated you, and nothing I did after that could repair the damage between us. For the rest of the summer you wouldn't speak to me. You were either holed up in your room or out all day with Matt."

"I needed you," Sean choked out as moisture filled his eyes. It was as if he were thirteen and helpless all over again.

"I know, son."

Sean glared at him. "Do you? Those…those hours at the hospital seemed like a year. Nobody would tell me anything—I was a kid. A *kid*—" Sean's shoulders slumped, the anger draining from him like air from a balloon "—who needed you to make everything all right."

A taut silence filled the room. James blinked several times and then said, "I let you down and it's been eating at me ever since. The more I tried to reach out to you, the more you pulled away. Before I knew it we were strangers sharing the same house. When you decided to become an actor I thought maybe we could find some common ground, but I'm afraid my desire to rebuild our relationship was perceived as trying to control you. Believe me, that's the last thing I wanted to do."

"I should have changed that battery," Sean whispered, reaching up to wipe his eyes.

"You didn't know she would try to change it herself. We both know she didn't like heights. It never occurred to me that she wouldn't wait for me to get home. But I guess she couldn't stand listening to that damn chirping noise it made. It was an accident, Sean. A horrible, senseless accident. You need to believe that and stop blaming yourself."

"Easier said than done."

"Maybe we could try to do it together." There was a tremor in his father's voice as he continued. "I came all this way because whether you believe it or not, I do love you." He paused. "I'd like a second chance. And, God knows, it's a lot to ask. But I hope you'll give it to me."

I happen to believe in second chances.

Kayla had said those words to him. And believed

them. That was the kind of person she was. He'd thrown the very qualities she truly possessed back in her face; the thought of it made him sick to his stomach. Because of his stupid stubborn pride he'd hurt the only woman who'd ever found her way into his heart. He was a damn fool for not recognizing what had been right in front of his face for weeks.

Glancing at his watch, he fought the urge to tear out of the room and go directly to her. But the banquet was starting in less than fifteen minutes. That wasn't enough time for him to say everything he needed to say to her. He *would* say it though. He just hoped it wasn't too late.

Twenty-Three

Jared: I don't want you to go.
Shay: Give me one good reason to stay.
Jared: After Rebecca died I didn't think I could ever fall in love again. But I did. With you.
Shay: That's a really good reason.

WHEN KAYLA CAME to, she was lying on a hard linoleum floor in a small room that reeked of pine-scented cleaner and other chemicals. She tried to move and winced at the pain that reverberated in her head. Panic seized her. Her arms were tied in front of her and her ankles were also bound. Whatever was binding her was tight and unyielding.

"It's about time you woke up."

The familiar voice confused her until she remembered opening her hotel room door and finding him standing on the other side. She heard steps. In her line of vision two highly polished black dress shoes appeared. Angling her head up, she locked eyes with the man she'd once cared about.

Greg Alamo.

He sank to his haunches beside her. Fear gripped her like a vice when she saw the hatred burning in his coal black eyes. "Surprised to see me?" he asked. She stared at him, amazed that she had ever found him remotely attractive. Right now he looked like the devil's disciple.

"Where am I?" The last thing she remembered was the foul smelling cloth he'd shoved over her face. She'd passed out within seconds.

"You're still in the hotel," he said, reaching out and brushing a finger over her temple. When she flinched his eyes flickered with amusement. "I thought about leaving you tied up in your room, but I figured your boyfriend would come back and find you." He stroked her cheek. She tried to pull away but he held her head in place, pressing his fingers into her flesh. "I'm not going to kill you, if that's what you're thinking. Despite what I may have implied in my letters, the intent was never murder."

"Oh, my God." Her body stiffened in shock. "It's you? You're the stalker?"

"Stalker?" His dark eyebrows slanted in a frown. "I really don't like labels. Actually, I was just doing a favor for a friend."

"What friend? Who would want to do this to me?" she asked and then remembered the picture of him and Rachel in *Soap Opera Journal*. "Rachel?" she whispered. "You're doing this for Rachel?"

"She inadvertently gave me the idea." Greg gave her cheek a hard pat before rising to his feet. He stared down at her, his dark eyes soulless. "Did you like the rat?"

"You're sick."

"I wish I could have seen your face. Did you scream?" He chuckled. It was an evil sound. "This little game has been *so* amusing."

"Game?" Her voice trembled. "What kind of monster are you? This is no game."

"It was genius—if I do say so myself." Greg stuck

his hands in the pockets of his slacks and looked at her with sick satisfaction.

"W-why did you do this?"

"Rachel's been bitching about you for months. I got sick of her damn whining."

He's crazy. Absolutely crazy.

"Rachel doesn't know?"

"If she had half a brain she'd figure it out. But she's pretty clueless." He pulled his hand from his pocket. Icy fear gripped her heart when she saw the switchblade.

"Do you remember what I told you that night you came to Malibu?" Greg's eyes flashed with unconcealed rage. "The night you broke up with me."

"Y-you said you'd make me pay."

A tense silence enveloped the room and a wave of apprehension swept through her. He was insane. For all she knew he could snap at any moment.

"I'm the one who says it's over." He sank down and grabbed her chin with his fingers. Fear roiled in the pit of her stomach as he lowered his head and stared into her eyes. "You belonged to me." His breath felt hot on her face. "Did you think you could make a fool out of me and get away with it? There are consequences for what you did. But since I'm not willing to risk spending the rest of my life in jail I decided to do the next best thing to killing you." His fingers dug into her skin. She winced and tried to pull away but he was too strong. "I wanted you scared. I wanted you to wonder if you were being watched and followed." His mouth curved with a smile that was made of pure evil. "I wanted you to believe that someone wanted you dead."

"You're insane," she whispered. "You won't get away with this."

"There's no proof I did anything to you. I covered my tracks very well." Now he was gloating.

"I'll tell the police everything."

"Your word against mine." The calm in his eyes was more terrifying than anything else he'd said. The pounding of her heart echoed like a drum in her ears; it was beating so fast she feared it might burst from her chest. "I haven't hurt you." She heard whoosh of the knife opening. Her body shook as he laid the cold steel blade against her neck. "But I will if you tell anyone I brought you here." He pressed the tip of the knife against her skin until she felt a sting and then the trickle of blood as it dripped down her neck. She bit back a sob.

Oh, God, was he going to slit her throat?

Loosening his grip on her chin, he rose to his feet and stared down at her. "Consider this payback," he sneered. "And always remember…you got off easy."

THE MOMENT LISA entered the Savannah ballroom, Sean knew something was wrong. For one thing, she was alone. His other clue was the way her lips were pressed together in a grim line as she wound her way around the tables set up in neat precision in the ballroom. When she reached his table, she sank down onto the chair next to him. "Have you seen Kayla?" she asked him a low voice and then glanced at the podium. The emcee was in the middle of his welcome speech.

"I saw her about an hour ago. In her room," he said, meeting her worried gaze. "Why?"

"I went to her room but she wasn't there." Lisa leaned back and craned her neck to survey the ballroom. It was filled with actors, soap fans, and assorted media. "I thought she might have come down early, but I don't see her." Lisa looked at him. "Did you two have an argument?" she asked in an accusing tone.

"No. We talked for about ten minutes and then I went back to my room."

"Was she upset when you left her?"

"Our discussion was civil. I apologized for something I said to her last week and then left." He didn't want to tell Lisa about the tears he'd seen glistening in Kayla's eyes. He felt like a bastard for causing them, but he didn't believe she was upset enough to miss the banquet. She would never do that to her fans. "Did you try calling her?"

Lisa nodded. "There was no answer in the room and when I tried her cell phone it went straight to her voice mail. Sean, if there was a good reason for her not to show up, she would have called me. I'm really worried."

"Let's go." He pushed his chair back and grabbed Lisa's arm.

Ignoring the speculative looks from the guests, he tried to tamp down the dread that had enveloped him and hurried her out of the ballroom and into the hallway. Once the door closed behind them, Lisa turned to him. "What should we do?"

"Talk to hotel security. They can get us into Kayla's room." They moved toward the lobby and it hit him. He stopped short. "Son of a bitch."

Lisa stumbled to a stop beside him, her eyes wide and filled with apprehension "What?"

"I just remembered the name of the guy I saw with Rachel." He met Lisa's confused gaze. "Greg Alamo."

"Greg? You saw him? Here?"

"With Rachel."

Lisa's face paled. "I don't like this."

Sick fear coiled in Sean's stomach. He didn't like it either. "Let's talk to security, then we'll find out what Rachel knows."

Fifteen minutes later, Sean slipped back into the ballroom, and after skirting the perimeter of the room, made his way to Rachel's table. She was in deep conversation with an actress from another show and treated him to an annoyed look when he wrapped his fingers around her too thin arm. "Come with me," he said putting his mouth to her ear. "Right now."

She turned and met his gaze with furious eyes. She opened her mouth and then snapped it shut and looked around. Then she pasted a fake smile on her face. "Why, Sean, *darling*, of course we can talk," she said and then let him pull her up out of her chair and guide her to the side exit.

The minute they left the ballroom she jerked her arm from his grasp and glared at him. "What's wrong with you? Why did you drag me out of there?" she demanded.

"Where's Greg Alamo?" he asked, not wasting any time. "Don't bother denying you know him. I saw you with him at the café."

"Why would I deny it?" Rachel asked. "I've been seeing him for a few months."

"What a coincidence. That's when Kayla started getting those threatening notes."

"What does that have to do with me? Or Greg?"

Sean tried to read her face. She looked annoyed and perplexed. But not nervous. "Either you've finally learned how to act or you're telling the truth. Which is it?"

Rachel's eyes flashed with anger. "I don't have to take this. I'm going back inside."

"Not so fast." He reclaimed her arm. "Cut the bullshit, Rachel. Just tell me where Alamo is." Out of the corner of his eye he saw Lisa approaching them from the lobby. "Any luck?"

Lisa shook her head. Her demeanor was calm but her eyes were filled with worry. "Greg isn't registered at the hotel."

Rachel looked from him to Lisa. "That's because he's staying with me. In my room."

"How come he wasn't with you on the plane?" Lisa asked.

"He caught a later flight. He told me he had an early morning meeting with his agent he couldn't get out of."

Lisa let out a derisive sound. "He probably knew Kayla would be on the same plane."

Rachel put her hands on her hips. "What's going on? Why are you looking for Greg?"

"Because I find it odd that he's here in Savannah. Especially now that Kayla has gone missing," Sean snapped, tired of her innocent act.

"Missing?" Rachel exclaimed. "I saw her just a few hours ago." She looked at Lisa. "With you."

"Why isn't Greg your escort tonight?" Lisa asked.

"He said it wasn't his thing. He was going to have dinner somewhere in the historic district, and then after the banquet we're hitting a couple clubs the concierge recommended." She paused and looked from Lisa to him. "Sean, I can assure you that wherever Kayla is Greg isn't with her. He hates her."

"That's what I'm afraid of," Sean said and met Lisa's

troubled gaze. "Did Alamo ever threaten Kayla when they were dating?"

"He was possessive and jealous but she never mentioned any threats. She did tell me he was livid when she dumped him," Lisa said in a voice edged with tension. "She said she'd never seen him that angry and that she got out of the beach house as quickly as she could."

"No." Rachel shook her head vehemently. "You're wrong. Greg wouldn't hurt anyone."

"Where were you two going to meet up?" he asked, not bothering to argue with her.

"My room."

"Take us there," Sean commanded. "Now."

THE MINUTE GREG closed door and she was alone, Kayla rolled to her back and was able to get into an upright sitting position. The restraints around her wrists and ankles were thin and made of plastic. They were tight—as in cutting off her circulation tight. Twisting her wrists, she let out a groan of pain when the plastic dug into her skin.

Okay, Kayla. Keep it together. You'll get out of here.

Looking around the small room, she saw shelves with cleaning supplies, rolls of toilet paper and plastic bins with travel size bottle of shampoo and soap. A couple of vacuums were sitting in the corner. She was in a housekeeping supply closet.

And probably on the same floor as her room. Greg wouldn't have taken a chance on going any farther with her passed out in his arms.

Be quiet. That's what he'd told her.

Oh hell no, asshole. You're going to find out just how loud I can be.

She screamed. And then screamed again. But it was futile. The gag Greg had fashioned from a towel and knotted tightly around her head and stuffed into her mouth muffled her cries. She grunted in frustration.

Damn you, Greg.

She should have known he was the stalker. Seriously, how stupid was she? His behavior the night she'd broken up with him should have been her first clue. But she'd been lulled into a false sense of security. He never called her or tried to see her after that night and she'd forgotten his threats. But he'd been biding his time, waiting for the perfect opportunity to get back at her. The sick freak.

He is so not getting away with this.

Using her hips, she scooted her butt along the floor toward the door. With any luck, it would be unlocked, but if it wasn't she'd bang her head or her feet against it until someone heard her.

By the time she reached the door, her dress had ridden up past her hips. Lying flat, she rolled to her stomach and after a few ungraceful tries was able to push herself to her knees. The gag in her mouth prevented her from getting enough air so she stilled and drew air in through her nose. Once her equilibrium returned she pressed against the floor with her hands, sat back on her haunches and then pushed herself up into a standing position. Elation filled her as she lifted her bound hands up to the door handle, but when it didn't budge she let out a frustrated groan.

Sweat trickled down her back as she considered her options. Angling her head to her right, she took stock of the items sitting on the metal shelving unit placed against the wall near the door. Her gaze rested on a crescent wrench. If she could get her hands on it, the wrench would be perfect to bang against the door. Certainly less painful then using her head, and easier than using her feet.

It was the perfect plan.

WAITING ALONE IN Rachel's room, Sean heard the sound of the card key being inserted into the slot on the door and tensed. Since Rachel was with Lisa in Lisa's room, the person on the other side of the door could only be Greg Alamo returning to pick up Rachel for their night of clubbing. His gut told him that Alamo was behind Kayla's sudden disappearance, but although the head of security had placed a call to the Savannah police department, they still hadn't arrived. Unable to stand by and do nothing, he'd decided to take matters into his own hands.

Rachel's room was exactly like his. One king-sized bed, one small round table with two chairs, armoire, dresser and nightstand. There was probably a Bible in the drawer, just like in his room. Unlike his room though, there were clothes strewn on every available surface. Rachel didn't pack light.

He didn't have a plan. There had been no time to concoct some elaborate plot to get Alamo to admit he'd taken Kayla somewhere. All he had was the element of surprise and a burning desire to find Kayla. That was all he needed.

The click of the door unlocking echoed even louder than his hammering heart. With his fists clenched at his sides, he kept his eyes trained on the door. He'd played a cop for six of his ten years on the show but it hadn't prepared him for this. This was reality, not make believe. His body knew it. Every single one of his nerves was on full alert.

When the door swung open, Alamo took one step over the threshold and then froze in his tracks. His eyes widened in shock and a split second later he bolted down the hallway.

Sean reacted immediately. Careening through the doorway, he hit the hallway and sprinted after Alamo, who was almost at the elevators. Alamo bypassed the elevators and skidded to a stop. After a quick glance back, he pulled open the door to the stairs and disappeared.

The elevator doors slid open and an elderly couple stepped out. Dodging them, Sean headed for the stairwell door. Pulling it open, he raced down the first flight of stairs and saw Alamo had already cleared them and was working on the next flight. Adrenalin fueled him and he flew down the stairs, gaining on Alamo. By the time the bastard had reached the next flight Sean was five feet behind him.

The sound of their shoes on the concrete stairs reverberated loudly in the empty stairwell. Alamo looked back just before he reached the landing. That look back cost him. He slowed, and Sean was able to shorten the gap between them. Launching his body forward, he flew through the air and tackled Alamo. Together they fell hard on the landing with Alamo grunting in pain as Sean landed on top of him.

Pushing himself up, Sean bent over, clenched handfuls of Alamo's shirt in his fists and hauled him up.

"Where is she?" He shoved Alamo against the wall.

"Don't...don't hurt me." Blood trickled from Alamo's nostril to his upper lip.

"Where the fuck is she?" Sean pulled him away from the wall and then shoved him against it again, even harder than the first time.

Alamo grunted in pain. "Stop."

"Not until you tell me where she is." He let go of Alamo's shirt and pressed his forearm across his windpipe. Alamo's eyes bulged. "I swear to God, if you've hurt her." He applied more pressure to Alamo's throat. "I'll kill you with my bare hands."

"Didn't…didn't…hurt…her."

"Where is she?"

"Can't…breathe."

"Too fucking bad." He pressed harder. "Where is she?"

"Sup…supply closet," Alamo gasped. "Her floor."

Sean released him and took two steps back. Alamo slumped to the floor gulping for air. Above them, he heard the sound of the door opening. "What's going on down there?" a male voice asked with concern. "Call security," Sean called out and then looked down at Greg. "You'd better pray Kayla isn't hurt. If she is—you'll answer to me."

Turning, he sprinted up the stairs until he reached Kayla's floor. He pushed open the door, ran past the elevators and then her room until he was at the end of the hallway where—just like on his floor—there was a door with the word Housekeeping engraved on a gold metal plaque.

"Kayla." He tried the handle. It was locked. "Kayla, sweetheart, can you hear me?"

There was no sound from inside the closet. That scared him. He couldn't wait for security. Kayla's life could be at stake. Every second counted. Moving away from the door, he lifted his leg and kicked the door—hard. It didn't budge.

"Shit."

Sweat dripped down his face. Turning, he lunged at the door, throwing his weight against it. He heard a loud sound and realized it was him, groaning. He ignored the pain shooting through his shoulder and rammed his body against the door with all of his might. The hinges gave way opening about a foot before becoming lodged against something solid.

"Kayla?" He stuck his head inside the room. He didn't see her. He did see what was blocking the door though. A metal shelving unit had fallen over, obstructing the entrance. Quickly, he scanned the room. There were rolls of toilet paper and other hotel sundries scattered around the floor. Angling his head, he peered just behind the door. Sheer black fright swept over him when he saw Kayla's feet protruding from under the bottom rung of the shelving unit.

"Kayla…oh, Jesus."

His only thought as he barreled against the door with more strength than he knew he possessed was that he couldn't let her die. He hadn't been able to save his mom, but he could save Kayla.

The door budged just enough for him to turn and squeeze through. His heart pounded frantically as he stepped over the metal shelves. Moving to the top portion of the unit, he crouched and grabbed the posts on either side of it. Bracing his knees, he heaved it up; it looked heavier than it actually was. As he pushed it upright, he glanced down and saw that Kayla was unconscious.

Consumed with dread, he righted the shelving unit

and then crouched beside her. She was on her back, her wrists and ankles bound with zip ties. And she had a gag over her mouth. He pulled it off and tossed it over his shoulder.

Her face was pale—too pale. He pressed his fingers against the side of her neck and felt a pulse. She was alive. Thank God.

Don't move her. He knew that much. Moving her could make things worse.

He brushed her hair from face and then heard the sound of footsteps running toward the supply closet.

"Sean!"

"Lisa…" he yelled. "In here. Call 911."

He looked just as Lisa appeared in the doorway. "Oh, my God," she whispered, and then covered her mouth with her hand.

"Call 911." Lisa didn't move. "Now!"

His harsh tone galvanized her—she took off and then he heard her nearly hysterical on one of the hotel house phones near the elevator.

Kayla groaned. He looked down just as her eyes fluttered open. "Sean…"

"I'm here." He met her unfocused gaze.

"Greg…stalker."

"I know, sweetheart." He stroked her forehead, feeling more helpless than he'd ever felt in his life.

It was his fault. If he hadn't gotten so angry about that damn audition she wouldn't have been alone in the hotel room. He would have been there with her; Alamo would never have been able to get to her.

"Sean…" Her voice was faint. "Don't…don't leave me."

"I won't."

Her eyes closed. Panic hit him like a tidal wave. He felt for her pulse again and breathed a sigh of relief when he felt its steady beat. He lowered his head to hers and pressed his lips to her temple.

"I love you," he whispered against her skin.

Stunned that he'd spoken the words aloud, he raised his head and gazed at her. Over the past few months he had seen her kindness on a daily basis. Initially, he'd been impressed by her beauty, and then by her talent. But it was her loving spirit that had captured his heart. He hadn't known it was possible to love someone so completely. But he knew it now.

Twenty-Four

Jared: Let's get married.
Shay: We already are.
Jared: I know. But I want to marry you again. In a church this time.
Shay: I'm like eight months pregnant. I think that's frowned upon.
Jared: So what? I love you, and I want the whole world to know it.
Shay: I love you too... Oh, my God! I think my water just broke!

SEAN WATCHED THE paramedics wheel a gurney with Kayla on it from the supply closet into the hallway. From his vantage point behind several fire and rescue personnel he could see she was still pale and unconscious. The sight of the plastic zip ties digging into her soft skin enraged him.

Two minutes.

That's all he wanted—two minutes alone in a room with Greg Alamo. That would be more than enough time to beat him to a bloody pulp.

"Where are they taking her?" he asked Curtis Trent, the head of hotel security, who was standing next to him and Lisa.

"There's a hospital not too far from here." Trent's voice was calm.

"I have to go with her," Sean said, moving toward the gurney.

When he reached her and saw her slack face, his heart plummeted to his stomach. She looked so still—so abnormally still—that it sent a wave of sheer terror through him.

"Is she…?" he asked, fearing the worst.

"She's unconscious," the female paramedic assured him. Her partner hit the call button and then reached under the gurney. He retrieved a pair of scissors and cut the plastic zip tie from Kayla's wrists, and then moved to cut the tie from her ankles.

"Sir, you need to step back," he said in a polite but firm voice.

"I'm going with her," Sean said, looking at Kayla. He couldn't leave her. Not now. "If she wakes up, I don't… she can't be alone."

"I'm sorry but only the patient and EMT's are allowed in the ambulance." The paramedic put the scissors away just as the elevator chimed its arrival.

"My partner is right, sir," the woman said, glancing at her partner and then back at him. Her expression softened. "If she wakes up we'll make sure she's okay. We've done this before."

The elevator doors slid open and after the paramedics wheeled the gurney inside Sean tried to follow but the male paramedic put his hand up, preventing Sean from entering the elevator.

"I'm sorry, sir, but if you want to go to the hospital you'll need to find another mode of transportation."

"We're taking her to Memorial," his partner said in a gentler tone just before the doors slid shut.

Sean felt a hand on his shoulder.

"I'll call for a cab," Lisa said.

"That won't be necessary." Recognizing his father's voice, Sean turned to find his father standing next to Curtis Trent. "I have a car at my disposal. I can have it ready to go in five minutes."

AN HOUR AND a half later, he and Lisa were alone in the hospital's sterile waiting room. She sat beside him, staring at a flat panel television mounted on the wall. It was tuned to a twenty-four hour news channel, that, for the past ninety minutes had been cycling the top news stories of the day on what seemed to be a continuous loop.

Because Lisa had been Kayla's publicist for so many years she was able to give the admitting nurse most of Kayla's personal information, including the name of her insurance company. The entire time she'd spoken to the nurse Lisa had been on the verge of tears.

There was a time when Sean had considered Lisa rather cold. But she wasn't. Underneath the steely reserve she wore like a cloak, Lisa cared very deeply.

He heard the sound of rubber soles squeaking on the linoleum and turned to find a very short, dark-haired woman wearing scrubs walking toward them. She had a stethoscope hanging around her neck. As she drew closer Sean could make out her name on her hospital badge: Vihba Dalal, M.D.

When the doctor halted in front of them, Lisa grabbed Sean's hand. "How is Kayla?" she asked, squeezing his fingers so tightly he winced.

"I have good news," Dr. Dalal said in a lightly accented voice. "The X-rays show no broken bones, nor did she sustain any significant internal injuries."

"Oh, thank God."

"But she was unconscious," Sean said, not as relieved as Lisa. Head trauma of any kind wasn't good.

"Ms. Maxwell regained consciousness in the ambulance," Dr. Dalal said, looking at him. "She was cognizant and answered all the usual questions correctly. However, we will monitor her throughout the evening. She will have some pain and bruising due to the incident, but I believe I should be able to release her tomorrow afternoon."

"I want to see her," Sean said.

"She's asleep right now and visiting hours are over." Dr. Dalal's eyes were filled with genuine compassion. "I know you're worried, but trust me, there's nothing you can do for her. It would be best if you went home and got some rest. You can visit her tomorrow."

Sean fixed the doctor with a stubborn stare. "I'm not leaving. I'll camp out in this waiting room all night if I have to, but I'm not leaving her."

"Is there any way he can just sit quietly in her room?" Lisa asked. "I know Kayla would want him there."

Dr. Dalal hesitated a moment and then said, "We occasionally make exceptions. Wait here and I'll see what I can do."

"Thank you." Sean turned toward Lisa after Dr. Dalal left the room. "I know you've been angry with me. It can't have been easy for you to plead my case."

"Just promise me one thing," Lisa said. "Don't hurt her again."

"I won't," he promised.

Lisa tilted her head and regarded solemnly. "I think you mean that."

"I do," he said and for the first time noticed the dark

circles under her eyes. "You should go back to the hotel and get some rest."

"Is that your way of saying I look like shit?" She gave him a wan smile. "I think I will go back to the hotel, but I won't be sleeping. My phone has been vibrating like crazy. I have to go into publicist mode and handle the media." She let go of his hand. "Will you call me if there's any change?"

"Yes," he said as she rose from the chair.

After she left, Sean unbuttoned the sleeves of his shirt and rolled them up to his elbows. He thought about finding some coffee but it would only make him more wired than he already was. Besides, he wanted to stay put until Dr. Dalal returned. He heard footsteps and when he looked up he was surprised to see his father walking toward him.

That was odd. He'd assumed his father had gone back to the hotel after his driver had dropped him and Lisa off in front of the hospital.

"How's Kayla?" James asked after settling in the spot Lisa had just vacated.

"Resting." Sean leaned back against his chair. "No broken bones and no internal damage."

"That's good news."

"How did you know what happened to her?"

"I went down to the hotel gift shop to buy a candy bar. I saw the paramedics," James said. "I didn't know it was Kayla until I got back to my floor. I'm on the same floor as she is."

"The mini-bar is stocked with candy," Sean said. "Why did you go to the gift shop?"

"I'm not going to pay five dollars for a candy bar

when I can get it for a buck-fifty," James said with a wry grin.

"You can afford a five dollar candy bar."

James shrugged. "It's the principle of the thing. Besides, I hate being cooped up in hotel rooms."

"Is that why you're here? Because you don't want to go back to your hotel room?"

James put his hand on Sean's forearm. It was the first time in years his father had touched him. Strangely, it comforted him. "You needed me once before and I wasn't there for you. But I'm here now." James squeezed his arm gently. "I'll stay as long as you need me to."

There was still a lot to resolve between the two of them. But his father had traveled across the country to talk to him. That was worth something. They were strangers, but it didn't have to stay that way. A very wise woman had once told him that everyone deserved a second chance. She was right.

"I'd appreciate the company." He met his father's moist eyes. "Dad."

THE FIRST THING Kayla saw when she woke up was Sean sprawled in a chair next to her bed fast asleep, still wearing the clothes he'd been wearing when he came to her room—minus the jacket. The buttons of his white dress shirt were undone at the collar and the sleeves were rolled up revealing his tanned forearms. His face was relaxed, but judging from the angle of his head, he would probably wake up with a stiff neck.

Like a dying woman thirsting for water, she let her eyes drink their fill of him. From the first moment she'd seen him on *A New Dawn* she'd been smitten.

And she still was. That school girl crush ten years ago had turned into something so much more.

Almost as if he sensed her watching him, Sean's eyes opened sleepily and met hers. "You're awake," he said as he sat up in the chair and searched her face. "How are you feeling?"

"Sore," she admitted. "Like one giant bruise actually. But I'm not hooked up to anything that's beeping so I guess I'm pretty lucky. Where's Greg?"

Sean's expression darkened. "They took him to the police station last night. I imagine he's still there. Hotel security said a detective will take your statement before we go back to L.A."

"He's the stalker," Kayla said, remembering the horrible scene in the supply room. "He did everything—the notes, vandalizing my car, the dead rat." She shivered, wondering if she would ever be able to forget the malice in Greg's eyes. "It was his way of paying me back for dumping him."

"He won't be doing any of those things anymore," Sean said grimly. "With your statement I'm sure he'll get some serious jail time. Stalking aside, he kidnapped you and held you against your will. That's a felony."

Plucking at the edge of the sheet with her fingers, Kayla managed a grin. "It's my own fault I'm in the hospital," she said, and saw the surprise on Sean's face. "I was trying to get out of that damn supply room and accidentally brought the whole shelving unit down on top of me." She couldn't help but chuckle at the irony of it. "This is the second time in less than two months I almost got a concussion."

Sean smiled. "But this time there was no arguing about going to the hospital."

She wrinkled her nose. “I hate hospitals.”

“I seem to recall words to that effect.”

“I hope I didn’t swear at the nurse.” She reached for the small remote lying near the edge of the bed and pressed the button to elevate the head of the bed so she was sitting up. “I’m pretty sure they woke me up a few times.”

“Don’t worry. You were very cooperative.”

“How do you…” She paused. “You were here all night?”

“Guilty.” Closing his eyes, he rubbed his neck and grimaced.

Surprised, Kayla tried to wrap her head around what this meant. When he’d walked out of her hotel room last night she was certain things were over between them. Now she wasn’t so sure. Nothing had changed, but he was here and he’d stayed all night.

That has to mean something, right?

“Where’s Lisa?” she asked when he opened his eyes and found her staring at him.

“She went back to the hotel late last night. She’s handling the fallout. I’m sure there are a lot of people who want to know why you didn’t show up at the banquet, and several hotel employees saw you being taken out by the paramedics. She wants to make sure the right information gets out to the media. She was shaken up last night. I’ve never seen her like that.”

“Lisa has a big heart, but she doesn’t let a lot of people get close to her.”

“You managed to. But that doesn’t surprise me.” Sean’s eyes shined with unexpected warmth. She tried to throttle the dizzying current running through her, but couldn’t. “I think you could soften the toughest of hearts." She felt her face growing warm. "You're blushing," he said with amusement.

Leaning forward, Sean rested his forearms on his knees. His amused grin faded as he held her gaze intently. Time seemed to stand still as he gazed deeply into her eyes. "I'm sorry, Kayla."

"For what?" she asked, hoping he wasn't blaming himself for Greg's actions. "What happened last night wasn't your fault."

"I'm sorry for accusing you of using me to get to my father, and I'm sorry I said all those vicious things to you." His paused. "You were right. I let the resentment I harbored toward my father blind me. And if I'm being totally honest, the day I walked into his kitchen and saw you two getting along so famously I was jealous."

"Jealous?" she asked. "Of what?"

"Of the easy rapport you had with him, and he with you. For one brief moment I wished it was me instead of you sitting there talking with him so easily—so comfortably." Sean's eyes shadowed with sadness. "I was jealous because you have what I lost when my mom died. A loving family. But instead of admitting that to you—or to myself—I took the first opportunity I could to lash out at you."

"The audition."

"Yes. The audition. Even if my father had set it up it was no excuse to treat you the way I did. You deserved to go on the audition and you deserved to get the part. You're an amazing actress. I can honestly say that working with you has made me a better actor. I just wish being with you had made me a better man."

"Sean..." she began, stunned not only by his apology, but at his high regard for her acting ability.

"No," he interrupted her gently. "I need to tell you this." He paused and gave her a long searching look. "When I found you last night..."

"Wait...you're the one who found me?"

"I saw Alamo with Rachel but I didn't recognize him right away. When Lisa said you were missing I remembered who he was."

"But I never told you about him. How did you know who he was?"

He shifted in the chair, looking slightly uncomfortable. "When we first started working together I looked you up on the internet. Just once," he added quickly. "I wanted to see if you were dating anyone. But all I found out was that you'd broken up with Alamo a few months ago. There was a picture of the two of you at some event."

"You could have just asked me if I was seeing anyone," she said with a grin.

Sean's eyes glinted with amusement. "The internet doesn't ask questions."

"Or make assumptions."

"I'm glad I saw the picture. If I hadn't I probably wouldn't have figured out that Alamo had kidnapped you." He reached for her hand, his warm fingers twining with hers. "I thought I lost you last night, Kayla." His eyes held hers and were filled with such tenderness she almost couldn't breathe. "And I swore to myself that if I got the chance I'd tell you exactly how I feel." He lifted his other hand and touched her cheek. "I'm in love with you. And I'm pretty sure I know exactly when it happened."

"When?" she asked. Joyful tears filled her eyes. She blinked to keep them at bay.

"The day of the fan club luncheon." His fingertips lightly grazed her skin. She tilted her head, leaning into his soft caress. "You were so kind to Donna and Stephanie. You paid their registration fee and arranged for them to sit with us. You didn't have to do that, but you did. Because that's who you are." He gazed at her with undisguised emotion. "How could I not love you?"

"Do you know what I want?"

"Whatever it is, I'll try my best to give it to you."

"I want you to take me home. And when we get there I'd like to go to the guest cottage on your father's estate."

Surprise flickered in his eyes. "Why?"

"Because that's where I realized that I'm totally and completely in love with you."

"You love me?"

"How could I not?" she said softly and smiled. "Now, there's something else I want. Something you can do for me right now."

"Name it."

"Would you kiss me?"

Another heart-stopping grin curved his lips. "Sweetheart, that is one question where my answer will always be yes," he said, then leaned forward to capture her mouth with his. His demanding kiss ignited a bone-melting fire that spread through her body and spilled into her soul.

"I love you," Sean whispered when they parted.

Gazing into his eyes, her heart overflowed with happiness, and there was something more—a feeling of completeness she'd never experienced before. Just like her character Shay, who'd found her soul mate in Jared, Kayla had found hers in Sean.

Life had imitated art in the best way possible.

* * * * *